FOR FREEDOM AND HONOUR

To Sandra.

With Best wishes

James R S Black

James.

July 2016

First published in 2010 by

WOODFIELD PUBLISHING LTD
Bognor Regis ~ West Sussex ~ England ~ PO21 5EL
www.woodfieldpublishing.co.uk

ISBN 1-84683-096-6

Front cover design by Shannon Mackisey

FOR FREEDOM & HONOUR

A historical novel set in World War II

JAMES R.S. BLACK

Woodfield

Woodfield Publishing Ltd
Bognor Regis ~ West Sussex ~ PO21 5EL ~ England

Interesting and informative books on a variety of subjects

For details of all our published titles, visit our website at
www.woodfieldpublishing.co.uk

~ CONTENTS ~

Acknowledgments

For all her help whenever I needed it, for all her patience and understanding, I'd like to thank my daughter Heather.
  Love you always. Dad.

For her vision and creative design work for the book, I'd like to thank Shannon Mackisey. Keep doing what you do Shannon; you have a flair for it. James.

Last but by my no means least, I'd like to thank Woodfield Publishing for the contribution they made in transforming my manuscript into a book. Writing a manuscript is one thing but finding the right person and publisher who believes in you is quite another. I found that person at Woodfield.
  Thank you Nicholas, from the bottom of my heart. James.

Preface

This story was written in memory of my uncle, who fought and died for freedom and honour in the First World War. I don't think there are any greater events in history than those of the First and Second World Wars; the colossal loss of life in both conflicts was staggering and unbelievable. The heroism, bravery, self-sacrifice, courage and endurance displayed by so many individuals should never be forgotten. There must be so many heroic stories that we will never know. I often think about the fighter pilots who engaged in aerial combat, the bomber crews who flew long missions deep into Germany, the infantrymen who leapt out of landing craft to run up heavily-defended beaches, the seamen whose ships were torpedoed and I wonder... how would I have handled the fear? Would I have had the courage to do what had to be done?

During the Second World War the destruction of cities and loss of civilian life was unimaginable. Maybe, if we keep the memory alive, we will never see its like again.

But there are also happier memories of the Second World War years, of camaraderie and people working together towards a common goal. The technological advancements and production levels accomplished were amazing. It was Britain's darkest hour but also her finest.

In 1939 Germany unleashed her military might and rolled almost unopposed through Belgium, the Low Countries and France, halted only by a narrow strip of water from invading Britain too. As Britannia took a stand she wasn't fully prepared for war and the future looked bleak but with help from New Zealand, Australia, Canada and others, she held out. America sent various supplies and even a squadron of American pilots who flew in the Battle of Britain in the summer of 1940, but the American public didn't want to send their sons to fight and die in a far-off country. They remembered only too well what had happened in the First World War. Fortunately, the Japanese attack in Hawaii in 1941 changed their minds.

Britain also had a defiant bulldog of a leader who had long warned of the threat posed by Germany. There is no doubt that Winston Churchill was the right man, in the right place, at the right time. With his articulate command of the English language he found the right words to inspire a nation.

But even the greatest leader needs to call on the talents of others and one such talent was Hugh Dowding, the man at the helm of RAF Fighter

Command prior to and during the Battle of Britain in 1940. Originally from Moffat in Scotland, he had been in the RAF since the First World War. It was due to his foresight that the RAF and Britain's air defences were as prepared as they were. As the Luftwaffe hammered RAF aerodromes in southern England, Britain teetered, but thanks to the tenacity of the pilots of The Few, Germany lost her opportunity to invade mainland Britain. It would not arise again.

Of course there were many other people and organisations without whose contributions the outcome of the war may have been very much different. One such man was Reginald J Mitchell, designer of the Spitfire. Despite being diagnosed with cancer, he worked tirelessly to complete his creation and died in 1937, before he could witness the invaluable contribution this remarkable aircraft made to British victory. He, along with Supermarine, which built the Spitfire and Rolls-Royce, which designed and built the Merlin engine that powered it, along with a wide variety of other aircraft, gave the RAF an all-important competitive edge.

When I think of the sacrifices and the efforts made by so many for our collective freedom, or of my Uncle and the many other brave young men who flew planes in the First World War, when survival expectancy was a mere few weeks, I am awed by it all.

Whether it was someone in the armed forces fighting in a far off land, a factory worker building planes, or a farmer at home producing food, they were all part of the fight and all part of the triumph. We owe it to all involved to make the most of every day in our lives and to be the best we can be.

If this story serves to make any reader a little more aware of the sacrifices that were made by so many during those far-off years of war, then it will have been worthwhile.

James R S Black, 2010

James Somerville Black

My Uncle, James Somerville Black, photographed at Roberton Mains Farm, Dolphinton, Biggar, Scotland, before leaving for France 1916/17.

Born at Fauldhouse in Scotland, November 23rd 1890, James moved to Canada and arrived in Winnipeg in November 1911. He must have wondered what he had done, for I have first-hand experience and other than the Arctic, I don't know if there is a colder place on earth at that time of year. He began work on November 21st 1911 as a bank teller for the Royal Bank of Canada in the Portage and Main branch in Winnipeg. The information I have is that he made his home in the YMCA on Mission, just a short distance from the bank.

Whether or not he requested it, I don't know, but he transferred to the Bank's branch in Regina, Saskatchewan in 1915. Sometime in that same year he volunteered for the 46th Battalion in Moose Jaw, Saskatchewan. Actual dates are unclear but at some point after that he transferred into the Royal Flying Corps. He was sent to France in 1916/17, where he flew with 16 Squadron. The pillar of RAF Fighter Command during the battle of Britain in the Second World War, Sir Hugh Dowding, was the commanding officer of 16 Squadron for a while but it's unlikely they ever met, as Dowding would have been back in England by the time my uncle got there.

On 29th April 1917, Second Lieutenant James Somerville Black was killed in action during a month in which the Allies lost 350 pilots. It has been known as 'Black April' ever since.

Buried at St. Omer in France, he died for freedom and honour.

James Somerville Black's medal of honour.

Introduction

Although from time to time this story relates to actual events in history, it is otherwise purely fictional. It focuses on a young man who was born and grew up in a particularly picturesque part of Scotland. There he shared with his family and those around him a warm and genuine bond at a time of great sacrifice and hardship. In his quest for freedom he admired and was admired, loved and was loved, cried and was cried for. The son of farming folk, he was taught by example that the way ahead was to work hard and to do what was right.

Some of the best farming land and certainly some of the most beautiful scenery in Scotland is to be found in Perthshire. There are fruit-growing areas, arable and stock farming, forestry – and it has one of the best salmon rivers in Scotland, the River Tay. Around Perth itself the land is quite flat but a few miles to the north it becomes more rolling and then, up around Pitlochry, it can be quite rugged.

James Somerville, the central character in the story, grows up on a farm just outside Pitlochry, a sleepy Highland town seemingly far removed from the threat of war but, with its young men heading away to the fight and later experiencing petrol and food rationing, it wasn't immune from the effects of the conflict that first engulfed Europe and then the wider world beyond.

Enlisting in the RAF at a young age, James becomes a fighter pilot and participates in the Battle of Britain in 1940. His squadron doesn't get through the battle unscathed; they were exhausted, and although they never confessed to it, were scared. Would they make it through? Would this be the flight they wouldn't come back from? The threat of invasion past and the enemy tactics changed from attacking airfields to bombing London. It was a turning point and eventually, weary, front line squadrons were withdrawn to less active aerodromes where the pilots could have a rest, James's back to Turnhouse, in Scotland.

While in Scotland he went back to Pitlochry and home as often as he could and, while there he always made the time to visit the teacher who had taught him in school, who meant more to him than he knew. He made frequent visits to Edinburgh as well and became particularly fond of the city and all her charm and history.

As the years went on the squadron was sent overseas and was eventually posted to Italy. After D-day, everybody thought the war would end by Christmas 1944 but it wasn't to be, Germany would fight on to the bitter end. Then the news came, Hitler was dead; the war in Europe was over. A few days later the squadron got the word they were going home to their old aerodrome in the south of England and, eventually back up to Turnhouse and home.

The war in Europe was over but it would be some time before the war in the Pacific would end. Eventually, with the surrender of Japan the world entered a new more frightening age. There was celebration at the end of hostilities, people could get on with their lives, some military personnel got home quite quickly after the end, but for others it would be many months. For some it would be years.

The war had dragged on. For many, including James and his squadron it was the thought of going home that kept them going. Sometimes they wondered if they would ever see home again.

Before going to war James had been told that he would be back but his experiences only confirmed what he had known from the start – that nothing compared to home or to the peace and tranquillity of the rolling hills of Perthshire.

1.   In the Beginning

It is mid-summer's day and so far it has been a peaceful day, warm with a quiet gentle breeze, the sun is shining down from a cloudless blue sky. Sitting hand-in-hand in our garden, waiting for our parents to arrive so we can have tea together, my thoughts drift to and fro with the sights, sounds and smells of summer. In the shade of the tree I close my eyes and listen to the sparrows above me. Farther away, I hear lapwings flap their wings, diving and swooping at any would-be predators getting too close to their nests. A curlew squawks. Off in the distance I can hear the afternoon train coming up the glen, on its way to Inverness. There is the smell of roses and other summer blossoms. Thinking about summer blossoms of a different kind, a host of happy memories come flooding back. It's a good day to be alive. I feel fortunate and privileged to be here. But for the grace of God, I could quite easily not have been. My mind is off in another place and time and I can't help but wonder why I was spared when so many perished. A twinge of guilt. Did I do enough? From deep inside I hear that little voice. 'Yes, you did enough. You did make a difference,' and I feel better again. I've been having these thoughts now and again but I've been told by my superiors that in light of what happened it's a natural reaction. Sometimes the whole thing just doesn't seem real.

The train is much louder now. Opening my eyes I watch it trudge upwards, pulling hard and billowing thick, black smoke, denying the light of day to everything around it. As the smoke slowly dissipates, the sanctuary of the glen is again revealed. How accurately that train reflected the recent past. Normality, the rumble of things to come, the noise and darkness and then, slowly, peace returns. Other than the brief moments of guilt, I feel lucky and I'm happy and content. We survivors will never be the same again. In fact, all those who went away and came home have similar stories and memories, some happy but many sad.

But still, in spite of everything I'm glad I was there at that point in time, to help fight the darkness. Privileged also to have met a number of people who have had a profound influence in my life.

It's been a little over a year since the war with Germany ended, bringing a halt to the bombing and destruction of so many cities in Britain, Europe, the Middle East, Russia, the Mediterranean and elsewhere. Not just the end of the killing in the air, on the battlefields or the high seas, but an end to the unspeakable atrocities committed in the concentration camps and P.O.W. camps – the indiscriminate and total disregard for human life.

Many innocent people found themselves in the wrong place at the wrong time. Those considered by the enemy to be of the wrong race, religion or beliefs. Those rendered homeless, maimed, orphaned or killed. For those of us who were in the armed forces for the duration of the war, or for the people in countries that were occupied, it is difficult to believe that it is all, at last, over.

Drowsy in the heat of the day, as the rumble and clickety-click of the train in the glen faded, I close my eyes and begin to reflect... right back to the beginning... about my mother, father, brothers and sisters and when I was a little boy.

On the 29th of April 1922, in a big, old and draughty two-storey farmhouse in Scotland, I was born the third son of William and Jean Somerville. A few weeks later I was christened with the name James. Years later Mum told me that when I came into the world I had a head full of thick, black hair and, for the most part, I didn't cry much. "The day you were christened you were like an angel," she said.

Altogether Mum and Dad had ten children, six daughters and four sons. William was the oldest, then John. I was next. Then they had their first girl, Isobel. They had another son, Richard, and after that five girls: Jean, Mary, Heather, Lisa and Grace.

My parents had moved to this particularly picturesque part of Scotland a couple of years before from Fauldhouse, a coal mining village about twenty miles west of Edinburgh, where the landscape and scenery is vastly different from where we live now. Before he married, Dad worked at home for my grandfather on his farm and part-time for others when he could. The only thing he ever wanted was to have a farm of his own.

Dad courted Mum for about two years before they married on 9th March 1919. Later that same year he took Mum, some belongings and a few head of Hereford cows to a farm northwest of Perth, not far from Dunkeld. Looking back, it was a courageous thing to do. They weren't very old and being so far away from their parents they really were on their own. This first venture together was three hundred acres of rented land, of which maybe one third was reasonably productive. The rest was steep and sloping, bracken and tree covered, a hiding place for rabbits and deer and a hunting ground for foxes and hawks.

Mum and Dad worked hard, doing what they had to do, tending to their small herd. Eventually the numbers grew. Not only did we have more cows but, to my dismay, Dad bought sheep as well. Then there was Daisy, an old Ayrshire cow that grazed in the little field beside the house. Mum milked that cow faithfully twice a day, every day. It seems the only time she didn't was a couple of weeks before and after she herself was giving birth. There were hens. We only had a few but they made sure Mum never had much of a garden. They were always in there, scratching out any seed she planted. Although she liked gardening, there wasn't much time in those early years.

As we grew up, the family got bigger and the livestock numbers increased, Mum and Dad had less and less time to themselves. But they thought the world of each other. I can honestly say we never heard them have a disagreement. There wasn't a lot of money around but we never went hungry. Mum was always baking something. Who knows where she got all her energy. The washing alone for our big and growing family was a daunting prospect. The workload did eventually get to be too much and she needed help, so for two, sometimes three days a week, she got a maid. A few months later Isabella moved into a little room of her own up in the attic. Bella was seventeen.

In the years that Bella stayed with us, my brothers and sisters and I had a lot of fun. We used to play hide and seek around the farm buildings but soon she knew all our hiding places. She would take us on picnics out on the hill, not far from the house, that was our favourite place to go. There was a stand of Douglas fir there that seemed to reach up and touch the sky; they were certainly big enough to hide behind. When we got fed up with that we would play in the burn that ran down off the hill into the river Tay below. The Tay was out of bounds for us. From a distance it looked majestic and serene, flowing through the valley. Dad didn't say a lot, so when he said, "do not go there," or "do not do this or that," you knew he meant it.

Most days Bella got us ready for school and walked with us part of the way there. In the afternoons she met us on the way home. At night, if we had homework, she would help us with that and then, all too soon, it was time for bed. Although I never found schoolwork that difficult, I didn't enjoy it very much. I only did what I had to do and couldn't wait for the weekends and holidays.

The summers and the years passed and, as we got older, we helped Dad on the farm. For the most part I enjoyed it, planting potatoes and turnips, making hay and harvest; the potatoes to quell our insatiable appetite, the turnips for the cows and sheep. I didn't like a few jobs, like picking stones off the fields after they were ploughed but we didn't get much sympathy from Dad. "Do what you have to do," he would say. "This too will pass." Over the years, whenever something had to be done that I didn't like doing, I heard that phrase resonate in my head.

Mum and Dad never stood still; if something needed doing, it was done. So it shouldn't have been a surprise when, at dinner one autumn Sunday, Dad announced we would be moving to a new farm. The oldest of us were horrified at first and didn't want to move. Would there be any hiding places at this new farm or Douglas fir or burns to paddle in? But he made it plain that we would be moving anyway. The following weekend he would be taking some of the livestock to the new farm and we three oldest boys would have to go along and help herd the cattle and sheep.

It was a dreary week and the weekend came all too quickly. On Saturday morning we were up early and just after eight o'clock we were heading down the farm road. Meg and Mhairi, our two border collies, were happy at least, keeping a keen eye on the livestock, doing what they loved to do. It never dawned on us to begin with, but if we were within walking distance, it couldn't be too far to this new farm.

We were so engrossed herding the cattle that it seemed like no time at all when Dad pointed up the hill and said, "that's where we are going." It didn't look like much from where we were at that moment, but the closer we got, the more we liked the look of it. It was on the north side of the glen. That was going to be different. It was also on the other side of the Perth-Inverness railway line and our river wasn't the Tay any longer, it would be the River Tummel, which flows into the Tay. We need not have worried. There were Douglas fir, a burn and buildings to play and hide in. When we got into the yard it looked like the house was a bit smaller and Dad said there was a hundred fewer acres, not that this meant a whole lot to us. But there was an inviting, comfortable feel about the place and I immediately felt at home.

We put the cattle in a field and did a bit of exploring. There was a nice fenced garden on the south side of the house, a place where Mum could at last do what she loved. There was already a big rhododendron to one side, with a rickety old seat under it. The view down the valley was spectacular. But more than all of that, this was going to be Mum and Dad's own farm; they had bought it. It seemed like Dad was ten feet tall that day, he had a smile on his face and a spring in his step; we had trouble keeping up with him on the way home.

The next couple of weeks were quite hectic. We all had to help pack our belongings to get ready for the flitting. Then the day came – Martimas – one of the two days in the year when most moves are made between farms in Scotland. With the help of a few friends and neighbours, everything we owned was loaded onto the horses and carts and at around eleven o'clock we made our way down the farm road for the last time. Mum and Dad were the last to leave. I was down the road a bit and had turned around to have a last look at the place. They were standing there, looking at the old house, then at each other. Mum put her arm through Dad's and then they turned and followed us. It was November 1932; I was ten-and-a-half years old.

The previous couple of weeks had been a bit unsettled weather-wise but this day was like a summer's day; not a cloud in the sky and a nice day for a walk. Everything was just right. For us kids it was an adventure. Unlike the day we moved the cattle, it seemed like we were never getting there. It was the middle of the afternoon before we arrived. Whether it was excitement or too much sun, I don't know, but we were all tired and just felt like sleeping. Nevertheless, we did a little more exploring and ended up by showing Mum her garden. It was plain to see just how happy they both were that day.

Before it got dark we moved our modest collection of furniture into the house. Mum gave us instructions where she wanted everything and then she and Bella made supper. Dad got the fire going in the sitting room and before long the house was quite cosy. Where everybody slept that night I don't remember, I was too tired to care.

The next morning, after breakfast, we unloaded the other carts. Before our neighbours left, Dad got a whisky bottle out and poured the grownups a dram. Whisky was something we usually saw only once a year, at New Year, but this was a special occasion. It wasn't every day you moved to another farm. Dad thanked them for their help and they in turn wished Mum and Dad good luck at their new farm.

The oldest of us spent the rest of the day familiarizing ourselves with our new farm and home. The more we saw, the more we liked. It was almost as if we had always been there. But what Dad hadn't told us yet was that we would now be going to a different school. Suddenly moving didn't seem such a good idea. The thought of going to another school had never entered our heads.

The next day was Monday and Dad said he would go with us. "Not to make sure you find the school, it's to make sure you go in," he said. Bella came with us that first morning as well. There was quite a sharp frost, so we got into the back of the buggy with her, where we huddled together under a blanket to keep warm. We could see our breath in the cold morning air.

Bella seemed to be full of little stories and tales. She could make light of the darkest moment. That morning was no different. Before we knew it, we were there. Looking over the side of the buggy it didn't look a big school. In some ways it looked just like the one we went to in Dunkeld. Jumping down from the buggy, Dad and Bella led us towards the schoolhouse door, where we were greeted by an old-looking lady who possessed the warmest of smiles. Dad shook her hand and introduced us.

"Hello, I'm Mrs Dunlop," she said. "How are you all this morning?"

None of us said a word.

"I know you are all a little frightened, so we will try to make your first day as pleasant as possible. In fact, we hope that all of the time you spend with us will be pleasant and that you have fun learning."

Still we said nothing. She looked at Dad and assured him she would look after us. Bella winked at us and then she and Dad left. Mrs Dunlop escorted my two older brothers to one room and then she came back, took my sister and me into another and introduced us to our new teacher.

"Hello, my name is Miss Campbell ... and you must be James and Isobel Somerville. I've been looking forward to meeting you," she said, shaking our hands. "I've got a desk all ready for you."

She was nice and did her best to make us feel at ease, but that didn't stop my knees from knocking but I could hear Dad's voice, "This too will pass." For the first few days Miss Campbell allowed Isobel and I to sit together and by week's end, thoughts of our old school, like our old farm, were fading. This new place of learning was just outside Pitlochry and, like our farm, it had a great view of the valley.

In no time at all Christmas and New Year were upon us and we had a few days off school. The weather had grown a lot colder and there was snow on the ground. We had a good time playing in it but Dad hoped there wouldn't be too much. It could mean buying more feed for the livestock. Although we all had fun in our new, cosier home, that first Christmas Mum wasn't feeling her best. Since the flitting she'd had a pain in her side. Some days it was worse than others and some days it wasn't there at all. Dad thought that maybe she had been overdoing it at the time of the flitting and pulled a muscle or something. He said if it didn't get any better in the next little while he would take her to the doctor.

All too soon it was time to go back to school. We had made new friends there. I liked Miss Campbell; she had a way of making learning fun. One day, early in the New Year, I wasn't allowed out at lunchtime. One of the other boys had been annoying Isobel, so I had punched his nose. Miss Campbell said that although defending my sister was the honourable thing to do I shouldn't have used my fist.

"You know James, you are a clever boy. You could be anything you want to be," she told me. In the next breath she went on. "What would you like to do when you leave school?"

The thought of being anything other than a farmer had never crossed my mind. I liked working with the cattle and helping on the farm.

"I want to be a farmer, like my dad," I told her.

She stared at me for the longest minute, not saying anything and then, quietly, she continued. "You can be anything you want to be." As time went by, I began to realize how wise she was.

Soon the cold winds of winter were replaced with something more moderate and the first signs of spring began to appear. Snowdrops and crocus were popping up everywhere, then daffodils and buds on the trees. There were so many trees in the valley, big grand trees, beech, sycamore and chestnut, good trees to climb. Dad too was relieved. The lambs were enjoying the better weather, either chasing each other up and down or stretching out in the sun. That first spring Dad was behind with his ploughing; it was usually done in the autumn but with everything else going, he hadn't had a chance to start. One of Dad's neighbours came over for a few days to help him to catch up. The field they were in had a steep slope, making the horses sweat on the way back up the hill. Both William and John had their first go at ploughing that spring. After an hour or so they had blisters on their hands where they had been hanging onto the reins and the shafts of the plough. Meg and I lay behind the dyke, watching them. We watched the crows and the seagulls too, flying around behind the plough and devouring worms as the sod was turned over.

The seagulls instinctively knew where there was food. Swooping down from a great height, they pulled their wings close to their bodies and dropped like a stone. Within a few feet of the ground, they spread their wings again and seemed to just settle on the ground. I found it fascinating watching them. Meg looked at me and then at the birds. She wanted to chase them but she was a little too fat for that; she was going to have pups in a few days, and a lot of them, judging by the size of her. After a while I went back to the house. I walked and Meg waddled. Mum and two of my sisters were working in the garden. I tried to sneak into the house but no such luck. Mum held up the spade. "Come and do some digging for me," she said. As I dug, Mum sat on the garden seat for a while, watching me, looking down the valley at the same time. Then she said she was going to help Bella make supper. As she disappeared through the front door I could see her holding her side. Later on, after we had gone to bed, I heard Dad say he would take her to the doctor the next day.

The day dawned and, as usual, Mum was up early and had breakfast ready, but as soon as it was over Dad took her into Pitlochry. It was almost dinnertime before they were back. We were anxious to know what the doctor had said to her.

"There is nothing wrong with me," she said, "the doctor thinks that maybe I pulled a muscle when I was digging. Nothing to worry about, I'm fine."

The next day or two she didn't do much and by the end of the week she seemed to be back to normal.

There is always something to do around a farm and spring is no exception. Dad was busy seeding and harrowing and when we got back from school he always had a list of jobs for us to do.

One afternoon Bella met us at the house door, saying she had a surprise for us. Meg had given birth to her pups. It was her first litter and she looked so proud of them. We picked one up. "Careful now," said Bella. "Dogs don't like you touching their puppies when they are new born." We were all excited and at suppertime we thought of names for them all.

"Don't be getting too fond of them now," Dad said. "We will only be keeping one."

That dampened our enthusiasm but I suppose we knew that's what would happen.

In the weeks that followed we did get attached to them, of course, and we were a bit sad when the day came for them to go, but Dad had decided which one he was keeping and the rest were sold. The one we kept looked like her mother; we named her Sally. Everything else was going fine; calves and lambs were growing like mushrooms, Dad was happy with his farm, Mum loved her garden and spent a lot of time in it when we were at school.

Before we knew it, it was the end of school for the summer. Miss Campbell told us that she was moving up a class, so it meant for those of us having to move classrooms we would have her for a teacher the next year as well. I was happy about that.

The summer weather was glorious, with lots of warm days for picnics and, for a change, both Mum and Bella went. Another unusual thing happened that summer. Dad took us fishing on the River Tummel. We didn't catch anything but we had a good time.

Who knows where the time went? Everything seemed to be perfect, except for the fact that school would be starting in a few days. Dad was up to date with his work and Mum actually found time to sit in and enjoy her garden. It looked like the doctor had been right; she had just been doing too much and didn't seem to be bothered with any pains now.

My sister Mary started school. Mum and Dad took us in the old car they had just bought. Once it started it ran fine, but it was just as well we lived on a hill. More often than not, we had to let it run down the hill to bump start it.

It was good to see Miss Campbell again. I hadn't realized I had missed her. As usual, the first day back we didn't do much but we certainly made up for it in the weeks that followed. At home, in his relentless pursuit to increase the size of the herd, Dad had been away at sales buying more livestock. By mid-October the weather had turned decidedly colder and already the leaves on the trees were beginning to change colour. A couple of nights had been particularly cold and wet and Dad decided to put some of the cattle in the shed. But the cattle had other ideas and didn't want to go inside, so Mum, Dad and Bella, with the aid of our two dogs, had to spend a number of hours rounding them up. When we got home they were sitting at the kitchen table, having a cup of tea, but it was clear from Mum's face that she wasn't well. Then she did something I'd never see her do before. She went to lie down. The next morning she was no better and was barely getting around. Even before we left for school, Dad had taken her to the doctor.

Again he told her she had just been overdoing it and to rest but, if she didn't feel any better in a day or two, he would get her into the hospital for some tests. When we got home from school Mum was already in bed. Nothing ever seemed to faze Dad but he was clearly concerned. We were like church mice that night, trying not to disturb her.

The next morning before we were up, Dad had taken Mum to the hospital. Bella told us that Mum had been up most of the night in pain. When we got home from school Mum wasn't there and we were anxious to know what was wrong. Dad, in his usual calm demeanour, said not to worry, the doctors had told him that Mum was suffering from a grumbling appendix and she may need a small operation to remove it.

"She'll be home before you know it," he said. "In a few days she'll be as right as rain. The doctor told me that is quite a common thing and that we shouldn't worry."

We had never heard of an appendix. What was it? Dad and Bella tried to reassure us she would be fine. I wouldn't have thought about it so much but Dad was clearly worried. When I went to bed, I tossed and turned all night and couldn't sleep. I had a deep, nagging feeling of impending doom. At school the next day I told Miss Campbell about Mum. My lip quivered and I could feel tears well up in my eyes. I just couldn't help it. Mum was in hospital, I loved her and wanted her home. Miss Campbell put her arms around me.

"Try not to worry. I'm sure your Mum will be alright."

The few days turned into a week, Mum still wasn't home and they still had not done the operation. If anything, the feeling I had inside was worse. Then, out of the blue, Dad announced that Mum was a lot better and would be getting home the next day. It was good news and I couldn't wait to see her. In anticipation we ran most of the way home and when we got into the yard there was a big black car sitting there, shining in the late afternoon sun. 'Someone else has brought Mum home,' we thought. Racing into the kitchen, we expected to find her there, but instead Dad was sitting at the table, talking to a burly-looking man dressed in a dark suit and a bowler hat. Mum had to be in the sitting room.

She wasn't there either, but Bella was, sitting on the couch with the rest of my sisters, tears streaming down her face. We heard the black car start and could see it through the window as it made its way down the farm road. Dad came into the sitting room, sat down on his chair and looked at each of us in turn. Other than Bella's sobbing there wasn't a sound. Dad wasn't someone who showed a lot of emotion but it didn't mean he didn't have feelings. We knew his family and those close to him meant everything to him. With eyes misting over and a crackled voice, he began.

"I'm afraid I've got bad news... Your Mum won't be coming home, she died earlier today."

Stunned, we stood there in total disbelief. How could this be? Everybody said it was a simple procedure and that she would be fine.

Bella was sobbing louder now, hanging on tightly to my younger sisters. They too began to cry. Dad said he had things to attend to in the town and left us with instructions to feed the cattle in the shed. We walked around in a daze. That little voice inside had been right all along.

We found out later that Mum's condition had been more complicated than normal. This is what had been troubling her off and on for almost a year. She hadn't just been overdoing it. Why couldn't the doctors have known that? We were told, in simple terms, what had happened, but I wasn't really listening. I just knew that whatever it was had killed her, that we would never see our mother again. We didn't get a chance to say good-bye or tell her how much we loved her. The hardest part for me was that she died alone. None of us was with her.

Mum's funeral was arranged for Tuesday of the following week. Our grandparents were there; Dad had phoned them from the town on the day Mum died. There were a lot of other people there, most of whom I had never seen before.

Born on September 7th 1896, Mum was christened Jean Robertson Bell. She had a younger sister, who died when she was five, and a brother who still lived on the family farm where they were all born. After Mum and Dad married and decided to move to Perthshire, Mum's parents hadn't been very happy about it and had often been a bit frosty towards Dad. For a while after Mum died they blamed him for her death.

Mum died on October 26th 1933; she was 37 years old. Three days later she was buried in the churchyard in Pitlochry.

The next months were a blur. We missed our mother desperately. Our grandmother stayed with us for a while. Friends and neighbours came to visit and at school our teachers tried to console us. Christmas and New Year came and went; needless to say, it wasn't very festive. Then, when spring came, we were hit with another bombshell. Bella told us she was going to be married and would be leaving in a month. Our whole world was falling apart. We were happy for her but what were we going to do without her? For almost nine years she had been there to help us and play with us.

Over the next weeks Dad interviewed a number of people and managed to hire a lady named Janet. All too soon Bella was gone. For a while Janet tried her best but she was never going to fill Bella's shoes. She just couldn't cope with all there was to do and started to scold us for silly little things. She often had my little sisters crying. Dad told her there had been enough tears in the house in the last six months and let her go. In the next couple of weeks Dad tried hard to find someone else but to no avail.

Then, in an instant, the world was again a brighter place.

It was the weekend and we were all in the kitchen having dinner when there was a knock on the door. William opened it and in walked Bella, suitcase in hand. After the excitement had died down my youngest sister Grace asked Bella what we had all been wondering.

"Where is your new husband Bella? Did you bring him to visit?"

You could have heard a pin drop. She looked around the room at each one of us and then she responded.

"No Grace, I didn't bring my husband and no, I didn't come to visit. I'm not getting married now." She hesitated, looking at Dad. "I've come to stay."

I don't think any of us could believe it. Even Dad was speechless. After we had stopped hugging her he put his arm around her and welcomed her back.

For a long time I never knew why Bella didn't get married. I didn't care. We were just happy that she was back.

Just over a year later, on midsummer's day 1935, twenty months after Mum died, Isabella Jean Duncan and Dad were married in a quiet ceremony in the Registrar's Office in Pitlochry. Bella was ecstatically happy as she held on to Dad's hand. Although they were happy and we were happy for them, on that day and in all the years since, none of us forgot our mother or the good, kind person she was.

A year or so later Dad and Bella had a little girl together. Named Margaret, she was born August 10th 1936. Dad had bought more land, more cows and even a second-hand tractor. William had left school and was working at home. John had also left school and he too was working at home and part time for neighbours. He liked fixing engines and, as there were more and more people getting tractors, he was becoming increasingly busy doing that. In a few months I'd be leaving school myself although it hadn't been all that bad as far as I was concerned. I'd been lucky with my teachers, especially Miss Campbell. She had helped, pushed and encouraged me when I needed it.

Although I liked the idea of working at home, a day came that changed my life and after it I could think of nothing else. It all started one afternoon in Miss Campbell's class. First, there was a distant drone, getting louder and louder. We looked at each other, not knowing what it was. Then we saw them... three aeroplanes, flying up the valley, skipping over the trees. I had seen pictures of planes but I had never seen a real one before and certainly never flying this low. We could see the pilots clearly.

In an instant, I knew what I wanted to do.

Miss Campbell saw the look on my face as they flew past.

"Do you know where they're going?" she asked

Peering out of the window still, I shook my head.

"There's an open day at Blair Castle this weekend," she went on. "They're going there. You can come with me if you'd like. There is someone there I want to see. I'll take a picnic."

It never dawned on me at the time to ask her how she knew the planes were going there. After Dad said I could go, the weekend couldn't come quickly enough and on Saturday morning I met Miss Campbell at the station in Pitlochry. The train was busy. It turned out that most of the people on it were going to Blair Castle. Travelling north, immersed in our own thoughts, we sat quietly and looked out of the train window. It was a cool morning with patchy fog, but it had all the makings of being a nice day. When we got to Blair Castle Miss Campbell bought a programme to see what activities were scheduled for the day.

"There you are, it says here that, weather permitting, the planes will fly after lunch."

Blair Castle is, in itself, an impressive building and although it's open to the public at different times of the year, I had never been there before. But I wasn't interested in any of it that day. I just wanted to find the aeroplanes. We walked around to the south side of the castle and there they were; bright yellow and in sharp contrast to the green grass they were standing on. There were a lot of people around them already, talking to the pilots. Miss Campbell made a beeline for them for some reason. This was a dream come true. Here I was, standing in front of something that could climb and soar in the sky and go wherever it wanted. Who knows how long I walked around, fascinated by the aeroplanes and the pilots. Then I heard a familiar voice call me. Turning around, I saw Miss Campbell beckoning me. I had completely forgotten about her. She was talking and laughing with an older-looking man in uniform.

"James, I'd like you to meet my father."

"Hello" he said, shaking my hand. "Catherine has told me all about you."

"Catherine?" I asked him.

Miss Campbell put her hand on my shoulder and laughed. "I'm Catherine."

In all the years I'd been in her class, somehow I'd never known her first name.

"What can I tell you about our aeroplanes young man?" He asked.

"Everything!" I replied.

As we walked around, he explained what everything was and how it worked and then he showed me inside the cockpit. It was fascinating. All the while Miss Campbell held on tightly to his arm. They smiled and laughed with each other. It was easy to see they got along well.

"We're going to be flying after lunch," he said. "Would you like to go for a ride?"

I was dumbstruck; the best I could do in response was a rather feeble nod.

Miss Campbell suggested we have a walk round for a while and return later for the picnic. As we walked, I spent more time looking over my shoulder at the planes. We went back, had our picnic, met the pilots and then, just before one o'clock, Miss Campbell's father asked me if I was ready to go. I wanted to go but now it was time I was scared to death. Miss Campbell already had a flying jacket and goggles on.

"Come on, I'll help you get your things on," she said.

Miss Campbell climbed into the front cockpit of one plane and her father helped me get into another. He helped with my harness and then climbed into the back cockpit. Seconds later, he leaned forward and asked if I was ready to go. Another feeble nod was all I could muster.

"Don't worry, you'll be fine," he said.

The engine started and immediately I felt the blast from the propeller. We taxied to the end of the grass strip and turned into the wind. Looking across at Miss Campbell in the other plane I could see she was laughing and had her thumbs up. I did the same. With engines screaming, within seconds we were racing along the grass. I hung on for dear life; the noise from the engine was deafening. Then we were up, the ground got farther away and, as the plane climbed higher, the feeling was indescribable. Suddenly, someone was talking to me.

"You take the controls for a bit."

Turning around I looked at Miss Campbell's father; he was laughing and nodding.

"Go ahead, keep her straight and level for a bit, then we'll go back and land."

Taking hold of the joystick, I couldn't keep it level, we were either going up or going down.

"Don't worry about it," he said. "Flying level is quite difficult, just move the stick to the left and we'll turn around and go back."

After a bit more of going up and down he took control and we started to go down. With Blair Castle's massive white walls sticking up out of the carpet of green like an oasis in a desert it wasn't difficult to find our way back. The ground raced up to meet us then the wheels touched; we were down. The engine stopped and we got out of the plane.

"Well young man, what do you think of that?"

Overcome with excitement and enthusiasm I was babbling. He gave me some information about the plane and the Royal Air Force to take home and then we shook hands.

"Maybe I'll see you again sometime," he said.

He turned to his daughter. They gave each other the warmest of smiles and a hug, him telling her to remember to write.

Sitting in the station waiting for the train, Miss Campbell told me a few little things about her family. She told me that her father was Squadron Leader John Campbell, an instructor stationed at Turnhouse, just outside Edinburgh, training young men to be pilots. "We phone and write to each other as much as possible. Like you, my mother died when I was quite young, but so far Dad has never remarried, there's just the two of us. So you see, we have some things in common, you and I."

When we got back to Pitlochry I thanked her for one of the best days of my life and told her that flying was what I wanted to do when I left school.

"You can be anything you want to be, James Somerville; I'm glad you had a good day today."

After that first experience at Blair Castle, Miss Campbell invited me on a number of occasions to go with her to see her father at Turnhouse. He took me around the airfield with him and I watched and talked to mechanics working on the aeroplanes. The highlight of these visits, though, was when he took me flying. I felt privileged, as indeed I was.

I turned seventeen and although I had left school, I kept in touch with Miss Campbell. The year was 1939. There were dark clouds over Europe and, if the wireless was to be believed, war with Germany wasn't far off. Adolf Hitler came to power and built up a frightening military arsenal, wielding an intimidating heavy hand in various countries in Europe. At the time he seemed invincible and thought he could do what he liked; for a while, he did just that.

Dad knew I wanted to fly planes but when I spoke to him about enlisting in the RAF I sensed he wasn't keen on the idea. Speaking to Bella about it one day, she said that it looked like there would be a war. If I were in the RAF there was a good chance I'd be in the thick of it.

"Your Dad just doesn't want to see you get hurt."

The thought had never occurred to me. I just knew I wanted to fly.

Miss Campbell told me her father had a few days leave and asked if I'd like to spend it with them. I accepted.

We had a nice, relaxing time together, not doing anything in particular. We walked, talked and discussed what was happening in Europe. Miss Campbell's father thought a war with Germany was inevitable. He brought forms for me should I want to enlist. I asked him if I would train at Turnhouse but he said he had no control over that. The R.A.F. had a number of training fields and I could be sent to any one of them. Before I went home, we reviewed and filled out the forms together. After I got home, I talked with Dad and Bella and told them what I had done. Dad wasn't happy.

"You could die," he said, quietly. "I couldn't live with that."

Explaining to him that if there was a war there would more than likely be conscription anyway and I would be sent where I was most needed. If I enlisted, I could go into the service I wanted. Flying was what I wanted to do. Reluctantly and with a heavy heart, he signed the forms. Before returning to Turnhouse, I met with Miss Campbell's father and gave him the forms. He said he would see what he could do about me being stationed if not at Turnhouse, somewhere else in Scotland. He shook my hand as usual and then gave his daughter the same warm affectionate smile and hug as always then he boarded the train. As we watched it disappear, Miss Campbell said she was going to go to the little café on the corner for tea and wondered if I would join her.

We both needed to talk. She was always a bit down after they parted. This time there might be a war and he could be posted somewhere else, to the south of England or even overseas. She feared for his safety, felt responsible for getting me interested in aeroplanes and feared for mine as well.

In the weeks that followed, I helped around the farm where I could. Sometimes I helped Bella in the garden and sometimes we would just sit on the garden seat and chat, looking down the valley. Then it came... an official-looking envelope with O.H.M.S. stamped on the front. It was lying on the table when we went in for dinner. After eating, Dad looked at the letter and then at me.

"Well... are you going to open it? I need to know if we need to find work for you this summer or if we need to help you pack."

Picking up the letter, I opened it and thought at the same time 'what have I done?' Bracing myself, I read the words on the page.

"Well... are you going to tell us what it says?" Bella asked.

Looking across the table at them both, I told them I had to report to RAF Turnhouse on June 1st to start basic training. Nobody said anything for a moment.

"Well," Dad went on, trying to look happy about it. "It looks like we'll have to help you pack."

We got up from the table, saying nothing more. Later on in the day I went into the town to see Miss Campbell and tell her. We went for a walk by the river. Except for the relentless movement of the water and the odd shriek of the hooded crows it was quiet and peaceful.

"Well, at least you know some people there," she blurted. "And my father's there if you need him."

We sat down for a while on a big flat stone beside the water. It was especially quiet there. The river ran deep and quiet.

"I should never have taken you to Blair Castle."

She was staring out across the river but I could tell by her voice that she was upset.

"There's going to be a war, Dad's going to be in it. You're only seventeen and you're going to be in it too. Why does this have to happen?"

For a few moments, I didn't say anything and then, in the most optimistic tone I could muster, I tried to console her.

"Miss Campbell, try not to worry, your Dad will be fine. He is a good pilot, that's why they have him doing training. If I had anything to do with the air force, I'd make sure he stayed at Turnhouse to do just that. As for me, I love this place. I can't imagine having lived anywhere else. In fact, there's a little cottage down the valley a bit I've always liked. In a year or two I'm going to buy it and live in it so I can grow old here."

She looked at me and laughed and then got up.

"Come on," she said. "It's getting late, we should get back."

Walking back to town she told me she was going to go and see her father and that maybe we could go down on the train together before the first.

The next two weeks flew past. Bella helped me pack the things she felt I would need, and then it was time to go. One minute I was excited and anxious to be away, the next I wished I wasn't going. Dad and Bella would take me to the station and so I said goodbye to my brothers and sisters at the farm. Dad put my suitcase in the car and told me to get a move on or I'd miss my train. By the time we got to the station, there were just a few minutes to spare. Miss Campbell looked a little anxious, scanning the platform. The train whistle blew and then the conductor's whistle. 'God tell me why I'm doing this,' I thought. Dad looked upset as he shook my hand. I gave Bella a hug. She reminded me to write and let them know how I was.

The second we got on the train, it started to move. Closing the door, I stood with my head out of the window, waving until I could see them no longer. Miss Campbell pulled on my sleeve.

"Come on, I've reserved a seat for us."

I followed her into the carriage where we sat silently, looking out of the window. Eventually the train arrived in Edinburgh where Miss Campbell's father met us. That first night I stayed with them. He told me where to report the next morning and said that if there was anything he could help me with in the weeks ahead to let him know. It was a comfort to know he was there, but I knew that however difficult things might get, I would have to find my own way. Sleep was difficult and when morning came I didn't feel good. We sat together to have breakfast but I couldn't eat anything. Miss Campbell and her father were looking at me and could see I was scared out of my wits.

"Don't worry about a thing," he said. "You'll be fine."

2.   Training Begins

Leaving the house together, Miss Campbell walked with us as far as the main gate where we said our good-byes. We turned and looked at each other. I had never noticed until then but I was a little taller than her now. With her eyes misted over, she gave me a hug and said quietly in my ear.

"You write to me, do you hear?"

Occasionally at school she would give me a little hug, like when Mum died. This was different. As she held me, I could feel she was crying.

I promised to write and she reluctantly let me go. Her father and I went through the gate and made our way along the asphalt to the building where I was to report. Looking back, I saw her wipe her eyes. We waved to each other and then I went inside. When I came out she was gone. I felt so alone. Turning around, I went to find the new home I would be sharing with twenty-nine other young men who wanted to be pilots. Finding a vacant bed, I put my belongings on top of it and sat and glanced at those of us already there. They looked as scared as I felt.

Miss Campbell's father had already warned me about the drill sergeant named Ferguson. 'What he says goes. You'll find him a fair man but his word is the law.'

We were to be on the parade ground at 10 o' clock, but one or two of our group were a few minutes late. Well, I have never heard anybody shout that loud before or since!

None of us was ever late again.

That first day we were allocated a bunk, which we were told had to be kept spotless, with bed made every day. We were then given a haircut, medical and also a uniform. By the end of the day I had become friendly with two other young men, Findlay Douglas from Dumbarton and William Gray from Stirling; they were both nineteen. I was the youngest in the bunch. We were all there because we wanted to fly, but were told that training would be tough and that by the end only a handful of us would become pilots. The rest would become navigators, wireless operators or some other type of aircrew. It was the topic of conversation among us before lights out. We looked at each other, all likely wondering the same thing. Who were the pilots among us? I'd never given any thought to the fact that for some reason I might not be good enough, but I made a commitment to myself right then that I'd do all I could to be one of the few.

Our days consisted of getting up and running around the airfield by 6 a.m., rain or shine. After breakfast we would spend most of the morning with sergeant Ferguson on the parade ground. After lunch, we learned about navigation, weather and more. There was a lot to learn but I didn't find it difficult. When night came we fell asleep instantly. Sunday was the exception and were allowed to sleep later if we wanted. After breakfast, however, we were expected to be in church. In the afternoon we could do what we liked and it was then I made an effort to write home. And sometimes, discreetly, I'd have a chat with Miss Campbell's father. I asked him about the percentage of cadets who would become pilots and he confirmed that it was correct. He hadn't told me before because he hadn't wanted to discourage me.

"Think only that you are going to do it," he said. "Immerse yourself in what has to be done. You can be anything you want to be." Where had I heard that before? "Anything I can help you with, I will, but it's up to you. You have to look at it from the R.A.F. point of view. They don't want young men flying their planes who don't know what they are doing."

And so that's what I did. As the weeks passed we spent less time on the parade ground and more in class. There were tests every other day to evaluate our progress, but so far, since getting to the airfield, we hadn't been near a plane.

One afternoon I got two letters from home; one was from Bella. It didn't have any news really, Everybody was fine. The other was from Miss Campbell, reminding me that I hadn't written to her. She said also that school would be finished soon for the summer and she would be spending time at Turnhouse with her father. Perhaps we would see each other? Feeling guilty, I sent her a note by return.

At last we were introduced to actual flying. One or two of my classmates were sick the first time they went up. They discovered they didn't like flying much. I, on the other hand, couldn't wait to fly again. We were now at the stage of our training where our instructors knew who the fighter pilots were among us. With a lot of the classroom stuff behind us and into more flying, this part of our training was enjoyable.

Speaking to Miss Campbell's father one Friday afternoon, he asked if I'd like to go to his house on the Sunday coming for afternoon tea.

"Just keep it to yourself though," he said. "I don't want the rest of your group to think you're getting preferential treatment."

It would be a change to get away from the airfield for a little while and I thanked him for the invitation. After church I discreetly made my way there. It was a short walk to his house and within a minute of knocking on the door it opened. There stood Miss Campbell.

"Miss Campbell! I didn't know you were here. You didn't write and tell me we you were coming."

"You don't write much either," she retorted.

Fumbling for an excuse, I told her that the R.A.F. gave me more home-work than she did and I didn't have a lot of time to write.

"You look very smart in your uniform," she said, ushering me in the door. Her father was sitting at the kitchen, grinning.

"Surprised?" He asked.

"Very. It's great to see someone from home."

Miss Campbell's father said he had arranged to have a car for the after-noon, so we had a quick lunch and at the same time Miss Campbell brought me up to date with what was happening in Pitlochry. Then we were heading for Edinburgh, or "The Smoke" as she was affectionately known. It would be my first time in the city. Walking along Prince's Street, looking up at the castle, I felt comfortable and at home somehow. Some-time, when I got the chance, I'd visit the castle; it looked impressive, sitting on the edge of the sheer rock face. Impenetrable. We found a little café where we could have tea and a chat. Although it was a Sunday afternoon the city was busy.

"Where do they all come from and what do they do?" I wondered.

"Funny," said Miss Campbell. "I was wondering the same thing."

After a while it was time to head back. Arriving at Turnhouse I thanked them both for the day and the surprise. Miss Campbell walked with me to the gate and at the same time gave me a letter from Dad and Bella. Looking at it and holding it, for the first time I felt homesick. She had gone to the farm one day to see them. They were fine and sent their love.

"Dad has been keeping me informed about how you are," she said. "About how busy you've been with your training, so I'll forgive you for not writing more."

She went on to say that she was planning on staying until the end of the month.

"Hopefully we can see each other again before I go back."

"I'd like that," I replied.

As our training progressed the workload was intense, I thought of little else. But I was determined to accomplish what I had come to do. Conse-quently the next weeks just vanished. We had by now done a fair bit of flying with an instructor and a number of us had also gone solo. It was unexpected when it happened. It had been a nice sunny morning with almost no wind and a few of us had been doing some circuits. One time after I landed, my instructor told me to taxi back to the apron. When we got there he said he was getting out and instructed me to do one circuit on my own.

He could see I wasn't keen on the idea and put his hand on my shoulder. "On you go," he said. "You'll be fine."

After taxiing out for my take-off run, I sat for a minute. Then I heard Dad's voice in my head. 'On you go. Do what you have to do.' Opening the throttle, the plane responded and on reaching take off speed I eased back on the stick. It was the most unbelievable feeling. I had full control of the plane. No one in the back seat to help if I got into trouble. I was on my own and free. My instructor met me when I got back to the apron. Getting out of the plane he shook my hand and congratulated me. I felt great. For those of us who flew solo that day there was much excitement, Findlay couldn't contain himself and wouldn't stop nattering. But until we got some leave we could only share our exuberance with each other.

Into the last few days of August and after three months of training, running true to form, the R.A.F. had made their selection. William, Findlay and Yours Truly were three of only seven who would go on to be fighter pilots. There was still a lot to learn and we couldn't take anything for granted, but it was indeed a milestone for us. We had made the grade and were ecstatic. We would not, however, ever forget the day when we were chosen. No need to wonder and have to look up the date. We would always remember it was the week when war with Germany was declared.

For the past number of weeks, our Prime Minister had been trying to reach some kind of peaceful agreement with Germany, but it wasn't to be. Nothing was going to stand in the way of Hitler's quest for whatever it was he wanted.

Sadly, war was declared.

It was the third day of September 1939.

3. Dark Clouds

After learning who would go to fighter pilot training we were allowed a couple of days off. I spent the Sunday with Miss Campbell and her father. The first thing they did was to congratulate me on my achievement. We talked as well about us now being at war, but we didn't dwell on it.

"Have you ever played golf?" Miss Campbell's father asked.

I never had, so he suggested we go and give it a try.

We went to the course not far from the airfield, where Miss Campbell's father tried in vain to teach me the art of hitting the ball. It had been a while since I'd laughed so much and the day passed all too quickly. Miss Campbell walked with me back to the airfield gate, telling me at the same time she would have to go back to Pitlochry. School was starting again.

"You've done really well," she said. "I'm proud of you."

"It's been good seeing you again," I replied. "Thanks for the really enjoyable day. It's a pity we didn't have a bit more time to spend together."

Telling her I had a week's leave coming up I suggested we could maybe get together then.

"It's a date," she said, taking my hand. "Now promise me you'll be careful when you're flying. If anything happened to you I'd never be able to look your family in the face again."

Promising I would, we said goodbye and I went through the gate.

For the first time since getting to Turnhouse, time seemed to drag. I couldn't wait to get on the train for home. We were now training on aircraft that were bigger, heavier and had a lot more power. There was a squadron of Hurricanes based at Turnhouse. Anytime we could, we watched them take off and climb out. We wondered how long it would be before they would allow us in one. What was even more exciting was, we heard a rumour that a squadron of Spitfires would soon be stationed on the airfield. 'Now that's what I'd really like to get into,' I thought.

At long last the day came. We had been away from home for four months, now we were going back for a few days. I couldn't wait to see my family. It had been a dull day with the odd spot of rain and by the time I got on the train it was pouring. It was a driech day. Sitting in the carriage with the rain pelting off the window it seemed we were never getting there. As slow as it seemed, the train pulled into Pitlochry right on time. Looking out of the window I could see a handful of people standing under the overhang of the station roof, but no familiar faces. It was raining heavier here than it had been in Edinburgh. It certainly wasn't flying weather, I thought, as I gathered up my belongings and darted across the platform into the waiting room. There were no familiar faces there either. Maybe they didn't get my letter. Then there was a voice I knew. Turning around Dad, Bella, two of my little sisters and Miss Campbell were there. It was they who had been sheltering under the overhang. Shaking Dad's hand I gave him a hug; by the time I got to Bella I could see she was a bit misty eyed. I asked my two sisters if they had missed me. 'Only a little,' Margaret answered. Laughing, I looked at Miss Campbell. She too looked a little emotional.

Wrapping our arms around each other, I thought how great she smelled, like fresh flowers.

"Hello," she said. "It's good to see you."

We stood chatting for a few minutes then bundled into the car. Dropping Miss Campbell off at her house, I arranged to meet with her on the Sunday. It was good to see all my family. I hadn't realized how much I 'd missed them. They wanted to know all the things I had been doing, what was it like to fly. It had been a busy exciting time for me and I had learned a lot, but when I tried to explain what I'd been doing it didn't seem like much. They told me what they had been doing. There really wasn't anything new. William was still working at home and John was still doing part-time work away. Nobody mentioned the war.

As we sat down for supper that first night home I was reminded of how good a cook Bella was. I hadn't realized how much I had missed it. The whole week I was home she pampered me, making all the things she knew I liked. By the time we got to bed I was tired, so with the familiarity of the bedroom I used to share with my three brothers I was soon oblivious to the continual downpour outside.

When I woke the next morning it was late. From the sanctuary of my warm bed I could hear it was still raining. Sometimes the weather is like that at that time of year, the transition between summer and autumn. It meant, though, that for a good part of the day we were housebound. Before venturing downstairs I peered out my bedroom window at the green, but now very wet fields and could see cows in some of them, huddled in the corners with their backs up. They didn't like cold, wet days.

For a house that had so many inhabitants it was strangely quiet for a Saturday morning, especially a wet one. Heading into the kitchen I found Bella there.

"Well good morning," she said.

I put my arm around her waist and said that she should have wakened me.

"You needed the rest. You were tired when you went to bed. Besides, it's still raining."

Later on, when it cleared up a bit, I went for a walk around the farm with William and John. Although they were wet, the fields looked nice and green and fresh. We talked about the war and what we thought would happen. William wondered if there would be conscription. Would he get called up? Time would tell.

After suppertime I had a chat with Dad, telling him I'd seen the new cows he had bought. He told me then that as soon as he could he would buy more. He felt that if the war was to drag on, food could be in short supply. From the very beginning though there was an unwritten rule in our home that we wouldn't talk about the war any more than we had to. Two of the younger members of the family had not long since started taking fiddle lessons. They played for me and asked what I thought.

"It sounds like two cats screeching," I said.

"Fine, we won't play for you again if that's what you think!"

Later I told them I was teasing and that it sounded great and then asked them how they were getting on at school.

"We have Miss Campbell this year. We like her a lot but she talks about you all the time, about how you were a model student."

Teasing them again, I said she was only telling them the truth.

On Sunday I awoke to a clear and somewhat cold morning. Looking out of the window down the valley there was wispy fog in some areas and in the garden Bella's flowers were looking a bit sorry for themselves. Before breakfast I went out and helped Dad and my brothers feed the cows and to make sure they were all right after the rain. Another month or so and some of them would be inside again for the winter. 'The cycle never ends,' I thought, but looking at Dad he never seemed to tire of it. Making our way back to the house, I could smell breakfast before we got there.

"Sit yourselves down," said Bella. "It's almost ready."

They say you never miss anything until you don't have it anymore. I was aware of how good Bella was to us, but having been deprived of the attention for a while and then coming back to it, I was a lot more appreciative. Although Bella wasn't our natural mother she pampered all of us. She was like Mum in so many ways. She had the same easy-going nature and a seemingly endless amount of energy. Although it had been almost six years since Mum died the memories were still so vivid.

By the time I got into town, with the sun warming the day the fog was almost gone. Miss Campbell was already in the café, waiting. She smiled as I made my way to the table and on sitting down we exchanged hellos.

"Am I late or are you early?" I asked.

Shrugging her shoulders she said it didn't matter, whatever it was it was only a minute or two one way or the other. We talked for ages and drank tea. I asked her if my little sisters were working hard in class then told her what they had said. She fumbled for words.

"Come on," I said. "Let's go fishing."

Heading for the river, we heard it long before we saw it. After all the rain it was a raging torrent. We sat on our big boulder. It was a bit quieter there but fishing was a waste of time. Miss Campbell, like me, enjoyed having a picnic, today was no exception. She had brought something to eat; I promised that the next time I'd provide it. Walking back after our fruitless fishing expedition I apologized for making her feel uncomfortable in the café earlier.

"You didn't really. Trying to inspire them I have mentioned your name a few times in class. Anyway, I'm proud to be able to say you were my student."

We parted company outside the café, agreeing to meet again at a ceilidh in the town the following Friday night. Between one thing and another, the week flew past. When my sisters were at school it gave the rest of us some quiet time for a chat. I had a heart-to-heart conversation with John, who was asking about the R.A.F. and the mechanics who fix the planes. I told him about the engines in the planes I flew.

"The engines in the Hurricane and Spitfire are twelve cylinder and more than a thousand horsepower."

"I don't believe it," he said. "Why would you need all that power to turn a propeller?"

He said he was thinking about enlisting to be a mechanic. I thought something was on his mind, since getting home he'd been unusually quiet.

"What about helping on the farm, doesn't Dad need you?"

Apparently he had talked to Dad and had his approval. Dad felt that if he was fixing planes he would hopefully be out of harm's way and that the R.A.F. would teach him all there was to know about engines. It sounded like his mind was made up and asked me to find out when I went back how to go about it. When I got the chance I talked to Dad and Bella. They said they would miss him if he went, but that they'd manage.

Friday night came and Dad and Bella had decided we should all go to the ceilidh. We met Miss Campbell there and found a place where we could all be together. We had a good time; nobody had given the war a thought. Before we went home I told Miss Campbell I'd be leaving on the midday train on Sunday and asked if there was anything she wanted me to take to her father.

On Saturday morning we slept late. It was dinnertime when my little sisters got up, giggling about how late they had stayed up the night before. In the afternoon I went for a quiet walk around the farm. When I got to the north field I stood, leaning over the gate for a while, looking down the valley and letting my mind wander. Where would I be next year at this time, I wondered.

Sunday morning I awoke to the smell of baking. When I got to the kitchen it was obvious Bella had been up for a while.

"Are you all right?" I asked her.

"Oh I'm fine. I couldn't sleep so I decided to get up and do something."

"Is there something wrong that I don't know about?"

There was no reply. She was standing by the oven with her back to me. I went over and slipped my arm around her waist, asking her what was wrong.

She turned around and at the same time wiped away a tear that was just starting to roll down her cheek.

"You're going away again," she began. "Who knows when you will be back. You're not much more than a boy. You just started shaving a little while ago and now you're going to fight in a war."

It was funny the way she said it and I couldn't help laughing. She began to smile herself.

"I'm not going anywhere yet, but I'll make a deal with you. If you promise not to worry, I'll promise to be as careful as I can."

She nodded, but I knew she would worry. And so would Dad. They couldn't help it, it's just how they were.

"You look so grown up in that uniform. It just seems like yesterday when I came to live with you to help your mum. The games I've played with all of you. The next thing we'll know is you'll have a girlfriend and will be getting married."

"When that happens you'll be the first to know."

By now Dad was in the kitchen and the three of us sat at the table, had some breakfast and chatted. Then it was time to go. Bella decided she would say goodbye at the house and, giving me some of her baking to take, she reminded me to be careful. There was still twenty minutes to spare when we got to the station. Dad spoke to Miss Campbell for a minute and then we shook hands.

"Be careful now," he said. "I worry about you."

"I know. I'll be careful." Then he was away.

Looking at Miss Campbell I could see her eyes were a little misty.

"You're so lucky to have the family you have, do you know that?"

I was lucky and I think I did know it. She went on to say she expected me to write occasionally and wondered if I knew when my next leave would be. Then the train's whistle blew and it was time to go. Walking with me to the carriage she gave me a parcel for her father.

"Oh, and there is one more thing I'd like you to do for me," she said. "From now on, you have to call me Catherine."

The porter blew his whistle again. I gave her a hug and then boarded the train. As we pulled out of the station I leaned out of the window and waved. It had been a good relaxing week, but in a way I was anxious to get back to flying. When I got back to Turnhouse I still had a couple of hours before I had to be through the gate so I went directly to Miss Campbell's father's house and dropped off the parcel. He was sitting writing a note to his daughter; he wondered how she was and also asked after my family. I told him about my brother John and he said he would look into it and let me know. Leaving him to finish his letter, I headed for the airfield where I found William and Findlay already checked in. All of us were curious to now know how the other spent our first leave. Until then I hadn't told them anything about my family. When I said that I had nine other brothers and sisters they were horrified.

"That's enough for a football team!" Findlay laughed. When he found out about my sister Isobel he said he wanted to go back with me on our next leave and meet her.

"I don't think so. You forget I've lived in this hut with you for the last four months, I've already told her what you're like!"

He didn't take it to heart. We often poked fun at each other. Although he did talk a lot, he was good fun. Both he and William were good company and we'd become quite close friends.

Monday morning came and we all awoke early and went for a run before breakfast. I felt charged and rejuvenated after our week off. At our 8 a.m. briefing our instructors confirmed the rumours we had heard. That first, the seven of us who were to go on to be fighter pilots were being moved to another hut to be on our own. And second, our training was being intensified. The RAF, in its quest for pilots, wanted the training time reduced. To quote one of our instructors, 'your backside is going to be sore from sitting in planes.' And third, we were stepping up to a bigger training plane.

And that's what happened. We were soon doing a lot of flying but I enjoyed every minute of it. There was, however, a bit of a hiccup one day when I was being checked out on the bigger trainer. We had done a few circuits and I was feeling quite competent with it. Whether I had got a little complacent and wasn't paying enough attention, I'm not sure, but we had just landed and just at that critical moment when there isn't enough airflow around the rudder, the aircraft began to ground loop. Fortunately my instructor was quick to take control and averted what was a bad situation into nothing more than a scary moment. He later called it a learning curve. I did learn from it. It never happened again.

By the end of the day, the rest of my group had heard about my little mishap; needless to say I was subjected to a bit of ribbing because of it. It didn't get out of hand. They all knew that tomorrow it could be one of them. That was one of the good things about training in a group. We did learn from each other's mistakes. Then came the part that scared the living daylights out of me. How to exit our aircraft and parachute to safety. Every time I was confronted with something I wasn't comfortable with, I heard Dad say "Do what you have to do."

As the weeks passed, however, we discovered our instructors had been right; our backsides were sore. In the meantime Miss Campbell's father made some enquires on John's behalf and discovered that a few of our mechanics were being moved to airfields in the south of England. Fields that would likely see more action and where there were more operational aircraft. So, yes, they would need apprentices at Turnhouse. There was a good chance that if John applied now he could be based right here. Sending a note home, I enclosed all the necessary forms to fill out. Miss Campbell and I also exchanged notes, but other than to say that training was progressing and that I was getting closer to the end, I didn't have any news to tell her.

Although we tried to fly most days sometimes at that time of year the weather didn't cooperate. East winds in particular could be a problem; sometimes they would bring a fog rolling in quickly from the North Sea, making it impossible to find the airfield from the air. Sometimes it was so thick it was difficult to find even if you were only walking.

Being stationed on one of the main aerodromes in Scotland the circuit was always busy. With different kinds of aeroplanes coming and going we got to know with the engine sound and beat what the aircraft was without looking. Occasionally there would be something different that would get our attention. One that would always turn heads whenever it was flying was the Spitfire. Once you've heard a Spitfire you never forget it. The sound of the big Rolls Royce engine was unmistakeable. Personally, it made the hair on the back of my neck stand on end. 'Maybe one day,' I thought, 'if I get good enough...'

But our training wasn't finished and we had been advised that sometime in the next few days we would be flying Hurricanes. We were excited and apprehensive at the same time. We learned all we could about them, take-off and landing speeds for one thing. But the biggest change was that this plane had retractable undercarriage. Although it had always been a part of our checklist in the other planes we had flown, now we would physically have to do something. Miss Campbell's father had flown the type often so I asked him if there was anything in particular I should watch for.

"It's not all that different from what you've been flying," he said. "It has a lot more power and speed, but you'll be fine. If your instructors didn't think you were ready they wouldn't have put you in it. Be confident in yourself knowing they have confidence in you."

So in the next couple of days whenever we got the chance we would familiarize ourselves with the plane and had actually started it and taxied around in it a little bit in preparation for our first flight. The nose of the aircraft was so long you had to zigzag and look either side of it to see where you were going. This was the last hurdle for us; if we got through this part we would get our wings to fly fighters.

Then the day came.

"Right gentlemen, who is going to be first to go up in the Hurricane?" Our instructor asked.

We looked at each other.

"We have a plan," they said. "To help you decide you could go by age, alphabetically or draw straws. Suit yourselves, you've got five minutes."

We were scared, but sooner or later we all had to do it. When the others were trying to decide what method to use I could hear Dad yet again. Standing up, I said that I'd go first.

For a few seconds there was silence and everybody focused on me.

"Right Somerville," my instructor said. "I'll take you to the aircraft."

As we walked out I thought 'thank goodness, not a puff of wind'. Getting closer to the aircraft, I tried to stay focused. He looked at me and could see I was scared stiff.

"Don't worry so much," he said. "You're a good pilot. You'll be fine. Just do two circuits for now and then come back."

When you start your training you're at the very bottom of the ladder but when you got to this stage it was different. Our instructors were our superiors but they realized how big a step this was. They had been there themselves. For the most part my instructor had been pilot officer Robert Findlay. He was much older than Miss Campbell but he reminded me of her. The way he taught, the ability of knowing when someone genuinely needs help and reassurance or when they need a bit of a push. It was why the R.A.F. had him as an instructor; he was good at his job.

Climbing into the plane, he helped me with the harness then indicated to the mechanic I was ready to start. Pushing the button, the propeller turned and the engine fired. He gave the cockpit one last check, gave me a thumbs up then jumped down off the back of the wing. The mechanic pulled the chocks from in front of the wheels. Collecting my thoughts I looked towards the control tower, waiting for my clearance to taxi. I didn't have to wait long. Pushing the throttle gently ahead, we began to move. As I put my foot on the rudder and swung around, I looked at my instructor one last time. Standing beside the mechanic, he smiled, one hand in his pocket and the other extended with his thumb up.

Taxiing out, I began to feel a lot better and by the time I got to the take-off point I felt ready. Turning into wind, I looked towards the control tower, waiting for my clearance. Again it wasn't long in coming and with one last check in the cockpit I slid the canopy closed then pushed the throttle all the way forward. Pushing the stick ahead just a little, the tail came off the ground; now I could see where I was going. Keeping the plane straight and then, in what seemed like an instant we were at take-off speed. Pulling back gently, I climbed very quickly to circuit height. Turning downwind, base leg and then finals, I ran through the pre-landing checks, carburettor heat, mixture, throttle, undercarriage down.

It was down. I hadn't raised it after take-off. Well, it was too late now. 'Just remember it the next time,' I thought.

The ground got closer and closer. Gently, I eased back on the stick and flared. The plane gently landed. Again I pushed the throttle all the way forward, took off and went around again. This time I remembered the undercarriage.

Back on the apron, I just sat there for a minute. I had done it. Sliding the canopy back I got out. My instructor was waiting on me getting down. I expected him to give me a talking to about the undercarriage on the first time around.

"Well done," he said. "Those were two pretty nice landings, congratulations."

I told him I forgot about the undercarriage on my first time around.

"Yes you did, but you remembered the second time. You won't forget again."

The plane had flown like a dream and I couldn't wait till the next time. Walking back to the operations room we met Findlay on the way out. He looked petrified.

"She flies great," I told him, and wished him luck.

Inside, the rest of my group congratulated me and wanted to know what it was like. I was glad I had gone first. It didn't strike me until a few days later about how far we'd come. Joining the air force a relatively short time ago and now able to fly one of the best high performance aeroplanes they had. All seven of us gained the right to enter the final phase of our training that day. All that remained was some cross country flights, target practice and some formation flying in the Hurricane. This part we would do with a new instructor. The ones who had taught us to fly were starting the process all over again with a new batch of students. But before they left us they congratulated us again and introduced us to our new instructor. It was Miss Campbell's father.

"Gentlemen, this is squadron leader John Campbell, he will take you on."

I couldn't believe it; we were going to be flying together. I had never given any thought as to whether or not we would, but I was pleased. He congratulated us on our achievement and advised us that it was customary for the new pilots to buy their instructors a dram to celebrate. Giving us the rest of the day off they expected to see us in the mess at night to do just that. We were all excited about having at last flown the Hurricane. It was indeed a milestone.

There was yet another first in store for me that day. In the mess that night to celebrate with our instructors a dram was duly poured. We raised our glasses, one of our instructors proposed a toast, then, innocently, I put the glass to my lips and promptly gulped the lot. Never in my short life had I tasted anything that bad. Putting the glass down with one hand and keeping my mouth closed with the other I swallowed and felt it burn all the way down. Coughing and gasping for air, I became, for the second time that day, the centre of attention.

"What's wrong Somerville lad?" my instructor asked. "Have you never tried the Highland Nectar before?"

I couldn't speak. My colleagues were in hysterics.

"Come on man," he said. "Have another to keep that one company."

Hastily I placed my hand firmly on the top of the glass. It was as much as I could do to shake my head. Now I know why you didn't get much at a time. For a while that night I was the source of amusement.

When the commotion died down our new commanding officer asked me if I had heard from his daughter. I told him that I hadn't recently but said I was going to be writing home to tell them about my day and intended writing to her as well.

"She's proud of you," he went on. "She feels privileged to have taught you in school. I don't know if you know or not, but the year you started school in Pitlochry you were in her first ever class. She had graduated from college only a few weeks previously and immediately got a job. At just turned seventeen she was a child teaching children. She made me very proud."

His daughter meant everything to him; from that very first day at Blair Castle when I saw them laugh together I had known that. They were completely at ease in each other's company.

"I'm the one who is privileged," I said. "Privileged to have had her for a teacher all these years. She helped and encouraged me, consoled me when my mother died. Wherever I go, I'll always remember her."

We shook hands again and parted company. I went to write my letters.

We were now half way through November and a passing out parade was being arranged for the end of the month but although we were almost at the end of our training there was no let-up in our busy schedule. Miss Campbell's father said he would hone our skills and teach us things that would hopefully keep us alive.

Since coming to Turnhouse we had talked quite a bit off and on, but in the last few weeks of training I got to know him a lot better and realized just how alike he and his daughter really were. They possessed an ability to reach into an individual and extract all the best qualities, to get them to do things they never knew they were capable of. Although these last weeks were intense we all enjoyed it and were better for it. One of the last flights we made before our big day was to fly up the coast to Aberdeen and then to Kinloss. The weather was good and the airfields were easy to find. At debriefing later we joked with Miss Campbell's father saying he was like a mother hen and we were his clutch. On the way back to Edinburgh later in the day our flight path would take us over Pitlochry. It was the first time I had seen home from the air. Looking down as we flew over, I wondered what everyone was doing. The squadron leader came on the radio, wondering if I could see anyone I knew.

It was good to get back to Turnhouse and familiar faces after our flight. Looking forward to lying down for a few minutes after debriefing, I headed for our hut. As we got in I could see someone sitting on my bunk. I got the surprise of my life. It was my brother John.

"Hello little brother," he grinned. "Surprised?"

"Yes I am. What are you doing here?"

We gave each other a hug then he went on to tell me that after he had sent his forms in he got an immediate reply giving him only a few days to report, not enough time to let me know he was coming. It was great to see him and he was excited to be there. For weeks after, until he got used to the size of the engines he was working on, he was awed by it all. What he never got used to, though, and a continual source of amusement to me, was the fact that I was his superior officer and he was supposed to salute me.

In another week our training would be finished. All the arrangements had been made for our passing out parade and we were advised that we should notify anyone we wanted to be there. I wrote to my family and to Miss Campbell.

4. Wings

The day came and I still hadn't heard from home. When the bus came from the station I met it, not knowing if any of my family would be on it. When the door opened, the first ones out were Isobel and Richard, then Dad and Bella appeared. It was good to see them and I asked them if they had a good trip down.

"We did," Bella answered. "Believe it or not, other than your Dad, none of us have been to Edinburgh before. It's exciting."

Then there was a tap on my shoulder; turning around I was pleased to see Miss Campbell. We smiled and gave each other a hug. As always, she smelled great.

"I didn't know if you would come."

"Are you kidding? I wouldn't miss this for all the tea in China."

From out of nowhere her father appeared. He said hello to his daughter and I introduced him to my family. Just at that moment John appeared. Miss Campbell and her father left us but said they would see us later at the ceremonies, so John and I showed our family around some of the base, ending up in the hanger where I showed them the planes I had been flying. We stood looking at the Hurricane. Dad and I got up on the wing and I showed him inside the cockpit.

"Why don't you sit in and see how it feels?" I said.

He looked at me momentarily, then, with his big frame taking up a lot of space, he did just that. Surveying the dials and controls around him and looking outside at the wings and at the big long nose stretching out in front of him he sat shaking his head.

"How the devil do you fly this thing?" he said. "There's no room in here and outside you can't see where you're going."

To a degree he was right, but I explained to him that when you were flying it was fine. Then it was time and so we made our way to the where the ceremonies would to take place. We again met Miss Campbell and her father. He showed his daughter and my family to the seats he had reserved for them but I was to sit with the rest of my fellow graduates at the front.

In true military fashion the base commander stood up exactly on time and began. He spoke for a few minutes, saying that after the presentations there would be a banquet in the mess hall and later, back in the hanger, there was to be a dance. Then it was on with the official part of the proceedings. He began by saying that in light of the current situation the

R.A.F. needed pilots and that he'd been asked to try and cut the amount of time it took to train young men to be pilots.

"Although they didn't know it, this group of graduates were an experiment," he said. "We have been pushing them hard, and I can tell you they haven't done any less training to get here. But I'm pleased to be able to say that we have cut four weeks off the training period. We are proud of them."

There was a little applause and we looked at each other. We had heard a rumour about that once but had forgotten about it. As usual Findlay had a comment.

"Bloody guinea pigs, that's what we are!"

No one paid any attention. He was just being Findlay. Then one by one we marched up onto the stage and saluted the commander as he pinned the wings onto our chest. As he shook my hand he congratulated me on my achievement and for being the youngest graduate they had ever had at Turnhouse. We had made it. I had made it. If someone had offered me a thousand pounds I wouldn't have traded it for that moment. After a few more words from the base commander the official part of the proceedings was over. Finding my family Dad shook my hand but didn't say anything. He didn't have to; the look in his eyes said it all. With tears in her eyes, Bella gave me a hug but didn't say anything either. Miss Campbell was the same as she gave me a hug.

"I'm so proud of you," she said.

"Thanks for everything," I whispered. "I couldn't have done it without you."

Her father shook my hand, patted me on the back and said well done.

Everybody admired our new décor, parents and colleague's alike. It was difficult to believe we had finally reached our objective.

After the excitement subsided everybody was hungry and ready for food. It was quite a lavish affair; Bella enjoyed it, who knows when she last sat down to a meal without having first spent a considerable time preparing it. And then, after eating, it was back to the hanger for the dance. There were a lot of people there already, sitting listening to the music. We found a table where Miss Campbell's father sat with us for a while. Dad, Bella and he seemed to hit it off and talked for ages. Findlay and William introduced me to their families, but I should have been prepared for Findlay.

"Well, are you going to introduce me to your sister?" He said, staring at her.

"She isn't seventeen yet, leave her alone."

"I just want to dance with her."

He persisted, so I did introduce them and he danced with her most of the night. The orchestra announced they were going to play a waltz. Miss Campbell looked at me.

"Well, are you going to dance with me?" she asked, smiling.

Getting up, I took her hand and we made our way to the dance floor.

"I'm afraid I don't dance very well," I said.

"Well, I'll just have to teach you that as well," she said, laughing.

Dancing with her was like being in her class, she somehow made it easy. As we made our way around the floor I told her I had a week's leave at Christmas and would be going home. I wondered what she was doing. There was a party at the school. She was going to be there for that and then planned on spending Christmas with her father at Turnhouse.

"If you're in Pitlochry in time for the party, why don't you come?" she asked.

"If I am, maybe I could do that."

"By the way, you're still calling me Miss Campbell."

"Well, somehow it just doesn't feel right calling you Catherine."

"Try it. Can it really be more difficult than flying? Come on, it's painless."

"Alright... Catherine."

She smiled and we danced on.

When we got back to the table we sat together. Bella took my hand and said that Dad had something for me. They all stood up and Dad proposed a toast.

"Congratulations on your significant achievement. May God always watch over you and keep you safe."

Giving me a present I removed the paper and opened the box. Inside there was most beautiful gold pocket watch I'd ever seen. There was an inscription on the back, 'To James, Wings Graduation, 15th December 1939. There was a note in the box. 'You've made us all so proud, love always, Mum, Dad and all your family. Looking at it and then at Dad I sat with tears in my eyes and a lump in my throat, unable to say anything. Catherine broke the silence.

"As we're opening presents, I've got something for you as well."

Unwrapping her gift, it looked like another pocket-watch but on opening the front cover and exposing the face I discovered it was a small compass. There was an inscription on the back. 'Graduation, 15th December 1939. Your friend always, Catherine'. She had put a note in the box too; it read: 'So you'll always find your way home'.

Lost for words, I could only give her a hug.

Our day was almost over. It was one of the most memorable in my life and I thanked them all for being there. Arrangements had been made for my and some other families who had travelled a long way to stay on the base overnight. Catherine was staying with her father. In the morning there would be a bus to take them back to the station for the train home. At breakfast, when I got the chance, I asked Bella if she would do me favour.

"If I can, you know I will," she answered.

Telling her I was going to get Miss Campbell a gift for Christmas I wondered if she could find out what perfume she wore. She looked at me with a mischievous smile.

"James Somerville, you're buying perfume for a woman?"

Still grinning, for a moment she said nothing. Who knows what was going through her mind.

"Leave it to me. I'll find out for you."

Then they were gone but the good news was that I'd see them all again in a few days.

The next week, however, the weather was atrocious, low cloud and rain, certainly not flying weather, so we got home sooner than expected. John was allowed leave as well and went home together. Wishing the rest of my colleagues a Merry Christmas when it came, Findlay said it would merry if my sister was with him and gave me a note for her.

"Will you see your girlfriend when you're home?" he asked.

"Girlfriend? I don't have a girlfriend."

"You don't think so?" he grinned.

With that we parted and with John's company the train journey home didn't seem as long. On the high ground around Pitlochry there was quite a bit of snow, but at least it was a lot clearer here. Nobody knew we were going home that day so no one was at the station to meet us. We just walked home. There is one place where there is a particularly good view and we stopped for a few minutes, admiring the scenery.

"You know," John remarked. "I never noticed before how peaceful it is here."

"Yes it is," I replied. "This will always be home for me."

When we got home, Dad and Bella were sitting at the kitchen table, drinking tea. We gave them a bit of a fright when we walked in. Later on, when Bella was by herself, I asked if she had discovered what perfume Miss Campbell wore.

"Yes I did," she answered smiling. "It's called Summer Blossoms. It's nice. I like it myself. She buys it in a little gift shop on the main street in the town." The next day I went into the shop and bought a bottle for both Catherine and Bella. I'd never known Bella to wear perfume. I also got sample bottles of different kinds for my sisters. The lady in the shop was laughing.

"How many girls have you got on a string then?" she asked.

I was going to explain but I could see she wasn't going to believe a word.

Thinking I'd surprise her, before going home I went into the school to see Catherine. It was no surprise, my sisters had told her I was home. We didn't talk long, but she did ask me if I'd go to the school for the party and to wear my uniform. She said also that after the party she was catching the train to go to Edinburgh.

As promised, I went to the school. Feeling out of place, I said I was over-dressed.

"No you're fine, you're my secret weapon. They've heard me speak of you, now they can see you for themselves. Hopefully you'll be their inspiration and make them want to work harder."

I smiled at her and said she was crafty. She smiled back and nodded. Later, walking with her to the station, I told her I'd be back at Turnhouse before New Year. Maybe we would see each other then. Thanking her again for the gift she gave me at my graduation I gave her the Christmas gift I had for her.

"You didn't have to buy me anything."

Opening the box and peering inside, she laughed.

"James Somerville, you went into a shop and bought me perfume?" Then she looked at the label on the bottle. "Summer Blossoms. How did you know that?" Searching my eyes for a clue I didn't say a word.

"Bella! It was Bella who told you."

Just at that the conductor blew his whistle. Wishing each other a Merry Christmas we embraced briefly then she boarded the train.

Christmas day came and everyone opened their modest gifts. By the time Bella and all my sisters had their perfume on the house smelled like the little shop in the town. Margaret was running around shouting.

"Smell me! Smell me!"

Isobel got her letter from Findlay and we all ate too much, Bella saw to that. If Mum was in a place where she could see us I know she would be happy and content with the way Bella had taken care of us.

It seemed like we just got home but already it was time to go back to Edinburgh. On our arrival the weather was as bad as the day we left. Checking in at the aerodrome I discovered there had been virtually no flying done. The next morning I got a note from Catherine wondering if I would meet her at twelve noon at the gate. It had only been a few days since I'd seen her and I thought the summons a little bit mysterious, but I was looking forward to our rendezvous nevertheless. After exchanging hellos she wondered if I'd like to go into the city later on and see a show.

"If I could, I would, but we just got back. I'd never get a pass. Besides, it wouldn't be right me getting a pass and the rest of my colleagues having to stay on the base."

"Alright, if I can get you all out, would you go?"

"If you can pull that off, yes I'll go."

Later, Catherine's father advised us that because of the continued bad weather flying had been cancelled. As well, the base commander had given us a six-hour pass.

"You are his blue eyed boys, so it wasn't difficult convincing him you should have it."

I couldn't believe it; she had pulled it off! The rest of my group had no idea what had just happened and I had no intention of telling them. There was a brief discussion about what we could do with our unexpected freedom. To fulfil my end of the bargain I was insistent that we go into the city and see a show. Looking at our squadron leader I could see him smile. Upon further discussion it was finalized; William and Findlay wanted to go and see a show with me and the other four members of our flight would go their own way.

"Alright then," said squadron leader Campbell, looking at me. "I'll have a couple of vehicles at the gate at six sharp and I'll let everyone else know what's happening."

Nothing else had to be said; I knew what he meant. This was going to be interesting, I thought, as we checked out at the gate. How was Catherine going to put this together without arousing any suspicion? She wanted us to go and see a show together, and apparently her father had no objections, but he couldn't give me a pass without the rest getting it as well. I didn't want that either. Neither did I want a ribbing from the rest of my flight about going to see a show with my schoolteacher, who just happened to be our Squadron leader's daughter. But she had it engineered to a tee; I only had to watch the event unfold. Our drivers had been instructed to stop just past the gate by the bus stop. Catherine was standing there, as if waiting for a bus. Findlay was the first to see her. He freely admits that on seeing a good-looking woman with nice legs he wants to go and rescue her, whether or not she needs to be.

"There's Miss Campbell by the bus stop," he said. "She is obviously waiting for the bus. Maybe she needs a lift to the station?"

And that was it. She fed Findlay a half truthful story about her supposed to be meeting an old school friend to go and see a show, but it looked like she had been stood up. Findlay fell for it hook line and sinker.

"Come with us!" he said. "That's where we're going."

"You don't mind?"

"We would consider it an honour," he said.

We bundled into the car and decided on the way that first we'd go to a restaurant and eat then go and see a show.

"Sounds great to me," said Findlay.

The night was a memorable experience. When I got the chance I asked her how she managed it.

"Manage what? I don't know what you mean," she grinned. "I was just standing there minding my own business when two young pilots asked me if I needed a lift."

She always told me I could be anything I wanted to be. Truth be told, *she* could be anything *she* wanted to be. With her father's help she had orchestrated with precision, a way in which we could spend time together without anyone having the slightest suspicion.

Getting back to Turnhouse we thanked Catherine for her company. With William and Findlay present we just said good night. The next day was New Year's Eve and at exactly eleven am we were scrambled; unidentified aircraft East of Edinburgh. We took off and climbed up through ten thousand feet but couldn't see any intruders. Then the controller instructed us to patrol the East coast as far down as Dunbar. Back in the debriefing room we discovered that the scramble had been a practice. Squadron leader Campbell also advised us that the take-off and climb out had taken much too long. We would have to do it in a lot less time. If we didn't and there was an actual raid, we'd be sitting ducks. We left the debriefing with our tails between our legs.

Later in the mess there was a get together to see the New Year in. Catherine and her father were there. It was a light-hearted, informal affair but I wondered, if the war continued, how many of the people present would see another New Year. It was also the start of a new decade, it was 1940. Catherine told me she was going back to Pitlochry the next day.

It would be another three months before I'd see her or my family again.

In Europe the war wasn't going well. Every day there was more bad news about how the enemy was forging ahead, crushing everything in its path. They had clearly been planning their strategy for a long time, building up over years a huge military killing machine of planes, tanks and men. Now unleashed, nobody could stop them. Some days their front line moved so far ahead, their supply line couldn't keep up. They had squadrons of dive-bombers that went ahead of the tanks and armies, softening up any resistance there might be. These planes not only brought destruction, they were designed to inflict terror on all those who saw and heard them. In France the R.A.F. were losing a lot of aircraft on the ground to the advancing armies, aircraft that were repairable but not flyable. In the air, Wellington and Blenheim bombers, in an effort to try and slow the enemy momentum, were being annihilated. They were no match for the fast and manoeuvrable enemy fighters. Hearing of all our losses, I wondered if I would soon be subjected to the same fate. Our squadron leader told us over and over to train to be the best we could be. We had a superior machine and to use it.

So that's what we did, we practiced intensely; each of us determined we wouldn't be a statistic. Getting to altitude in the shortest time possible was going to be crucial. Anything we could think of to be better and more efficient, we did it. Every time we went on patrol we ran to our aircraft, trying to improve upon the last time. As well as the endless training we were now flying regular patrols up and down the coast. There were numerous reports of hostile aircraft and the possibility did exist that the Luftwaffe would sneak in at low level, but for a while we never saw any. Although the war wasn't going well, the R.A.F., for the time being, were aware that we did need time off. It was coincidental I know, the R.A.F. doesn't give someone leave because it's their birthday, but that's what happened. I would be home for a few days at the end of April.

It was a nice run up to Pitlochry, the countryside was starting to freshen up again after the winter. Regardless of what was happening with the war, the daffodils in our valley didn't care, they grew just the same. When I got home I was exhausted and so Bella chased me to my bed. In the morning, like so many in our house, I awoke to the smell of baking. Bella always said it was the best time of the day. It was quiet and she could get more done. Getting out of bed, I followed my nose to the kitchen. She had her back to the door, so I crept up behind her and covered her eyes and asked her who she thought it was it was.

"Mm... I wonder," she said. "Could it be our boy in blue?"

"Well there is just no deceiving you," I said, letting her go.

Looking over her shoulder, I could see she was icing a cake.

"Where do you get all your energy?" I asked. " Don't you ever get tired?"

"Mothers aren't supposed to get tired, there isn't enough time."

We sat at the table for a while, sipping tea and chatting in the quiet of the morning. She said that Dad had bought a few more cows again. They were having the telephone installed and were also thinking about getting electricity as well; that would undoubtedly make everyone's life a lot easier. With the wick lamps and candles we used, it was a wonder the house had never burned to the ground. As my little sisters appeared, our peace was shattered. Bella handed me some candles.

"Here," she said. "Stick these in your cake and I'll make breakfast."

Later on in the morning I went for a walk around the farm. It was becoming a ritual. I took the dogs with me for company. It looked as though Dad was up to date with his work. I don't know where he got his energy either. Both of them somehow kept going. As usual at this time of year, there was new life, with the sheep lambing and cows calving. Back at the house I peered over the fence into the garden; there were daffodils everywhere. 'Bella needs a few for her kitchen window,' I thought, jumping the fence.

Later on in the day I borrowed Dad's car and went into the town to see Catherine. When I got there she was digging in her garden.

"You're just in time," she said. "You can help me plant some potatoes, it's time they were in."

Although she was chatting away, I could see there was something troubling her. After we finished we went inside and she made us tea. I asked her if there was something on her mind and she gave me a fleeting glance. I could see her eyes instantly mist over. She got up, went to the window and stared out at her garden. Getting up, I followed her.

"What's wrong?" I asked her again. "Did we plant the potatoes upside down?"

Forcing a smile, she said she had just received a note from her father. There was a strong possibility that he, and a number of pilots, would be posted to the South of England. It could happen at any time.

"There was always a possibility it could happen," she said. "I thought I was prepared for it, but it doesn't look like I am. Then there is you. If anything happened to either one of you I'd die. I wish I hadn't taken you to Blair Castle that day."

Holding her hand, I tried to console her, saying that if it hadn't been that day it would have been some other. If it hadn't been with her it would have been with someone else. I was doing what I felt I was supposed to be doing.

"There is a compass I have that a friend gave me,' I said. As long as I have that, I'll always be back."

Giving me a forced smile and a hug, she thanked me for reassuring her.

"Look, why don't you come to the farm tomorrow. It's my birthday and Bella made a cake. You can help me eat it."

She looked at me for a moment.

"Alright," she said. "I will."

As always Bella pampered me; she made the things she knew I liked. I said to her that I'd asked Miss Campbell and hoped she didn't mind. All she said was that she liked her and was glad she could come. Catherine had been to the farm before but it was the first time she had been in our house. She looked a little uncomfortable at first and my little sisters, who were in her class at school, definitely were, but everybody got used to it after a while.

Before Catherine left she asked if I had anything else planned to do when I was home. The only thing I knew for sure I wanted to do was to go and visit my mother's grave. What had brought the feeling on I couldn't say, it's not that I hadn't been there before, but I'd had, for some time, an irresistible urge to go. Maybe it was to show her my uniform and to let her see what I had accomplished, or maybe it was to ask her if I would soon be joining her, I couldn't tell.

"If you want some company, I'll go with you," she said.

After Mum died, Bella made every effort to keep our day-to-day lives as normal as possible. Because of her, her nature and the way she did things we saw our mother everywhere. If it was within her power, she would do anything for us. We all thought the world of her but still there were times I missed my mother desperately.

The following morning I borrowed the car and went into the town, taking a few daffodils with me for Mum's grave from the garden she had enjoyed for so brief a time. When I got to her house, Catherine was working in her garden. I gave her a few daffodils.

"Flowers for the teacher? Thank you," she smiled.

She looked around the garden then I felt like a right twit. Giving her daffodils was like taking coal to Newcastle. It would have been difficult to walk on her grass without standing on a clump. She knew what I was thinking.

"It's the thought that counts," she said, grinning.

After putting them in a vase, she went with me to the cemetery. It was quiet and peaceful the sun was shining, there wasn't a puff of wind, the apple trees dotted around were in full bloom and daffodils were everywhere. We walked up through the churchyard to where Mum was and I looked around at what little view she had and then I knelt down and put the flowers in the vase by her headstone. Getting up, I began to read the inscription on the stone, only getting as far as 'beloved wife and mother'. With my eyes fixated on these words the tears began to well up in my eyes. Catherine didn't say anything; she instinctively knew how I was feeling and slipped her arm through mine. Then there was the weirdest thing. I felt a shiver and the hair on the back of my neck stood on end. Although I never spoke it was like I was having a conversation with Mum.

"Do you know how proud of you I am? I feel fortunate to have been part of your life, even though it was only for a little while." Tears were rolling down my jaw now and falling on the ground. "Be careful flying and you will come home, there's someone waiting for you here."

As quickly as the feeling had come it was gone. At the same time I felt an overwhelming sense of peace and well-being.

"I'm sorry," I said, squinting at Catherine. "I feel a bit silly."

"You don't have to feel sorry or silly because you loved your mother," she answered, pulling on my sleeve.

We stood there for a while, saying nothing, lost in our own thoughts. Then we turned and walked slowly back towards the gate. Catherine broke the silence.

"Would you like to share a little secret of mine?"

We paused for a moment and looked at each other. I nodded.

"If I ever get married and I'm lucky enough to have a family, I hope and pray that my children will love me like your mother's children loved her. Your mother's life was short but she was fortunate and blessed. She lives on in you and your brothers and sisters."

Again I could feel tears burn my eyes.

"Come on," she said. "Let's go to the café and I'll buy you tea."

We had the place to ourselves and sat for ages. I can't remember half the things we talked about but I felt completely at ease with her. She had had a tremendous impact on my life. We had met as teacher and pupil but now we were more than that, we were the best of friends.

Catherine was an attractive woman. Slim, with blue eyes and the shiniest dark hair, she had an infectious laugh and was fun to be with. But it dawned on me, sitting in the café, that I'd never seen her with, or heard her talk about a boyfriend.

"Would you mind if I asked you a personal question?" I asked.

"That depends," she answered.

But I got cold feet, saying it was none of my business.

"Ask me. How personal could it be?"

Looking everywhere except at Catherine, I thought, 'Somerville, you're an idiot. You can't ask her this.'

"No... it's none of my business."

She put her hand on mine, looked me straight in the eye and said again.

"Ask me. I promise I won't bite you."

The words dribbled out of my mouth.

"Well, I just wondered if you had a boyfriend. I've never heard you speak of anyone."

She kept looking at me, the way she did sometimes, searching from eye to eye, like she is trying to reach into my soul.

"I'm sorry," I said. "I shouldn't have asked you that. It's none of my business," and tried to pull my hand out from under hers.

But she wouldn't let it go. She slowly shook her head, smiling at the same time.

"Yes I do," she answered. "But I don't think he knows it yet. I've known him for years. He is the nicest, sweetest person I've ever met. He isn't here all the time and so, sometimes we write. I really can't imagine my life without him."

Having asked her I felt a lot better but at the same time I felt envious of this person. It was obvious she thought an awful lot of him.

"Why don't you tell him how you feel?"

"Maybe one of these days I'll have to do that."

The difficult part over, I asked her where he came from and if I knew him, but she wouldn't say.

Looking at the clock on the wall I commented that it was getting late.

"We should go. I'm going back to Turnhouse tomorrow and I still have to pack."

She let my hand go and got up to leave; she wondered when my next leave would be, but there was no way of knowing that. Normally we should get regular leave, but things weren't normal. It would depend on the war.

"You don't have to come to the station tomorrow, unless there is something you want me to take to your father."

She said there was and that she'd be there. Giving her a hug I thanked her for going to the cemetery with me and for buying tea.

"It was a pleasure. Next time it's your turn."

When I got home Bella had some things laid out on the bed for me to take. When I was packing she came in and sat on the bed.

"So how did it go today?" she asked.

"Good. Catherine went with me to the cemetery. It was so unbelievably peaceful, with the sun shining and the daffodils everywhere. Heaven couldn't be better than that."

Sitting beside her, I told her about my experience.

"You know, I had the eeriest feeling that Mum spoke to me. It only lasted a few seconds but it was so vivid. Almost like you talking to me now."

"What did she say to you?"

"She told me that if I were careful I'd be back... and that somebody here was waiting for me. What did that mean?"

It was Bella's turn to take my hand.

"Hopefully it means just that. That this war will end quickly and you will be alright."

"Do you believe in life after death?" I asked.

She thought for a moment, then slowly she exposed thoughts and beliefs I'd never heard her talk about before.

"Sometimes in your life there are little things that happen that are unexplainable, like you today. You felt the need to go and see your Mum and when you were there she reached out and touched you."

She paused for a moment collecting her thoughts.

"Yes, I believe in life after death. I believe that God created heaven and earth and everything on it, the trees the flowers and the animals, you, the sun that warms everything on a summers day. When you think about it all, how everything is dependent on everything else, it's truly amazing. Then there are the times when a little voice deep inside tells you things. Sometimes you get a feeling that you should do something. You can't explain it but you can't shake it either. To me, that's God's way of telling you which way to go."

"Have you had feelings like that?"

She laughed and tried to lighten the mood of our conversation.

"Of course! It can happen a dozen times a day."

"No, I mean about things you can't explain, weird things that happen."

"Yes, I know what you mean," she said. Hesitantly she went on. "When I came to help your Mum and Dad at first, I remember I was supposed to go and work in an old hotel in Dunkeld. I went to see the place and the people, but I just had a feeling it wasn't where I was supposed to be. At the same time there was an advertisement in the paper from a farmer up the valley who was looking for a maid. A farm maid, out in the country and miles from anywhere, children to look after? No, I don't think so. It wasn't for me. But from the moment I read it I couldn't get it out of my mind. The next thing I knew I was meeting your Mum and Dad and their family. I asked myself. What are you doing here? But your Mum and Dad must have liked me; they asked me to start as soon as I could. I said that I would, but on the way home and in the days between the interview and me coming back I told myself over and over it wasn't the right job for me. But that voice inside said I should go and I found myself walking back up the farm road. Then there was the time after your Mum died. There was a man I'd been seeing for a while; we were going to be married. That's why I left, remember?"

How could I forget? It was etched in my mind as being the worst day in our lives after Mum died.

"After I left," she went on, "and as the wedding day got closer, it just didn't feel right. I tried to convince myself that it was probably just wedding jitters but as I tried to focus on my life ahead it wasn't the man I left to marry I saw there, it was this place. When I thought of you, your brothers and sisters and your Dad, I felt peace inside; I knew this was my home. I couldn't wait to see you all again. If I hadn't listened to my little voice, I don't know where I'd be now. I can't imagine my life without your Dad and all of you in it."

We sat there for a bit; immersed in our own thoughts. Mine drifted back to Catherine.

"Do you know that Catherine has a boyfriend?" I said.

Bella was grinning from ear to ear.

"Well I know there is somebody she is absolutely nuts about."

"You never told me. I didn't know that."

"She didn't tell you who it was then?"

"No, she said I'd maybe find out sometime."

"Well she'll tell you when she's ready. It's not for me to say."

Bella squeezed my hand and got up.

"You finish your packing," she said. "Then you could help me make tea."

After we had eaten Dad asked me to go for a walk with him to see the cattle. We got to the gate we all liked to lean on and look down the valley. As always, he was a man of few words. When he did speak, he intended you to listen.

"Now you be careful, we want you back here in one piece, do you hear?"

Nodding my head, I didn't say anything; he had my attention.

"That idiot in Germany is going to make it tough for all of us. This war is just getting started. You're in the R.A.F. now, so there's nothing I can do about that, but you can do something for me?"

"Anything," I said.

"You promise me you'll do all you can to be as safe as possible. If you do that, tomorrow when we say cheerio at the station I know I'll see you again. Do what you have to do, but be careful."

Be careful. That was twice I'd heard that in the last two days, from both my mother and father. I admired Dad an awful lot, he seemed to know what was going to happen long before it did and was seldom wrong about anything. But more than that he loved all of us and I wanted to be around so I could share his life.

"You know that little house down the road a bit?" I asked. "You know the one, it's got nice granite walls and trees around it?"

"Aye, I know the one."

"Well I've always liked it and if it ever comes up for sale, I'd like to buy it. I love it here. I don't know of any other place I'd rather be, so I promise you I'll do all I can to come back."

His eyes began to mist a little but he said nothing. After a minute he put his hand on my shoulder and said we should head for home. As we made our way back it dawned on me that he hadn't really needed to see the cattle, he just wanted to talk to me.

Then, with the relentless march of time it was morning again. We had breakfast together and sat chatting for a while until it was time to leave. Dad was taking me to the station by himself again, and when it was time to go I gave Bella a hug and thanked her for my birthday cake and also for the chat we had the day before. Dad and I didn't say much on the way into the town, he didn't wait at the station either; he just gave me a quick hug and told me to look after myself. As he was leaving, Catherine was coming in.

"You're early today," she said to him.

"Oh, a little bit," he answered, getting into the car at the same time. "Come out to the farm some day if you'd like." Then he was gone.

"Your father seems to be in a hurry today," Catherine commented.

"It looks that way, but he said his goodbyes and didn't want to linger."

Catherine handed me two envelopes, saying there was one for me and one for her dad. I nodded, and put the one for her father in my pocket. I was going to open mine but she said to read it on the train.

"About yesterday... I didn't mean to pry into your personal life," I mumbled.

"Don't worry about it," she smiled. "It was amusing in a way. What about your next leave? Have you any idea as to when it might be?"

"No, but there is a girl I know who can arrange things like that. If I talk to her it could be anytime."

She laughed and as she did the porter blew his whistle. Looking at him and then at me she gave me a hug.

"You be careful James Somerville."

As the train left she stood there until I couldn't see her any longer. After getting comfortable on the train I began to read the note she had given me.

> Dear James,
> Remember to write. I look forward to hearing how you are. Take care.
> Your friend always,
> Catherine

'She is a good friend,' I thought. I missed her when she wasn't around.

Getting back to Turnhouse I caught up with our squadron leader to find out what had been happening since I'd been away, and to give him the note from his daughter. After that I found my brother John to see how he was. It had already been six months since he had enlisted. 'Loving every minute,' he said.

The next morning in the briefing room our squadron leader told us that the British forces in France were taking a beating and may have to be evacuated. The RAF had lost a lot of aircraft. The bottom line was, we were an operational unit and could be posted out of Turnhouse at any time.

"But until that happens," he said, "we will keep ourselves in a high state of readiness."

We reviewed again techniques on dog fighting, because, as he put it, it would be evasive aerobatic manoeuvres that would keep us alive, not formation flying. We felt ready. On one hand were anxious to see action, on the other my colleges and I didn't discuss the fact that some of us may not survive. Every day the news was worse, the Germans had pushed our armies onto the beaches at Dunkirk. How would they get home? Would they get home? The RAF were losing bombers to the fast enemy fighters, it was depressing news. Everything seemed hopeless. But even though there were reports on the wireless that didn't sound good there were more and more young men wanting to be pilots. Training was stepped up yet again at Turnhouse. As for us, for weeks there were rumours we were to be posted south and one day after being summoned to the briefing room we thought 'this is it' but instead of us being moved to another field we were told that we were being taken out of our Hurricanes and given Spitfires. None of us could believe it. It was a dream come true. All the reports said it was the best fighter aircraft available. It wasn't any bigger to look at but it was faster and had a lot more power. For the next two months we flew them day in and day out. I fell in love with it. But although there were air raids in the South, and even sporadic ones in Scotland, as yet we hadn't even seen an enemy aircraft.

So far I'd managed to write home fairly regularly and they to me. In one note from Catherine she reminded me it had been a year since I'd started my training. Squadron Leader Campbell was still our mother hen and we did see a lot of him every day. Although he was our superior officer, he didn't think anything about going golfing with us on a Sunday afternoon whenever we got the chance. He had instilled in us to stay alive we would need to be good airmen, but showed us also the need to relax and to have an interest in something else, to get away from flying if only for a little while.

Then, out of the blue, we were told we would be moving to another air-field in the North of England the next day. That was one thing about the RAF, they didn't give you a lot of time to think about it. We didn't know, either, if this was just a temporary move, only time would tell.

After packing our belongings we checked that our aircraft were ready to go. Later on I caught up with John and in the course of conversation asked him to be at the plane in the morning.

5.   Into Action

It was now the 7th of August 1940, the sun was shining; it was a calm summer morning. As arranged, John was on the apron beside my plane.

"Take care little brother," he said. "Let me know where you are and get some of those Jerries for me."

After starting our engines we followed the squadron leader out for take-off. We climbed out to the East and then headed South. Taking a last look at Edinburgh, lying peacefully under her smoky shroud, I wondered when we would see her again.

Our destination was just across the border at Newcastle, so it didn't take us long to get there. Other than our squadron leader, none of us had ever been out of Scotland before. It wasn't as big a field as Turnhouse but it was to be home for a bit. As we were shown around, our aircraft were refuelled. After lunch we were going on patrol farther down the coast. It was a nice day for flying and I made the comment on the radio to the rest of the squadron. The squadron leader came back quickly.

"It is, red four, but keep your eyes peeled. Jerry could be anywhere, sneaking in under our radar."

As always, he was right. We couldn't afford the luxury of a sightseeing flight. We didn't see the enemy that day, or in the next few but there were plenty of raids in different areas further South. Then, on the 12th of August, there were reports of hundreds of enemy aircraft bombing aerodromes along the South coast. Everyone was expecting the enemy to launch an offensive against Britain. Was this the start? Up and down the East Coast, the enemy would sometimes sneak in under the cover of darkness, but as yet we hadn't seen him on our daily patrols. Then we were scrambled. On climbing up, it went through my mind was this another drill? It didn't take long to find out. "Ten plus bandits," the controller said. "Angels fifteen."

Then we saw them and the squadron leader came on the radio.

"Alright red wing, this is what all that training was about. Try to stay calm."

If the rest of the squadron was like me they were scared to death. I was, quite literally, shaking. Briefly I thought of home and I heard Dad. "Come on now, get on with it." This is what we were trained for and it's why we were there. Again the squadron leader said to try and stay calm and then we peeled off one after the other, bearing down on the still unsuspecting enemy. Then they saw us and began to scatter. They were twin-engined Heinkel 111 bombers, a lot slower and a lot less manoeuvrable than we were.

I was catching one of them fast, but with my shaking and fumbling I flew right past him without firing. Trying to control myself, I came back around in a tight turn. By now he was darting in and out of cloud, so it was difficult to get him in my sights. Then, suddenly, there was no cloud and nowhere to hide. Pushing gently on the firing button, almost immediately the enemy aircraft seemed to shudder and there were wisps of smoke behind the starboard engine. Again he found sanctuary in the clouds. It was the last I saw of him. Suddenly, the squadron leader came on the radio, telling us to head for home. We all made it back unscathed. At debriefing we were asked if we had any kills, none of us did, although, like me, some said they were sure they had hit their targets.

"That was your first encounter with the enemy," squadron leader Campbell said. "You'll do better next time."

Later I sat and discussed the encounter with my colleagues. All confessed to be scared out of their wits. I personally was determined to be more productive the next time.

A couple of days later it was almost the same scenario; we had been scrambled and were in position. Pressing home the attack they didn't see us until the last moment. Pushing the firing button he banked right, there were wisps of smoke and an engine blew up. I expected him to level out but instead he rolled over on his back and went straight down. Pulling hard on the stick I went the other way. 'They know we're here now,' I thought. Looking around I could see a handful of bombers limping back out over the water, being chased by Spitfires. Then again, it was over. At debriefing there was some jubilation that we had four confirmed kills, and it was possible a few others were too damaged to make it home. We discovered the enemy had come from bases in Norway. I could only imagine how the crews felt as they made their way home. The North Sea was a dark and foreboding place at the best of times. Attempting to cross it in a damaged aircraft didn't bear thinking about. I was glad it wasn't me. Our peers congratulated those of us who had a confirmed kill. Today I had been a lot more relaxed, but for the benefit of those of us who did have a kill, our squadron leader brought us back to earth.

"Congratulations to those who found their mark today," he said. "But don't let your success go to your head. In combat, if you lose concentration for a minute you could be the next one who buys it. These bombers are slow and clumsy but it will be different when you encounter fighters."

Later, he took me aside and congratulated me again.

"As I said at debriefing, don't let it go to your head. Stay focused. If you don't, they'll get you. Besides, that daughter of mine said I have to keep an eye on you, to keep you out of harm's way if I can."

"That's funny. She said the same thing to me about you."

We looked at each other and laughed.

"It's her birthday soon," he said. "Will you be writing to her?"

It had been a few weeks since I had written home and I was thinking about doing so, but I didn't know Catherine had a birthday coming up, or how old she was.

"Yes, it's on the 3rd of September. She'll be twenty-five. It's a pity, but I don't think we'll be home to help her celebrate. This is the bad part about being away all the time," he went on. "We miss the things that matter the most, the things that keep families together."

With that, we went to check on our aircraft. We were scrambled again later on in the day but by the time we got there the raiders had disappeared.

We didn't go without loss, however. No one knows what happened but one of our flight didn't make it home. No radio transmission, nothing, just the wreckage of a Spitfire in a field. Gordon Turnbull was a quiet individual but a good pilot nevertheless. His death shook us. What happened to him is a mystery. Whether it was an engine failure or whether he had in fact been hit by enemy fire no one could say. His loss made us acutely aware that war wasn't a game and that it could happen to any one of us. Catherine's father now had the unpleasant task of writing to his parents.

The next couple of days were quiet. About the only thing that happened really was that Gordon was replaced by John Ferguson. I found time to write letters home though, and to John at Turnhouse. But other than telling them about our move south and that we had seen some enemy planes there didn't seem to be a lot to write about. I didn't want to worry them so never said anything about shooting one down or telling them either about losing one of the squadron. As I wrote it dawned on me that Catherine would be on school holidays and wondered why she hadn't been down to Turnhouse to see her father before we left. Maybe she had been. If she had been why had I not seen her? Maybe she had taken offence at my prying after all. It also dawned on me that Catherine was only about six and a half years older than I was. Maybe it was because she had been my teacher she just seemed older. It was, in the end, just a short note wishing her a happy birthday, reminding her to write.

When I got the chance I asked her father if Catherine had been at Turnhouse during the school holidays. He hesitated for a moment and then said that she had, in fact, been down for a weekend. My heart sank as he went on to explain there had been something she wanted to talk to him about. They both felt that under the circumstances it would be better for her to go back to Pitlochry and not say to me she had been down. When I asked him why she didn't want to see me he said it wasn't that she didn't. She felt I had enough on my plate, training on the Spitfire. Thanking him for telling me, I accepted his explanation. I was disappointed but tried not to think about it again.

Although my colleagues and I all got along, we realized that each of us needed our own space sometimes. For me, I just liked some peace and quiet when I could find it, to maybe sit and watch birds soar on a thermal, or listen to the rain rattle off the windows on a wet night. Somehow things like that reminded me of home, not that it rained a lot there, on the contrary.

Findlay's sanctuary was to sit and draw, mostly of aeroplanes. But it could be of anything, even cartoons with funny little captions attached. I tormented him, saying that it was his warped sense of humour coming out. William possessed a deeper personality. As it happens, he too liked to draw. He was interested in architecture so his were usually of houses he said he would build after the war.

Then, in the briefing room one morning, our squadron leader told us we were moving again, this time to a field just north of London. More than likely we would be posted again a few days after that, rotating with one of the front line squadrons who were in need of a rest. Some of them had been flying two and three sorties a day for the last few weeks.

Taking off, we headed south and in less than an hour were on the ground at our new location. Immediately the squadron leader had us in the briefing room, going over maps, showing us where all the different airfields were in the area. There were a lot of them, quite close together. Until we got used to the area it would be easy to land at the wrong one.

We didn't get a lot of time to familiarize ourselves with anything; we were scrambled shortly after arriving. As we ran to our aircraft the squadron leader shouted at us to keep a sharp look out for fighters.

We were one of a number of squadrons up. Again the controller got us up and behind the intruders. When we caught sight of them, a formation of bombers was being escorted by a formation of fighters. There was little point in attacking the bombers directly; the fighters would have just pounced on us. The plan was to come down on the fighters first, then follow through and try to get to the bombers. Attacking the fighters, I tried to think of them as just another target, but it was difficult to erase the fact that this fighter was the ME 109, the German equivalent of the Spitfire. But I was comforted by the fact they only had enough fuel to stay in the area for about ten minutes. This was going to be the first true test of our flying ability. The squadron leader came on the radio.

"All right red wing, follow me down. Focus now, these characters can be slippery."

He peeled off and started the attack. The first Spitfires down chopped pieces off their targets but the remainder scattered. The rest of us continued with our attack on the bombers. By now they too had seen us and were taking evasive action but for four of them it was too late and their aircrews baled out. The squadron leader came on the radio telling us to break off the attack on the bombers as the fighter were now on our tail. Pulling back hard on the stick I went straight up. There was a 109 following me up. That's when I discovered that although he had similar speed, my Spitfire was more manoeuvrable. We gyrated around the sky, trying to get at each other, and then he was gone. Pursuing the bombers, I managed to get behind one, pushing the firing button. It lurched and then I ran out of ammunition. Just at that moment we were told to regroup and head for home. When we landed we discovered that Findlay had a few holes in his aircraft, which were hastily repaired. Fortunately there were none in him. Although I hadn't shot anything down this time, some of the squadron had. With every encounter with the enemy we gained a bit more experience and confidence. The grim reality for the enemy aircrews was that if they survived getting shot down, they would spend the rest of the war as prisoners.

As expected, we were moving again, this time to Eastchurch, rotating with a squadron there. On the south side of the Thames estuary, it was just east of London. A day or so after we got to our new home the weather took a turn for the worse, or the best, depending on your state of mind. During the short period of unsettled weather there had been the odd raid at bases further west but on the whole there wasn't much activity by either side. On the 24th of August, however, the enemy came back with a vengeance. The raids on the fighter aerodromes intensified, some being hit two and three times a day the hangers were reduced to piles of rubble. There were reports on the wireless about what was happening, but we didn't pay them much heed. It was difficult enough for those of us in the RAF to get accurate information, so how could they? But one thing was clear; the enemy was trying to eliminate the RAF. During these intense attacks we would be up, trying to defend the aerodromes, only to find on our return that they had been bombed. Dodging the craters made landing tricky.

Flying as often as we were in that kind of environment was both mentally and physically exhausting. but our squadron leader had us as an added responsibility. We were his "clutch" still, so he kept an eye on us but it was a heavy load. He too was tired and needed a rest. As a squadron we had been lucky so far, most of us had a few holes in our aircraft but nothing any more serious than that. That changed on the 2nd of September.

We had already been up once in the morning, but immediately after lunch we were scrambled again. We had just started our take-off run when a formation of enemy fighters strafed us. My aircraft wasn't hit and from somewhere I found the presence of mind to keep going. With my hand on the throttle I pushed it hard against the stop. As soon as she had enough speed I lifted off, pulled the undercarriage up and immediately swung right and left to see if there was anyone behind me. There was no enemy, just three Spitfires. My hand on the throttle still, I pulled back on the stick and with the big propeller clawing at the sky I climbed to five thousand feet. As the three other Spitfires pulled up alongside, I looked to see who was with me. The squadron leader, red one, two and five were still on the ground. It wasn't a good time to reflect on what had just happened, we had to stay focused. Just at that moment the sector controller came on the radio wondering where we were. It was the squadron leader's job to talk to him, but he wasn't here. Again the radio crackled into life.

"Red flight, this is sector control, do you read?"

Turning around I looked at the rest of my flight. I could see they weren't keen on talking to sector. Without any more thought, I called the controller.

"Sector control this is red four. Four aircraft airborne at five thousand overhead Eastchurch. Squadron Leader Campbell and three other aircraft strafed on take-off."

The controller acknowledged my transmission and our status and instructed us to head west to Gravesend and join up with squadron leader Simpson and his flight. It only took a few minutes to get to there and after talking to the squadron leader he instructed us to fall in behind them. They were heading southwest to intercept a formation of bombers. When we got sight of them the squadron leader didn't waste any time getting on with the attack. There was no sign of fighters, so I for one was going to take advantage of the situation.

One by one we peeled off and followed the leader down. Without their fighter protection they were sitting ducks. On my first pass and with only a few seconds on the firing button, pieces of fuselage peeled off one enemy plane. Slowly it rolled over on its back and went down. Pulling up, I checked for enemy fighters. Nothing, so I looked for another bomber. Before the attack was over I would be able to claim one raider destroyed and another damaged. Anything on the receiving end of the Spitfire's firepower didn't stand a chance. If you could get a target lined up in your sights, the cannon fire in particular was devastating. We kept company with Squadron Leader Simpson back to Gravesend and then headed for our own aerodrome. As we landed and taxied in we could see the aircraft sitting there with mechanics working on them. They didn't look badly damaged, but what about their occupants? As we walked across the grass towards the briefing room we didn't know what to expect. Reaching the door I put my hand on the handle and hesitated, looking at my three colleges.

"Open the door," said Findlay. " Good or bad, we have to find out."

Turning the handle we went in. To our amazement and relief the squadron leader and the other three members of our flight were sitting, waiting on our return.

"You alright?" I asked.

"We're fine," the squadron leader answered. "Just a bit shaken."

"We were fearing the worst, it's miraculous none of you were hurt."

We're all fine," he said again. "None of us have as much as a scratch, there isn't much wrong with the aircraft either. The mechanics say they'll have them fixed in a few hours."

He wanted to know how we got on. When I told him we had all downed some raiders, he grinned from ear to ear.

After the debriefing the squadron leader wanted to talk to me privately.

"Can you do me a favour," he asked.

" If I can I will," I replied.

"I don't want you to say anything to Catherine about what happened today, she'll only worry more than she does already."

"Alright, I won't say a word."

"There's something else I'd like you to do for me," he continued. "If anything should happen to me, I'd like you to make sure that Catherine is alright."

Shaking my head, I said that nothing was going to happen to him.

"Listen," he went on. "We were lucky today. Catherine means everything to me, I need to know there is someone there who she can depend on to help her if she needs it."

"And who will help her if something happens to both of us?" I asked him.

"Well, hopefully that won't happen. I just need you to tell me that you'll help her if she needs it."

Why he was asking me, I couldn't understand. Catherine and I were the best of friends. I thought the world of her and would help her if I could. But she had someone else in her life she obviously thought a lot of and would have thought she would have preferred that he help her.

"Well, will you do it?" he asked again.

"Yes, of course, I'll help her if she needs it."

Walking back to the briefing room he reminded me it would be Catherine's birthday the next day, September 3rd. It was also a year since war with Germany had been declared. Thankfully there were no more raids that day and so we made the most of it. We sat around playing cards, chatting about what we would do with our lives when the war was over.

It was a couple of days before the damaged Spitfires were fit to fly again and so, until that happened, and because I had taken the initiative on the day of the raid, I was designated red wing leader. For the next little while most of the airfields in the southeast corner of England were attacked and we were up trying to defend them. Then, into the second week of September, the enemy changed their strategy from bombing airfields to bombing London. No one knows why, but it was, in a way, a welcome change for us. We knew where they were going every day; it was just a case of getting up there and trying to stop them. But we couldn't stop them all. Consequently, parts of London were badly damaged. Bombs and incendiaries started huge fires. There was a short respite in the middle of the month when there was a spell of very low cloud that made flying impossible and we were hoping to get posted out to a less active field for a while but it didn't happen. We had been told there were indications the enemy was about to make an all-out effort to beat us, and the country, into submission. What had they been doing so far, we wondered?

On the 14th of September the weather cleared and the bombing resumed. But it was on the 15th we saw the biggest concentration so far of enemy aircraft. The sky was black as they kept coming, wave after wave. We were grossly outnumbered; all we could do was to keep going up and try to get as many of them as possible.

We, as a squadron, all shot down raiding aircraft that day but we didn't go unscathed either. First to go was red seven, John Ferguson. He managed to get out of his aircraft and parachute to safety, none the worse for his experience.

George McDonald in red six was next. An enemy fighter had got to him and before he could get out of his plane it caught fire. He was alive but he'd been badly burned and would be in hospital for a while. Again it was brought home to us just how vulnerable we were. We were all tired and needed a few days rest but as long as the enemy kept doing what they were doing we would not get it. Thankfully the next few days were a bit quieter.

Then, on the 22nd of September, it was my turn to have a brush with death. We had been sent up to intercept a formation of bombers but couldn't find them at first. There were big blobs of cotton wool type clouds everywhere, the kind big enough to hid in. We did eventually find them, but before attacking, the squadron leader reminded us to be on the lookout for fighters. As the clouds had concealed them they did us also, before they could do anything we were right on top of them. On the first pass we all hit our targets, either destroying them or damaging them enough that they just dumped their bombs right there. The rest scattered and hid in the clouds. When I found them again they too were heading for home. Although they were just leaving the coast they weren't too far away so I decided to pursue them. Closing in for the attack I pushed the firing button and almost immediately one engine began to smoke. As if in slow motion the bomber rolled over and the crew baled out.

'Another one less,' I thought, and turned for home. Then, suddenly, I was head-to-head with a fighter. Appearing out of nowhere he obviously didn't know I was there either. We both banked hard right and at the same time I instinctively pushed the firing button. He must have done the same, I felt machine gun fire sink into my plane and immediately it began to vibrate violently. Trying to bring her back level I applied opposite aileron and rudder but there was no response. The joystick moved around its axis like stirring porridge in a pot. Being in a tight turn to begin with it didn't take much for my aircraft to go right over on her back and into a spiral. My mind racing, I looked around and discovered I was still over water. 'If I bale out here I'm going to get wet,' I thought. 'but at least she isn't on fire. Maybe I can get her level again.' By now the engine was screaming. 'What are you doing?' my inner voice screamed louder than the engine. 'Get out of here.' Undoing my harness, I slide the canopy back and pulled myself up and out. The blast of freezing cold air was unbelievable and for a few seconds I couldn't breathe. Fumbling for the ripcord I managed to find it. After what seemed like an eternity my parachute billowed out above me and things began to slow down. Looking around I could see I was about three miles out over the Channel. I was definitely going to get wet. The enemy fighter responsible for my predicament was now no more than a speck in the distance, visible mainly by the wispy trail of smoke behind him. Had I hit him too, I wondered.

Drifting downwards, I hung there and watched my plane hit the water and disappear. Another minute or so I'd be in it as well. At least the water wasn't rough. A few seconds before I went into the water my spirits lifted when I heard the familiar throb of a Spitfire. Looking around to see where he was, the next thing I knew I was in the water. Quickly undoing my harness I swam out from under my chute before I got tangled up in the cords. I wouldn't be the first pilot to drown because of that. When I surfaced, the Spitfire was circling above me, it was Findlay. As we were the only squadron in the area at that time he would have known it was one of us. Waving up at him he waggled his wings and then he climbed higher and stayed there for a while. Turning around I began to swim for shore, it didn't look all that far from the plane but clearly it would take a while. As I swam on I could hear that Findlay was still there, then after a while there was a different noise. Looking around I could see a boat heading in my direction and Findlay was down, skimming the water, leading them straight to me. It was a welcome sight, I had only been in the water about fifteen minutes but already I was cold.

A big, burly man with a bushy beard and a heavy Scottish accent pulled me into the boat.

"Come on laddie, let's get you in here," he said. Effortlessly and singlehandedly he hoisted me out of the water. Shivering uncontrollably, I couldn't speak.

"Come on then," he said. "Let's get these wet things off you."

With his help I got my flying jacket off then I heard the Spitfire getting closer again; turning around I watched it down, skimming the water. As it passed it pulled up into a victory roll and then headed home.

"That must be a friend of yours," he said, shaking my hand. "My name is Jock Fraser. Stand still till I get the rest of these wet things off you."

The other man on the boat opened the throttles, turned the boat around and headed for shore.

"O aye," he went on. "That's Fergus that's driving the boat."

Before I knew it he had me stripped down to not much more than my birthday suit and then he wrapped a blanket around me.

"Here, get this in your belly," he said, thrusting a glass in my face. "Some Highland nectar to warm you up."

With the first experience of whisky still fresh in my mind, I motioned him to take the glass back.

"No laddie, you *have* tae drink it, it'll do you the world of good. Believe me when I tell you, if it was a wee bit later on I would keep you company. Come on now, one gulp and she'll be down."

It was plain to see he wasn't going to take no for an answer. 'God help me,' I thought, as I tilted the glass. Instantly I could feel it burn as it slide down my throat. Jock stood staring at me.

"I see now you were just being mannerly not wanting to drink, but I can see you have experience."

Shaking my head, I could feel the whisky heat my insides.

"You don't say much, do you?" he said, looking at me. "Here, you're not a Jerry are you?"

Turning to his partner he shouted, "Fergus! I think we picked up a Jerry. I'm going to put him back over the side."

Looking at him, I laughed, and since my teeth had stopped chattering I could speak.

"No, you've got the right man," I said.

"Man laddie, you're a Scotsman yourself. What a relief! I thought for a wee minute I would have tae put you back beside the fish. I would hae done it too. I don't like those Jerries. Where are you from?"

"Pitlochry," I replied.

"Pitlochry? Aye, they say it's a nice place. I've never been there myself, though. Have you ever been to Pitlochry Fergus?" He shouted to his partner, barely taking time for a breath.

Fergus shook his head and kept steering the boat.

"Myself, I'm from Aberdeen, and Fergus is from Fraserburgh. We still have a trawler there but we're here doing our wee bit. They were needing folk to scoot up and down the water here to pluck loons like you out. We feel a wee bit like Jesus, instead of fishing for fish we're fishing for men."

In just a few minutes we'd be into the harbour. I'd been on the boat maybe half an hour and in that time I hadn't been given the chance to dwell or reflect on my recent experience. I was grateful to my two fellow Scots for picking me up, but at the same time I was relieved we were almost back on dry land. Fergus manoeuvred the boat alongside the harbour wall and Jock jumped out and tied it up.

"Common laddie," he said. "We have tae go and see the harbourmaster just to let him see you're not a Jerry. Fergus, if you could be bringing the loon's clothes, we don't want folk to think we're starting a Chinese laundry on our wee boat."

The three of us walked along the harbour wall and towards the harbourmaster's office, Jock leading the way and Fergus and I tagging on behind. We looked like The Three Stooges. Getting to the office, Jock opened the door and breezed in.

"We brought you another one Freddie," he bellowed.

Freddie, in a way, looked like Jock. He was a big man with huge hands and a beard. He could have been a fisherman as well, I thought, but the resemblance ended there. Freddie was soft spoken and seemed a gentleman.

"Hello, I'm Freddie," he said, shaking my hand. "Are you all right, you're not hurt?"

I shook my head but before I could utter a word Jock spoke.

"He doesn't say much, this one Freddie."

Freddie went on to ask me my name and squadron.

"Let me just phone and if everything confirms we'll get transport arranged for you."

He was only on the phone for a minute and then he suggested to Jock that he and Fergus head back out into the channel in case somebody else needed their help.

"Oh, right you are then Freddie," said Jock, writing something on a piece of Freddie's paper at the same time.

Jock and Fergus shook my hand and he gave me the paper, saying it was their address.

"If you're ever up in Aberdeen you have tae look us up. You take care now son and if they give you another aeroplane, try and keep it flying!"

"Thanks for picking me up," I smiled.

"It was no bother son, that's what we're here for. After the war we'll get together and have another wee dram."

As they went out of the door I felt exhausted and couldn't decide if it was because of trying to get out of my plane, trying to swim for shore or Jock's never-ending chatter. Freddie found me dry clothes and then arranged transport for me. Putting the clothes on I thought they must have belonged to Jock at some time; they were much too big for me. As my transport rumbled north there were still enemy bombers going in the same direction. 'How much longer are they going to keep this up?' I wondered.

When we eventually got to Eastchurch, the field seemed quiet. No one took any notice as the lorry pulled up to the briefing room door. Thanking the driver for the lift, I picked up my wet clothes and got out of the lorry. Standing there for a minute I looked at my attire. There was no doubt about it, I resembled a scarecrow. The first thing I did as I began to head for the door was to trip on one of the trouser legs and make a fairly undignified crash landing. Lying there helpless for a minute, I casually looked around, wondering if anyone had seen. Somehow, I picked myself up, got to the door and went inside. There, as always, was the briefing officer. He smiled.

"Been for a swim have we?"

As we sat together I told him what had happened and he went on to tell me that it hadn't been a good day for the squadron. We had lost another two planes besides mine. I wondered who it was.

"Don't worry," he said. "They're both basically alright; it was red two and five."

"That's William and David. And they're alright?"

"Yes, but we'll have to get a few new aircraft, the squadron is down to just four planes."

Just then the door opened and the squadron leader walked in.

"Thank the lord," he said, shaking my hand. "Are you alright?"

I just nodded, then he smiled, saying that he had seen the lorry drop me off and wondered how a drunk had got onto the airfield.

"Why don't you go and get tidied up, find some clothes that fit and then we can have a chat."

So, holding up the trousers with one hand and my wet clothes under the other arm, I shuffled out of the door and headed for our hut. There I found the rest of my weary mates. They were as pleased to see me as I was to see them. Before I did anything else I thanked Findlay for staying with me when I was in the water.

"I suppose I owe you one."

"Big time," came the reply. "To be honest I didn't know who it was at first. I just noticed the Spitfire going down and then the parachute. It wasn't until I tried to contact you and then saw your scrawny frame standing in the boat that I knew for sure it was you. But you still owe me. I still want that date with your sister."

Shaking my head, I turned to William. He was sitting in a chair, his arm in a sling and his face cut and bruised. He looked a bit worse for wear.

"Looks like you've been in a war," I commented.

"I was really lucky," he said, forcing a smile. "But I survived and I'll fight another day."

Looking at David, I asked him how he was.

"I'm fine, don't have a scratch," he smiled.

After getting cleaned up we all sat together, telling each other about our experiences. When I told them about Jock thinking I was a Jerry, Findlay just about split his sides laughing. Later on we had a chat with the squadron leader. He informed us the squadron would be stood down for a day or two. We only had four planes and some of them had holes in them. New planes were coming and also another pilot to replace George McDonald. Then he said he wanted to have a private word. We went outside and walked across the grass.

"You're all right?" he asked.

"I'm fine."

"What happened?"

"The enemy fighter appeared out of cloud, we just missed each other. Another second or so and I wouldn't be here."

"Well you are," he said. "And I'm thankful for that. The last thing I want to have to do is to write to your parents and Catherine."

If there was a good side to our every misfortune it would have to be that we learned from them. We all got along well together; we talked about our individual experiences and became better pilots for it. For myself, I learned that day that it didn't matter what kind of pilot you were. Good or bad, if you were in the wrong place at the wrong time, it was over. As I lay in my bed, trying to get to sleep, the experiences of the day very clear in my mind, I pondered on just how close I'd come to death.

The next day, four shiny, new Spitfires were ferried in, along with a new pilot. John McDonald. But he had come right out of flying school and had no combat experience. Those of us getting a new aircraft checked them over and discovered there were a few changes here and there. Later in the day the squadron went flying for half an hour to check them out and, I believed, so that the squadron leader could check us out, making sure those of us who had to bale out earlier in the week didn't have the jitters. The rest of the day was quiet, but after that until the end of the month we were up twice a day. All of us had minor damage inflicted upon us but we never lost anyone, and although our replacement pilot, John McDonald in red six didn't have any enemy planes to his credit yet, he could look after himself.

We were now at the end of September 1940 and it looked like the enemy were changing their tactics again. We were still getting daylight raids but there were a lot fewer of them and most of those were flown at high altitude. For the time being the Spitfire was the only fighter the RAF had that was capable of intercepting them but by the time we were scrambled and up to 30,000 feet, the raiders had dropped their bombs and were heading home again. So the RAF changed their tactics as well. We were sent on 'standing patrols', flying at high altitude, waiting for the raiders to appear. It was exhausting being on constant lookout, intercepting and attacking the incoming planes. Sometimes they would show up, other times they wouldn't. The intense bombing of London and other cities continued but was now being carried out during the hours of darkness. Although there were anti-aircraft batteries and searchlights probing the night sky, the enemy did pretty much as they liked.

Over the next couple of weeks we all had yet more brushes with death and the mechanics were kept busy fixing holes in our aircraft. We had scrapes and bruises but the most seriously injured was John Ferguson in red seven. Subjected to the wrath of an enemy fighter he did manage to get back to the airfield but couldn't get the undercarriage down and so he had to belly land. Between bullet holes and damage from the crash his plane was written off. John himself had a leg injury from a piece of shrapnel. He would be all right but wouldn't be flying for a while.

Although the squadron had lost aircraft recently and there had been a number of injuries, there had been no deaths. That changed on the 15th of October. The close-knit family we had become had to cope with the grim reality of our second fatality. David Cleland in red five was gone. After being jumped by an enemy fighter he limped back to the airfield and managed to land. Sadly he died from his wounds later in the day. Before he enlisted he had lived in Scotland along the Solway coast with his parents and younger brother; they had a small hotel there. He often spoke of how quiet and peaceful it could be, especially in the long summer days. He spoke of the times he went fishing in the estuary and about the thousands of migratory birds that would congregate there at certain times of the year. He loved his home and planned to go back there after the war. The squadron leader now had the unpleasant task of writing to his family. How do you go about telling a mother that her twenty-one-year-old son is dead?

But the squadron's misfortune didn't end there. The next day it happened again, but this time it was our invincible squadron leader. We were up over thirty thousand feet, engaging the enemy. Somehow, one of their fighters got on his tail and riddled his aircraft. It went over on its back and went straight down. I couldn't believe it and for a few moments I couldn't do anything. It must be one of us, I thought. But there was no mistake and I began to relive my own bailing out a few days earlier. You don't have time to be scared, it's something that has to be done. To stay with the aircraft was certain death. But the force of the wind as you fight to get out is indescribable. Then it dawned on me. He would have to stay with his plane for a little while if he could, there was no air up here. I decided to stay with him to see if he got out of his plane, praying that he would.

There was a thin layer of wispy cloud below us that made it difficult to see if he had managed to bale out. Descending through it I eventually caught sight of his plane spinning wildly far below. But there were no parachutes and a moment of disbelief and fear swept over me. This can't be. Then, my prayer was answered, above me there was a chute somewhat camouflaged against the cloud. Fixated on his plane I'd passed him on the way down. Pulling up, I went around him; he gave me a half-hearted wave.

He was alive but he didn't look great. His aircraft hit the ground and exploded and a few minutes later the squadron leader landed not far from it and just lay there. If there had been enough room to land I would have done just that. Radioing the sector controller I told him where they could find him and stayed in the area. Within minutes a handful of people were running towards his motionless body. Yesterday he had the unpleasant task of writing to David Cleland's parents; was I now faced with the prospect of telling Catherine? Please God, let him be alright.

As his rescuers reached him there was nothing else I could do and so I headed back to the airfield. After debriefing, the duty officer phoned the police in the village close to where he had landed and was told that he was alive. He had a broken arm and was unconscious. They told him which hospital he had been taken to. They confirmed his injuries. We wanted to go and see him but there was little point until he regained consciousness. The good news was that he would survive. As we retired for the night I thought of what Bella used to say. 'Your bad luck comes in three's.' I tried to erase the thought from my mind. The squadron didn't need any more of this kind of luck.

In the morning, besides the duty officer in the briefing room there was a Group Captain Thomson; he had come to speak to us and to bringing us up to date with the Squadron Leader's health.

"First of all," he said. "Let me put your minds at ease by telling you that Squadron Leader Campbell is now awake and is expected to make a full recovery. He should be out of hospital in a few days. After that, he is going to Scotland to spend time with his daughter and recuperate". He went on to say there would be a car made available for anyone who wanted to go to see him. As well, the squadron would be getting three replacement aircraft and pilots.

"That brings me to my next point," he went on. "In my conversation with Squadron Leader Campbell last night, there was no doubt in my mind how much he thinks of each and every one of you, how capable all of you are and how much respect you have for each other. We talked about how the squadron would need a leader. I explained to him how the RAF was so desperately short of squadron leaders. Even if we had a replacement you may not be compatible and that's no good, so we at sector control, with the help of Squadron Leader Campbell, have taken the rather unusual step in deciding that the best person for the job was one of you."

We looked at each other, probably all thinking the same thing, that we didn't have enough experience.

"Who's it going to be?" he asked.

Findlay stood up. Good I thought. He's going to volunteer.

"Sir," he began. "There is one man we all admire and respect. The fact that he has the best looking sister I've ever seen doesn't enter into it. I think I speak for everyone when I say Somerville should be the one."

If ever there was a humbling experience, this was the moment. Finding out what my peers really thought of me.

"Looks like you're elected Somerville," the commander reacted.

"Sir, I don't know the first thing about being a squadron leader. I wouldn't know where to begin."

"Yes you do Somerville," he went on. "You know a lot more than you think."

With that, the briefing was over, for everyone except me that is. I suggested to the commander that I'd do the job until Squadron Leader Campbell came back.

"You may as well know right now Somerville, Squadron Leader Campbell will not be back."

"Won't be back? But sir, we need him. Besides, what will he do?"

"Believe me, he won't be out of a job."

Hesitating for a moment, he looked at me and then went on. "There is something else you should know. When I asked him who he would recommend to lead the squadron, without hesitation he said you were the one. There is no doubt he thinks very highly of you."

Lost for words, I didn't say anything. He went on to say that we, as a squadron, because we had Spitfires, would continue to intercept the high-flying intruders. He told me also that there were indications the feared invasion of Britain by the enemy had been postponed.

"For their Channel crossing to have succeeded the Germans first had to crush RAF Fighter Command and they haven't been able to do that. The indications are that they will step up their night bombing campaign of London and other cities, but time alone will tell".

It was clear that I was now privy to information that before I'd been elevated up the chain of command had only been told on a 'need to know' basis.

After the group captain left I rounded up my newly acquired responsibilities. As we sat talking, I told them I really didn't want to be the one to tell them what to do. I was, after all, the youngest. Again Findlay elected himself spokesman.

"You're the best man for the job ... and besides, I do want a date with your sister!"

He was persistent, I told him, and I thanked them all for their confidence in me.

"Confidence?" Findlay said, smiling. "We just didn't want all the paperwork that goes along with the job!"

"There is going to be extra paperwork," I replied. "But there is one thing I am going to like about the job. I'm now your superior officer and you are going to have to salute me and be nice to me."

"No way!" he said, smiling and shaking his head.

6.   The Chain of Command

After lunchtime three new planes and three new pilots arrived, none of them had any combat experience. I stood there looking at them and they at me. All at once I realized I had become the "mother hen" and immediately I was thrust into my new role and responsibilities. It was my job to do my best to protect them and to make sure that the squadron was operational. Turning, I stood staring out the briefing room window. 'I'm not ready for this,' I thought. 'How am I going to manage?' I didn't want to be there but I *was* there and, like every other time I was faced with a new challenge and uncertainty, I drew strength from Dad. 'Just get on with it', I could hear him say. 'You can do this. Be the best you can be.'

Taking a deep breath, I turned and faced my new charges and at the same time asked the duty officer to summon the rest of the squadron. When they appeared a few minutes later I introduced them to the new members of the squadron, then they took a seat and stared at me. Staring back, wondering what to do next, you could have heard a pin drop. What would Squadron Leader Campbell have done at that moment, I wondered? First, tell them only what they needed to know, and second, go for a short flight to see how everybody fits. So that's what I did; instructing the duty officer to make sure our aircraft were fuelled and ready to go I reminded my "clutch" of what our role had been, and would continue to be for a while.

With that, we headed to our aircraft, Findlay and I walking out together.

"Why did you get me into this job?" I asked him.

"James old buddy, you got yourself the job," he said, patting me on the back. "You're the best man for it."

With that, we climbed into our aircraft. On our return the duty officer, who was now my right hand man, reminded me I should phone sector control to tell them we were operational again.

We didn't fly again that day. Instead we got the car we were promised and the five old members of the squadron went to the hospital to see Squadron Leader Campbell. He looked tired, but after seeing him lying in that field the day before he was better looking than I expected.

"I just did this to get away from you lot," he smiled.

"And you're no sooner away and this scoundrel steals your job," Findlay commented.

"So I hear," came the reply.

Somehow feeling guilty that maybe I had, I changed the subject, telling Findlay to go and chat to the nurses. He looked at them momentarily.

"No, I don't think so. There's only one girl for me."

We didn't stay all that long. Before we left, however, the squadron leader wanted to talk to me in private.

"You didn't steal my job," he began. "I can't be there and the squadron needs a leader. They asked me who I thought was the best person for the job. You're all good pilots but the best person to lead them got the job. It could be a bit awkward for a while, until your colleagues come to terms with the fact that you are their superior officer. Under the circumstances though, we felt it was better this way. Just be yourself and everything will work. The duty officer is a good man, he will do all he can to keep you right. Remember the things I taught you and remind them. You'll be fine; they're your clutch now."

He was saying goodbye and somehow I felt an enormous weight rest itself on my shoulders. The gravity of my new responsibilities was beginning to sink in. How was I going to manage without him? He was like my father. He was the rock I had leaned on. He saw I was overwhelmed by it all and said again. "Don't worry, just remember what I told you once before. If the RAF didn't think you were capable they wouldn't have you doing the job. I know you can do it."

He went on to tell me that he was going to Pitlochry to stay with Catherine.

"Can you take me with you?" I quipped. "I'd love to go back and see everybody."

"No can do, old man, but according to sector the enemy attacks will fizzle out in a bit. If that happens you'll get some leave."

We had been so engrossed in flying we hadn't had time to pine for home, but now the squadron leader was going I felt homesick.

"It seems like a hundred years since we've been home," I said. "I miss everybody."

"Well, if you want me to take a note to them, I'll make sure they get it," he said.

Just before I left him he told me he was being promoted, that when he got back they had a new job for him. He would be flying a Spitfire fitted with cameras, taking aerial pictures of potential bombing targets. For the most part he would be flying on his own. No "clutch" to look after. With that, we parted company and we headed back to the airfield.

When we got back, there was another development. My promotion came with a room of my own, complete with a phone. Was this the price of advancement, being deprived of the things I'd grown accustomed to? Sharing our concerns and lives with each other in our hut at night, the camaraderie, listening to Findlay ramble. Maybe I could change my mind about the promotion. I decided to phone the Group Captain in the morning. In the meantime I used the solitude and privacy of the room to write a note home but as I put pen to paper I couldn't think of anything to write, we hadn't been doing anything else but flying, and I didn't want to alarm them by telling them I was shot down, or about how black the sky had been with enemy aircraft. It took me an hour to write a few short lines.

In the morning I gave the envelopes to the duty officer and asked if he could make sure that Squadron Leader Campbell got them. At the same time I asked him if he had the phone number for Group Captain Thomson. Just at that moment the phone rang. The duty officer answered it, then handed me the phone and whispered. "Speak of the devil."

"Good morning sir," I said.

"Yes good morning Somerville, I thought I'd phone and say that if you need anything at all just let me know, good luck."

There wasn't a chance to say how I felt. I just managed to utter a 'thank-you' before he hung up. Maybe just as well. Although I didn't think I was capable of filling the void left by Squadron Leader Campbell, it seemed everyone else thought otherwise. After sleeping on it, part of me did want to give it a go. Besides, "Squadron Leader Somerville" didn't sound so bad. Before the members of the squadron made their appearance I spoke with the duty officer.

"Mr Sloan, I'm going to lean on you a lot. Keep me up to date with all the things I need to attend to."

"You can count on me sir," he smiled.

With that the members of red flight filed into the briefing room. Thus began my first full day in my new duties. We had just exchanged good mornings when the phone rang. The duty officer advised me we were on standby.

"Are our aircraft fuelled and ready to go?" I asked.

He nodded and then, five minutes later, the phone rang again. "Red Wing scramble!" he shouted. In the days that followed until the end of October we were up twice a day, either to intercept the enemy or to fly standing patrols. Fortunately, in that time we never lost any aircraft or had any casualties. By the first part of November the enemy were flying only sporadic daylight raids, as our superiors had predicted most of the enemy bombing was now being done during the hours of darkness.

Then, out of the blue, there was an announcement on the wireless by Prime Minister Winston Churchill, lavishing praise on the pilots of RAF Fighter Command.

"Never in the field of human conflict," he declared at one point, "was so much owed by so many to so few."

After listening to the announcement I experienced an overwhelming sense of pride. I was one of the few and had survived the most intense air battle in history.

As the weeks passed we were still flying a few standing patrols but saw little of the enemy. The bombing of London, on the other hand, was relentless and caused great fires. An orange glow lit the night sky. Sometimes we could hear the distant rumble and feel the vibrations. Sometimes as I watched I thought of my family and drew comfort from the thought that at least they were far removed from the chaos, terror and destruction.

Being a Squadron Leader didn't mean I could do as I pleased, it did have its advantages though. Because of the long winter nights and not being able to fly as much I arranged to have the odd one off the airfield. Occasionally a few of us went into London to see a show. In spite of the bombing, in an effort to maintain some kind of normality some theatres and pubs stayed open. It was on one of these jaunts we experienced firsthand the terror of bombing and then witnessed the consequences of it. Getting caught in an air raid, we had to go into one of the underground stations. They were deep and safe. Hundreds of people had been using them as shelters since the Blitz began. Families with children were sleeping and spending the nights together in a hole, not knowing if in the morning they had a home to go back to. They were fighting their own war, I admired them for the way they coped with it all. When we emerged after the "all clear" there were fires everywhere and firemen fighting a losing battle trying to extinguish them. There was a woman screaming that there was a family trapped in a house and so we helped the firemen look for them. There we discovered two little girls standing in the remnants of what used to be their Mum and Dad's bedroom. Holding each other's hand they cried, "Mummy and Daddy won't wake up."

They were the first dead people I had ever seen, killed in their bed by falling masonry. It was a sad scene. Those little girls, so vulnerable and helpless, wouldn't be tucked up in bed or cuddled by their Mum or Dad again. Then there was another first for me; using the word hate. I knew I didn't like Hitler for what he was doing but after witnessing this, suddenly I felt an overwhelming sense of hate and revulsion towards the whole German nation. It was they who started this. With the amount of flying we had been doing in the recent weeks, we were all extremely tired and needed a rest, but on the way back to the airfield we somehow forgot how weary we were and vowed to continue the quest against evil and try to do all we could to end the suffering as quickly as possible. It was a sad ending to our day.

7.   Home for Christmas

On the last day or so of November, Group Captain Thomson called to say they were trying to arrange leave for the pilots of Fighter Command for Christmas and New Year; he wanted to know what would suit us best. Christmas was best for us, I suggested, and arranged with him to be away from the twenty-second until the twenty-ninth of December. When I told the rest of the squadron we would be going home for a week's leave it was difficult to contain the excitement. As soon as he got the opportunity, the first thing Findlay asked was if he could come home with me to see Isobel.

I suggested he should go home and spend the time with his own family, but in the end I relented.

For those of us who stayed in Scotland, I made the arrangements to fly up to Turnhouse later in the afternoon of the twenty first. I also sent a note home, telling them when to expect us. As I wrote, I thought about the trouble I'd be in when I got home for not writing more, but there hadn't been a lot of time somehow, and whatever the reason was none of us had been getting all that much mail from our respective families. Then, wondering if my brother John would get leave from Turnhouse to go home at Christmas, I called the base commander. I was a little apprehensive about talking to him to begin with; it didn't seem all that long since he had presented me with my wings, but he couldn't have been nicer.

"I hear they made you a squadron leader," he said. "You leave it to me, I'll arrange it and I'll look forward to seeing you on the twenty-first."

After I laid the phone down and thought about the conversation it sounded like he was going to meet us in person.

Although there were things to do, the next three weeks just dragged past, however, we did manage a day in London to do some Christmas shopping. When the twenty-first came the weather wasn't the best but we managed to get away on time to be in Edinburgh before dark. Although there wasn't a lot of daylight left, the city looked great as we flew over on our approach into Turnhouse. When we landed and got out of our aircraft, the first thing we noticed was that it was a lot colder than it was in London. Almost immediately the mechanics got our aircraft into the hangar out of the weather. As they were doing that, the base commander appeared.

"It's good to see you," he said, shaking my hand.

He welcomed us like long-lost relations, almost celebrity status. It felt good.

"Before you go back to London next week," he said, "I'd like you to drop into your old classroom and share some of your experiences with a few students who are almost finished their training. We told them there were a few Battle of Britain pilots flying in. They wanted to meet you."

"It would be a pleasure sir."

"Right you are then, we'll see you next week. There's a car waiting to take you to the station ... and it's been arranged that your brother will be going with you."

Just at that moment John appeared. Both of us were a little choked and for a moment neither one of us said anything.

"Hello little brother," he managed to say. "How are you?"

"A lot better now I'm home; let's go and get our train."

Turning to the base commander I shook his hand again and thanked him for his help.

"No, thank *you* squadron leader. If there's anything else we can do for you while you are here, just let us know."

With that, we piled into the car and headed for the station. Findlay blethered all the way there. He was always like that when he was nervous. John wanted to know how many "Jerries" I'd shot down. 'A few,' I told him, then told him off for not writing more.

"You didn't write either," he countered.

"Not enough, anyway. I'll be in trouble when I get home."

The train ride north seemed to take ages and looking out of the carriage windows we couldn't see a thing; it was a moonless, pitch-black night. But, as always, the train pulled into Pitlochry right on time. Gathering our belongings as we got off I knew Dad would be there, but I didn't know about Catherine. After her being down at Turnhouse during the summer and not telling me, I didn't know where we stood. Dad saw us before we saw him and was almost beside us before I noticed him. We shook hands and gave each other a hug.

"It's good to see you," he said. "You're looking well."

"It's good to see you too," I replied. "I've missed you."

As he said hello to Findlay I looked up and down the platform through the people mingling there but couldn't see any other familiar faces. Dad saw me looking and caught my arm and smiled.

"She's standing under the roof overhang."

After he told me I could see her standing there, hanging onto her father's arm. That was typical of her, I thought, letting the family say their hellos first. She never barged in. I made my way over. She looked at her Dad and then at me and smiled. Even under the dim lights of the station she was absolutely radiant. I had forgotten how good-looking she was and noticed in the same dim light her eyes glistening. I shook her dad's hand I asked him if he felt as good as he looked.

"I feel great," he said, looking at Catherine. "But I've had a good nurse."

For a few seconds Catherine and I looked at each other. Letting go of her Dad's arm we hugged each other.

"You look great," I told her. "I've missed you."

"Not as much as I've missed you," she answered.

She was wearing her favourite perfume.

It was good to be home.

We didn't tarry long at the station; we arranged to meet at the café the next afternoon, where we would have peace to catch up with each other's lives.

When we got to the farm there were hugs all around and I introduced Findlay to the family He was now as quiet as a church mouse. All he could manage was a feeble 'hello'. Isobel and Findlay glanced at each other. Bella was a bit upset and didn't say much for a little while but she knew we would be hungry and had something ready for us to eat. As we sat around the table I wanted to know what everybody had been doing for the past eight months. One by one they brought me up to date with their lives.

When I got to Isobel she said she had applied to go to nursing college and was supposed to start training after the New Year. As she was telling me, Findlay was mesmerized.

Isobel was an easy-going, caring person. She would make a great nurse.

"What about you?" Bella asked. "Tell us what you've been up to ... we haven't had a lot of letters."

"I know and I feel bad about it. But honestly, up until a few weeks ago we've had very little time to ourselves. We've spent countless hours in the air."

"I know," Bella answered. "I'm teasing you. We've seen Catherine's father a few times since he's been here. He told us you haven't had a lot of time to yourself."

Bella turned her attention to Findlay and asked him if he wrote home regularly.

"Like James, I haven't written enough either," he began. "And I'll likely get told off about it when I get home, but it has been hectic."

Findlay went on to thank Dad and Bella for letting him stay for a couple of days and that he had been looking forward to meeting all of my family.

"Think nothing of it," said Bella. "You can stay any time."

We sat around chatting for a while after tea but it had been a long day and I was looking forward to getting to bed. For the first time in weeks I had to share a room with Findlay.

"Just like old times eh?" he grinned.

"Just like old times."

When we woke the next morning it was nine o'clock. We lay there for a while, chatting.

"Do you know how lucky you are to have a family like you have?" Findlay remarked.

"Catherine has told me that as well. I am lucky, but it's the way it's always been."

"Catherine... now she is something else," he went on. "She is gorgeous. She's still not as attractive as Isobel, but gorgeous nonetheless."

"Findlay, quit while you're ahead," I warned.

But he still wasn't finished. "Do you know how lucky you are to have a girlfriend like that?"

"Findlay, she was my schoolteacher, now we're friends."

"Friends? Aye right. And I'm a Dutchman!"

"The last time I was home she told me she had a boyfriend and Bella told me there was somebody she was really keen on."

"You know," he said, jumping out of bed and getting dressed, "It's a true saying, 'love is blind'. Come on, let's make the most of this leave. God only knows when we'll get another."

I knew he was right. When we got to the kitchen Bella was in the midst of making goodies for Christmas. She was her usual cheery self.

"Oh you're up at long last," she smiled. "Would you like some breakfast?"

Findlay and I looked at each other and agreed we would go for a walk first and eat later. It was a cool morning with a touch of frost and could see our breath as we made our way up through the farm to the 'gate with a view'.

"No wonder you like it here," Findlay commented. "It's beautiful. I could live here myself."

Standing there, admiring the countryside, London and the war seemed a long way off. Eventually, we made our way back to the house. By the time we got there, it was lunchtime. Now we were ready to eat. Over lunch I asked Dad if we could borrow the car to go into Pitlochry, but he said if we were going we would either have to walk or go on the pushbike.

"They started petrol rationing a while back," he went on. "We get enough to do the essentials every month and that's about it."

It maybe seemed like the war was a long way off but it wasn't all that far and, it was certainly affecting everybody's life.

"That's all right, I forgot there was rationing. We can go on the bike. Or should I say, I'll go on the bike and Findlay can run."

"That will depend on who gets to it first," Findlay laughed.

After we ate, Findlay asked me to ask Isobel if she wanted to go. In a flash she said yes. Before we left, I spoke to Bella for a minute, asking her if it would be all right to ask Catherine and her father to come for their Christmas dinner. She looked at me, smiled and slipped her arm around my waist at the same time.

"You're too late. I already asked them last week."

I gave her a long lingering hug and whispered in her ear.

"Thanks Bella. You'll always be my angel."

"Oh, not for much longer," she laughed. "Somebody else is going to steal you away. Now away you go, and try and be back before it's dark."

Getting the bikes out of the shed, Findlay realized I had been pulling his leg about there being only one. Racing each other along the road, within a few minutes we were outside the café.

When we got inside, Catherine was sitting waiting.

"Hello again," she smiled and before I got a chance to say anything Findlay, in what I thought was a very bold move for him under the circumstances, had a suggestion.

"If it's all right, why don't you two sit there and have a chat and we can sit over here and do the same."

It was fine with me, it was the way I wanted it.

Catherine and I sat at our little table, looking at each other, not saying anything for a minute.

Then I told her she looked great. She just smiled.

"How have you been?" I asked her. "Tell me what you've been doing all summer. The potatoes we planted, did the grow?"

The tea came and she began to tell me some of the things she had been doing.

"We must have planted the potatoes the right way up because they all grew and I've got the garden dug for spring again. School is busy as usual. There isn't really anything new, it's just more of the same."

"But what about you though? How have you been?" I asked.

As she sipped her tea I could see her blue eyes begin to glisten and as she put the cup down on the table they were about to boil over.

"Hey, what's wrong," I said, taking hold of her hand. "Whatever it is, it can't be that bad, can it?"

She cleared her throat. " I'm sorry, I promised myself that this wouldn't happen."

"Come on, tell me what's wrong."

"It's just that I'm so pleased to see you," she began again. "There have been so many reports on the wireless about how many pilots have been killed or seriously injured. Then when Dad came back injured, I just didn't know if I'd ever see you again. I've lived in fear for months. Fear of the phone ringing, or the postman with a letter telling me that one of you, or worse still, both of you wouldn't be coming home. Sometimes when I thought of it, it was almost unbearable."

"I'm sorry," I said. "I should have written more. I promised I would, and if I'd put my mind to it, I could have. But when I discovered you'd been down at Turnhouse during the summer and I hadn't seen you, well, I was disappointed and just thought you didn't want to see me after my prying the last time we sat here. I thought I had offended you."

"Believe me, I wanted to see you, but I reluctantly agreed with Dad that you had enough on your mind at that time without me clouding it. When we heard you were coming back for Christmas I spoke to Dad about it again. He agreed that this was a better time. And the last day I was up at the farm Bella and I talked and she thought this may be a better time as well. She and I have gotten really close this last while."

"What do you mean, a better time for what?"

She looked across at Findlay and Isobel, who I could see out of the corner of my eye were looking at us. At the same time I overheard Findlay's comment to Isobel. "Your brother is a good pilot, but he sure is blind."

Catherine briefly held my hand and asked me to walk with her for a bit. Leaving Findlay and Isobel in the café we walked down the hill towards the river. As we went, she slipped her arm through mine. We were almost at the river and she still hadn't said anything. I asked her if she was going to tell me what was troubling her.

"Oh dear," she said. "This is going to be more difficult than I thought."

We found a place to sit by the water out of the cool December breeze. Clinging tightly to my arm she took a deep breath and began.

"When I went to Turnhouse it was you I wanted to see but, as I said, Dad convinced me you didn't need anything else to think about at that time, something that may affect your judgement. So I came back home. Both Dad and I knew if I'd seen you I would have told you. So we both agreed to say nothing about me being there. Then, a while after Dad told me that somehow you guessed I'd been there, and about the look of disappointment on your face, I hated myself for not seeing you."

"Catherine, I'm getting more confused than ever."

"Ssh," she said, putting her finger to her lips. "This is difficult. Remember the day when you and I went to see your mother's grave and you felt that she had spoken to you?"

"How did you know that?" I interrupted. "The only person I told was Bella."

She looked a little sheepish and said that it was Bella who had told her.

"There was something I desperately needed help with, after giving it a great deal of thought I felt Bella was the right person to ask. When I went to the farm and told Bella what was on my mind I expected her to be annoyed and chase me away. But instead we talked for ages. That's when she told me about the cemetery, and she also told me what I wanted to hear."

"Catherine, I'm having a hard time following you. I never had this much trouble when you were teaching me in school."

"Yes, I know. I feel like I'm babbling, but I just want to get it right."

There were tears in her eyes again and she was shaking.

Giving her a hug I asked her to tell me what was making her hurt so badly. She leaned back and looked at me and with tears running down her face. I had never seen her so upset.

"Just take your time and tell me what's wrong."

"This is difficult," she began again. "I never thought it would be this difficult but I'm just going to say it. Remember your mother saying there was someone waiting here for you. Well... I'm the someone. I love you James Somerville."

Now she was crying and shaking uncontrollably.

"You love me? But what about your boyfriend?" I asked.

"There never was a boyfriend."

"But in the café before, you said you had a boyfriend."

"I said there was someone in my life, but that he didn't know it yet. The times I wanted to tell you how I felt, in the café, before you got on the train the last time. Then when I went down to Turnhouse intent on seeing you, I wanted to tell you in case I didn't get the chance again. If you die, I swear I'll die with you."

"Come on, don't cry. I'm not going to die," I said, helping her dry her eyes.

"You know, it's just dawned on me. Everybody knew about this except me, didn't they?"

Still looking at me she nodded.

"Bella and Dad, your Dad, Isobel ... everybody."

Again she nodded. We sat there for a while, holding each other, not saying anything, then I quietly told her how I felt.

"When I discovered you had been at Turnhouse I was disappointed. We were so busy training on Spitfires that summer was almost over when it dawned on me you would have been on your holidays from school. I thought it strange you not being down, so I asked your Dad. When he told me you had been, I was disappointed, maybe even devastated, and I was so annoyed with myself for prying into your life. I felt I had lost my best friend."

We sat for a few more minutes and then I remembered Findlay and Isobel.

"We should get back to the café. Do you think Isobel and Findlay will still be there?"

She shrugged her shoulders, neither one of us cared if they were or not. We got up from our seat but before we took a step she put her arms around my neck and kissed me for the first time.

"I love you James Somerville, I always will," she whispered in my ear.

As we stood there hanging on to each other I could smell her perfume.

"Do you know how many times I wanted to tell you how good you smell, you and your Summer Blossoms."

"Come on," she smiled. "We should get back."

As we began to walk back up the hill the tears had stopped and she was smiling again. This was the Catherine I knew. When we got back to the café Isobel and Findlay were chatting away.

"I'm such an idiot," I remarked. "Findlay isn't going to let me forget this."

Catherine squeezed my hand and we went in. As usual Findlay had something to say, he looked at his watch and then at Catherine.

"You've been away for an hour and a half. Does he know now?"

Catherine and I looked at each other and smiled.

"Thank the Lord!" he sighed. And in the next breath suggested we make tracks for the farm before it got dark.

Before we left I said to Catherine that Findlay would be leaving on the morning of the twenty-fourth and I would be in to see him off. Maybe we could meet again then.

"It's a date. I'll look forward to it," she said.

When we got home Bella was in the middle of making supper. As we walked into the kitchen our eyes met. Slipping my arm around her waist I whispered in her ear.

"You've been naughty haven't you, telling other people our secret?"

She looked at me and smiled. " She told you didn't she? How she feels."

I nodded and smiled.

"Thank the Lord! On you go and get cleaned up, your tea will be ready in a bit. We can talk tomorrow."

Later, sitting around the table, Dad was looking at me and grinning.

"Good day today James?" he asked.

Smiling back, I didn't need to say anything, he knew.

The next morning I was up early, it was the one time of the day I knew Bella and I could talk in peace. Leaving Findlay snoring, I made my way to the kitchen. Expecting me to be up, she had two cups on the table and a pot of tea made.

"Good morning," she said. "You slept well?"

"Like a log."

After pouring our tea we sat down at the table opposite each other; Bella wasted no time in getting to what we both wanted to talk about.

"So how was Catherine when you left her last night?"

"She was happy and looked great," I replied.

"Well I can tell you this much," she went on. "I've never seen anybody so head over heels in love as she is with you. It started back in the summer, just before you went to England. She came to the farm one day wanting to talk to me. Sitting where you are now she told me she needed advice and could I help her. We sat looking at each other for a minute, me wondering what was coming next, then those bonny blue eyes of hers filled and the tears began to roll down her cheeks. 'What is it lassie?' I asked her. 'What could be making you hurt so much?' Then she said what I had known for a while. 'I love him. I love James.' That girl cried over you for ages. She was frightened you wouldn't come back, that you would never know how she felt. That's when I told her about the cemetery. You didn't mean for me to tell anybody about that I know, but she was making herself ill, she needed something to cling to. We talked about everything that day. About her being older than you, about her being your teacher and about what people might say. 'You're only a little older,' I told her, and the fact that she was your teacher didn't matter. The main thing was that you felt the same way about her. That made her cry even more, thinking that you might not. She has been such a big part of your life already, I told her, and I know you think the world of her but it wasn't for me to say you loved her. I know how you feel about her but I've never heard you say it. Then she said she was thinking about going to Turnhouse to see you. I suggested she wait till you came home on leave but she had it in her mind she was going to see you. The next thing I knew she was away. When she got there her father told her the same thing and a day or two later she was back home. She came up to the farm again, sat in the same spot and cried her eyes out worse than the time before.

We sat and talked and talked and eventually she settled down. Since then she has been to the farm regularly and we've gotten quite close. She is a true sincere person and I like her a lot. Then, her Dad came home injured, that unfortunately set her off again. But between the two of us we got her settled down again. It didn't help that we didn't get enough mail, and I promised myself I'd get onto you for that. But then her father told us how much flying you were doing and how exhausted you all were. Instead of getting on to you I just wanted to hug you. Her Dad being home has helped and she has brought him to the farm when she comes to visit. He and I have had long chats about the two of you, and he and your Dad, although they don't appear to have much in common, can sit and blether for ages. He is a good person and his personality has rubbed off on Catherine."

"So there you have it. You've been such a big part of each other's lives already, nothing can change that. This still may not have been the best time to have told you, but she had to. She had her mind made up that you wouldn't leave this time without knowing how she felt. So you see, I maybe was your angel once but now there is a brighter light."

We sat in silence for a few minutes, looking at each other, me trying to absorb it all.

"What an idiot I've been!" I began "I had no idea all this was going on. Thanks Bella, you've been so good to all of us over the years, you've always been there. I'll never forget you..." I could feel a lump in my throat and my eyes begin to burn. "What made me ask her Dad if she had been down at

Turnhouse, I don't know. I just had a feeling. When he told me she had been there, I have to say I was hurt. And then both of you led me to believe she had a boyfriend. I couldn't explain it to myself at the time but I know now I was feeling jealous. Thinking she was seeing some one bothered me."

"I didn't tell you she had a boyfriend," Bella remarked. "I told you there was somebody she was keen on. I could see it long before she said anything about how she felt about you."

"Well it doesn't matter now. It's just that I feel like a right twit. You all must have been having a good laugh."

"We weren't laughing at you James. Yes, we maybe did find it amusing, even Catherine did. She told me about your conversation in the café. But it was nice, magical. You were completely oblivious to it all and we loved you all the more for it. We've all known for a long time what you mean to each other. You come home and you have to see her. She means as much to you as you do to her, don't you?"

We sat looking at each other for a moment and as we did, somehow I could feel a peace and contentment inside. How I always felt in Catherine's company.

"She's my best friend Bella, she is everything."

"Well, have you told her that?"

"Not yet, but I will."

With that, Findlay appeared and our heart-to-heart was over.

"Morning," he said. "I hope I'm not interrupting?"

"Good morning Findlay," Bella answered. "No you're not."

She squeezed my hand and got up and set about making breakfast. Findlay sat down and I asked him if he slept well.

"Like a log," he said. "I don't think I moved all night."

He wondered if I had anything planned for the day. He wanted to go into the town. There was something he needed to do.

"We can go in this morning if you like. There is something I'd like to do myself."

Bella looked at me and smiled, she knew what I meant. By now my little sisters were filing into the kitchen, sleepy eyed and tired. As I watched them I recalled those two little girls in the bombed out house in London and inwardly shuddered.

After breakfast Findlay and I went into town. It was a bright and sunny Perthshire morning and as we pedalled to keep warm our eyes watered with the cold wind. In Pitlochry Findlay wanted to know where the shops were.

"I'd like to buy something for Isobel," he said. "But I don't know what."

"She's going to nursing college. Maybe you could get her one of these watches nurses wear on their lapel," I suggested.

"That's a good idea," he said. "Let's do that."

After we finished our shopping we went by Catherine's house. She wasn't expecting us and when she opened the door she was covered in flour.

"What are you two doing here?" she asked. "You said tomorrow. Look at me."

Flour or not, she looked radiant and I just wanted to hold her again. As we made our way inside I slipped my arm around her waist and whispered in her ear.

"You look great."

"I don't think so!" she answered, rolling her eyes at the same time.

When we got to the kitchen her Dad was sitting there; he had been reading the paper.

"Well hello," he smiled. "It's a bit chilly outside."

Catherine made us tea and at the same time wondered why we were in town.

"Oh, Findlay wanted to do a bit of Christmas shopping, that's one reason."

"Would this be for anyone I know?" she asked, smiling at Findlay and for the first time in my life I witnessed Findlay blushing and lost for words.

Drinking tea and eating some of Catherine's baking we sat talking for a while, staying off the topic of war. As we were leaving Findlay told Catherine's Dad he would be leaving on the early train the next morning to go to Glasgow. As they talked I took hold of Catherine's hand and asked her how she was feeling. She looked at me and smiled.

"A lot better, but you're supposed to let a girl know when you are going to call so she can get cleaned up. You didn't tell me the other reason why you came into the town."

"I wanted to see you," I answered squeezing her hand. "I wanted to tell you..."

"Tell me tomorrow when we're alone," she whispered, interrupting me.

The rest of the day we spent at the farm, keeping company with my family and catching up with what was new. Findlay wanted to go for another walk around the farm, only this time he and Isobel went themselves. When they were away I talked to Bella for a while. I wanted to know how Dad and William would manage after Isobel left to go to college, but Bella was more interested in Findlay. What was he really like?

"Well there isn't really a lot to tell," I began. "All of us who started flying school on the same day, for the most part, got along well. But he, William and I just seemed to hit it off. They are my two closest friends. Findlay is the most outgoing and sometimes I do get fed up with his chatter. I like flying with him though. He's focused and I know he wouldn't intentionally let you down; he could quite possibly have saved my life."

Bella looked at me, wondering what I meant.

"It's not important right now," I went on. "I'll tell you about it sometime. He is a good person."

"He seems to have an eye for Isobel."

"Oh, they like each other, but that's as far as it goes. This is only the second time they've seen each other. Besides, I don't think Findlay is Isobel's type."

That was basically the end of our discussion. It was the time of year when the days were shortest and it was getting dark by four o'clock, but after supper we sat and talked and played cards and the night passed.

The next morning Findlay was up a lot earlier to catch his train. We had breakfast and then it was time to go. Giving Bella a hug he thanked her for letting him stay.

"You're welcome Findlay, come back again sometime."

He shook Isobel's hand and said that maybe he would see her again.

"Maybe," she answered with a little smile.

It was another cold morning, not one for hanging around. We got into the car and five minutes later we were at the station. Catherine and her father were there, waiting to say goodbye.

"Be careful," Squadron Leader Campbell said. "Remember the things I taught you."

They shook hands and then Findlay turned to Catherine and shook her hand.

"Merry Christmas Catherine. I'm glad James knows ... finally."

"So am I Findlay," she replied. "Have a Merry Christmas."

The train whistle blew and as he boarded the train he gave me a present.

"Can you make sure Isobel gets this?"

"I'll make sure. Merry Christmas Findlay. I'll see you back at Turnhouse in a few days."

The train disappeared quickly, swallowed by the darkness, and as we stood there Catherine slipped her arm through mine.

"Come on," she said. "Let's go back to the house and I'll make some tea. It's too cold to stand here."

Getting into the car, we were there in a few minutes. Catherine's house wasn't big but it was cosy. As she made tea, her father and I chatted. Sitting in the chair, watching the fire licking at the chimneybreast, I felt drowsy and Catherine's father's voice got farther and farther away.

I was awakened by the phone ringing. It was now broad daylight and the sun was shining in the window. Someone had put a shawl around me. Looking around, I was alone, the fire was still nice and warm and I could hear Catherine speaking on the phone.

"Yes he's here, he fell asleep on the chair. I was making tea and the next thing I knew he was asleep."

That'll be Bella wondering where I am. It was comfortable and I could have sat a while longer, but I got up and went into the kitchen.

"Well if it isn't sleeping beauty?" she said, giving me a hug. "Do you feel better now?"

" I think so. I could still sleep though."

"Have some tea, that will wake you up."

"In a minute, just let me hold you for a bit."

It felt good to be close to her.

"How is it you always smell so nice?" I asked.

She giggled her infectious giggle and shrugged her shoulders.

"That was Bella on the phone, just wondering where her little boy was."

"Bella was telling me you've been up at the farm quite a bit this summer."

Evading the question, she said that she'd pour the tea. I sat at the table and she sat beside me. She took a sip then pushed her arm through mine and held on tightly.

"I have been at the farm a lot," she began. "If Bella hadn't been there I don't know what I would have done. I needed someone to talk to and as it turns out she undoubtedly was the right person. She never got flustered or short with me. How she made time for me I'll never know, she has so much to do all the time. There were days we sat and talked for ages. Looking back, she must have been fed up with me. But she was the closest thing to you, and I wanted to be close to you. Because of it all, because of you, she is the best friend I have."

She went quiet again and as I looked at her I could see her lip quiver. Finding her hand, I held it.

"Come on," I said quietly. "Don't do that."

She cleared her throat and went on.

"I was so upset and she made the time and consoled me. If she hadn't been there I don't know what I would have done. And when she told me about the cemetery I felt so much better. Your mother reached out and touched you. For some reason you felt the need to go there that morning. We're all so glad you did. We've all drawn strength from it. Any day I was feeling down I would think of it and be uplifted by it."

For a moment again there was silence, then I spoke.

"You know, there have been three women in my life. First there was Mum, and then Bella, and now there is you. All of you have done so much for me, seeming to fall into place one after the other. I really can't imagine my life without any one of you in it. I love all of you so very much and wonder sometimes how I got to be so fortunate."

Catherine turned in her seat and looked at me.

"You love me?" she asked. Her crystal clear blue eyes were almost overflowing, begging me to say it again. Leaning over I whispered in her ear.

"Catherine Campbell, I love you."

"Is that what you were going to tell me yesterday?"

Telling her it was, she leaned into me and tears rolled down her cheeks. I was still holding her when her father walked into the kitchen a while later.

"Are those happy tears or sad tears?" he asked.

Catherine looked at him, half crying and half laughing.

"They're happy tears. Thank the Lord. At last, I don't have to carry a secret around with me any longer."

Catherine let me go and got up, disappearing through the door. After she left the room her father said that he would always be indebted to Bella for all the support she had given Catherine.

"She confided in the one person who had the compassion and found the time for her," he went on. "I know what she was like when she came to Turnhouse during the summer. Rhyme reason or none she was going to talk to you. She was convinced that she wouldn't see you again. Eventually I persuaded her that it wasn't a good time. She was upset enough then I know and I felt bad when she left to come home. But I felt you had enough on your mind. When I got back here she was getting along better and then she got your letter saying you'd be home for Christmas. Well the time wouldn't pass quickly enough. Anyway, now you know everything."

Catherine reappeared, looking better and wearing a smile.

"Are you all right?" I asked.

She nodded and asked me if I wanted more tea.

Declining the offer, I said I should get back home. We hugged each other and as I made my way out the door they said they'd be at the farm around lunchtime the next day.

Although there was some snow on higher ground to the north, on Christmas Day 1940 we were looking at green fields, and compared to the last few days it was quite mild. The family were up earlier than usual, in anticipation I suppose. All my sisters got something to wear, between that and the perfume, again, they were happy.

Giving Isobel her present from Findlay, I told her it was from an admirer. She opened the box and looked at the watch.

"This is just what I need," she beamed, and read the note aloud. "Have a Merry Christmas. Will be thinking of you, Findlay."

"Will you tell him thanks from me?" she asked.

"Why don't you write him a note and I'll see he gets it."

"That's what I'll do," she nodded.

Catherine and her father arrived on time. I was looking forward to spending Christmas with them. Exchanging gifts her father thanked me for the pen and writing paper I had given him. I told him he didn't have an excuse for not writing home now. Opening the present they had given me we looked at each other and laughed.

"It looks like you don't have an excuse for not writing home now either," her father smiled.

"Merry Christmas James," Catherine said, giving me a hug, and whispering that she loved me.

Like any other, the day came and went and we ate and drank too much. Catherine wanted to go for a walk and so we went up to 'the gate'. Her hand in mine, occasionally she looked at me and squeezed tighter. Content to be in each other's company we said little as we walked. Getting to our vantage point she pointed things out she hadn't seen before. Full of enthusiasm she commented on how lovely the valley looked and as she did I looked at her and thought the same. At that moment it seemed like she didn't have a care in the world. With her dark hair shining in the December sun and the sparkle in her eyes, she looked positively radiant.

As she talked, my mind wandered, thinking that the two most beautiful things in the world were right in front of me. The valley that held all the memories of my childhood, where I grew up and felt secure, where my family were, knowing that if I wanted their company I could have it. But at the same time I knew of a hundred places I could go to find solitude and peace. Places I could walk or just sit on a stone and watch birds soar, or watch the valley come and go with the seasons.

Then there was Catherine. She had, for a long time, been a big part of my valley. She was my guiding light and I had come to realize, like Dad, she was seldom wrong about anything. As the sun danced on her it made me all the more determined to do what I had to do in whatever lay ahead and hopefully I'd be back to spend time with her. Reaching for her hand I interrupted her.

"Have I told you today how beautiful you are?"

Slowly she shook her head and looked at me for a moment. Then, her eyes began to glisten and she put her arms around me.

"Now look what you've made me do."

I didn't want the moment to end. Eventually though we made our way back to the house. They had been waiting for us; Catherine's Dad had brought a camera with him and wanted to take every one's picture. For some members of the family it was their first time and because of that, it turned out to be a memorable occasion. He froze the moment in time. It took a while to get around everyone but when he was done Dad announced he wanted to propose a toast.

"We've all had a good Christmas I know. Let me first say thanks to Bella and to friends and family, the people who made it that way and, also for our health in the New Year when it comes. Cheers," he said, and we all chinked our glasses, wishing each other good health.

"I'd like to propose another toast," he continued.

He hesitated for a moment, looking at Catherine's father and then at me.

"I want us to drink to the health of James and John, and for the health of all the other souls who are flying against the enemy. To them and to the memory of those who made the ultimate sacrifice, we will be forever indebted. Nobody said it better than our Prime Minister, 'Never in the field of human conflict was so much owed by so many to so few'.

"To the few, and to our two of the few," he said, raising his glass again. "To James and John."

As Dad, followed by the rest of my family, hugged us, I could feel a lump in my throat and the room blurred.

"Do you know how proud I am of you both?" Catherine managed to say.

Dad never said any more than he had to. It was humbling. I did feel an enormous sense of pride in myself though, and felt privileged to be one of the few. But at the same time I knew it wasn't over.

It was late when Catherine and her father went home, and as soon as they left everyone just disappeared and went to bed.

The next day, after helping feed the cattle, I biked into Pitlochry. The town was quiet but as I got close to Catherine's house I could see a sign that life within this house at least had stirred. A thin column of smoke was rising from the chimney and with no wind to influence its direction it was going straight up. Just as I got to the door it opened. Catherine stood there grinning.

"Good morning," she said, holding my hand. "I've been watching for you."

"Good morning. You look happy today."

"That's because I am happy," she replied.

In the kitchen her Dad was sitting reading the paper.

"Good morning," I said. "It looks like you've recovered from your visit to the farm yesterday then?"

"Good morning James. Yes I have. Catherine and I were talking about it this morning. It was a very enjoyable day."

I sat opposite him at the table while Catherine made tea and he continued.

"We were just saying that your home is a happy home."

As I nodded in agreement I thought it wasn't the first time I'd heard someone say that but I'd never given it any thought. It was the way it had always been.

Catherine disappeared for a few minutes and as soon as she did he commented on what he'd been reading.

"Look at this paper. It's full of stories about the war. Who knows where they get all their information or how much is accurate."

He went on to say there was a lot of speculation about what the enemy may do next. Intelligence reports would seem to suggest they were going to concentrate on Russia for a while.

"The buggers can't get the better of us," he continued. "So they are going to harass somebody else."

Just at that moment Catherine reappeared, poured our tea and then sat down beside me.

"You know," she said. "We could go into the front room and sit by the fire."

"We could," I replied. "But I'd likely fall asleep again."

"And what would be wrong with that?" Catherine laughed.

"Nothing I suppose. But I was thinking we could go for a walk down to the river and back."

"That's a good idea, it'll work up an appetite for supper."

"You two go by yourselves," Catherine's father said. "I'll stay here and make something so you can eat when you come back."

Sipping our tea I asked him if his arm was healed now. He said that it was as good as new.

"I've had more time off than I needed really, but they told me not to report back until January 2nd. They are giving me the latest model Spitfire fitted with cameras. It doesn't have armament of any kind. I'm going to be part of a new reconnaissance squadron taking pictures of potential targets or whatever else the powers that be deem necessary."

He could see me looking at him in disbelief, but I didn't say anything that would alarm Catherine.

"They've been doing it for a while now," he went on. "It's quite safe. We fly so high and fast they don't have anything to get us with."

Maybe so, I thought, but I don't think I'd like to be doing it if I couldn't defend myself.

"You'll likely have a lot quieter time at Eastchurch now as well," he continued. "In fact, because of the change in focus of the enemy, some squadrons may even be posted overseas. But don't get complacent. Keep your pilots razor sharp. When you're not flying keep yourself up to date with what's happening so you can keep them informed. Do all you can to keep them and yourself alive."

He was right, they were my responsibility, I knew that. Then reality began to set in. It would soon be time to go back. It's not that I didn't want to be there, it was just that I'd had such a carefree few days at home. After finding out how Catherine really felt about me, it was going to be difficult to say goodbye when the time came. Catherine's father knew the risks and the responsibility. He was concerned and was tactfully reminding me of them.

"I'm sorry," he said. "I didn't mean to lecture you."

"No, that's alright. I was just thinking of how much I was going to miss everybody when I go back."

"Come on, let's go for our walk," Catherine said, holding my hand. She asked her father again if he would come.

"No, you two go on. I'll finish reading my paper then I'll make supper."

Getting up from the table, Catherine gave her Dad a hug and I heard her whisper 'thanks' in his ear.

"On you go," he said again. "Take your time. I'll see you later."

As we walked and talked the Catherine I knew was back to her old self. Like the rest of us she had views and opinions, but at the same time she had a light-hearted approach to them. She knew there were things she could change and that there were things she couldn't. But she had the wisdom to know the difference. Like her father and I going back to war, I know she didn't like the thought of it but she couldn't change it either, so accepted it. When we got to the river we sat together on 'our' big stone, watching the water flow on we got lost in our own thoughts for a bit. Then she picked up my hand and began to speak to it.

"Now hand," she began. "You have to promise faithfully that you will write to me once a week, no more and no less. You have to tell me everything about your master, if he is tired or lonely and what he is doing. But most of all I want you to tell me if your master meets another girl who he likes better than me. Will you do that?"

Laying my hand back on the stone she again looked out over the water. Snuggling up a little closer to her I slipped my arm around her waist and held her hand and did the same thing.

"Hand, tell your mistress I promise to write every week. Tell her also she has to be strong and not to worry. She has to look after herself so I can remember her as she is now and yearn for her. Tell her there will be no other girls. Where would I find someone who has done as much for me or would love me like she does? Tell her I love her and that everything I want is right here."

Putting her hand back on her lap she turned and looked at me.

"I love you James Somerville. You come back to me."

Holding her tighter still, I told her to be strong.

We sat for a while longer, watching the water; eventually we got up and made our way back up the hill into the heart of the town and the sanctuary of her little house.

"You have to leave the day after tomorrow?" she asked.

"Yes, we have to be back on the airfield by the 29th so that other squadrons can be home for New Year."

"You don't know when your next leave will be do you?"

"No, I'll just have to wait and see."

When we got back to the house we had supper and later the three of us sat together beside the fire in her little sitting room, talking but staying off the subject of war. Catherine had a lot of little things on the walls and on her sideboard, the kind of things that make a house a home. She had a tale to tell about all of them and went from one to the other telling me where she got them and from whom. The letter opener I had given her at one point was lying there. Picking it up she looked at it for a moment and then at me.

"This is my most precious possession. I'll treasure it always. Mind you," she went on, grinning. "It might get worn away opening all the mail I'm going to get from the two men in my life."

Her father and I looked at each other, smiled and slowly shook our heads. Then, in further conversation, Catherine asked me what I was going to do with my last full day of leave. Up until then I hadn't given it a thought.

"If it's a nice day," Catherine continued. "We could go for a walk up the hill behind the town, it's ages since I've been up there."

It was one hill I'd never been up and we agreed that's what we would do.

"We can go after dinner, I'll help at the farm in the morning then I'll come in."

The only bad thing about staying later at Catherine's was that I had to bike home in the dark. As I left I had visions of running into something on the way. Fortunately, although there was a frost and was quite cold, it was a clear, bright, moonlit night. After I got going I quite enjoyed the ride home. The only negative thought I had was wondering if I'd be like 'Tam O'Shanter' and meet three witches somewhere on the way.

When the next day came, I helped at the farm but as soon as I had lunch I biked the short distance into the town. When I got there Catherine was dressed for the occasion and ready to go. She gave me a few biscuits to take, saying I'd be hungry before we got back. Thinking of taking a few biscuits wasn't such a big thought, but as I stuffed them in my pocket I thought to myself it was one of the things I loved about her. She was always thinking ahead. Maybe it was her job that made her like that, or maybe she inherited it from her father. Telling her father which way we would be going we then headed out. We walked briskly at first but the pace soon slowed as we climbed ever higher on the sometimes very steep, winding path. On one of those spots I had walked on in front, and as I looked back Catherine was at times almost on her hands and knees, pushing her slim, agile frame on.

"Do you need a pull?" I asked laughing.

"Do you?" she replied, passing me.

We couldn't have had a better day, there had been some frost and it was still cool but it was fine for walking. We had been away for more than an hour and although the summit was ahead of us still we thought we had gone far enough. Daylight goes quickly at this time of year and didn't want to get caught trying to making our way in the dark, so we found a place out of the December breeze then sat and ate our biscuits, admiring our surroundings.

"God's creation," Catherine commented. "Where could you find a place better than this to live?"

She was right, where indeed? Catherine had moved to Pitlochry years ago now with her work, but like me she was passionate about where she lived. Neither one of us has ever taken it for granted. We could see for miles and although the countryside wasn't as picturesque as it was in summer, with all its different shades of green, the winter season brought with it its own particular beauty. The mountains around us were cloaked in snow. Somewhere to the west there was Ben Nevis, Scotland's highest mountain. Behind us were the Cairngorms, another mountain range, and Aviemore. Neither one of us had been to these places but maybe someday, when there was more than a few day's leave, we would see them together. In the valley below and to the south there was no sign of snow. There still were shades of green and the river snaking its way down through the middle, shimmering in the winter sun.

"I can't imagine living anywhere else," I said, holding her hand.

"Nor can I. We are so fortunate."

We sat for a little while longer and then reluctantly picked ourselves up from our vantage point and headed back. By the time we got to the house daylight was fading fast.

Catherine's father was in the kitchen, sitting reading the paper. Again he had supper ready and the table set. He was a good cook. It seemed to come easily to him, certainly a lot more capable than I.

"The wanderers return," he smiled. "Did you have a good walk?"

"Yes we did," Catherine replied. "And it was a good day for it. The only thing was James was getting tired, he was on his hands and knees part of the way up so we didn't go all the way to the top."

"Don't believe her," I replied laughing. "I had to carry her most of the way home."

"Well, somehow," he said, grinning. "I don't believe either one of you."

After supper we sat in the sitting room and kept each other company for a while, staring into the fire my mind wandered, then I heard Catherine's voice.

"I'll give you penny for your thoughts James Somerville?"

I looked at her and she smiled and then asked again.

"What are you thinking about? You were a hundred miles away?"

"Yes I was, but I'm back now. I was just thinking about how nice the day has been. About how much I've enjoyed being back home over Christmas and that by this time tomorrow I'll be back in Eastchurch with the squadron. Sitting here at this moment it's difficult to believe there is a war."

Catherine grabbed my hand and put her finger to her lips.

"Ssh, it's been a beautiful day, don't spoil it."

It had been a nice day but still I couldn't help thinking as we sat in the comfort and safety of Catherine's sitting room about the two little girls in the bombed-out house in London, losing their Mum and Dad. Or David Cleland's family. It had been two months since their son was killed. How were they coping this Christmas knowing he was gone? We were all living on a knife-edge, hoping for the best but fearing the worst.

"When you get back to the base," Catherine's father added. "You have to stay focused, remember your training and you'll be fine."

We looked at each other, knowing what the other was thinking, not saying anything more about the subject. We both knew it wasn't just about training. You could be the best pilot that ever lived but if you were in the wrong place at the wrong time it was over. His seemingly light-hearted statement was to try and appease his daughter's concern about us both going back to fight the fight.

"I should get back home, it's going to be a long day tomorrow."

As I made my way out, Catherine's father said he would see me at the station in the morning and then Catherine walked with me into the evening chill to the garden gate. She put her arms around me and we kissed.

"You should go in before you get a cold."

"Ssh," she said. "Just hold me for a minute and then I'll go. God alone knows when we'll get the chance again."

With our arms around each other we stood not saying anything. I felt her warm body against mine. Then she whispered in my ear.

"I'll love you always."

"I know you will," I whispered back.

We hung onto each other for a few minutes and then I felt her shiver.

"Come on, in you go. I'll see you in the morning."

She kissed me again and I wished I could have stayed.

When the morning came Bella as usual had breakfast ready and pampered John and I. She made something for us to eat on the train. Isobel gave me a hug and told me to look after myself and gave me a letter for Findlay.

"You take care, and have fun at nursing college."

"It's been a long time since you've been home," Bella said as she hugged me. "Hopefully it won't be as long till the next time."

After saying cheerio to the rest of the family Dad took us to the station. We didn't say anything on the way there. I was thinking about how difficult it was going to be to say goodbye to Catherine. In the last little while I had discovered just how much I meant to her and the feeling was mutual. From the first day I met her she had been my guiding light, we always got on well together. I loved her and her company. Mum was right, there was someone here waiting for me. When we got to the station Catherine and her father were waiting on the platform; there wasn't a lot of time before the train would leave. Hanging onto her father's arm she smiled when she saw me. We walked hand in hand to the end of the platform and back, talking gibberish. Then the conductor blew his whistle. Catherine's father and Dad shook our hands and issued a last instruction.

"Do what you have to do, but be careful."

Catherine slipped an envelope in my pocket and then put her arms around me.

"Just something to read when you get a chance. Be careful. I love you. Did you notice there are no tears?"

"I noticed. Take care."

Again the conductor blew his whistle. At that moment if Catherine had asked me to stay with her I would have been sorely tempted.

"Come on James," John stressed. "We have to go."

As soon as we boarded the train it began to move. Closing the door behind us we peered out of the window and waved, Catherine was standing between her father and ours waving back. In a few minutes they were out of sight.

"Do you know how lucky you are?" John said as we sat. "I hope when I find a girl she will think as much of me as Catherine does of you, she worships the ground you walk on."

I could feel a lump in my throat and could only nod. I was missing her already. As the train rumbled south John and I talked about a lot of things. He thanked me for pulling strings at Turnhouse so he could get leave at Christmas. He wanted to know how many Jerries I'd shot down, wondering if I'd managed to get a few for him.

"What's it like to be in a dogfight?" he asked.

"Believe it or not, most are over in a few seconds. You have to keep your wits about you or you won't last long. You can be the best pilot that ever lived, but if you're in the wrong place at the wrong time it counts for nothing."

Thinking back to the day just a few short months ago when I was in the wrong place at the wrong time I thought of my rescuers, Jock and Fergus, I couldn't help but smile.

"Something amusing you?" John asked.

When I told him about what happened he looked stunned.

"You were lucky, you might not have been here."

Then he saw the funny side, Jock giving me brandy to heat me up then him thinking I was a Jerry. We had a good laugh.

Although I had enjoyed every minute of my leave I was in a way anxious to get back. I loved flying and I missed my aircraft. She and I still had things to do together. When we got to Turnhouse the rest of the squadron were already there and had our aircraft on the apron ready to go. The weather was clear; it would be a nice flight south. After chatting briefly with Findlay and the rest of the crew I called in on the base commander.

"Well squadron leader, that was a quick week was it not?"

"Yes sir," I replied. "Much too quick."

"You'll want to get away, I know, so I won't keep you long. Just have a word with this graduating class then you can be on your way."

In our old briefing room we were introduced to the six young men who were going to be fighter pilots. The base commander bestowed so much praise upon us about being 'Battle of Britain' veteran pilots. It felt good. They sat there looking and listening to someone who only a year before was at the stage they were at now. The only words of wisdom I could think of to share with them were what had been instilled in us. Train, and then train some more. Train until you're tired of it. Be the best you can be. If you do that, you'll have given yourselves a fighting chance. We are living proof.

Shaking their hands, we wished them luck and then, as we headed to our aircraft, I thought, we'll have to practice what I've just been preaching. War wasn't a game; in an effort to stay alive we had to be ready to fight. The harsh reality of war was that one had to be prepared to confront the enemy and to destroy him. There was no doubt that's what he wanted to do to us. The base commander thanked me for inspiring the new graduates and then shook our hands and wished us continued good luck. Meeting John at my aircraft he gave me a hug and then helped me to strap in. It was good to be back in the cockpit.

Ignition on and throttle set, I shouted 'clear'. Pushing the start button the prop turned and almost immediately the big Merlin engine sprang to life. There is no sound like it. I motioned to John and he pulled the chocks from in front of the wheels. Advancing the throttle we began to move and I waved farewell to John.

8.   Back to the Fray

The flight south was uneventful and we touched down in Eastchurch on schedule. For an hour or so I kept company with my 'clutch', finding out how they spent their Christmas and I gave Findlay his letter from Isobel. He was one happy man and opened it immediately. Then I went to the sanctuary, or the solitude, depending on what frame of mind one was in, to my own quarters, where I began to write my letters home. The plan was to write a few lines every day so that by the end of the week they were almost ready to post. Before I started, I read the note that Catherine had given me at the station. She had written what she had told me in person, that she loved me more than anything. She had always managed to bring the best out in me, she made me determined to be the best I could be now so I could go home again.

Over the New Year we didn't fly much, it looked like the enemy wanted some time off as well. On New Year's eve a bottle of whisky appeared from somewhere. It was one of these times when, as their commanding officer, I wasn't all that popular, telling them they could have one drink only, although they knew themselves that we were on standby and that drinking and flying didn't mix.

In the first week in January John Ferguson was reinstated to flying status. He had spent longer in hospital than was expected after his crash landing last year. He looked alright but three months away from combat flying is a long time. During his first few days back, whenever he got into his aircraft he didn't look comfortable. In my opinion he should have been posted to a quieter squadron for a while, but the RAF were desperately short of experienced pilots, so he was sent back to us.

One of my duties was to keep up to date records of the status of the pilots of my squadron. Not only their flying capabilities and achievements but also their health and opinions as well. John was no exception. Some of it I didn't think was necessary and in those areas I kept my comments to the minimum. They all knew that this sort of information was kept; someone, somewhere was collecting the same information on me. After all, that was partly the reason I got my promotion.

Fortunately for John, in the first few weeks he was back, although we were scrambled a few times, we didn't see much of the enemy. None of us complained about that. I'm not sure what the reason was but everyone was a little down in the mouth; even Findlay wasn't his usual cheery self. The weather hadn't been the best; low cloud, dreary and drizzly days. For lack of a better reason, I attributed the squadron's mood to that.

As January passed, the bombing of London and other cities continued. On more than one occasion we visited the city and again witnessed first-hand the devastation caused by it. It was obscene. Vast areas were just shells of buildings or reduced to piles of rubble. Everything would have to be totally rebuilt. But although thousands of innocent people were dying or suffering, the mood was determined and defiant. Everywhere we went there was someone who wanted to shake our hand or pat us on the back, telling us, 'we can take it. The next time you're up, get one for me.'

Such visits always had a profound impact on us. These people could do nothing about the bombing. They were depending on us, the RAF, to do something about it. Seeing their pain and suffering at first-hand was humbling. Seeing their determination and resolve always renewed our commitment and determination to do what we had to and were expected to do. Any time a squadron member was complaining about his lot, which wasn't very often, to be honest, I threatened to take him to London. That always put an end to it.

We were determined to stop the intruders and during daylight hours we did all we could. But the sad truth was that we, as a Spitfire squadron, could do nothing about these night-time raiders. There were squadrons being set up with radar-equipped aircraft that could find the enemy in the dark, but as yet they were having limited success. For the time being, enemy losses were minimal.

The first week in February brought the return of another member of our old squadron. George McDonald, who'd been badly burned in his aircraft back in September, was again deemed fit to fly. His face was a bit scarred but it was his hands and forearms that bore the brunt of his injury. He told me that his hands and arms were still tender to touch, but he felt confident to fly and said he couldn't wait to get up. He had been away for fourteen weeks, though, and I tried to put myself in his shoes. But it was the same old story, the RAF needed pilots and he had been certified by the doctors as being fit to fly. It didn't look like George had lost any of his skills and when I mentioned it to him he said it was like riding a bike. Once you have it, it never leaves you.

Our squadron was now bigger than it had ever been but that could change at any time, with pilots being transferred or whatever. In the meantime I tried to follow in the footsteps of my mentor and keep us tight, more in a family kind of way than by barking orders.

For the time being I was into a routine for writing home but there still wasn't a lot to write about. Other than flying and the occasional visit to London, we didn't do much. Catherine, on the other hand, seemed to have no trouble filling a page. Bella also wrote, telling me all that was happening at the farm and about Catherine, but I wondered if she gave me all the facts. I knew she didn't want me to worry. Apparently she was still seeing a lot of Catherine and since Christmas she was more her old self. I looked forward to these letters but always felt a twinge of homesickness whenever I read them. I missed the valley and everything in it, my family and my best friend in life. Her notes always ended the same way. 'Missing you, love you always, Catherine'. The pictures her father had taken at Christmas had been developed. In one of her letters she sent one of her and I together. I placed it on my desk beside the compass she had given me when I got my wings.

Getting to the last day or two of February, although we were still flying standing patrols we didn't see much in the way of action. There were still daylight raids but they were focusing more on the southwest side of the country for the time being. Again, no one was complaining. Group Captain Thomson from sector paid us a surprise visit one day.

'Just wanted to make sure everything was all right,' he said. He told me that some of the bombed-out buildings on the airfield would be replaced before long.

Catherine's father had now been back on duty for a number of weeks. Although he was stationed not all that far from us, to date I hadn't seen or heard from him. Then, out of the blue, one day he dropped in. He had a couple of days leave. He had been busy, he said, flying all over for whatever branch of the military wanted pictures taken. The missions were flown alone, at high altitude and usually deep into enemy territory. It sounded daunting to me but he said that since he started he hadn't seen one enemy aircraft. He felt quite comfortable doing it. He talked about his daughter and about how much happier she had been since Christmas.

"She is so like her mother," he said. "She has the same eyes, the same hair and build. Even the same mannerisms. It seems the older she gets the more like her mother she becomes, it's uncanny really."

That was the first time I'd heard him say anything about his wife, other than Catherine telling me once that her mother had died when she was young she had never mentioned her either. It was just never talked about, and to be honest, I'd never given it any thought about what had happened to her. He took a picture from his wallet and showed it to me.

"This was my wife," he said. "Like your mother, she died young too."

"Can I ask you what happened?"

"Yes. It was a simple, stupid thing really. We had been out walking one Sunday afternoon and got caught in a shower. She got a chill and never recovered from it. She died a few weeks later of pneumonia. Catherine was only twelve when it happened."

Looking at the picture in my hand and then at the woman standing beside me in the picture on my desk they could have been the same person.

"I can see what you mean, they are very alike. She meant a lot to you, I'm so sorry."

"It was a long time ago now, I've got over it."

He might have said that but it didn't look like it to me.

"You've never met anyone else?"

For a brief moment he had a rare annoyed look on his face and immediately I wished I hadn't asked.

"No, I didn't want to. Besides, between my work in the RAF and taking care of Catherine I had enough to do. In keeping company with someone else I would have felt very guilty."

Pausing, he looked at the picture on my desk and then continued.

"But maybe now I'll give it some thought. Catherine doesn't need me as much now. It looks like she has someone else to take care of her."

I could see he was smiling and then he turned and looked at me. The last time we had a conversation similar to this was last summer when he could quite easily have been killed when the enemy fighters strafed his aircraft.

"The only thing Catherine ever said to me about her mother was that we had something in common, that both our mothers had died when we were young."

"As you know, Catherine is an emotional, caring person. When her mother passed away she missed her desperately and cried for weeks. I was beginning to wonder what I was going to do with her. But we leaned on each other and time passed. They got along really well together, sharing the little secrets that mothers and daughters share. There is only one person I know of who she has got really close to since and that is your stepmother. As long as Bella is there I don't need to worry about Catherine. I owe Bella a great debt."

'You and I both,' I thought. Before Catherine's father left he wanted to take a picture of the members of the squadron, 'for his scrapbook,' he said.

There was another welcome visitor at the end of February, snowdrops and crocus were flowering and at the same time clusters of daffodils were starting to grow after their long winter sleep. It was invigorating to see them; they somehow brought renewed faith and hope that one day the war would be over. But it wasn't yet, and short of a miracle it wouldn't be for a while. As a reminder to the squadron of how real it all was, death came calling again.

We had been scrambled by sector to intercept enemy aircraft along the south coast. When we caught up with them we discovered they were twin-engined fighter-bombers; no match for our Spitfires. They were hedge-hopping, terrorizing the towns below. I instructed five aircraft of red wing to make the attack while the other five would cover them. George McDonald in red nine was one of the attackers and Findlay was his cover. Even before George got properly lined up to take a shot, the rear gunner in the enemy aircraft found his mark. George's Spitfire rolled over and went down. Being so close to the ground he never got the chance to bale out. It was all over in a few seconds. His aircraft hit the ground and exploded. Findlay didn't waste any time and was immediately all over the enemy plane; it exploded before it hit the ground. Of the eight enemy aircraft we encountered, only four made it back across the Channel and two of those were damaged. There was nothing we could do for George; he was gone. Heading back to the aerodrome, I was stunned at how quickly it had happened, the rear gunner just got a lucky shot in.

After debriefing we sat and talked about what had happened. This was the first combat he had seen since he had come back from sick leave so we all felt so very sorry for him, especially after the pain and suffering he must have endured after being burned. At least he wouldn't be suffering this time. Until he joined the RAF, George had lived in Dunbar with his mother and his sister. He was twenty-one years old.

As I retired to the solitude of my office I remembered Catherine's father telling me that the moment would come when I would have to write to one of my pilots' next of kin. The only advice he could give me was to be compassionate. This person who had just paid the ultimate price had been someone's son, a brother or friend. Sitting at my desk I began to write but the words came slowly. Looking out of the window I felt the heat of the sun on my face. George wouldn't feel that again. Glancing at the picture on the desk of Catherine and I, I wondered if he had known love. Somehow I felt like I had neglected him. His death shook me. Slowly the letter came together.

I gave it to the briefing officer to post, also asking him to arrange for a telegram to be sent to the family. I could only imagine their response. I know how I felt myself. Some weeks later I received a letter from George's mother, thanking me for my kind words. They had been a comfort, she said. To know that his peers thought so much of him meant a lot.

But we couldn't dwell on his loss. We were too busy trying to stay alive ourselves. We had to stay focused or it would be someone else's turn. Every squadron was the same.

Time doesn't stand still and, as the days passed, enemy intrusion again became more frequent. Then it happened again; we lost another two pilots in one day. We were flying a standing patrol when a handful of enemy fighters jumped us. Before we could react they had disappeared into cloud. In the brief encounter James Lamb and Robert Smith were killed. Neither one of them made any attempt to get out of their aircraft as they spiralled earthwards. The rest of us, with the exception of Findlay, had holes in our aircraft but we made it back to the airfield. There had been no warning, nothing from sector control advising us of any hostile aircraft in the area.

As we limped home I advised sector what we were doing and why but left it at that until we landed. Phoning sector I got hold of Group Captain Thomson and told him what had happened. He said he would look into it and get back to me. Within the hour he called back.

"It appears there are a number of factors," he began. "Apparently radar picked up something but no one was sure what to make of it. There was a bit of confusion at the time. There had been a few false alarms earlier, something to do with atmospheric conditions. To top it all off, the controller on duty was training another controller. The way everything happened, it isn't really anyone's fault, but you can be sure I'm going over there right now to read the riot act. In the meantime you stand down and get your aircraft fixed."

Needless to say, we were all shaken. We all knew any one of us could have suffered the same fate as James and Robert. As the mechanics began to repair our damaged aircraft I was again faced with the unpleasant task of writing to the next of kin.

By the time our aircraft were airworthy again, daylight raids in our area were few, but the raids at night continued relentlessly. The enemy wasn't getting everything their own way, though. Our night-fighter squadrons were now better equipped and having considerable success. One month alone at the height of the Blitz they were responsible for shooting down almost a hundred enemy planes, a comforting thought.

Another month passed and mail arrived, reminding me of my birthday, my nineteenth. I had almost forgotten. There was no real news from home; it was a busy time at the farm, calving and lambing season again. Catherine didn't have any news either, just busy teaching and missing me, wondering if I had any leave coming up. It would be nice to have another week off and go home, but all we were getting was the odd day. Most of us spent that sleeping.

Although we had been seeing a lot less of the enemy, in Europe the fighting was everywhere. Germany controlled everything all the way to Russia in the east. Germany and Italy between them had a stranglehold on the Mediterranean and North Africa. These were dark days. Britain had stood alone against a formidable foe; if it hadn't been for the Channel we wouldn't have stood a chance either. It was a depressing thought but we didn't let it get to us.

Although Great Britain had been fighting alone we had been getting some supplies from America but other than that they didn't want to get involved in 'our' war. That lifeline was in danger of being cut, however, as ship after ship was being sunk by German submarines. Aircraft from Costal Command were flying patrols trying to locate the enemy. It had to be done but I was glad it wasn't me going to look for them. The thought of being shot down in the cold north Atlantic didn't bear thinking about, even if one was fortunate enough to survive the ditching, the chances of being rescued were slim to none.

As Spring rolled into Summer we didn't see much of the enemy, he was too busy elsewhere. When Group Captain Thomson called one day I told him we felt we weren't contributing very much.

"You may feel that," he answered, "but for the time being we have to keep you here. We haven't forgotten about you and I'm willing to bet the enemy hasn't either. For the moment you are a deterrent and are doing more good than you know. Stay in shape. The way things are going, some squadrons may be posted overseas."

Catherine's father called in on us one day. He didn't have any news either, just that he was spending a lot of time flying, so much so that the squadron was going to be expanding to try and keep up with the workload. He didn't stay long saying he had another appointment. Two weeks later I discovered what the other appointment had been. He called me on the phone and asked me to meet him at a little cottage about three miles along the road, saying he would explain when I got there. Later in the day I got a vehicle and followed the directions he had given me. It was off the main road a little but I didn't have any trouble finding it. He was sitting outside the door on one of two deck chairs. I got out of the vehicle and he motioned me to have a seat.

"Well, you made it," he said. "What do you think of the view?"

Looking out to the east, there was a bit of a view of the Thames estuary but nothing great. I looked at him.

"It's not like home is it?" he said.

"No, but nothing compares to that."

We sat talking gibberish for a bit and then he said what he was doing there.

"I've rented the cottage for a month. I needed a place to get away from the aerodrome for a day or two. What do you think?"

"It's good. Maybe I'll rent it after you're done with it, I know what it's like hanging around the base, there is always something you feel you should be doing."

"Oh, I almost forgot, I've got someone to keep me company."

Thinking the obvious, that he had found a female companion, I asked him if I would meet her. As he answered, saying that I definitely would meet her, someone crept up behind me and covered my eyes. The hands were soft and gentle and almost at once I detected the faintest hint of a familiar perfume.

"Guess who?"

It sounded like Catherine and it was like the perfume she wore, but it couldn't be. She wouldn't come all the way down to London without saying. Then I thought, yes she would!

"Catherine, is that you?"

"Right first time," came the reply.

Jumping out of my chair I turned around. I couldn't believe it. She was standing there, looking at me with the cutest smile, with the sun behind her shining through her hair she looked like an angel. Dumbstruck, I couldn't believe it.

"What's wrong?" she asked. "Cat got your tongue?"

I vaguely remember extending my hand and her taking it and then she put her arms around my neck. As always she smelled great.

"You look fabulous," I whispered.

Until he spoke we had almost forgotten about her father sitting an arm's length away.

"Why don't the two of you sit here and catch up a bit and I'll go and make us some tea."

As he disappeared into the cottage I told Catherine about how much I'd missed her.

"I've missed you too. Hopefully over the next month we'll be able to spend some time together. You could take me to London."

"You can't stay here," I blurted. "You have to go home."

Her face changed from a warm glow to sadness.

"You don't want me to stay?" She feebly asked.

"Catherine, I'd love for you to stay, but it's much too dangerous for you here."

As we held each other I went on to explain that there were air raids and that I just didn't want to see her get hurt. As I did so her eyes began to cloud.

"You're right, it is dangerous. But the two people I care most about in the world are here and I haven't seen either one of them in months. They can't get a long enough leave so I came to see them. Dad said the same as you but I managed to persuade him and he agreed to find a place where I could stay."

Her eyes were full now and just as her father came back with the tea a tear rolled down her cheek. He was quick to notice and asked her if they were happy tears or sad tears.

"They're sad tears," I replied. "It's my fault, I'm frightened she could get hurt staying here."

Handing us a cup each he took a sip of his tea and then he answered.

"She could," he began. "But I don't think she will. The daylight raids are few now and I can't see them intentionally attack a lone cottage out in the country anyway. As long as she keeps the lights off at night she should be alright."

Catherine put her cup down and went into the cottage, saying she would be back in a minute.

"Don't worry," he said. "She'll be fine, I thought all the same things you are thinking. I was going to tell her not to come but I changed my mind."

"It is good to see her."

"Have you ever noticed how she seems to have the uncanny ability to do the right thing at the right time."

I had thought that often in the past. I nodded.

"Well this is most likely one of those times. When we were making arrangements, the first thing she said was not to tell you, to keep it a surprise. To be honest, I wish I'd had my camera at the ready, the expression on your face was priceless."

We smiled at each other and at the same time I thought about how much she liked to do things like that. Just at that Catherine reappeared in the doorway, looking at her father and then at me. Offering her my hand she quickly took it.

"Alright, you can stay, but you have to be really careful."

Again she threw her arms around my neck and promised she would be.

"Let's go for a walk and I'll tell you about what's been happening at home."

As we strolled down the quiet country lane she held onto my hand and told me what she had been up to.

"I haven't been doing anything out of the ordinary really. School is just the same. The kids ask for you sometimes, wondering where you are and what you're doing. I go up to the farm every week, sometimes twice. Bella must get fed up with me. Your Dad and her have so much to do all the time. But I really look forward to going and talking to her and I feel really close to you when I'm there. They're both the picture of health, they told me to give you a cuddle from them."

Thinking of them and home I could feel the lump in my throat. Catherine could see what was happening.

"Come on now, don't do that, you know I've got tears enough for both of us."

As we strolled on she continued.

"You know I can never make up my mind what it is I love most about you and I ask myself often. Is it because he is a kind and sensitive person, or is it because he is such a handsome devil? Could it be because he is so young and carries undaunted an awesome responsibility, or is it because at heart he is a simple person who wants only to go home some day and live in his valley. The answer is always the same. It's everything. With all of my heart I love all of you. There are few minutes in the day when I don't think of you. If anything ever happened to you I'd die, I know it."

We stood there for a while, holding onto each other and I told her I loved her too.

Eventually we made our way back to the cottage where her father was still sitting outside on the old deckchair. Although he had been flying quite a bit lately, over the next week or two it wasn't going to be so intense. He said he'd bring Catherine to the airfield. There wasn't a lot to see but she wanted to see where I spent my time. Now that she was here beside us I didn't feel like going back to the airfield; it was difficult dragging myself away. Before leaving I gave her a hug and thanked her for coming.

"Go on, I'll see you tomorrow."

The next morning we were airborne just after eight. Sector wanted us to patrol along the south coast. Lately we never saw hide nor hair of the enemy. We never complained about not seeing him but these missions were still tiring. On constant lookout, never knowing when we might run into them. When we got back to the field Catherine and her father were waiting. I had forgotten they said they would come by. As I got out of my aircraft they made their way over, his camera in hand.

"Stay there," he shouted. "I'd like to take a few photo's."

We sat in, or stood in front of our aircraft until he said he had enough. As he photographed the squadron Catherine gave me a hug.

"Good morning sunshine," she smiled. "How are you this morning?"

"I'm great. I still can't believe you're here though."

As we held each other Findlay walked over. Saying hello to Catherine he then looked at me.

"Man you're a crafty beggar! You didn't tell me the love of your life was coming to see you."

"Didn't know myself until last night."

"A likely story," he retorted. "You know you're getting more and more like an officer every day. You don't tell your friends anything."

Laughing, I let Catherine explain and then I introduced her to the squadron members she'd never met. When lunchtime came we sat together and as we dined on some of the RAF's finest bully beef I watched the members of my 'clutch' admire Catherine as she laughed and fitted in. She had a magnetism about her, a genuine knack of making people feel good about themselves and wanting to be around her. Findlay stood up, clutching his glass of water and in his posh Glaswegian accent said what I think what we were all thinking.

"Gentlemen, I'd like to propose a toast. Please be upstanding and drink to the health of the most beautiful creation to grace us with her presence, more refreshing and lovely than the first flower in spring. To Catherine."

It was true, and it was all taken in good fun. As Catherine smiled at him she took an envelope from her purse and got up to reply. She knew what Findlay was like. He always had something to say, to the point of being annoying sometimes. But, like me she liked him. She knew he was inclined to flirt with the fairer sex.

"Why Mr Douglas I'm truly flattered by your kind words. Perhaps I should give you this note a certain young lady asked me to give you so that you can reply to it with due haste and woo her with similar words of affection."

As the note was passed to Findlay and Catherine sat down we all had a good giggle. But Findlay didn't care. He looked at the envelope and as he ran his fingers over it the expression on his face changed. He was eager to open it but instead slipped it into his pocket. When everyone else was focused on Findlay, Catherine and I looked at each other and smiled. Catherine's father had another little announcement. For the next few weeks Catherine would be at the airfield from time to time taking pictures. He explained that the RAF wanted pictures of various operational aerodromes and that Catherine had been commissioned to take them at Eastchurch. After lunch I asked him how he managed to do that.

"It was easy, the RAF actually do want pictures and were looking for someone to do it. After I knew for sure that Catherine was coming I managed to get her the job, this afternoon we're going into London to get her a camera and everything else she needs."

Like the night before I was lost for words.

"Cat got your tongue again," Catherine asked.

"All I can say," I answered smiling. "If intelligence find out about the two of you they'll want you to go and work for them. I don't know anyone who can keep secrets better, except maybe Bella."

"But they are nice secrets aren't they?" Catherine laughed.

Squeezing her hand I smiled and with that they left to go into London. When I caught up with Findlay he was sitting on the grass under the wing of his aircraft reading his letter. He didn't look very happy and I asked him if there was something wrong.

"This war sucks. We're stuck here on this base for weeks at a time. We can't get enough leave to visit the people we care about. Do you know how lucky you are, your girlfriend comes to see you. I'd like to see your sister again but God only knows when that's going to be."

"When I discovered Catherine was here you could have bowled be over with a feather. I didn't know she was coming."

"Aye, I know," he answered. "She told me all about it."

He was right, we hadn't had a lot of time off lately and that was my fault. I just hadn't arranged it. But there was something else bothering him, his mood had changed a lot since lunchtime.

"What was Isobel saying to you in her letter that's troubled you?"

He looked at me for a few seconds and then handed me the letter.

"You're like my mother," he went on. "You sense everything. It looks like she's found somebody else."

"It doesn't say anything in here about finding somebody else," I answered, reading the letter through. "It says it's difficult to have a relationship with someone who's so far away, but to stay in touch."

"The way it's written it means she has found somebody else."

"Well to me it says she is busy with her studies and might not have the time to write. Can you remember what flying training was like? We were so absorbed in it weeks would go past. We were so tired we didn't feel like writing to anyone."

"You know," he said. "You are just like *my* mother. She always has an explanation as well."

Sitting beside him, I told him he was right.

"I am fortunate and happy that Catherine is here. And you're right about what you said at lunch, it was a really nice thing to say. I wish I had said it. In fact, if you ever say anything like that to her again, I'll have you locked up."

We looked at each other and laughed and then I got up.

"If you like Isobel that much, do what she asks and stay in touch. Faint heart never won a fair lady, you know."

Leaving him thinking on that thought, I went back to the briefing room and immediately phoned Group Captain Thomson and arranged to have time off. He told me to take the time we needed and relax a bit. He also said that it was becoming more likely that a number of squadrons would be going overseas and that if that happened leave would be out of the question.

It was the next morning before I saw Catherine and her father again. Sporting a new camera she seemed to have mastered already, she was photographing everything. She had enjoyed her first visit to London and said she would like to go back again.

"How about this weekend?" I said. "My 'clutch' have been complaining about not getting enough time off, so I made some arrangements with sector to do just that. You could arrange it if you like. You decide what you want to do and that's what we'll do."

"You mean just you and me or for the squadron?"

"We can ask them what they want to do and then go from there. But I thought we could spend a day in London and then maybe go down to the south coast the next day. You could take your camera and photograph pilots on leave."

Catherine thought it was a good idea and so the squadron were summoned to the briefing room. When I told them we were having the weekend off the mood changed and there were 'about time' comments. Telling them also what Catherine and I had talked about there was a brief discussion. They unanimously decided we would spend the weekend together so, with the help of the briefing officer, who knew his way around the city, Catherine planned our weekend.

Over the next day or two there were reports that a vast number of enemy aircraft had been sent to the Russian front as part of the onslaught against that nation. If that's why we had been seeing less of them it was bad news for the Russians, but we certainly appreciated the lull in activities.

When Saturday came it was a nice calm Summer morning. Everybody was up at the crack of dawn, eager to get away from the aerodrome, just in case the phone rang at the last minute. Catherine was there at eight, camera in hand and ready to go. Hastily, we all piled into the back of one of the base lorries and headed for the city. Everybody was in a good jovial mood as we bumped along the road, but that changed as we got to the east side of London and were reminded yet again of the devastation caused by the enemy bombing. The only one of us who said anything as we made our way through the destruction was Catherine. She had been to London a few days before with her father but he had taken her a different way, she hadn't seen the extent of the bombing. Taking pictures of burned out shells of buildings and houses as we went, she kept saying over and over, "These poor people."

As we got to the city centre there was little evidence of any bombing. Stopping at a little café, we invaded the place and as we sat drinking our tea Catherine told us where we were going. Buckingham Palace, Tower Bridge and the Houses of Parliament were on the itinerary. At night we were going to see a show. It was a good day. The weather and the company were perfect. By the time we got to the theatre at night we were all bushed and had a hard time staying awake. Rest and relaxation was almost as tiring as flying, we decided.

After the show and as we were heading out of London, the air raid sirens began to wail; it still was almost a nightly occurrence. It was difficult to go to London and not get caught in a raid. Then, a few minutes later, in the distance there was the muffled sound of exploding bombs. Not everyone went into the shelters during a raid, but it was the safe thing to do. We grabbed our belongings out of the lorry and sought the sanctuary of the underground, Catherine hanging onto her camera with one hand and me with the other.

As we went deeper we could feel and hear the bombs above us. The lights flickered but decided to stay on and there were the occasional puffs of dust coming out of the cracks in the walls. Going deeper still the sound of the explosions was almost inaudible and was replaced by voices. Getting to the bottom of the steps we were confronted with the same scene I remembered from before. Catherine couldn't believe it. As we got talking to a few of them and they told their own particular story she discovered for herself most of them didn't have a home now, they had been bombed out, this is how they lived, working during the day and then spending their nights in the underground. They had no idea when they might live in a house of their own again. Catherine took pictures of people sleeping, children playing, and then she put her arm around my waist and said again, 'these poor people.' Seeing how they made the best of their lives was a humbling experience. As always, it made us all the more determined to fight on and do all we could.

The all-clear siren went off and as we made our way back upstairs, our newfound friends wished us luck. It annoyed us that we personally couldn't do anything about the raiding aircraft, but it was of some comfort to know that the night fighters would be giving them a hard time. On one hand there was sorrow and sympathy for the thousands of people who were being killed, injured, or were being made homeless, then on the other the anger and resentment we all felt towards the enemy. Catherine, with a few words described how we all felt.

"Thousands of poor people suffering. Bloody Germans! Who do they think they are, anyway?"

As we made our way outside into the mayhem we were confronted with just one of the many inconveniences the local people put up with on an almost daily basis. It looked like our transportation had taken a direct hit.

"Oh lovely!" said Findlay. "Just what do we do now?"

What indeed, I wondered. Do we try and get someone from the airfield to come and pick us up or will we go back into the underground and spent the night with our new friends? What would be best? Maybe someone would give us a lift, but who would that be? The only people around were firemen and rescue services. God knows they had enough to do.

"Does anyone know where we could find a phone?" I asked.

Someone remembered seeing a phone box at the end of the street so we headed in that direction, threading our way through the fallen rubble and intertwined fire hoses. Amazingly, the phone box was unscathed, and even more amazing, the phone still worked. The operator connected me and I spoke to the duty officer at the aerodrome. After telling him of our transport's demise he said he could have someone drive into London to pick us up.

Until the lorry arrived, an hour or so later, we did what we could to help the firemen. Catherine took yet more pictures of the aftermath and of the firemen working. There are no words to adequately describe what it's like to be in an air raid, how terrifying it is to have bombs falling and exploding around you, to witness first-hand the wanton destruction and loss of life. To know what it is like, one has to live it. The people in this part of London did that all too often.

Eventually our transport arrived and we all piled into the back, huddling together to stay warm for the trip back to the aerodrome. It had been a long day and we were all tired. As the lorry made its way out of London and into the darkness, immersed in our own thoughts, nobody said a word. A few, including Catherine, fell asleep.

When we got to the cottage, Catherine's father was standing outside, waiting. Helping Catherine down we explained why we were so late.

"Well, everyone is alright," he said. "That's the main thing."

We arranged with Catherine to meet the next morning again and then the rest of us headed back to the aerodrome and bed.

The morning came all too soon. When I awoke, rays of sunshine were filling the room. No sooner had I dragged myself out of bed and our tour organizer arrived.

"Have you only just got up, you lazy thing?" Catherine asked.

"I have, and although it's late, I could have slept for another couple of hours."

As we all sat having breakfast together I asked Catherine what she had planned for the day.

"We are going to the seaside," she replied. "We're taking a picnic and we're going to relax for the day."

We headed south towards Dover; Catherine wanted to see the white cliffs. The sun was shining, it was warm and Catherine took yet more pictures, 'to remind us of the day,' she said. But we couldn't escape the war. There were constant reminders of it everywhere – RAF and enemy aircraft flying overhead, barrage balloons dotted here and there. Determined to have a good day, however, none of us said anything about any of it. Catherine saw and stood beside the white cliffs, and as proof Findlay took a picture of us doing just that. I held her hand and we paddled in the cool English Channel and as we did I relived memories of the year before – being shot down and Jock and Fergus fishing me out of the water. The harbour they operated from wasn't far from where we were, so as we had our picnic I suggested we go and see if they were still there. Locating the harbourmaster's office I discovered that the same big burly man was in charge. As he swung around in his chair I could see he didn't remember me. He probably didn't recognize me wearing clothes that fitted. Telling him that we had met the year before he was still at a loss.

"We meet a lot of people here," he said. "I just can't remember everybody. What can I do for you today?"

"I'm looking for Jock and Fergus."

"That's their boat along at the end," he said, pointing through the window.

As we made our way along the harbour wall I could see the two of them sitting in the back of the boat, playing cards. Looking down into the boat I shouted. "Hello." Jock turned in his seat.

"Aye hello," he responded in his broad Aberdonian accent. All his time in this part of the world hadn't changed that.

"What can we do for you? We don't do tours if that's what you're thinking."

"We don't want a tour," I told him. " I just wanted to see if you were still here and to say thanks again."

"Do I know you?" he asked.

"We met last summer."

The two of them looked at each other and shrugged their shoulders. Getting out of the boat they climbed the steps of the harbour wall. Taking a closer look at me slowly Jock began to nod his head.

"Ach aye," he said, turning to Fergus. "Mind this one Fergus?" Fergus didn't look very sure but nodded anyway. Introducing Catherine and the rest of the squadron I told them we were having a couple of days off and were doing some sightseeing.

"Couple of days off, sightseeing, very nice. So is this young lass somebody's girl then?"

Catherine and I looked at each other then she took my hand. "Yes I'm his," she smiled.

"My you're a lucky man son! I can tell you my wife doesn't look like that. And I can tell you another thing, you haven't changed. You still don't say much. Aye we fished this man o' yours out of the water last summer," he told Catherine. "We thought he was a Jerry at first, mind that Fergus?"

As Jock looked over his shoulder at Fergus, Catherine tugged on my hand.

"What were you doing in the water?" she asked.

Then I remembered I hadn't told her about my brush with death.

"My, lassie," Jock went on. "I can see he didn't tell you that wee bit."

There was no secret now; she was going to get the whole story from Jock.

"One of these Jerries nailed him and he ended up in the drink. Me and Fergus were sent out tae pick him up. He wasn't hard tae find though, another plane showed us where he was at."

As Findlay and I looked at each other Catherine noticed but never said anything.

"But my, my," Jock went on. "We're not doing much just now. No that many fleers in the water. In fact, Fergus and me were thinking about going back up to Aberdeen, but the coastguard wanted us to stay a wee bit longer. I can tell you though, I'm getting a wee bit fed up playing cards."

Looking around at the rest of red wing, their eyes fixated on Jock. They obviously had never seen or heard anybody like him before. Nevertheless, I liked him and would be forever grateful to the two of them for rescuing me.

"Do you mind if Catherine takes your picture?", I asked him.

"Picture, ach no I don't think so, I'm not very photogenic.

Well... on you go then," he said, changing his mind in the next instant. "But only if we can stand beside this bonnie lass of yours."

Catherine handed the camera to Findlay, then stood sandwiched between the two of them.

"My you smell grand. If you were mine I wouldn't let you out my sight."

"Thanks for the picture," she said, smiling at him. "But most of all, thanks for rescuing James."

"Man lassie, that's what we're here for. Would you like to go out on the water for a wee tour?" Jock went on. "There's not much too see besides water, but it might be a wee change for you."

Findlay and the rest of red wing looked at each other, I could see they were getting a bit weary of Jock's continual chatter and hastily declined the invitation. Catherine, on the other hand, was keen to go, pulling me down the steps and into the boat.

"You get her started up there Fergus," Jock bellowed. "I'll get the lines."

Catherine clicked away with her camera as Jock and Fergus moved about the boat, Fergus engaged the drive and slowly we pulled away from the harbour wall. As soon as we reached open water Fergus opened the throttles and moments later the boat sat up. Catherine was sitting up in the front, her dark hair blowing in the wind. It wasn't just the speed of the boat, the further away we got from shore the breezier it seemed to get. Standing beside Jock I could see him looking at Catherine, then he looked at me and then gave me a dig in the ribs with his elbow.

"My you're a sly one, you didn't tell us you had a bonnie quine like that. Man, she's just a fair picture and I can see she just thinks the world of you."

Catherine was beckoning me to go and sit beside her.

"Would you look at that," Jock went on, grinning from ear to ear. "Get yourself up there and keep her company."

Sitting down beside her, Catherine held my hand and then, barely audible above the noise of the engines and the boat cutting through the water she said in my ear. "Do you know how much I love you?"

Life couldn't be any better than it was at that moment, I thought. Spending a sunny afternoon at the seaside with someone who meant everything to you, someone you felt completely at ease with.

"I'm glad you're here," I told her.

She just smiled and sat closer. It had turned out to be a really warm hazy summer day, altogether the kind of day you wished wouldn't end. Jock and Fergus left us alone to enjoy our short trip. All too soon Fergus was manoeuvring the boat alongside the harbour wall and Jock was securing the lines. Reluctantly we picked ourselves up and thanked them for our short excursion.

"It was nae bother," Jock answered. "If you're ever in this neck of the woods again, mind and look us up. Would you like a wee dram before you go?"

Simultaneously shaking our heads, Jock then took hold of Catherine's hand. "It's been a real pleasure meeting you, hasn't it Fergus?"

As usual, Fergus never got a word in.

"If we're real lucky", Jock went on. "We'll get to see you again sometime."

Then he shook my hand. "Now you take care of this lass. Do you know how lucky you are?"

I told him I did know and thanked them both again for everything they had done for us. Getting out of the boat we climbed the steps, looked back and waved. Catherine held onto my arm but didn't say anything as we made our way back towards our transportation. Getting into the back of the lorry we sat with our legs dangling over the back, then Catherine took my hand and looked at me.

"You didn't tell me you were shot down."

Wriggling closer, I put my arm around her waist.

"There was no point in telling you, you would have worried more."

"Would you tell me if it happened again?"

"No I don't think so," I said, after thinking about it for a moment.

"Your father and I agreed we would write home and keep everyone up to date with our daily lives, but something like that we would keep to ourselves for the time being. As long as we were alright we didn't see any point in worrying you all any more than you were already."

"You're right," she answered eventually. "I'm just so scared that every time we say goodbye it could be the last time."

"You remember what Mum said to me in the cemetery that morning?"

"Yes, I remember, it's what keeps me going every day."

"Often I think of it too and I do try to be as careful as I can every day. I want to come home. There's nothing I want more than to be there in the peace of the valley. There is so much I miss about it, my family, the early morning chats with Bella at the kitchen table, sharing secrets, the little café ... and a certain little house in the town I've been visiting. But most of all I miss someone who lives in that little house. She is waiting for me. When this war is over I would like to spend time with her."

The sad expression from a few moments ago was replaced with a little smile. She kissed my cheek and whispered in my ear. "You're a charmer James Somerville."

'Who knows when the war will be over?' I told her. For the time being I had to do what I was doing, fight the enemy. But I didn't have to tell her that, she knew it.

"Findlay was right the other day when he said you were the most beautiful creation. It was a really nice thing to say, I wish I had said it. When I spoke to him later I told him that, but told him also if he said anything like that to you again I would have him locked up."

"Why James Somerville, were you just a wee bit jealous?"

"I think maybe I was."

She wriggled closer and put her arm around my waist.

"It was a nice thing to say and it made me feel wonderful at the time but it didn't mean anything. You know what Findlay is like, he would have us believe he is Casanova himself. You know what he is like in Isobel's company though, with someone he really cares about he's like a church mouse and gets flustered."

Nodding in agreement I looked over my shoulder to see if the rest of the squadron were making their way back yet but there was no sign of them. Lost in our own thoughts for a moment, Catherine went on.

"Your friend Jock is quite a character. Poor Fergus, I don't think he got a word in at all."

All at once I felt tired and began to yawn.

"You know, all this rest and relaxation is really tiring. I could sleep."

Just at that moment I could see my 'clutch' coming back. The closer they got to the lorry I could see they were feeling like I was. Jokingly, I asked them where they wanted to go now. As usual, Findlay had to have some input.

"Well I don't know about the rest of you," he said. "But I'm knackered. That's Glaswegian for tired."

Maybe it was the heat of the day, or the sea air. Maybe it was rest catching up with us, who knows, but we were all tired and the general consensus was that we go back to Eastchurch.

Over the next five weeks or so we didn't see much of the enemy. Although we did fly every day it was mainly on patrol up and down the east coast. At some point every day I saw Catherine; she either came to the aerodrome or I went to the cottage. She took a lot more pictures of us and our aircraft and of all the people who worked on them to keep them flying – people who refuelled and rearmed them, the mechanics who fixed them and, wherever possible, she had names and dates. The RAF kept a lot of the pictures but she was allowed to keep a few 'for her scrapbook,' she said. Catherine also kept a journal about the squadron, documenting the things we did on and off duty. She entitled it 'a month in the life of a fighter pilot'. No doubt it would make interesting reading sometime.

All too soon it was time for her to go back to Pitlochry. Before she left she wanted to go for a picnic. We didn't go very far, just a mile or so from the cottage where we got a bit of a view of the Thames.

"It's going to be difficult to settle down again when I get back," she said. "It's been a real experience being here, meeting the people I've met, seeing how they cope with the danger in their daily lives. We are so lucky to live in Pitlochry away from it all."

It had been months and months since I'd been home. When Catherine spoke of it, I felt a twinge of homesickness.

"Have you any idea when you might get a leave long enough to come home?"

There hadn't been any more rumours lately about us being posted overseas. If we were to go, who knows when we would be back on British soil. I decided to tell her.

"No. I'll have to have a word with sector and try and arrange something."

Hesitating for a moment, she looked at me.

"There's something else, isn't there?"

"Well, there is. I know I've never mentioned it before but there is a possibility we may be posted overseas. If we do I've no idea when we would be back."

Immediately there was a look of shock and despair on her face. "Tell me you're joking?"

I slowly shook my head and for a moment she said nothing as she digested what I'd just told her. "Bloody Germans! Who do they think they are anyway?" she exclaimed.

Again there was silence, and then, with misted eyes and a crackly voice, she continued, "Will you still write every week?"

Putting my arm around her she leaned into me and then I whispered in her ear. "Every week. I promise I'll write every week."

In an effort to get her mind off what I'd just told her I reminded her it would be her twenty-sixth birthday in a few days. She just commented she would have to go to the farm for company.

"Thanks for coming down to stay with us. Everybody's enjoyed your company. We're going to miss you when you go home."

Still a bit emotional, she answered, "Every day I hope and pray that someday soon all of this hell will be over and you can all come home, so we can get on with the rest of our lives. None of us can make any plans. Everything is on hold."

She was right, there was so much uncertainty. It was almost two years since the war had started and there was no sign that it would end soon. How much longer it would go on was anybody's guess. With our picnic and our time alone almost over, with her hand in mine we headed back to the cottage. When we got there we sat talking with her father for a while, and then, reluctantly, I made my way back to the aerodrome. On getting back I summoned the squadron to the briefing room and advised them that Catherine would be coming by in the morning to say goodbye.

When morning came, everyone, including the briefing officer, were shining like new pins, standing waiting for her. As Catherine and her father got out the car I greeted them and advised her that the squadron was ready for inspection. She laughed and made her way along the short line. As each pilot saluted her and told her what a pleasure it had been meeting her, she gave them a hug.

"You all take care," she said. "When this war is over we'll get together again."

She turned and, taking my hand, we went back to the car.

"You promise me that wherever you are you'll write?"

"Thanks for coming," I said, giving her a letter for Dad and Bella. " I'm so glad you were here."

"This has been the best four weeks of my life," she smiled. "I'll never forget it."

Giving me her camera she instructed me to take lots of pictures and then, after hugging one another one last time, she was gone. Looking around at the rest of the squadron I could see they were feeling the same as me. Already they noticed the void. For the last four weeks Catherine had flowed among us like a soft summer breeze, bringing warmth and compassion to those she met. At that moment I had no idea when I'd see her again.

Their car had no sooner disappeared when sector called to say they wanted us on patrol along the south coast. It was a nice day for flying, cool air and clear skies. We didn't see any signs of the enemy and all of us got back to the aerodrome safely. Whether or not we saw the enemy, the briefing officer wanted his report, so after landing we headed for our briefing room. Inside I was surprised to find Group Captain Thomson from sector waiting on our return.

"Good morning Somerville," he said, in a jovial tone "How are you today?"

"Good morning sir," I replied. "I'm fine. I didn't know you were coming today."

"Well, I haven't been here for a while and I needed to have a word with you, so I decided to drive out rather than phone." Going by the clock on the wall it was almost midday, so I suggested we could have a chat over lunch.

"That will be fine Somerville, you make your report and then we'll do that."

After giving the briefing officer a few details of our patrol, I left the rest of the squadron to fill in the blanks and went to have lunch. As we sat across from each other, waiting for our food, he talked in generalities about what was happening with the war effort. As he did so, I began to feel uneasy and wondered again why was he here. Then it struck me. He was going to tell us we were going overseas.

"You'll be wondering why I'm here," he went on. "So I won't keep you in suspense any longer. We are in the process of moving a few squadrons around and you are going to be one of them. We need to get aircraft to Gibraltar and to North Africa. Some squadrons who haven't had a lot of time off are being posted to less active aerodromes where hopefully they can catch up on some well-deserved rest."

As he talked, I braced myself; it looked like the moment we had all been dreading had arrived.

"In all probability you and your squadron will be going to the Mediterranean," he went on. "But not yet. Sometime in the next few months. You have seen a lot of combat in the last year so for the time being we are sending you back to your old aerodrome. Effective noon tomorrow you will be relieved here. We want you and your squadron to fly up to Turnhouse. Get some rest. Once you go overseas it could be a while before you are home again."

We were going up to Scotland, I couldn't believe it. We were going to be nearer home for a while and who knows, maybe I'd manage to get enough days leave strung together to get home.

We talked about other things at our rather casual meeting but after he told me about our posting I found it difficult to focus. We would no doubt still be flying patrols but at least for the Scots among us we'd be on native soil.

After the Commander left I summoned the squadron to the briefing room and tried to look as stern and solemn as possible.

"As you know we've just had a visit from Group Captain Thomson,' I began. 'He informed me that effective tomorrow we are being relieved here and are being posted to another aerodrome...'

They knew about the rumours, it was just a question of where and when. There was a look of apprehension on all of their faces. Prolonging their agony, I turned and looked out of the window for a minute.

"Where are we going?" Findlay quizzed. "We can take it."

Turning around, I couldn't help but smile.

"Unless there is a change in the next few hours, tomorrow we are going up to Turnhouse. We will have to fly some patrols but the powers that be feel we are in need of a rest."

For a minute they sat in stunned disbelief and then the place erupted.

After the excitement died down I suggested they get organized for the flight north. For a little while, at least, we were going to be somewhat removed from the war.

9. Turnhouse and Safety

Sleep came slowly that night. When I did wake in the morning I felt like I'd just gone to bed but we all had breakfast together, so between that and Findlay's continual excited chatter I was now fully awake and anxious to get going. Our ever vigilant ground crew had our aircraft ready to go, we climbed in and roused the sleeping giant lying under the cowling. A few minutes later we were in a climbing turn and the Thames slipped away below us. The flight to Turnhouse was smooth as silk and the landing similar. Spitfire squadrons were a common sight here now, so nobody paid us much attention as we taxied in and parked on the apron. By the time I got out of our aircraft, though, ground personnel had appeared to attend to them. Heading to the office inside the hangar I spoke with the head mechanic and asked if he would manage to look after our aircraft for the next few months.

"It's good to see you again, sir," he said, shaking my hand. "We'll look after you alright".

"Is my brother on duty today?"

"The old Tiger Moth," he said, pointing through the window.

Thanking him, I made my way towards the plane John was working on. He was on the other side of it. I could only see his legs. With a gruff and somewhat disguised voice I asked him how long it would be before the old bird was ready to go.

"She just came in this morning and I don't have her apart yet. I think a piston is gone so it will be a day or so."

He still didn't come around to my side of the plane. I tried hard not to laugh.

"That's not good enough. I need her operational first thing in the morning. You'll have to work all night."

I heard him put something in his toolbox and then he appeared around the front of the engine, wiping his oily hands with a rag.

"I'm sorry sir," he said, looking up. "James! What are you doing here?"

"Was that you giving me a hard time?"

"It was. You didn't recognise the voice anyway."

"No I didn't, but then I wasn't expecting you either. I just thought who-ever it was had an attitude. What are you doing here?"

"We've been posted here, so for the next while we'll see quite a bit of each other. We were advised only yesterday about the posting. I still can't believe it. We thought we were going overseas. If we get a day or two off I'll go home and surprise them."

"Well I just got back from leave so I won't be able to keep you company."

"You'd better get back to work. I'll go and check in and I'll talk to you later. It's good to see you."

After leaving John I checked in with the briefing officer. He explained that there were an unusually high number of personnel on the aerodrome at the moment and consequently he was struggling to find accommodation for us. He assured me that by the end of the day he would have somewhere for us to stay. Group Captain Thomson had said at Eastchurch that squadrons were being moved around at the moment and we discovered that Turnhouse was no exception. The Hurricanes that had been based here for the last while were being posted overseas.

It was now two years since the start of the war and a year since the Battle of Britain, when our victory had done so much to boost not only our morale but also that of the people of Britain. We did, however, have the feeling we were now entering a new phase. It looked like pilots and their aircraft were being moved to where we could maybe go on the offensive. I was glad it wasn't us who were going, not yet anyway. We were tired and needed rest. We left the briefing officer with the problem of our accommodation and made our way to the mess hall to see if we could scrounge some lunch. In the early afternoon I left my clutch with the task of familiarizing themselves with the aerodrome and went to pay my respects to the station commander. Group Captain McKenzie always had a good memory for names and faces so I wasn't surprised when he remembered me. The trouble I had was getting past his secretary. She was quite good-looking but very officious. She assured me in no uncertain terms that there wasn't the remotest possibility of seeing the commander that day.

"He's having a very busy day," she said. "But if you'd like to make an appointment for tomorrow morning."

Just at that the door to his office opened and he walked out. "Miss Jenkins, could you get the driver to bring the car around to the front."

Then he saw me and in what seemed to be in the same breath he continued.

"Squadron Leader Somerville, how are you?"

"Couldn't be better Sir, but Miss Jenkins tells me you're too busy to..."

"I am", he said, cutting me off. "Come in for a minute though."

"Excuse me sir," Miss Jenkins said as we turned to go into the office. "Your car is around and waiting."

"Alright, I'll be right there."

As I disappeared behind the door I had the uneasy feeling that Miss Jenkins eyes were drilling into my back.

"Your secretary doesn't like me disrupting your schedule sir. If you're busy I can see you tomorrow." Again he cut me off. "You know Somerville, she's the cutest little thing and I love her to bits, I've told her that. But more than that, she's so damn good at her job she doesn't let me forget a thing. She told me earlier there was a squadron being posted in today but she didn't know yet which one it was, is it yours?"

As I answered him he was watching the clock on the wall. He was busy so I apologized for detaining him and said I'd see him in the morning.

"Well it is a bit hectic today," he said, hesitating for a moment. "I have to go over to Pitreavie Castle for a meeting. Why don't you come with me? We can have a chat on the way."

He advised Miss Jenkins on the way out to inform anyone looking for either he or I that we'd be off base for the rest of the afternoon. As we sped along the country roads towards South Queensferry he told me there had been quite a few meetings at Pitrievie recently and that he usually went over on the train. Today had been hastily arranged and it was decided he'd go over by car and the ferry. We had our chat on the way over to Fife, about the war and our role during our forthcoming stint at Turnhouse but he seemed to have a lot on his mind and was, from time to time, preoccupied.

We managed to get to the ferry just in the nick of time and as our driver manoeuvred our car into its parking spot on the deck I thought to myself I'd never been on a ferry before. I decided to have a look around. Leaving the Commander with his thoughts, I got out of the car and made my way to the front of the boat. It's only a short distance across the river Forth from South Queensferry to North Queensferry and doesn't take all that long. As I leaned over the railing, watching the water part before us, I thought that certainly this trip wouldn't take us as long as it took Mary, Queen of Scots, who is reputed to have made this crossing numerous times. As I turned and looked up to marvel at the railway bridge beside us I wondered what would she think if she were here now? Bridges and trains ... and what would she think of aeroplanes and the war? She had her own conflicts in her time with England and sought allegiance with France for support. Now her Scotland was united with England to try and help France fight an even deadlier foe. There was a blast from the ferry's horn; the ramp was only a few hundred feet away now. It was time to go back to the car.

Security at Pitrievie was tight. It was, after all, the headquarters for the northern defences and was often the venue for high-level meetings with chiefs of staff. Before going into his meeting the Commander arranged for me to have a tour of the unrestricted areas of the castle and then, with his meeting over, it was time to go back to Turnhouse. He didn't make me any the wiser as to the nature of his meeting but he was certainly more relaxed on the way back, even suggesting we have dinner together one evening.

Arriving back at the aerodrome the briefing officer wanted to see us.

"There's a problem with accommodation for you and your squadron sir," he began. "There's been a bit of a mix up apparently. The Hurricane squadron won't be leaving for another week and then there are other personnel staying this week as well. I just can't find anything on the aerodrome. But I have an idea though," he went on. "First I have to speak with you group captain."

"Right oh," the commander answered. "Give us a minute squadron leader if you don't mind."

The Group Captain and the briefing officer talked in private for a few minutes and then they told me what they had in mind.

"Sir, I've found accommodation for you and your squadron in the city for tonight. Transport is arranged to take you in. Then, effective tomorrow, you and your unit can take a week's leave. We have a squadron that can fly the patrols we need, so we're covered in that respect."

I couldn't believe it. A week's leave. Just yesterday we thought we were being posted overseas. How quickly things change.

"Well, squadron leader," said the commander. "Enjoy your week. We'll have dinner one night when you get back."

"Thank you sir, I will. And thank you sergeant, you've gone to a lot of trouble."

With that, I found the rest of my squadron and gave them the good news. As usual Findlay summed it up.

"A night in the city, and then a week's leave. Life couldn't be better!"

Before I left, I went back to the hangar and spoke briefly with John.

"You're going on a week's leave, you lucky beggar? Still, I suppose you need a few days off. I'd like to see their faces when you get home."

"I'm looking forward to seeing them. I can't believe it either. Anyway, I have to go. I'll see you when I get back."

The squadron made the rendezvous with our transport and were driven into the city. At the east end of Princes Street our accommodation was a hotel no less and only a stone's throw from the station. We wouldn't have far to go in the morning. Later on we had supper together and then Findlay suggested we sit in the residents lounge and have a dram. It was during this red wing social he decided to remind the old members who bore witness to the event and tell the new members who did not, about my first encounter with whisky. He made a pretty good job of dramatizing it. Needless to say they had another good laugh at my expense. It was a nice evening, probably the most relaxing I'd had since joining the RAF.

Wanting to catch the early train in the morning, I didn't stay up late. It took a while to drift off but when I did, I slept like a log. In the morning I was keen to get going. The rest of the crew wanted to sleep late so I went to the station on my own. As the train made its way out of Edinburgh and across the Forth Bridge I looked down at the ferry I'd stood on the day before, wondering how many times it crossed the narrow strip of water every day. I was daydreaming and must still have been tired. The next thing I knew we were in Perth, stopping just long enough to allow passengers to get on and off. Leaving the city and into open countryside the farmland looked so fertile and giving and then, as we followed the river Tay, it quickly changed to fir trees. Beyond Dunkeld the valley opened out a bit again. This was my valley, my home. Then, for some reason, the countryside blurred. I had said it a few times to different people in conversation but, alone there in the train, I knew in my heart I'd never leave this place. This was where I wanted to spend my life.

The train didn't like the long steady incline up to Pitlochry and usually it made lots of smoke and as I looked out of the window today was no exception. It was, however, right on time as it pulled into the station. As I disembarked the engine seemed to sigh with relief as it blew and hissed steam. Making my way out of the station and up the lane to the main street, I stood there for a moment and looked both ways. The town looked just the same, picturesque and sleepy and far removed from the threat of war. I breathed in the fresh, crisp Highland air. This week I was going to relax and for the next few months, when we flew out of Turnhouse we'd do so in relative safety. The train whistle blew behind me, shattering the peace of the town. Making my way along the street, first I was going to the school and then home to the farm.

It had only been three days since I'd seen Catherine at Eastchurch. She'd had just enough time to get home and get organized for work. This was the first day of the autumn session and as I walked the short distance to the school I knew I was the last person she was expecting to see. Making my way first to the headmistress's office I spoke to Mrs Dunlop. Years ago she had welcomed us when we started at this school and she was still here, and still just as welcoming. I knocked on her door and there was a prompt "come in."

"Good morning Mrs Dunlop, how are you?"

"James Somerville!" she said, with a startled look. "I'm fine, but what are you doing here? Catherine was just telling us this morning she didn't know when she'd see you again."

"Well it all happened quickly, the powers that be decided we needed some rest. When Catherine left the other day we didn't know we would be getting time off."

"You haven't seen Catherine yet, have you?"

"No," I replied, shaking my head.

"Why don't you stay here and I'll go and tell her that someone is here to see her. I'll watch her class for fifteen minutes. Oh, it's good to see you again."

Leaving me there in the silence of her office, the only sounds I could hear were the ticking of the clock on the wall and her footsteps echoing along the hall and then, a few minutes later, softer footsteps coming back. There was a knock on the door and then it opened. When Catherine saw me she froze. Standing there in stunned disbelief she looked me up and down and for a few seconds didn't say anything. I stretched out my arms and she took my hand and closed the door behind her.

"I don't understand, how come you're here? Is there something wrong?"

"No, there's nothing wrong, we have a week's leave."

"But the other day you said you didn't know when your next leave would be."

"I know, believe it or not just after you left we were told we were being posted to Turnhouse for a bit, when we got up there they didn't have accommodation for us so they gave us a week's leave."

Catherine put her arms around me and gave me a hug. As always she smelled great.

"You scared me. I thought you'd been hurt or something."

"I should have phoned but I thought I'd surprise you."

"Did I hear you correctly, you've been posted to Turnhouse?"

"Yes, for a few months. At least that's how it is at the moment, but you know how things can change."

"That's great", she said, giving me another hug. "Have you been home yet?"

"I just got off the train, I wanted to see you first."

As we stood there, holding each other and I told her how great she smelled.

"You can tell me better later. I have to go back to my class. I'll come up to the farm later. I can't believe you're here."

We kissed and she walked with me to the steps of the school.

Making my way out of the town I wandered up the country road towards the farm. I hadn't gone far when I heard a car coming up the road behind me. It looked familiar. Sure enough, it was Dad. He stopped and got out, shaking his head and with an ear-to-ear grin.

"Well if this isn't a sight for sore eyes," he said, walking around to my side of the car and giving me a hug. "We didn't know you were coming back."

"Didn't know myself until last night."

"Come on, get in, we'll go home and give Bella a surprise."

A few minutes later we were in the yard.

"Let me go in first," Dad smiled. "I'll keep her busy, then you slip in."

As Dad and Bella talked he made sure her back was to the door while I crept quietly into the kitchen. Dad's smile widened as I stood there.

"What's amusing you, William Somerville?" Bella asked Dad.

I tapped Bella on the shoulder and she turned around. For a moment she was speechless.

"My Lord, James! Is it really you? Where did you come from?"

"Aye, it's me", I replied.

"My, my this is a surprise," she said, giving me a hug. "We didn't know you were coming. Does Catherine know you're here?"

Dad put the kettle on and I sat down at the table with Bella. No sooner had I finished explaining how we managed to be get home when William appeared. We all sat and chatted for a while and then William and Dad went back outside to work. Bella and I continued as we'd done so many times in the past.

"How have you been?" Bella asked, taking my hand. "We've missed you."

"I've missed you and the way you pamper me."

"I know, but how have you been?"

"Fine really, just a bit tired. We thought we were being posted overseas, there's been enough rumours about it. When I found out we were being posted to Turnhouse for a bit I couldn't believe it. They said we needed a rest. Now that we're here I think maybe we do."

"Well Catherine will be happy you're home. She was up yesterday telling us all about her stay in England, how much she enjoyed being there. She's just nuts about you, you know that."

"I do know," I smiled. "She's coming up after school today for a bit."

"That's fine, we're always pleased to see her."

Squeezing Bella's hand I thanked her for always being there. Like Mum before her she just did what needed done and was uncomfortable if someone lavished praise on her or thanked her for anything.

"Get away with you James Somerville," she said, smiling. "Like your Dad, you can be a smooth talker sometimes. Away and see what your Dad and William are up to and I'll see to your bed."

It had been about nine months since I'd been home so I wondered if Meg and Mhairi would remember me. Opening the door to the doghouse Meg bolted past me, looking back only briefly to see who had let her out. Following her up through the yard towards the shed I found her peering through the railings. When I got closer I could see Dad and William in there working on a cow.

" Did you let that dog out?" William scowled.

"I'm afraid I did, I'll put her back in."

"It doesn't matter, we're done."

They had a cow tied up and had a sling on one of her back legs, fixing her foot.

"Has she got foot rot?" I asked.

"No, she was a bit lame and we thought that's maybe what it was, but it was a little stone stuck between her hoofs."

They let her down and untied her and then I gave them a hand putting her back in the field where she was reunited with her calf.

"The cows and calves are looking quite well," I commented.

"They're looking not too bad, hopefully we'll get good prices for the fat cattle again this year."

You probably will, I thought to myself. Petrol was rationed and it seemed with every passing week there was something else that was going to be. Some food was getting more difficult to come by. Dad said they still had a few jobs to do before suppertime so they went to get on with them. When I got back to the house my sisters were back from school. Bella hadn't told them I was there so like everyone else they were surprised to see me. 'Now we know why Miss Campbell walked home with us,' they said.

When I got to the kitchen the two of them were standing by the stove together having a laugh about something.

"What are you two up to?" I asked them.

Catherine crossed the kitchen and, putting her arm around my waist, looked at Bella and then giggled.

"We were trying to think of some prank we could play on you," said Bella. "After what you did to us today."

Catherine looked at me with a devilish grin but said nothing.

"You know," Bella continued. "I hope the two of you will always be as happy as you look right now."

Catherine and I looked at each other and then she whispered in my ear, "I hope so."

"Come on," she said, "let's help Bella get supper ready."

Last night I'd spent a relaxing night in Edinburgh with my squadron, tonight was a family affair. It had been a while since I'd spent such a leisurely night, laughing and joking with each other. I had almost forgotten what it could be like. Later on I took Catherine back to her cottage.

"Why don't you come in and have a cup of tea before you go back home," she asked

"If I come in I might not want to go home again."

"Yes you will. I won't let you stay."

We had tea and talked some more about maybe going for a hike on the weekend. Half an hour later it was time to go. Catherine walked with me to the end of the street and then, kissing and hugging me, she whispered in my ear.

"I'd like for you to stay with me but you can't, it's not right."

We held each other for a while longer and then I made my way back to the farm.

The next few days we settled into a bit of a routine. During the day I helped around the farm, later on I went into the town and had supper with Catherine. When the weekend came the weather was fine so we went for our hike. As we walked I thought, in all the years I'd know her she hadn't changed. She liked to have things organized and to have a plan, she was always more comfortable and happier that way. When she had things sorted in her mind she gave herself completely. Maybe that's why she was such a good teacher.

"What are you thinking about, squadron leader? You haven't said a word in the last half mile."

"What are you thinking about, Miss Campbell? You haven't said anything either."

We stopped for a minute to catch our breath and she laughed.

"It's a while since you called me that. What were you thinking about, anyway?"

"Well, I was just thinking how lucky I was, about the first day I met you and all the things you've done for me since. I liked you from that very first day you know, and now..."

"And now what?" she asked.

"And now I don't know what I'd do if you weren't there, I love you so much."

She looked at me like I'd seen her do often, flitting from one eye to the other, soul searching.

"What do you see in there?" I asked her.

"I see the soul of the person I met and liked from day one. The person on the day of his graduation from flying school it dawned on me I was in love with. I can see the soul of the person that if anything should happen to him I'd die on the spot, I just know it".

Again we stood, holding each other and for a brief moment I thought of the war. Would I be spared to come back to spend time with her? It was a brief thought. There was nothing I could do about it anyway. Other than do what Mum had said to do in the cemetery that morning.

My weeks leave passed all too quickly and it was time to go back but in that week and in the four weeks previously when Catherine at been at Eastchurch we had spent a lot of time together, good times. Times that memories are made of.

As usual, Bella gave me some of her baking to keep me going for a few days and told me to let them know in plenty of time when my next leave was. As usual Dad took me to the station and also as usual Catherine was there to see me off. In all the times I'd left on the train she had never missed being there.

"You've always been here to see me away, haven't you?"

She looked at me and smiled, nodding her head.

"I want to be here as the train leaves so that when you look out of the carriage window and wave I hope and pray it won't be the last time I'll see you. I've told you what will happen if anything should happen to you."

"Nothing is going to happen," I said, taking her hand.

For some reason I had always got to the station only five or ten minutes before the train was to leave, today was no exception. I don't think any of us liked long goodbyes anyway. When the conductor blew his whistle Catherine's grip on my hand tightened. It was time to go. It's difficult to explain but as soon as I got on the train I missed her and part of me wanted to stay while most of me still wanted to go. I had a burning desire to get back to flying and my squadron. We walked to the carriage door where she kissed me and I got in and closed the door. The train began to move but she held onto my hand as long as she could.

"You take care, do you hear. Maybe I'll come down to Edinburgh in two or three weeks and spend the weekend."

I smiled and waved, watching her get smaller and smaller.

The journey back to Edinburgh was uneventful. When I got to Turnhouse the briefing officer told me the aerodrome had returned to something resembling normal and the problem of our accommodation had been rectified. But more importantly, the commander wanted to see me as soon as I got back. As I made my way over I thought, 'here we go, we're being posted out already'.

Miss Jenkins was a lot more accommodating this time, and must have remembered me from the week before.

"Squadron Leader Somerville, good afternoon. Group Captain McKenzie is expecting you, I'll tell him you're here."

Phoning through she spoke with him briefly and then she showed me into his office. He was sitting behind his desk, engrossed in paperwork.

"I'll be with you in a minute squadron leader," he said. "Have a seat."

"Too much paper, squadron leader," he said, after a few moments. "Some days I seem to get bogged down in it."

He picked up his phone and spoke with his secretary. "Miss Jenkins, could you bring us some tea. You take both in your tea squadron leader, don't you?"

"That would be fine sir."

"You'll be wondering why I wanted to see you squadron leader" he said, laying the phone down. "So I'll get right to the point."

But before he got the chance to say any more there was a knock on the door and Miss Jenkins appeared with our tea. How could she do that so quickly I wondered! She gave me a fleeting glance, laid the tray on the desk and then smiled at the commander.

"Thank you Miss Jenkins," he said, as she closed the door on the way out.

"How did she do that so quickly?" I asked him.

"James my boy, some days I find it quite uncanny. I'm sure she can read my mind. As often as not she's one step ahead of me. I'd be lost without her. Anyway, getting back to why I wanted to see you. A few days ago we had, unfortunately, a couple of accidents here at the aerodrome. One aircraft had an engine failure on take-off and crashed into trees at the end of the field. Both the instructor and the student were killed. The very next morning another aircraft crashed on to the golf course just to the east here. The instructor and student are in hospital.

For a minute I was a little lost for words and then I asked him if he knew what the problem had been.

"Oh yes, in both cases it was birds. Both planes were in the wrong place at the wrong time and flew into a flock of seagulls. Birds around aerodromes are a problem. I wish I could think of something to alleviate the situation. It's very unfortunate, these things happen from time to time but we have to move on. We have other aircraft we can train with but we're short of instructors. You've never done any instructing, I know, but I need you to fill in for a while until we can find someone else."

This was going to be a new experience. I'd never thought of myself as an instructor but I would have to try. And then I remembered something Catherine's father once said. 'The RAF don't beat around the bush. If they don't think you're capable of a task they won't have you doing it'. It was a little intimidating. The commander was a fair man but he expected results.

"If you check in with Squadron Leader Timmons, he's in charge of all flight training," he continued. "You'll be working with him, he will bring you up to speed with the training programme. He and I have discussed what we'd like you to do. In a nutshell there are students at three levels. The cadets doing their basic, Squadron Leader Timmons will look after them. There's another group doing their transition from the biplane to the Hurricane, we'd like you to choose someone from your squadron who you think would be best suited to do that. And then there's a group who have made the transition and need a bit more time on the Hurricane doing gunnery training and the like. If you personally could take care of that, we feel your combat experience will be invaluable to them. Finally, what's left of your squadron, if you can appoint someone to lead it they can fly the patrols. This isn't what your stay with us was supposed to be like I know. You came here for a rest. Hopefully you'll get it before you go back to frontline flying. Just as soon as I can find replacement instructors you'll have your squadron back together. In the meantime if you can help us carry on with our training programme I'd appreciate it."

Drinking my tea I tried to digest all he was telling me. There was a lot to do. I voiced my concerns about my teaching abilities, for I knew there are those who can teach and those who cannot.

"You'll be fine squadron leader, there's no better person to take care of the situation. We're fortunate you're here. In a few days when you've had a chance to settle, we'll get together and have dinner. In the meantime, if you need to see me call Miss Jenkins, she'll adjust my schedule so that you can.

Anything else you need, anything at all, the briefing officer will make sure you get it."

As I sat for a minute, it was obvious he was anxious to get back to his mountain of paper. On the way out I spoke with Miss Jenkins briefly, saying that I may be in to see the commander from time to time and also apologizing for maybe getting off on the wrong foot the week before.

"You don't need to apologize squadron leader, it's just that the commander in the last few weeks has been extremely busy. It's got to the point if you don't have an appointment you just about can't see him. But you have a lot of influence around here," she said, smiling. "He's told me if you need to see him you have priority. If you need anything to facilitate your work here at Turnhouse I've to do what I can to help."

I thanked her for the tea and suggested that because of my most recent assignment she could be seeing a lot of me.

She smiled and nodded and then I made my way back to the briefing room where I discovered the rest of my flight were checked in and waiting for me. I welcomed them back and then asked them to go and check on our aircraft, saying I'd see them all again later.

Retreating to my office with the briefing officer he gave me his input on the situation and then he tracked down Squadron Leader Timmons for me. An hour later I had a meeting with him and we discussed at length the way ahead. He was an older man, maybe about the same age and build as Catherine's father. There was another similarity between them, their temperament. Squadron Leader Timmons too was easy-going and efficient. Again it was apparent about the RAF's ability to pick the right people for the job. He obviously knew his instructors and all of his students well and he was clearly distraught about the fatalities and injuries involving four of them in the past few days. There was something else about him; he too was overworked and tired. One of the many unsung heroes of the war, I thought. Agreeing to meet with him and the students I would be primarily concerned with first thing in the morning, I took the rest of the day to familiarize myself with the student progress reports and decide who in my squadron would fly the patrols and who would do the transition training. When the commander mentioned it I knew immediately who I would have do what. I just needed to talk to the officers I'd chosen so that they could get themselves organized. I had to speak with them first. When I got back to the briefing room my clutch were all there. I gave them the outline of what was happening and then I talked with Findlay in my office.

"Findlay, I want you to take what's left of the squadron and be responsible for flying the patrols. The briefing officer will keep you advised as to where he wants you to be, but I want you to report to me every day."

He acknowledged with a little wave as he left and a few seconds later William appeared.

"William," I began. "I don't think our stay at Turnhouse is going to be particularly restful. As I said a few minutes ago there's a group of students doing their transition to the Hurricane. I would like you to take responsibility for that. You organize the day to day flights of the students and keep detailed reports on their progress, but I want you to report to me every day. It will mean you going back in time to your biplane days for a bit, but you're the best person for the job."

Giving him the dossiers on the half dozen young men who'd be in his charge he didn't look enamoured.

"It won't be for long. I've been assured that as soon as they can find instructors we'll be off the hook. Who knows, maybe you'll get promotion out of it."

"That would be nice but I'd like it better if the squadron could stay together."

"Well, we're still together. It's just that for the next while we won't be flying together. Group Captain McKenzie asked for our squadron to help them out so that's what we have to do. Who knows, you might like throwing that old plane around the sky."

"You know, it's funny. When we were in the hangar earlier, checking on our aircraft, I noticed an old biplane trainer sitting in there and said to Findlay that thankfully we didn't need to fly in that draughty old bundle of canvas and wire any more. He'll be wetting himself laughing now, you know what he's like."

"Well I do, but you're the best man for this job. You take some comfort in that."

He left me in the solitude and peace of my office and for a few minutes I sat thinking back a couple of years to when I was in the midst of my own training. As my gaze fell on the seven files on my desk, files containing the history of the young men I'd meet in the morning, I felt glad to have that behind me. George Hamilton's name and number was stamped on the top right hand corner of the top folder, identifying this individual. Picking it up I opened it and began to read. It revealed everything, from his favourite colour to his religious beliefs. Twenty-six years old, above average student, vocal, but quick to learn. Vocal. What did that mean? Was he opinionated like Findlay or did it mean something else? I would soon find out. Reading through the files was interesting. All of them quite different. They had only one thing in common, a love of flying. I discovered as well that I was younger than they were. The thought hadn't crossed my mind but as I read the files I wondered what the RAF had said about me in mine.

An hour or so later I got together with my squadron and over supper Findlay told me they were going out on convoy patrol at 7am. William, in turn, told me the aircraft he'd be using was the one he'd seen in the hangar and had arranged to take her up in the morning for an hour, just to get the feel of her again.

"What was that you said?" Findlay asked William, laughing. "Something about a draughty old bag of canvass and wire, or was it a canvass and wire old draughty bag, or was it just a plain old bag, I can't remember?"

That was typical of Findlay, if there was an opportunity to have a laugh he would certainly try and seize it. But it appeared William had got used to the thought of flying the old plane again. He brushed Findlay's teasing aside. There was no doubt though, that of the three of us William's job was the most arduous and dangerous. There was no doubt either that he was more than capable of doing it. William looked at me with a wry little smile after Findlay's taunting and I acknowledged with a wink, Findlay oblivious to both. It wasn't late, but somehow it had been a long day. I was tired and decided to retreat to my room and bed. Before I turned out the light I started a note to Catherine, telling her about the developments of the day and about my reservations in my ability to teach anybody anything.

In the morning I was awakened by the unmistakable sound of Spitfires taking off. Thinking that my alarm hadn't gone off and I'd slept in, I jumped out of bed only to discover it was 6am. No sooner had I put it all together when the alarm went off behind me, giving me the fright of my life. Reaching back to switch it off I knocked the clock over. When it hit the floor it disintegrated. Bella always said bad luck came in threes. Sitting on the side of the bed I tried to decide if what just happened could be construed as three times unlucky. It was too early in the morning to try and sort it out in my mind. Hopefully the rest of the day would be better.

As I washed and shaved it dawned on me I'd forgotten to unpack my clothes the previous night, I'd just have to find something to wear for now and would unpack the rest later. Finding underwear and a shirt I went about putting them on but I couldn't get them on, my legs would go in the tops of the underpants but wouldn't come out the bottoms. I tried the shirt and it was the same, I couldn't get my arms down the sleeves. What the devil is going on, I wondered? On checking the rest of my attire it was all the same and as I stood there in the middle of my clothes that were now scattered everywhere, thinking about how rotten the day was so far, it dawned on me... Bella and Catherine! Finding scissors I set about undoing the stitching on one of everything so I could dress. As I sat on the bed I could picture the two of them having a good giggle. Cutting the thread on one of the trouser legs a note fell out.

Sorry, but we just couldn't let you off with the scare you gave us last week, all our love, Catherine and Bella.

Putting the note on my bedside table I shook my head and laughed. Already the day was brighter.

When I got to the briefing room it was seven a.m., the briefing officer, Sergeant Ferguson, brought me up to date with the day so far. Findlay and the squadron had been scrambled just before six a.m. to intercept a radar plot east of Dunbar and William had gone up in the trainer to do a few circuits. He wanted me to wait on him so we could have breakfast together.

Over breakfast William told me about his early morning jaunt in the old plane.

"It was neat to be in an open cockpit again," he said. "But I was right, she is a draughty old bag of canvass and wire, or whatever it was I said. Compared to the Spitfire it has no climb rate and is just so bloody clumsy. Hopefully I won't kill myself in her."

"You'll be fine," I reassured him. "Just fly around in her for a few days until you get the feel of her again and until you get to know your students. They're supposed to have been taught aerobatics already, if that's so, basically you're just along for the ride. You know how it goes, they just need the time on the bigger aeroplane to do the transition. Between us we have to decide when they're ready to do that."

"*We* have to decide when they're ready," he went on. "That's quite a responsibility."

"It is, but between us we'll manage and, after all, Squadron Leader Timmons has the last word."

Just at that moment the squadron leader appeared. I introduced him to William and then we went to meet the students we'd be working with.

Squadron leader Timmons first introduced us to William's group. They were all in their early twenties and sat like church mice as the squadron leader outlined the day ahead. As I looked at William, I didn't know who looked the most apprehensive. I put my hand on his shoulder and told him again he'd be fine.

We went next door to where I was introduced to my group.

"Blue flight," the squadron leader began. "This is Squadron Leader James Somerville. For the next few weeks he will take you on to hone your skills and teach you the finer points about flying Hurricanes."

I watched for a moment as they looked at each other, one or two of them rolling their eyes, a few had other facial expressions, it didn't bother me. 'What a cocky bunch,' I thought. They're in the final stages of their training and probably think they know everything already. They'd likely be wondering what I could possibly teach them about combat flying. Squadron Leader Timmons saw their reaction. He looked at me and smiled and then he clued them in.

"Squadron Leader Somerville is a squadron leader because he earned it flying in the Battle of Britain. Gentlemen, you're looking at one of The Few. If you pay attention to what he has to say then maybe you'll learn something that will better prepare you for combat flying. It may just keep you alive."

That seemed to get their attention and then the squadron leader left me with them. For a minute we looked at each other and then I began.

"Good morning gentlemen," I said, taking their files from under my arm. "Before we do anything else I need to know who everyone is, so when I call your name, identify yourself."

I was curious to know which one was George Hamilton, the quick learning 'vocal' one. He was sitting right in the front and he bore no resemblance to Findlay. As the day went on I got a better idea of their progress so far and told them what I expected of them. I also asked them if they'd been for their morning run. They laughed and said they hadn't done that since basic training.

"Right then, six a.m. tomorrow morning I'll meet you outside the briefing room and we'll go for a canter."

In the days and weeks that followed we went for our morning run, they complained a bit at first but for the most part they enjoyed it, and as we spent time in the classroom and in the air I got to know them and their little habits and idiosyncrasies. Thankfully George Hamilton wasn't nearly as vocal as Findlay, but he was, like his colleagues, a quick learner. Then came the presentation of their wings, the last one I had been at was my own. Needless to say it brought back happy memories and reminded me of what a monumental occasion it is for all those involved.

Williams group progressed well, they made the transition and moved up to my care, and so the cycle began again. William himself also discovered that within him lay an extraordinary talent to pass on what he knew and he actually enjoyed teaching.

True to his word, a few days after arriving back at Turnhouse, Group Captain McKenzie called me to go and have dinner with him and his wife. It was a leisurely evening and I enjoyed the informality of it, but I didn't stay late. He reiterated, however, that if I needed anything just to let him know.

Three weeks into my stay at Turnhouse, Catherine came down for the weekend. Meeting her early on the Saturday morning we planned to spend the day together. First we found a café and did a bit of catching up.

"So tell me, how have you been?"

"Busy, from the day we got here this is the first full day I've had off."

We talked for ages. I told her about the carry-on I had trying to get dressed that first morning back. She laughed. Later on we went up to the castle, Catherine had been there before but it was my first time. It's an impressive piece of history, of which Edinburgh is full. At night we went to a restaurant for something to eat and after that we went to see a picture, 'The Wizard of Oz'. I wasn't keen on it but Catherine liked it. That was my first time in a picture house, another new experience. Before the picture started they had news highlights and ran film showing some of the war in Europe and the Mediterranean. Until that moment neither one of us on our day together had given the war a thought. Walking with Catherine back to her guesthouse I arranged with her to meet in the morning outside the little café she and her father had taken me to on my first visit to Edinburgh, then I had to run to catch the last bus back to Turnhouse.

The next morning being Sunday there weren't as many buses running into Edinburgh from Turnhouse, so I ended up being a few minutes late. As I walked along the pavement towards our rendezvous I could see her standing, leaning on the railing, looking up at the castle. With her suitcase at her feet and her long black coat buttoned up against the cool breeze of the early October morning, her hair had blown around the side of her face. For a moment I stood and admired her slim frame and thought of the focused mind and soft heart within. About how lucky I was and then, she turned her head, smiled and held out her hand. We went into the café where we sat together and had a late breakfast and talked. After a while I walked with her to the station, it was time for her to go home.

Weeks had gone by, we were into December and William and I had finished with our second group. There was still no word of replacement instructors and then, a call from Miss Jenkins, the commander wanted to see us. As we sat, momentarily waiting to go into his office, I watched Miss Jenkins and William throw fleeting glances towards each other and then the door to the commander's office swung open and he asked us in.

"Good morning squadron leader, Pilot Officer Gray, have a seat. That's ten weeks you have been instructing now squadron leader, any problems?"

"No sir, Squadron Leader Timmons seemed to be happy with what we were doing so I didn't see the need to call you."

"He *is* happy, squadron leader. I've had almost daily contact with Squadron Leader Timmons and I have to say we're impressed. In spite of being thrown in at the deep end the way the two of you were, you've allowed us to continue with our training programme almost uninterrupted and we are delighted. At last we've found replacement instructors who can be here in a few days but I can tell you that if the two of you want to stay on a permanent basis and continue with the good work, the job is yours if you want it. Take a couple of days to think about it and let me know. Pilot Officer Gray, if you could wait outside, I'd like to have a few words with Squadron Leader Somerville."

What was coming next, I wondered, as William left us alone. As soon as the door closed the commander got right to the point.

"Squadron leader, forgive me for saying so, you're not very old, but we left you alone to choose someone in your squadron who you felt would have the right characteristics to do the transition training. In choosing Pilot

Officer Gray you fulfilled one of the RAF's primary objectives, finding the right person for the job. You are undoubtedly an asset and this will look good on your service record. We hope the two of you will stay with us, let me know what you decide."

When I left the commander's office I was walking on air and felt great. He was a fair man but wasn't one for lavishing credit if it wasn't warranted, so the praise was especially uplifting coming from him.

In the outside office William and Miss Jenkins were flirting with each other. They had broken the ice and were getting along famously.

"She's nice," William said, as we left the building. "I'm going to ask her out one night."

The statement was out of character for William. It was the kind of thing Findlay would say. "She's cute alright, you'll just have to ask her and see what happens. But first I need to know what your thoughts are about staying on at Turnhouse as an instructor. They are more than happy with the work you're doing, the job is yours if you want it."

"What are you thinking?"

"My instinct tells me to go back to combat flying, but I'm going to take the couple of days they've given us and think about it. It would be safer staying here and I know my nearest and dearest would want me to stay. Let's talk about it again in a couple of days."

Two days later I got a call from Miss Jenkins; the commander wanted to see us. Before we went over I got William into my office for a minute and asked him what he had decided.

"I've decided I'm going where you're going. We've been together since the beginning and I like flying with you, and God alone knows why, I like flying with Findlay. It would be nice if the squadron could stay together."

"If we go back to combat flying the chances are we'll be posted overseas. With that in mind it's been difficult enough making the decision, I can't make it for you too."

"You don't need to. Wherever you're going, that's where I'll be."

William wasn't going to say one way or the other, the only thing he had decided on for definite was that he wanted to be with me. If we went back to war and something happened to him I didn't know how I would cope with that. Walking to the commander's office he didn't know what I'd decided. It was a difficult decision to make, Catherine and my family were pulling at my heart strings, if they ever found out I'd had the chance to stay at Turnhouse and didn't take it they'd be very unhappy, especially if we went back to combat flying and the unthinkable happened. Miss Jenkins let the commander know we were there and, as we sat waiting to go in, William couldn't take his eyes off of her. Fortunately for me, we waited only a few minutes.

"Good morning gentlemen, come in, have a seat. Tell me, what have you decided?"

For a few seconds I looked at William and then at the commander.

"Tough decision, squadron leader," he went on.

"Yes sir. It was a very tempting offer but we've decided to go back to combat flying."

"We were hoping you would both stay, squadron leader, but that's what we expected the answer would be. I'll work on getting the new instructors here. When they arrive you can get your squadron back together."

The commander wished us luck and as we left his office I spoke briefly with Miss Jenkins and then left William and her together. Waiting for him outside on the path, I stood in the shelter of the building, it was a nice sunny clear morning but there was a cold north-westerly breeze blowing. December 7th 1941 and no snow yet. Being so close to the sea the Edinburgh area never got much snow, it was more likely to rain. The door opened behind me and William came out, grinning from ear to ear.

"She said yes then?"

"Aye, we're going to the pictures on Saturday night in Edinburgh. And, by the way, I knew that's what your answer would be."

As we walked together back to our students I said that I hoped I'd done the right thing. When I thought of all the advantages of staying it was tempting, but that little voice inside was telling me it wasn't the right thing to do. I had to get back to frontline flying. Before we went our separate ways I asked him if he could do me a favour.

"Sure," he replied without hesitation. "What is it?"

"Can you keep the commander's offer to yourself? If my family and Catherine found out they wouldn't be pleased."

"My lips are sealed. I won't say a word."

"You'd most likely have been promoted if you'd stayed here, you know".

"Maybe, but we're young and we should be doing the combat flying anyway. In a way I'm anxious to get back to it."

Later on when we'd finished for the day, all of us had congregated in the briefing room, sergeant Ferguson asked if we'd heard the news.

"The Japanese bombed and torpedoed ships of the American navy this morning, they were tied up in Pearl Harbor in the Hawaiian Islands."

We looked at him in stunned disbelief, then Squadron Leader Timmons asked if there was any other information.

"The only thing they said, sir, was that a large formation of Japanese aircraft made an unprovoked attack on ships of the United States navy without warning."

"Well," said Squadron Leader Timmons. "The Americans didn't want to be in a war but they've certainly got one now."

None of us knew what to say. We quietly dispersed, with our own thoughts. Supper together an hour or so later was a subdued affair. Findlay wondered what I thought would happen and if I thought the day's events would affect us.

"At this point in time there's no way of knowing, but it could. I'll tell you what I know for a fact," I went on. "In the next week or so we'll be flying as a squadron again. After the New Year I think we'll be posted back south and sometime after that I'm virtually certain we're going to be posted overseas. Just hope and pray it isn't to the Far East."

The next few days were a bit of a blur and then there was more gloomy news, Germany had just declared war on the United States. It was December 11th 1941. A few weeks ago I thought that maybe the war was entering a new phase, Germany hadn't been getting it all her own way, but I don't think anybody was thinking about Japan attacking the United States. Everything seemed dark and bleak. Italy, Germany and now Japan against the rest of the world. Thinking about it like that for a moment it didn't seem possible, how could they? I came to the conclusion that they wouldn't get the better of us and then I felt better.

A few days later the new instructors arrived. We worked with them for a while and then red wing got back together. Just a few days after that I got a call from Miss Jenkins; Group Captain McKenzie wanted to see me. When I got to his office Miss Jenkins saw me and grinned from ear to ear.

"Good morning Squadron Leader Somerville, how are you today?"

"Very well thank you, but I don't know if I'm as good as you."

"I'll tell the commander you're here," she went on.

No sooner had she told him, his office door opened and he invited me in.

"Good morning squadron leader, have a seat." He got right to the point. "Since you and your squadron arrived here, squadron leader, we've kept you fairly busy. You haven't had a lot of time to yourselves. I've arranged to have another squadron fly your patrols so you can have a week's leave and go home for Christmas, but I need you back here New Year's day."

"Thank-you very much sir, the squadron will be happy about that."

"We appreciate everything you've been doing since you got here squadron leader. Go home and relax, give my regards to your parents. Oh, and give my regards to Wing Commander Campbell's daughter, I hear you've been keeping company with her."

I was somewhat taken aback by his statement, I knew he knew Catherine, she had spent a lot of her life at Turnhouse, Catherine's dad must have told him about us.

"Thank you sir, I'll tell her."

Leaving him to his endless mound of paper, I spoke again briefly with Miss Jenkins in the outer office. She smiled.

"So you're going home for Christmas squadron leader?"

"Yes, it was unexpected, but it looks that way. How did you know?"

"I know everything," she said, still grinning. "I know all about red wing and it's fearless leader."

After I said it I thought to myself it was a silly thing to say, working closely with the commander she would know about most things that happened on the aerodrome.

"After William asked me out I wanted to find out what I could about him. He's nice, I like him."

"That's good, because he likes you too."

We talked for a few minutes longer, wishing each other a Merry Christmas and then I went to find my 'clutch'. Needless to say they were happy about the leave we had just been granted and couldn't wait. Remembering the scare I gave Catherine and my family the last time I went home, I immediately sent a note to let them know.

The next few days passed slowly, when the twenty forth finally did come, Findlay said he would like to have come home with me for a day or two but felt he should go home and spend all the time he could with his own family. We shook hands on the platform and wished each other a Merry Christmas. He also gave me a letter to give to Isobel. Sitting on the train as it made its way out of the station it dawned on me that he hadn't spoken of her lately. Was his obsession waning? They were two people who meant an awful lot to me, I knew they liked each other but somehow they were as alike as chalk and cheese.

I fell asleep on the way home. I didn't intend to but it certainly made the journey shorter. When I got off the train in Pitlochry it was early afternoon, immediately I saw two familiar faces.

"You've made it home again for Christmas," Dad said, still smiling.

"I have, I wasn't sure it would happen but I'm here."

Catherine, as always, was a picture. As we looked at each other and exchanged smiles, conscious of Dad's presence she gave me a very brief hug.

"Did you have a good trip?" she asked.

" I did, and for the second time now I slept part of the way."

"Come on then," Dad said. "Let's go home."

"You don't have to go back to school?" I asked Catherine.

"No, school is out until after New Year so I'm coming to the farm with you."

We bundled into the car and in five minutes we were home. Almost at once Bella was pampering me. As soon as we had said our hellos she poured tea. We sat around the kitchen table for a while, chatting and in the course of conversation I said I needed to go back into town for an hour.

"You just got here," said Bella. "Now you're away again."

"There's just a wee thing I'd like to do, it shouldn't take long."

"Well, you'll have to go on the bike then", Dad added. "Rationing is getting tighter, I just don't think I can spare the petrol in the car."

"It's no bother, I can go on the bike."

"Do you want company?" Catherine asked.

"If you feel like pedalling you can come."

Being mostly downhill it wasn't bad going to town, coming back was always more difficult. Scooting down the hill, and only a minute or two away from the farm Catherine asked if we could stop.

"Sure, what's wrong, have you got a flat tyre?"

She stopped beside me, laid her bike down on the grass and then took my hand.

"No the tyres are fine, I just wanted to cuddle you for a minute, I've missed you."

We stood holding each other for a minute and then I whispered in her ear, telling her I loved her.

"I know," she whispered back.

As we stood there Catherine asked why I needed to go into the town.

"Well, I wanted to do a little Christmas shopping, but we should get a move on or the shops will be closed."

"You don't have to do that, we're all just glad you're home."

"It won't be a lot, just a little something. Besides, I want to."

Getting on our bikes again in a few minutes we were in the town. The first place I wanted to go to was the little shop that sold the perfume, my little sisters seemed to get a lot of pleasure out of that before. The lady in the shop knew Catherine from always getting her 'Summer Blossom' there, I didn't expect her to remember me.

"Well, if it isn't the young man with the ten girlfriends!"

"No," I replied smiling at Catherine. "There's only one girlfriend, but I've got seven sisters and a mother."

"Well, if you've come in to do some Christmas shopping again, I've got just the thing. Sample packs of perfume, face powder and lipstick, just the thing for your sisters."

Catherine and I laughed as we imagined them spending hours in front of a mirror putting it on.

"Alright, that'll be fine, can you wrap them?"

"You come back in half an hour and they'll be ready."

We left the shop and went to the ironmongers across the street to get something for Dad and my brothers. But most of all, there was something I wanted to get for Bella. I had a plan in mind. As luck would have it they had exactly what I was looking for. I tried to be discreet buying them but Catherine was there all the time.

"I didn't know they sold these in here," she said.

The shopkeeper answered, saying that they'd sold them for years. I found it difficult not to laugh. Fortunately Catherine didn't say any more. Wishing him a Merry Christmas we then hurried back to the gift shop.

"Same time again next year," the lady smiled as we left.

"Hopefully," I replied looking over my shoulder. "Merry Christmas."

Outside it was getting dark and it was also noticeably colder, there was also the odd flake of snow falling.

"Well," Catherine remarked. "Isn't this magical, snow on Christmas eve?"

Looking up at the heavy grey sky we watched them flutter to and fro towards earth.

"It is nice, isn't it, but we should go, it'll be pitch dark in a little while and Bella will have supper ready."

Then it dawned on me that Catherine would have to come back into the town later on. I mentioned that it would be nice if she could have stayed the night at the farm.

"I am staying," she answered, grinning. "Bella asked me the other day if I'd like to stay."

"Bella and you are a pair," I said, smiling at her. "You're both full of little surprises, wait till I see her."

"But they're nice surprises, aren't they?"

Putting my arm around her waist, I squeezed her. "Yes, they're nice surprises."

As always, pedalling uphill it took longer to go home and now it was dark. It was also snowing a little heavier. We got in the door just in time to hear Bella saying that supper was ready and as we sat around the table I looked at my family and thought how good it was to be home.

"Did anyone know it's snowing?" I asked.

"No, I don't think anybody did," Bella answered. "But that's nice, there's something magical about when it snows on Christmas Eve."

"Hopefully there won't be too much," Dad added. "Or it'll mean a lot more feeding out to the sheep."

"Well, whatever happens I'll come out and help you in the morning, maybe you'll get finished up a bit earlier and then we can have a lazy day. We could spend the rest of it eating Bella's baking."

"There's baking there alright, but I didn't make it all this time," Bella said, looking at Catherine. "This year I had help."

We teased Catherine, saying it would have to be up to Bella's high standard. It was all in good fun, but nevertheless Bella defended Catherine.

"Well, you know I'm not a gambling woman, but tomorrow maybe we should have a tasting test to see if anybody can tell the difference. I've got a shilling in my purse that I'll bet nobody can." Bella winked at Catherine.

After supper we had a quiet night together. Catherine told me her father wouldn't be home for Christmas but should be back for New Year. I would see him. It was getting late. Before we went to bed Catherine and I looked outside. It was still snowing but it wasn't as cold as it had been earlier. With no wind it was deathly quiet, the freshly fallen snow muffling any sound. Standing watching the snow, Catherine asked me to wake her in the morning.

"If you're going out to help feed the cattle and sheep, I'd like to come with you."

"Maybe we could make breakfast for Bella in the morning as well, so she can have an easy morning."

"That's a nice idea. Let's go and tell her."

To begin with Bella said she'd just get on with things as normal but then she relented and said she'd look forward to it. Saying goodnight we went to bed. Catherine slept in Isobel's bed, just through the wall in the next room. So near and yet so far.

It must have been habit, I awoke at six a.m. Lying in the quiet, I looked towards the window and thought for a few minutes. Not about anything in particular, but the moon was shining, made all the brighter with the reflection of the snow. If the moon was shining it must have stopped snowing. And then, with the creaking of a floorboard the silence was broken. Someone was up. When I got to the kitchen Dad was just about to go out the door.

"Well good morning," he said. "Merry Christmas. Did you sleep alright?"

"Merry Christmas, and yes, I slept great. It was good to sleep in my old bed."

He went on to say he was going out to feed the cattle, I told him I'd be out to help.

"Right then, I'll see you in a bit."

Tiptoeing into Isobel's room I woke Catherine.

"It can't be time to get up already, it feels like we just went to bed."

"You don't have to get up yet, just lay still."

"No, it's alright, give me a few minutes, I'll be right there."

Going back to the kitchen I livened up the stove in preparation for making breakfast. When Catherine appeared she looked more asleep than awake.

"You're tired, why don't you go back to bed for an hour?"

"Ssh", she said, putting her finger on my lips and then put her arms around my waist.

"Did you sleep alright?"

"I did", she smiled. "Just not long enough. Come on, let's go and help your Dad."

It had long since stopped snowing, the sky was clear and the moon was shining bright and sharp, but it was cold. We did what we could to help and then went back into the house to organize breakfast, and my prank. The house was still quiet and for a while there was just Catherine and I in the kitchen. Together we set the table and put a few eggs on to boil. It was strange her being there first thing in the morning and I told her so.

"It's strange being here actually, but I'm enjoying it, Merry Christmas James Somerville."

We held each other for a moment and then, one by one the rest of the family began to appear. Each wished the other a Merry Christmas and then we sat around the kitchen table to have our modest breakfast.

"This is very nice," Bella said as she picked up a knife to cut her egg. "I don't know when last my breakfast was made for me."

She hit it a fair crack, but other than a chinking sound nothing happened. Again she hit it with the same result. She looked around the table; everyone except Catherine, who was having difficulty with hers as well, was getting on with the business of eating it. One more time Bella tried to cut the egg.

"How long did you boil the eggs for James?" She asked.

"Three minutes after they boiled Bella. That's about right isn't it?"

"Yes, that's about right, but this one's like a stone, I can't cut it."

"This ones the same," Catherine added.

"Let me see it," Dad said. "I'll do it for you."

Dad hit the egg and to his amazement he couldn't cut it either. He looked at it more closely and then Bella peered at it. I was finding it difficult not to laugh and as I wondered if I should confess or let the charade go a little longer but my hand was forced.

"What do you find so amusing, little brother?" William asked.

"Are these the eggs you got in the ironmongers last night?" Catherine asked.

"The ironmonger doesn't sell eggs," Dad said, with a mystified look on his face, looking at the egg again. "Wait a minute, this is a china egg!"

Now Bella was totally lost, she didn't know what was happening.

"Why are you buying eggs James, the hens are laying plenty, we don't need to buy eggs."

It was time to confess and I put my arm around Bella's shoulder.

"Last night when we were in the town I went into the ironmongers and bought a couple of china eggs, so I could play a wee prank on the two women who sewed up my clothes the last time I was home."

Bella and Catherine looked at each other and began to laugh. "I had forgotten about that," said Bella. "I'd like to have seen the expression on your face when you were fighting with them."

"They sewed up your clothes?" asked Dad.

"They did." And as I went on to tell them about that first morning back, about how I thought I'd slept in, about my alarm clock, and then about the antics of trying to get my arms and legs into my clothes, everybody laughed. Eventually the commotion died down and we finished our breakfast. Then my little sisters, wondering if Santa Claus had come scurried off into the sitting room to find out. Snow on Christmas Eve is magical, but for those of us still young enough to believe in Santa Claus this too was magical.

"He's been", little Margaret shouted ripping the wrapper off a parcel.

The adults stood back and watched for a while and then I gave everybody the modest present I had for them.

"You didn't have to be getting anybody anything," Bella said. "We're all just glad to see you home."

Giving Catherine her present, I told her it was just a little more of her favourite perfume and apologized for not being more imaginative. The truth was I just hadn't had the time to do a lot of shopping.

"You didn't have to," she said, taking my hand. "You being back is enough."

Going to her bedroom she was back in a moment and handed me a gift. Wrapped in red and green Christmas paper it was tied with red ribbon with a little piece of holly in the bow.

"I love you James, Merry Christmas," she whispered in my ear.

Inside was a gold pen and a note, 'I've given you note paper before and I know you haven't used all of that, so this is to make sure you are fully equipped to write home. Love always, Catherine, Christmas 1941'. Admiring it, it must have cost her a fortune.

"You shouldn't have", I said, putting my arm around her and whispering in her ear. "I love it."

We could have been in the room by ourselves, although the rest of the family were there talking and laughing, we were oblivious to them and the commotion.

On her way back through to the kitchen Bella asked us if we'd like some tea. Catherine and I looked at each other and said that we would.

"Come on through then, I'll put the kettle on. Maybe we could share one of these china eggs," she laughed.

"You know, that was pretty crafty James Somerville, I thought there was something funny when we were in that shop."

"It was difficult keeping a straight face, I thought you were going to guess they weren't real."

"Well, all I can say is, we'll just have to think up another wee prank we can play on you."

We were joined at the table by Dad, William and Jean, as we sat there talking before we knew it, it was mid-morning. The sun had risen to a clear blue sky, although it was frosty and a bit cool, shrouded in its winter white the countryside looked pure and clean.

"Why don't we go for a walk up to the gate?" I asked.

William and Jean didn't feel like it, saying they had enough walking to do every day they just wanted to relax, but Dad and Bella said they'd go.

The view from the gate was spectacular, summer or winter. With the river in the valley bottom winding its way towards Dunkeld, and across the valley on the opposite hill, different kinds of trees and different colours, in sharp contrast to the white blanket around them. Hundreds of acres of fir trees stood like vast armies.

"I don't think I'll ever tire of the view from here, there's always something new to see it seems."

"It's a while since I've been up here," Bella replied. "I'll have to do it more often, it's certainly a special place."

She was looking at Dad as she said it, and they smiled at each other. It occurred to me that there was something else besides the view that was special.

"I get the feeling I'm missing something."

Still smiling at one another Bella held on to Dad's arm.

"Will I tell them?"

"It's no big secret," Dad replied. "Tell them if you want."

If ever there had been any doubt about how they felt about each other it certainly would have been quashed at that moment. Like Mum before her, Bella thought the world of Dad and they were happy together. It had never showed more than it did at that moment as she clung to his arm and revealed their secret.

"It was on this very spot on the 29th of April 1935 that your Dad proposed to me."

Dad looked down at her, still smiling, and gently shaking his head. Catherine slipped her arm through mine and pulled me to her. For a moment we stood there looking at them. Their secret became ours. I think if we'd asked Bella what time of day it was when Dad asked her she would have known that as well. Catherine gave Dad a hug.

"That's really nice", she said. "Romantic."

For a moment Dad seemed to feel a little uncomfortable, embarrassed even. And then, as Dad and I looked on Catherine also gave Bella a long lingering hug and said simply, 'Merry Christmas'.

Eventually we made our way back down to the house and a warm fire. Later on we all had Christmas dinner together. Everybody had forgotten about Bella's taste-testing wager from the night before, everybody except Bella that is. As it turned out, none of us could tell the difference, and Bella got to keep her shilling. The night passed quickly, Christmas day almost over for another year. Before we turned in for the night Catherine and I went out for a breath of fresh air. As we wandered down the farm road, leaving our footprints in the snow, it felt good to be home beside her and my family, to be safe, if only for a little while. Where would I be next Christmas, I wondered?

Although I hadn't said anything to anybody, I'd had a nagging feeling about going to the cemetery to see Mum's grave. It had been a while since I had been there and I still missed her an awful lot and needed to be close to her for a little while. It still saddened me greatly that none of us were with her when she died.

"You're very quiet James Somerville, what's on your mind?"

We had walked almost to the end of the farm road. I'd been so far away I hadn't noticed how far we'd gone.

"I was thinking about Mum and about maybe going to the cemetery tomorrow."

"It crossed my mind that you may want to go," she replied, her grip on my hand tightening a little. "We could go after dinner time."

"That sounds like a good idea, maybe we could go to our café after."

"You know, it's eight years since she died," I went on. "I can remember it like it was yesterday. About us getting back from school that day and seeing the big black car sitting in the close. About us being so excited to see her, wondering who had brought her home, and then, the hurt began."

"I can remember it as well, you coming back to school after her funeral and about how sorry I felt for you. You looked so vulnerable and, it brought back memories of when my own mother died."

"Do you think the hurt ever goes away?"

Catherine thought for a moment as we stood looking at the moon lit snow covered landscape.

"Losing someone you love is difficult and it affects different people in different ways. For myself, for the most part the hurt is gone, but I still miss my mother desperately. When I think about the things we used to do together and the giggles we had. I miss talking to her and asking her things. Like your Mum she was a good person and I know she would have loved you. For a long time after at times I wanted to die. Every night for weeks I cried myself to sleep. But I still had Dad, although I was quite young I realized that he ached for her too. We consoled each other and moved on with time, but I'll never forget her. In a way we are both very lucky, we didn't have our Mothers for a very long, but the time we had was good. That's why we miss them so much. It's not how much time we have in this world, it's making the time we have count. Our mothers did that."

We stood for a few minutes longer in the cool, with the sounds of the night around us, then Catherine turned and put her arms around me.

"I love you James Somerville. I wish Mum was here now and I could tell her about you. She would see for herself how happy I am to be with you."

She gave me a long lingering kiss and then whispered in my ear.

"Come on, let's go back before they send out a search party for us."

The next day we got up early again to help with the cattle. Needless to say Bella wouldn't let me make the breakfast. After lunch we stuck with our plan and went to the cemetery. It wasn't nearly as sunny, but it wasn't as cold either and most of the snow had melted already.

"Let's go by my house first," Catherine said. "There's something I need to get."

Leaning our bikes against the side of the house Catherine opened the door.

"Your house is as homely as ever, but it's a bit cool in here. Maybe we should light the fire for a little while."

"The kindling is all there in the hearth, if you would like to light it for me I'll put the kettle on."

The fire lit easily and after watching it for a few minutes I went into the kitchen to find Catherine pouring the tea. We stayed for a little while just to make sure the fire would be all right when we went to the cemetery.

There was a wreath lying on the table.

"I had a feeling you'd want to go to the cemetery, so I got this to take with us," Catherine said.

Staring at the wreath, for a minute I didn't know what to say.

"You never met Mum," I said looking at her. "You would have liked her."

"No, I never did meet her. But I know how all of her children feel about her. That tells me all I need to know."

I could feel my lip quiver and my eyes well up.

"I can't remember what she looked like."

Catherine put her cup on the table and sat beside me, she put her arm around me and whispered.

"Your Mum was a lucky lady, all her family loved her. My life is a whole lot richer for knowing her family and, I love her son with all my heart."

"Why can't I remember what she looked like?"

"That happens sometimes. Come on, finish your tea and we'll go and see her."

The cemetery was quiet, other than Catherine and I, there wasn't another person to be seen. Making our way through the manicured churchyard, past the rhododendrons and crab apple trees that stood beside the church, they looked a bit drab on this dull day. In a few months they'd be bursting with new life and colour once again. Walking up the incline towards Mum's grave I could see the headstone, somehow it stood out from the rest. When we got there we stood for a minute looking at her resting place and then Catherine placed the wreath up against the grey stone. My gaze went from the wreath to the inscription above. When I started to read I didn't get very far before feeling a lump in my throat.

Although we didn't stay long I felt the better for going. I'd never sensed that mum had spoken to me this time, but going back down the incline I got the feeling she was watching us. If we'd looked back I felt we would have seen her there smiling. Catherine hadn't said a word, she had gone with me to keep me company. She didn't need to say anything.

As planned we made our way to the café. It was open and cosy inside but like the rest of the town it was quiet. The lady brought us our tea and a few of her fancy looking cakes and chatted for a minute. Her cakes looked good but Catherine and I made light of the fact that they didn't match either hers or Bella's for taste.

"Thanks for getting the wreath, you didn't have to."

"It wasn't much, it came to me one day that you may want to go and see your Mum when you were back and that we should take something with us."

"Thanks", I said again reaching for her hand. "That was a nice thing to do."

Then, for a few brief moments the war was part of our conversation, Catherine's tone more sombre. She wondered what I thought would happen now that Japan had attacked America. Things had become a whole lot worse and she looked afraid. Still holding her hand, I tried to reassure her.

"You know, when I got the news I felt like you. But the more I thought about it the better I felt. They might make things complicated, but I can't see them winning any war. We just have to keep doing what we've been doing and we'll come out on the right side."

Although I did have doubts it was what I'd been telling myself. God alone knew what the outcome would be. With my optimism Catherine seemed to feel better and our topic of conversation changed. She spoke of her father, saying he'd be back in a couple of days.

"The two of you will have to get together and have a good blether."

"I'm looking forward to it, I haven't spoken to him since August, when you were both at Eastchurch."

"You could stay with us at the cottage when he's here if you'd like."

As we sipped at our tea I said that I would like to, and then Catherine had another question.

"Have you ever given any thought to what you'll do after the war is over?"

"Not really," I answered, shaking my head. "I do know I want to come back and live here, and I'd like to do something with flying, but I just don't know. First I want to get through the war in one piece."

Catherine again looked uneasy. I got the feeling that's not what she wanted to hear. In an effort to lighten our conversation I quickly moved on.

"What about your dad, have you got anything planned to do when he's back?"

"No, not really, if the weather's all right we may go for a walk the odd day, but he'll be tired and will likely just want to relax."

"What do you think he'll do after the war is over?"

"It's difficult to know. Flying and the RAF have been his whole life. It would be hard for him to give it up, he doesn't know anything else."

"What about you?" I asked Catherine. "Do you think you will always teach?"

"No, I don't think so. Maybe I'll buy this little café."

"No you won't, you love your job."

Catherine smiled and sipped her tea. She did love her job and I couldn't see her doing anything else.

A couple of days later I went with Catherine to the station to meet her father. Watching him step out of the carriage he looked tired, but when he saw his daughter his face smiled from ear to ear and they embraced. What would one do without the other, I wondered? We shook hands and said hello and then I walked with them back to the cottage where I stayed for a while and had yet more tea. Catherine giggled when I made the comment that because of my tea intake over the last few days I'd probably fit right in at the local W.R.I. meetings. Catherine and her father needed some time to themselves however and so, saying that I'd see them the next day, I went home.

Back at the farm I found Bella trying to keep ahead of the endless housework, but she always had time for a chat.

"Come on," she said. "Sit yourself down and we'll have some tea."

"Please Bella, no more tea," I answered, laughing.

"What's amusing you?" Bella asked.

"I've just had tea with Catherine and her Dad."

"Maybe you have drank more than usual," she laughed. "But I won't tell if you don't, come on, keep me company."

Bella put the kettle on and asked if Catherine's Dad had arrived safely.

"Aye, he's here. He looks tired though. I thought I'd leave them in peace today and maybe go back and have a blether with him tomorrow. Catherine wants me to stay with them for a couple of nights."

"She said she was going to ask you and wondered if we'd mind. She's on cloud nine when the two of you are here; when you leave she's a bit sorry for herself for a while. Some day though this war will end and maybe we'll all get back to something resembling normality. But now with Japan attacking America, who knows when that will be."

Other than what Catherine had said in the café, since coming home the war had never been mentioned. Again I tried to be optimistic.

"Don't worry about it, they don't have a chance. Before you know it it'll all be over."

"Let's not talk about it, it's depressing. Tell me how you've been."

"There isn't much to tell really. Although it's been busy, being at Turnhouse has been good. William and I have been doing some instructing, but that's over now and when I go back the squadron will be back together."

I didn't dwell on the subject. If Bella had known I'd had the chance to stay at Turnhouse and didn't take it she would have been annoyed.

"We're all just doing our jobs, trying to live our lives the best way we can until the war is over. Until then all our lives are on hold."

Bella was right, it was depressing. Our little chat wasn't as upbeat as most we'd had.

The next day I went into the town and met Catherine and her Dad. He looked refreshed. Maybe it was the cool Scottish mountain air, I suggested.

"Maybe it is," he answered. "Maybe it's a combination of things. Compared to the aerodrome and the continual activity it's certainly quiet and peaceful. It's good to get away from the noise for a few days."

Catherine's sitting room was inviting and as we sat by the fire he was anxious to know what I'd been up to. There wasn't much to tell but he wanted to know every detail. He asked about Group Captain Mackenzie at Turnhouse.

"He seems to have a mountain of paperwork to attend to every day. I don't know how he does it."

"He has a big responsibility, I don't envy him. I wanted to have a chat with him when I came up but he wasn't available. Maybe I'll manage to see him on the way back down to London."

"You'll be lucky to get past Miss Jenkins."

"Is she the cute little thing I spoke with in his office?"

"Yes. The commander says he couldn't function without her. She's like a mother hen with him. Says if he was twenty years younger, well, you know what I mean."

Catherine's father laughed and Catherine smiled and slowly shook her head.

"What about you, what have you been doing?" I asked him.

"Like I said, your story is more interesting than mine. We are doing the same old thing, flying high and taking pictures, just more of it. More and more departments wanting photographs of potential targets, targets that have been hit or were supposed to have been. I'm not saying it's not interesting, it is, but sometimes I miss the target and I have to go back and do it again."

Catherine listened for a while and then she said she needed to go to the shop, but before she went she put more coal on the fire and made some tea. When she brought it into the sitting room she watched my reaction and laughed.

"Am I missing something?" her dad asked.

"James thinks Bella and I are making him into a tea Jenny," Catherine answered, running her fingers through my hair.

"He's probably right, but on the other hand we both like to be pampered when we're back."

"That was a good answer," Catherine replied. "Is there anything either one of you need from the shop, a paper maybe?"

"A paper would be nice," her Dad said. I nodded in agreement.

When Catherine left, it gave me a chance to ask her Dad what he felt about Japan attacking America.

"To me it's like Japan has awoken a sleeping giant," he began. "America was caught off guard. I don't think they thought they could or would be attacked."

He paused for a moment, watching the smoke from the new coal disappear up the chimney. "It would have been very reassuring for us," he went on, "had the American government been more decisive, but the administration were waffling. Some of them, I think, would like to have been playing a more decisive role helping us, but public opinion swayed them. The majority of Americans didn't want a part in any war, especially one so far away. But now that they themselves have been attacked, in a heartbeat public opinion has changed. These are dark sad days indeed, the whole world at war. God willing we will overcome the evil."

"Do you think we will?"

Staring into the fire he thought for a few moments, the new coal now alight it producing long fingers of flame where the smoke had been, and then he continued.

"It'll take a while, but in the end I think we will. I pray that we will. You know, we've been at war with Germany for more than two years now. They thought they would walk all over us like they did in Poland and all through Europe but we're still here. It may not seem like it sometimes but with every passing day we get stronger."

Just at that moment Catherine came back in, carrying her shopping bag. As we turned and looked at her she smiled.

"There's the paper you wanted Dad," she said, handing it to him. "It's almost lunchtime, would you like to come and help me make something Mr Somerville?"

Leaving her Dad with his paper and the exhausting heat of the room I followed Catherine into the kitchen where she laid her bag on the table. Slipping my arm around her slender waist I whispered in her ear.

"Have I told you today how much I love you?"

Quickly, she spun around, put her arms around me and with a devilish grin she replied.

"You do? And what about Miss Jenkins then?"

I suppose it was one of those things you had to be there, but I found it amusing and entered into a fit of laughter.

"Ssh," she said. "Dad's going to wonder what's going on in here."

Putting my arms around her we stood for a while, gently swaying back and forward, sometimes almost off balance and then she asked again.

"Is she cute?"

Leaning back, I looked at her and smiled.

"Yes, she's good looking and she's a nice person to talk to but in spite of all her qualities she isn't a patch on you."

Looking into Catherine's eyes I watched them begin to glisten.

"Dad and you are full of good answers today."

We stood for a few minutes longer and I told her about William and Miss Jenkins the first time they saw each other.

"It was love at first sight. At that moment they were head over heels. Her name is Alison."

"I like that name," Catherine replied. "Sometimes I think I'd like to have that name."

"It is nice but I like Catherine better. Catherine sounds more powerful and authoritative. When I think of Catherine I think of great people, like you and Catherine the Great."

"You do have the right answers today, don't you?" she said, smiling. "Come on, let's make some lunch."

When it was ready Catherine called to her Dad to come through but he didn't answer. We found him fast asleep on the chair, the unopened paper lying on the floor at his feet. Catherine took hold of my hand.

"Look at him, he's exhausted. I think he's been overdoing it."

"He is tired but after he's had a few days rest he'll be as right as rain."

We left him to sleep and went to have our modest lunch.

"It's a pity the weather wasn't a bit better," Catherine remarked. "We could have gone for a picnic somewhere."

"We could go for a walk later, but I think the picnic should wait till I come back the next time, it'll be warmer then."

Catherine's expression changed. Coming back meant I was going to have to leave first. I only had one more full day. As we sat there a hundred things went through my mind. When would the war be over, when we go back will we be posted overseas, if we do, to where. Will I come home? 'Stop thinking thoughts like that,' I told myself, and immediately Mum's words flashed into my head, 'be careful and you will come home, there's someone here waiting for you'. Catherine was watching me more closely now and I couldn't conceal the fact that I was upset. She reached across the table and took my hand.

"What's wrong James, you're a hundred miles away, what are you thinking about?"

"I think I'm eating too quickly," I answered, clearing my throat. "In too much of a rush. I do that sometimes these days."

Catherine seemed to accept my explanation and we finished lunch and then decided we would, in fact, go for a walk down by the river. It would be sheltered there, away from the December breeze. Before we left, Catherine woke her Dad and told him what we were doing and that his lunch was on the table. With her hand in mine we strolled down into the glen towards the river, which can sometimes be a raging torrent. Maybe if we walk slowly, I thought, time would slow down as well, but it didn't. As we wandered on I sensed Catherine was looking at me but she never said anything.

Other than a few squawking crows flying around it was quiet beside the river. Catherine sat on our big flat stone and I sat on the edge beside her. The river today was flowing quietly on, winding and weaving towards the sea. At times after rain it would pick up speed, if it rained a lot it would flow faster still. In any event the result is the same, like time it was relentless. Catherine was looking at me again and then she held my hand.

"Tell me where you are James Somerville, you've hardly said a word since lunchtime."

"I'm here with you," I answered, smiling at her.

"No you're not", she replied quietly. "You can't fool me. I know you as well as you know yourself. You didn't choke at lunchtime."

She kissed me with her soft lips and I smiled.

"No I can't fool you, sometimes I forget that. Do you remember you used to teach us proverbs in school? When we learn these things we don't always get our mind around them until one of them applies to our life. You remember that one, 'time and tide will wait for no man'. When I was little I used to wonder what it meant but when we walk down here and watch the river as it flows on and time just keeps ticking away... At lunchtime I was thinking that my leave is almost over and about how quickly time has ticked away. I wondered also when I might be back. I was thinking about you and how I would miss you when I go."

Catherine turned away, I knew she didn't like to think of me leaving and was often quite emotional about it. For a while we sat there, watching and listening to the river we said nothing.

"You only have one more day before you go back," Catherine began again. "When you leave, I never know if I'm going to see you again, how many times have we said good-bye. It's not fair. Sometimes I feel like screaming, 'when will this nightmare be over'."

Whether she was angry or just cold I wasn't sure, but she was trembling. Wriggling as close to her as I could I held her tight.

"You have to stay strong; it will all be over soon. Time doesn't stand still, remember?"

"How much more can we take though? We're all living on a knife edge. Bloody Hitler."

She was right. How much more could we take? Right now there was no end in sight. All we could do was keep going and, hopefully, if we all did our part we would conquer. If one allowed oneself to dwell on the seemingly insurmountable odds it was depressing. On the other hand, when you thought about how far we'd come it was encouraging. We in RAF Fighter Command had staved off a German invasion of Britain. Maybe if we'd known beforehand exactly what we were up against we'd have thrown the towel in before we got started. The simple fact was we had beaten the overwhelming odds. The main thing was to stay focused. For me, the quickest way to do that was to think of the two little girls I saw in that bombed-out house in London, standing beside their Mum and Dad's bed, trying to wake them after they'd been killed. It worked every time. Nothing made me more determined than that to grit my teeth and press on and do all I could so that the fighting would end sooner rather than later. Catherine was assertive and one of the most focused people I knew. She also possessed one of the softest, caring hearts. I loved these qualities and everything else about her but in all the time I'd known her I'd never seen her as vulnerable as she was at that moment. She needed something to hang onto. Suddenly, I felt really guilty. I should have taken the opportunity when Group Captain McKenzie presented it and stayed at Turnhouse to instruct.

"Listen..." I began again. "I've got an idea. Why don't we try and get together more often, say every couple of weeks, you come down to Edinburgh one weekend and the next time I'll come up to Pitlochry. There is a war on and we have to accept that, but there's no reason why we can't get together and make the best of it. What do you think?"

Catherine looked at me. Even though she felt sad she looked stunning. With her black coat buttoned all the way up, keeping her Black Watch tartan scarf tight around her neck, wisps of her hair flickered in the cool breeze. There were no tears in her eyes now and with my proposal there was optimism in her voice.

"Do you think we can do that? Will you be able to arrange time off?"

"You leave it to me. I'm in the commander's good books at the moment. I'm sure if I talk to him I'll manage it. By the way, he said that he'd heard I'd been keeping company with Wing Commander Campbell's daughter and asked if I'd convey his regards."

Catherine smiled. "I used to see him a lot when we stayed at Turnhouse. Dad must have told him about us."

Getting up, we held each other for a moment. Catherine leaned back and looked at me.

"Tell me, tell me again you'll always come back."

"I'll come back, remember what Mum said, we'll get through this."

"I'll remember, I've thought of it often, it's what's kept us all going I think."

When we got back to the cottage, Catherine's Dad had the fire stoked up again and was in the midst of reading the paper.

"Well, the wanderers return. I was beginning to think you had got lost. You both look frozen, sit by the fire and heat up and I'll go and make some tea."

Catherine looked at me and laughed, I knew what she was thinking.

"It is quite cold," I answered. "Tea would be great."

I sat on the big chair and Catherine sat on the floor between my legs and thawed out. It wasn't frosty outside but it must have been colder than we thought. The fire felt good and in no time at all I felt drowsy, but before I could nod off her Dad was back with the tea.

"The two of you are just about to fall asleep, you must have walked for miles."

"We went down to the river and sat and talked. It's just colder than we thought."

After our tea, Catherine's Dad said he was going out for a breath of fresh air. He wondered if I'd keep him company.

It was chilly outside so we didn't venture all that far, but it gave us another chance to chat on our own. I told him about the opportunity I'd had to stay at Turnhouse.

"Actually, I know about it. I'd been on the phone to Group Captain McKenzie about something else a few weeks ago. He told how impressed he was with your work and that he was going to offer you the position. Neither one of us thought you would take it but he wanted to try anyway."

"It was very tempting and I wouldn't mind having a crack at it sometime in the future, but at the moment I felt my place was with a front line squadron."

"It would have been safer staying at Turnhouse but I can understand why you didn't. Does Catherine or your family know?"

"No one at home knows and I don't intend telling them. If they found out I wouldn't be very popular."

"Isn't that the truth. Well your secret's safe with me, just be as safe as you can be and come back."

"What about you? You looked tired when you got off the train. Are you doing too much?"

"I was tired and it's nice to be back for a few days. I haven't been doing as much flying myself, we have a few new pilots and so I've been delegating, but there's still plenty of other things to do."

"I hope that you return safely too, so that after the war we can reminisce."

We looked at each other, smiled and walked on.

After supper we sat and played cards, had a laugh and tried to forget about the state the world was in. When bedtime came, Catherine's Dad said he was going for a walk before he turned in. As he went out Catherine handed me a blanket and pointed to the couch.

"Can I not come to bed with you?" I said, joking with her. "You know I'll get a terrible sore neck lying here."

"I know you will", she answered, giving me a cuddle. "And I'm sorry about that, but you can't. God knows I would like you to, but you can't. But it's going to be difficult getting to sleep knowing you're only a few feet away."

Holding each other we stood in the shadows, the room lit only by the light in the hall and the odd flicker of the fire, then we kissed. A few seconds later there was the familiar squeak of the gate at the end of the path.

"Dad," she said. "Why did you have to come back now? Good-night James, I love you."

Catherine disappeared and a moment later the front door opened and her Dad came in.

"Man, she's a cool one tonight," he said, kneeling down in front of the dying embers rubbing his hands. "Has Catherine gone to bed?"

"Yes, she went a few minutes ago".

"That's a good plan," he said, as he got up and sat on the chair. "You've only got another day at home, she won't be happy about that."

"She isn't too bad. She was down in the dumps this afternoon but we came up with an idea where we could see more of each other, after that she perked up a bit. We're going to alternate, one weekend Catherine will come down to Turnhouse, two weeks later I'll come up here."

"It's a good idea, but how much longer are you going to be at Turnhouse?"

That was something I didn't know and with that we turned in. Between one thought and another it took ages to get to sleep.

The next morning we awoke to sunshine and a clear blue sky but there had been a scuff of snow during the night, just enough to give everything a wintry look again. At breakfast I said I would have to go home and spend some time there before I left the next day. Catherine and her Dad said they would walk up the road with me. Before we left, Catherine's Dad swept the snow off the path and I helped Catherine wash the breakfast dishes. As she was putting things back in the cupboard I slipped my arm around her waist and asked her if she had a nice sleep.

"Not really," she said quietly, leaning into me. "I tossed and turned all night, hugging the pillow and wishing it was you. Will you stay here to-night again?" she asked, almost pleading.

"I'd like to but I should sleep in my own bed and hopefully get a good sleep before I head back tomorrow. It took a long time for me to doze off last night as well, I kept hoping you'd come through beside me."

"You know, I had a thought last night. Maybe I could get a transfer to a school in Edinburgh somewhere, so we could be closer. What do you think?"

For a moment she looked at me in her soul-searching way, and then she sighed and answered her own question.

"No, this is where I should be. I just miss you so much."

"We'll get through this," I said, holding her tighter. "Another day more is another day less."

We finished tidying up and then the three of us strolled along the street out of the town and up the hill towards the farm. It was just after ten when we got into the house, Bella smiling from ear to ear when she saw us.

"Sit you're selves down," she said. "I was just about to make some tea."

Catherine and Bella looked at me and then giggled.

Catherine's Dad wondered what was so amusing. As we sat at the table waiting for the kettle to boil I explained and also told him about the two of them sewing up my clothes the last time I was home. They all laughed.

As it turned out, Catherine and her Dad spent most of the day at the farm, only leaving in time to be home before dark. Dad had an extended lunch, spending a while talking with Catherine's Dad. It never ceased to amaze me, their interests were so different but in spite of that they liked a good blether. Catherine and Bella had a good laugh and blether during the course of the day as well, when I asked them what they found so interesting, they told me they were plotting, trying to come up with another good prank to play on me. As they laughed all I could do was laugh along with them. Before they left to go home Catherine said they'd meet me at the station in the morning, and then after refusing Dad's offer to give them a lift they set of down the road.

I had a quiet night with my family and although I hadn't done a lot I was tired, so had an early night as well.

Sleeping in a familiar room and bed I drifted off quickly. In the morning I awoke again to the creaking of a floorboard. Not knowing what time it was I dragged myself out of bed and headed for the kitchen where I found Bella setting the breakfast table.

"Good morning, did you have a good sleep?"

"Great, I don't think I moved all night."

"I thought you would be through early, so I made some tea. We can have a cup before your dad comes in for his breakfast."

Bella wondered when I thought I'd be home again. I told her what Catherine and I were planning on. If it came to pass I'd be back in a month. In fact, it was Catherine we spoke of most in our early morning conversation.

"We went for a walk down to the river yesterday, she was upset about me leaving, but more than that, I can't explain it exactly. She was annoyed and seemed depressed about the war. She said she didn't know how much more she could take. I've seen her upset before but this was more than that. I just hope she'll be alright."

"Catherine is made of the right stuff, she'll be fine," Bella said, holding my hand. "But I'll keep an eye on her. When you leave I'll likely see her most days until she settles down again. However bad you think she is right now, it's nothing to what she was when she was so desperate to tell you how she felt about you. If we got through that we'll get through this. We've all had enough of the war, quite frankly, but we all have to get on with what we have to do every day and try not to think about it too much. There are a lot of folk in London and in occupied countries who are a lot worse off than we are. At least we don't have bombs and the like."

Bella's words about Catherine were reassuring and I felt better by them. Catherine was tough and she was focused, but she was a sensitive little thing as well. All of us have our breaking point. Bella's grip on my hand tightened.

"There is one thing I do need you to do for me," she went on. "For all of us. You have to promise that wherever you are you'll do all you can to be safe. If anything happened to you I don't know how any of us would get through it."

Bella's voice wavered and her eyes clouded. Clasping her hand in mine I promised.

"Come on now, this isn't like you. I'll be fine."

Just at that the door opened and Dad, William and Jean walked in. We hadn't heard them coming and both got a bit of a fright.

"William Somerville, you scared the living daylights out of me."

"You two having one of your wee heart to hearts again are you?" Dad laughed.

Bella and I exchanged a smile and then she got up and made breakfast.

"Well James," Dad said. "Your time at home is over again. Any idea when we'll see you again?"

Telling him what we were planning on doing he hoped it would come to pass. During breakfast Dad wondered if I wanted to leave a little earlier.

"Maybe the love of your life would like to spend a bit more time with you before you go," he said, smiling.

"That would be fine," I answered, looking at him. He didn't usually say things like that.

"Just give me a shout when you're ready then," he said, disappearing out of the door.

If it was anything like usual I'd be fine once I got going, but just at that moment I felt like staying at home. Saying good-bye to my family I gave Bella a hug and asked her if there was any practical joke she or Catherine might be playing on me. Leaning back she looked at me and smiled.

"No, this time you're safe. On you go, look after yourself."

It was just after nine when Dad dropped me off outside Catherine's cottage. He gave me a quick hug and said he'd look forward to seeing me in a month. I stood and watched the car as it disappeared at the end of the street. Knocking on the cottage door I waited for a minute and then it opened. Catherine's dad let me in. As we got into the kitchen and I was taking my coat off I was somewhat hidden by the door. Catherine came in and stood there in her housecoat, brushing her hair. She hadn't seen me.

"Who was that at the door Dad?" she asked.

He smiled at her and then nodded in my direction. She turned around and jumped, for a moment she went quite pale. Giving her a hug, she sniffled and I heard her swallow.

"James Somerville why did you do that? You scared the living daylights out of me."

"I'm sorry, I didn't mean to."

"And look at me, I'm not dressed, I look a mess."

"You look great to me."

She leaned back, looked at me and smiled. "You're a charmer James Somerville. How come you're in town this early anyway? We were going to meet at the station."

"Well I thought I'd come earlier and spend a bit more time with you before I left, instead of the usual hello and cheerio at the station."

"You are a charmer James Somerville," she said, hugging me again.

"Well, actually, I've got a confession. It was Dad's idea."

"Huh!" she said, half laughing and letting me go. "Maybe it's your Dad who should be courting me then. I'm going to get dressed."

Disappearing out of the kitchen door I could see she was still smiling as she eyed me sideways.

Her Dad laughed as he poured the tea and we sat at the table. "For a minute there you were ahead until you said whose idea it was."

Laughing with him, he asked if I was looking forward to getting back.

"For the most part," I answered. "You know what it's like, you're anxious to get up there again but you miss everybody at home when you're away. The worst part is not knowing when the next leave will be."

"There's no doubt that is the worst part. Is there any word on when you might be going back down south?" he asked, in a hushed voice.

"No, there's been nothing about it yet. What bothers me a little is that when word does come it'll be to go somewhere overseas."

Just at that Catherine reappeared. "You two are whispering, it's obviously something you don't want me to hear so I won't ask."

"I was just asking James if he was looking forward to getting back," her Dad said, taking her hand.

As I watched Catherine and her Dad together, knowing how much female intuition she was blessed with, I realised she knew there was more to the conversation than that. Being in the RAF sometimes there were things we talked about that we just couldn't share with anyone. Then there were times, like now, when we wanted to spare those nearest and dearest to us any unnecessary anxiety.

"I understand Dad," she answered, smiling. "Honestly."

Catherine sat down beside me, held my hand between hers and watched her Dad pour her tea. As the cup filled up she looked at me and smiled. "No more cups of tea every hour or so James Somerville, at least not until you come back."

"No, I don't know how I'll manage."

Catherine produced a half-hearted laugh. "Have you got everything?" she asked. "By the time we walk to the station it will be train time."

Telling her I had, we finished our tea and left the three empty cups on the table. It was a quiet day, the kind where sound can travel for miles. In the distance I heard the train whistle. Catherine and her Dad must have heard it as well, but none of us said anything. When we got to the station it was just pulling in.

"Well, we timed that nicely. Take care now James," her Dad said, shaking my hand. "We'll see you before long."

Telling Catherine he'd wait for her in the waiting room, we smiled and said goodbye. As soon as Catherine's eyes met mine hers began to cloud. As she grabbed me and held tight I could hear her sniffle and swallow.

"This isn't fair," she said. "I don't want you to go."

"Two weeks, remember. You come down to Edinburgh in two weeks."

Out the corner of my eye I could see the conductor about to blow his whistle, then the ear-piercing shrill. Catherine was still hanging on as the train whistle blew, then the conductor shouted 'all aboard'.

"Come on, walk with me to the carriage."

Just as we got there, the train began to move. Catherine reluctantly let me go.

"Two weeks," I said, kissing her quickly. "It won't be long."

Closing the door, I stuck my head out of the window and as the train gathered speed we watched each other get smaller. She looked so vulnerable and alone, then she was out of sight. I closed the window and went to find a seat, 'somewhere I can be on my own,' I thought. Solitude, on the first part of the journey at least, wasn't going to be difficult to find. There wasn't another soul in my carriage.

As the train rumbled south I sat looking out of the window, daydreaming, thinking about Catherine mostly. We had said goodbye at the station many times now, but each time it became more difficult. With every passing day the bond between us grew deeper. She had said a number of times that if anything happened to me she would die on the spot. If anything happened to her I'd probably do the same. I would be absolutely lost without this person with whom I'd shared the most secret thoughts. My mind flashed back to our most recent parting and the image of her standing alone on the platform. I swallowed and suddenly the landscape blurred. At that moment I wanted nothing more than to go back to her. The picture of her and I, taken last Christmas, was on my desk in my office. That would be a comfort, I thought, then I remembered the pen she had given me this Christmas. I'd put it back in its box and hadn't looked at it since Christmas day. Opening my bag, I rummaged through my belongings to find it. Opening the box I admired it and then I took it out and held it, turning it around in my fingers. The engraving on it was a work of art, but there was something else, an inscription I hadn't noticed before. 'You are the air that I breathe, love Catherine'. Instantly, my eyes burned and overflowed. I'd often heard Bella say that the way to a man's heart is through his stomach. Catherine had another way, she could do it with words. How many times I read the inscription I can't say, there was only one thing I knew for certain, she meant more to me than anything and I'd love her always.

The train slowed down and stopped in Perth. There I was reminded of the grim reality that we still had a war to fight, the carriages filled up with all kinds of military personnel. Mostly they were soldiers who'd been on some kind of survival exercise in the Perthshire hills and were returning to their barracks in Edinburgh. They were a young carefree bunch and over-hearing some of their conversations and statements, anxious to get to war. The language and terminology used to describe Germans and Hitler in particular was quite entertaining. Needless to say, with them on the train I didn't sleep on the way back to Edinburgh and, the farther south we got the more anxious I was to get back into the fray myself.

Checking in with the briefing officer at Turnhouse I discovered that the rest of my squadron were already back. He also advised me that first thing in the morning we would be escorting a convoy down the east coast, they'd be leaving Rosyth at high tide. After that I went to the hanger to check on our aircraft. Wanting to see my own plane I wandered up the hanger towards her. This was the other lady in my life and I missed her too when I wasn't with her. Running my hand along the wing's leading edge and then up the blade of the propeller, I'd almost forgotten how big it was. Then there was the big Merlin engine underneath the cowling. I couldn't wait to get her airborne again. Deciding to sit in her for a minute I climbed up and was about to slide the canopy back when I noticed my name on the side of the fuselage, just under the canopy rails. Squadron Leader James Somerville. It's difficult to explain the impact of seeing my name there had. I knelt and ran my fingers over the letters. This was me, somehow it didn't seem possible, I was still only nineteen. The R.A.F. had entrusted me not only with this machine but the responsibility of the rest of the aircraft in my squadron and the lives of the men who flew in them. It wasn't a charge I was daunted by. For me it was more of a humbling experience than anything. Feeling the letters again, my chest expanded so much with the pride inside I expected the buttons on my tunic to pop off. Then there was a familiar voice behind me.

"What do you think, squadron leader?"

Turning around, my brother John was standing at the end of the wing. Getting down we gave each other a brief hug.

"Did you have a good visit home?" he asked.

"It was great. I had a nice relaxing time."

"You didn't answer me, what do you think?"

"It looks great. Who did it?"

"I did. I hope you don't mind."

"If you knew how it makes me feel to see my name there, with that small gesture you've probably done more to boost my morale than the RAF has since we all got our wings."

"It's something I heard about a while ago. The Americans paint the names of their pilots on the side of their aircraft. First I made sure that the powers that be didn't have a problem with it. She's ready to go, oil changed and serviced by yours truly."

After thanking him once again we went our separate ways, then I caught up with my squadron. All seemed to be in a very jovial frame of mind and recharged.

10. Training Young Men

The next ten days or so were uneventful. There was the odd time we were scrambled, but for the most part it was routine patrol flying. Catherine's dad stopped in on his way south. We were quite busy that day and so I didn't get much time with him. A day or so after that there was a notice from Miss Jenkins; Group Captain McKenzie wanted to see me. Was this it? Were we being posted out already? On my arrival in the outer office Miss Jenkins was as efficient as ever and immediately let the commander know I was there. Almost at once the commander opened his office door and asked me in.

"Have a seat squadron leader, I'll ask Miss Jenkins to bring us some tea. You take both in it don't you?"

Just as I responded Miss Jenkins did it again, she knocked on the door and came in with a tray and two cups of tea.

"Thank you Miss Jenkins," the commander smiled.

"Well squadron leader, did you have a good leave?"

"Yes sir. It was good to see my family again and to catch up. What about you? Did you manage to get away from your desk for a few days?"

"Actually I did. Jerry was pretty quiet, so I took advantage of it. You'll be wondering why I wanted to see you, squadron leader. I'd like you to do more instructing for us. The instructor who replaced you hasn't been keeping well and is, in fact, in hospital, suffering from pneumonia. He's going to be off for some time. Your squadron will manage to fly the patrols without you but as soon as it's possible you'll be reunited with your group. Like last time you'll be working with Squadron Leader Timmons. If you can advise your squadron and then report to him immediately that would be fine."

Another reprieve. It looked like we'd be at Turnhouse for a while yet. This was an ideal opportunity to ask him about leave every couple of weeks. I'd been meaning to call him a number of times about it.

"Sir, there's something I've been meaning to ask you. Would it be possible to arrange to have time off the airfield on a weekend every two weeks."

"I don't see why not, squadron leader. Work with Squadron Leader Timmons on the matter. Between you, I'm quite sure you'll manage to work it out."

"Anything else you need?" he added.

"No sir, that's it."

"Very well then... if you can, report to Squadron Leader Timmons."

Our meeting over, I got up to leave, but before I got out the door he stopped me.

"Oh, squadron leader, I nearly forgot. My wife asked me to ask you if you can come to dinner on Friday night, say about seven thirty?"

"Yes sir, I can manage that. I'll look forward to it."

Vacating his office I spoke for a few minutes with Miss Jenkins in hers. I had to ask her how she could make tea so quickly.

"Ah well, if I told you that squadron leader," she said, grinning, " I'd then have to shoot you. It's a secret, you see."

Before I could say anything else her phone rang, so I went to get on with the task at hand. First I wanted to speak with Squadron Leader Timmons to arrange for the weekend. I found him in his office, taking a few minutes between training sessions. He greeted me with a warm, enthusiastic smile but I could see he was exhausted. He needed time off or he was going to burn out. After filling me in with the current status of his students it was obvious to me that we needed more help so I suggested to him that we get William back. He thought that was a good idea and asked me to arrange it. Then I asked him about the weekends I'd like to have off. He said there wouldn't be a problem and told to me to arrange it to suit myself, but I should jot down the weekends I wanted away so that he wouldn't forget. 'That was easy enough,' I thought, as I left his office. Being at this level does have its privileges.

The next thing on the agenda was to talk to my squadron. Findlay was tickled pink that he'd be leading what was left of the squadron again and William was equally enthusiastic about doing more training. Then, so that the note would get away in the evening mail, I wrote to Catherine to confirm the weekend.

In the next day or two we settled into a bit of a training schedule again but the more I worked with Squadron Leader Timmons the clearer it became that if he didn't get some rest he would be off on sick leave. When I mentioned to him that I thought he looked tired and should take a few days off he said he felt he couldn't, that the commander expected him to be there to take care of flying training. Later on, as soon as I got a chance, I called Miss Jenkins and asked her if I could see the commander right away.

"Come right over," she said. "He has a few minutes now."

When I got there his office door was half open. Miss Jenkins said he was expecting me and to go right in.

"Have a seat squadron leader. What's on your mind?"

Now that I was sitting in his office I thought 'I shouldn't be doing this, Squadron Leader Timmons is going to be annoyed.' "Permission to speak freely sir?" I began.

"Go ahead squadron leader, you have my attention."

"Sir, this is difficult and I wonder if I should be doing it at all but it's Squadron Leader Timmons..."

Before I could say any more the commander interrupted me.

"He needs some time off squadron leader, I know. What do you have in mind?"

"Sir, I could use another member of my squadron to do what I'm doing and I would assume Squadron Leader Timmons responsibilities for a week."

The commander sat looking at me for a minute and as he did so I thought, 'he's probably thinking what a cheeky young pup I am.'

"That's a good idea, squadron leader. Starting Monday you take care of the squadron leader's agenda. I'll have a word with him."

"Sir," I said, as I got up to leave. "I would prefer if you didn't mention to the squadron leader that I talked to you. I like Squadron Leader Timmons a great deal and wouldn't like him to think I'm trying to undermine his position."

"Don't worry about it squadron leader, I won't say a word. By the way, everything still all right for dinner tomorrow night?"

"Yes sir," I smiled. "I'm looking forward to it."

Leaving his office, I sighed in relief and the observant Miss Jenkins, who was working on almost as big a pile of paper as the commander, noticed.

"Forgive me for saying so, squadron leader, but you look better now than you did when you went in."

Miss Jenkins was a very neat and tidy looking person, medium build with blonde hair, she spoke with a soft but posh Edinburgh accent. She was the kind of person who could say things to her superiors or otherwise that could sometimes be construed as cheeky or insubordinate but somehow you'd still like her regardless. But she instinctively knew whom she could be like that with and at the same time the wisdom to know how far she could go. Her smile, good looks and charm would take her wherever she wanted to go, I thought. William and she were keen on each other, but in some ways they were quite different. According to him she was funny and outgoing, where I knew he was quiet and composed, but for the time being they were enjoying each other's company.

"So tell me," I continued. "Are William and you going out on Saturday night?"

"We are, but you likely know that already. I'm quite sure he tells you everything."

"Well I have to confess, I did, and yes he does," I answered, grinning. She eyed me for a minute as I let her wonder if he did, in fact, tell me everything.

"He doesn't tell me everything, but he tells me enough to know that there are few minutes in the day when he doesn't think of you."

As I said it I knew I'd gone too far. It wasn't for me to say things like that to her. Sitting in her chair, her back poker straight, she clasped her hands in front of her and smiled.

"That's nice to know, squadron leader."

"I shouldn't have said that," I replied, stuttering and stammering like a fool. "It's William who's head over heels about you."

"Yes I know he is, and I feel the same way about him."

Making the excuse that I'd some urgent business to attend to, I beat a hasty retreat.

Later on the same day, as I was speaking with Squadron Leader Timmons, his phone rang. He spoke only briefly and when he came off he said that the commander wanted to see him. It was the next morning when I saw him again. Right away he told me why the commander wanted to see him. He was to take a week off and rest.

"The commander was quite definite about it. I told him I was fine and didn't need time off but last night, the more I thought about it, I'm quite looking forward to it. Maybe I'll even get a few rounds of golf in. It looks like you'll be in charge for a week James."

"You do need time off squadron leader, it's only for a week. We'll manage somehow."

As we left his office to continue with our day, with just the thought of time off he looked refreshed.

After he came back from patrol I spoke with Findlay, telling him he would have to fly in the trainer for the next week, doing conversions. Needless to say he wasn't too enamoured about it and said that William was going to have the last laugh, after he had ribbed him about flying in it.

As the day wore on it dawned on me that I hadn't heard from Catherine whether or not she was coming this weekend. There was time yet. She may not even get into Edinburgh until the morning. Before I left the aerodrome I spoke with sergeant Ferguson, advising him where I was going and that there could be a phone call for me. And then, it was time for my dinner date with the commander and his wife. The last time I was there, in the course of conversation they told me they still had a house in Edinburgh. But after the war started, so as to be close to his office he was assigned a house at Turnhouse. Once out the main gate it was only a few minutes' walk. Knocking on their door, he answered it almost immediately.

"Come on in squadron leader, you're right on time."

Showing me into the sitting room he asked at the same time what I'd like to drink. "Whisky, port ... or maybe a sherry?" The way he asked, refusing it wasn't an option. We sat for only a few minutes when Mrs McKenzie joined us. She was a petite lady and shone like a new pin. She was easily a head smaller than the commander but in spite of that the two of them seemed well matched. She apparently played an active part in the social side of life at Turnhouse, entertaining and the like. Tonight, for the second time since the squadron had been posted to Turnhouse last autumn, she was entertaining me. We got up as she walked into the room.

"Mrs McKenzie," I said, shaking her hand. "It's nice to see you again."

"It's nice to see you too squadron leader," she replied, holding onto my hand. "You know Colin, I think he looks even younger than he did the last time he was here."

"Jean," said the commander. "You're embarrassing the squadron leader."

"Mrs McKenzie, I was thinking the same thing about you," I answered, smiling at her.

"Why squadron leader, if I didn't know better I'd say you were flirting with me. Why can't you say things like that to me Colin?" she said, poking the commander in the ribs.

He slowly shook his head and smiled and was about to sit down again.

"Oh Colin dear, could you help me, dinner is almost ready but I need your assistance for a minute."

"Is there anything I can do to help Mrs McKenzie?" I enquired.

"No squadron leader, you stay there and finish your drink, we can manage. Oh, by the way, I hope you don't mind but we have another guest dining with us this evening, you'll meet her in a few minutes."

As they disappeared I sipped on the whisky he'd given me and wondered who the other guest might be. At the same time I admired some of the artefacts they had in the room, things they had accumulated over the years from the places they'd been. And then, the door creaked behind me. Turning around I expected to see either the commander or his wife, but instead there was an apparition, a vision. It was the most exquisite thing. Maybe it was because of the whisky, I thought, looking at my glass, but I hadn't drunk that much. The vision smiled and moved closer, took my hand and then it spoke.

"Hello James Somerville. Why don't you give me a cuddle and say hello back."

Putting my glass on the table I put my arms around this hallucination before it disappeared.

For a few moments Catherine and I just held each other. At the same time I tried to sort out in my mind how she'd got there, how she knew I'd be there. I was about to ask her when Mrs McKenzie and the commander knocked on the door and came in.

"Ah, squadron leader," she said, with a twinkle in her eye. "I see you've met our other guest."

Catherine and I look at each other and smiled.

"You used to look at me like that Colin," Mrs McKenzie said, holding onto the commander's arm. She was teasing him, but in a nice way. It was evident, even from the short time I'd seen them together, that they got along well. She was the hostess and was paving the way for us all to have a relaxing evening.

"Come on then," said Mrs McKenzie, laughing. "Now that I see James has survived the shock, let's go and have dinner."

We did have a relaxing evening, for each of us it was memorable for different reasons. For Mrs McKenzie and the commander, I don't think it was just another night of entertaining. They had, I discovered over dinner, conspired with Catherine's dad, and Catherine for that matter, to spring this surprise on me. They were amused by it and Mrs McKenzie grinned from ear to ear as she explained the plot. "I think it's so romantic,' she said, laughing. And Catherine, I know she just loves doing things like that. 'But they're nice surprises' I could hear her say. I could see her Dad smiling to himself as his daughter kept her rendezvous in the commander's house. Suspecting nothing, it was yet more evidence of just how much I meant to Catherine. She would have gone to any lengths to prove it.

Looking at my watch, I suggested to Catherine that it was getting late and we should go, she would have to get her to her guesthouse in Edinburgh. Mrs McKenzie and Catherine looked at each other and smiled.

"Catherine is staying here tonight James," Mrs McKenzie said. "In fact, she told us about the plan the two of you have. It's been agreed that once a month, when she comes to see you, she's going to stay here. We used to see quite a lot of her when she was a little girl; it won't be the first time she's stayed with us."

"She sat on my knee long before she sat on yours, squadron leader," the commander laughed.

"You can stay a bit longer if you like James," Mrs McKenzie continued. "Keep each other company. But you're right, it is getting late. Come on Colin," she said, reaching for his hand. "We should retire."

"Thank you very much for everything this evening Mrs McKenzie, commander, I've enjoyed the evening immensely."

"The pleasure was ours James," she said, taking my hand and giving me a hug. "You're such a good sport, if anyone had pulled that kind of prank on me like we did on you tonight, I think I would have fainted on the spot. Take care now, I'll see you again."

Leaving Catherine and I alone in the peace of their dimly lit sitting room, she looked at me and I at her. We stood for the longest time in the gloom, holding each other, not saying a word.

"Why don't we sit down before we fall down," Catherine murmured in my ear.

Sitting on the couch watching the fire flicker and fade she told me about how excited she had been about the weekend. And again, in her own words this time, how she came to be there.

"It was the commander's idea really. You know that Dad had gone to see him on his way back to London, when he was there he asked Dad how I was. That's when Dad told him I was coming down this weekend to see you, one thing led to another and the commander suggested instead of staying at a guest house in Edinburgh I could stay here. Then, when I got here Mrs McKenzie told me you were coming for dinner. So you see, I really didn't have a lot to do with it."

"It was weird seeing you standing there, you were the last person I was expecting," I said, admiring her. "You look absolutely fabulous."

"So do you," she said, kissing me. "There's nothing I wouldn't do for you, James Somerville.

Looking at her, I smiled. "You won't let me stay with you during the night though, when it gets late you send me home."

"Yes I do, and tonight isn't going to be any different," she said, getting up off the couch.

"I'd like you to stay more than anything," she whispered. "But you can't. Maybe one day."

Making arrangements about when and where we'd meet the next morning she walked with me to the door where we stood for a few more moments, holding each other.

"I don't want you to go," she said, kissing me again.

But we both knew I had to. Which one of us opened the door I can't remember, what I do remember was the sharp contrast of the penetrating cold outside that January night to the comfort of the commander's house and the warmth of the woman I loved.

Although I'd made arrangements to have the weekend off, in preparation for the next week when Squadron Leader Timmons was away, there were a few things I would have to attend to.

It was a busy morning. The remnants of my squadron were away on patrol and William, Findlay and I had a meeting with Squadron Leader Timmons. We had just finished when there was a knock on the office door. William opened it and the same apparition from the night before appeared again. Seeing the look on both William's and Findlay's faces was priceless. They hadn't seen Catherine since Eastchurch. We exchanged good mornings, smiled at one another and there was a brief silence.

"Ah, true love," William commented.

We heard him and our smile broadened, then I realized that Catherine and Squadron Leader Timmons hadn't met.

"I'm sorry, Squadron Leader Timmons, this is Catherine Campbell."

They shook hands and smiled, then the squadron leader went on. "So you're the reason Squadron Leader Somerville is taking the weekend off."

"I hope I am," Catherine answered, taking my arm. "But I'm beginning to think he's forgotten about me."

"Well I think we're all done here, he's all yours."

Our meeting over, we decided to go and have a late breakfast. Sitting in the canteen, chewing on our bacon and eggs, as usual, Findlay did the most talking.

"You're a crafty beggar Squadron Leader Somerville, you didn't tell us Catherine was coming this weekend or that you were taking the weekend off. Must be nice to be in a position of authority," he said, grunting.

William asked if we had anything special planned for our weekend. Other than spending time together we had nothing arranged.

"I've got a date with Alison later on, maybe the four of us could get together?"

Catherine looked at me and then said what I was thinking.

"That would be great. I'd like to meet Alison. Do you have anything in mind?"

"Well, I wouldn't mind going to the pictures," William went on. "But I think Alison wants to go dancing."

"Dancing sounds like fun," Catherine answered. "Why don't we do that?"

"Well this is just great," Findlay chimed in. "The four of you are going out and I don't even have a date."

"Why don't you come with us?" Catherine added. "Maybe you'll meet someone there."

There was a hint of a smile as he thought of the possibilities and then Catherine continued. "But there's a problem doing that, what about Isobel?"

As Findlay gave me a fleeting glance, it dawned on me that he hadn't mentioned her name in a while. She hadn't been at home for Christmas and so I hadn't spoken to her in some time. I waited for Findlay's response.

"I haven't heard from Isobel in ages," he answered, with a depressed look. "She's likely going out with a doctor or something."

"Listen, why don't you come with us?" Catherine said again, feeling sorry for him. "You'll enjoy it. And anyway, I would like to dance with you," she continued, smiling at him. "But only once, because I'm going to be dancing the rest of the night with Mr Somerville here."

After some gentle persuasion from Catherine, Findlay agreed to come. Deciding where we'd all meet in the city later on, we went our separate ways. Walking across the tarmac, heading for the main gate, we bumped into my brother John. He too was surprised to see Catherine. As we talked for a few minutes and he discovered what we were doing later, he said he'd like to come as well. We told him to talk to Findlay. Maybe they could go into the city together.

Later than intended, we made it into the city. Princes Street, as always, was busy. Catherine wanted to do some shopping so we went into a few stores. After lunch we sauntered through the Princes Street gardens and sat on a bench for a while, watching people coming and going. And then there was the hustle and bustle in Waverly Station in front of us. Where did all the people come from and where were they going? Later on, still on Princes Street, we walked through St Gilles cathedral. Catherine had taught us a little about it in school. It was the place where Jenny Geddis supposedly threw a stool at John Knox, the minister at that time. She didn't like his views.

Sightseeing was tiring. When it came time for us to meet our companions for the evening I felt drained. However, with their enthusiasm about the night ahead I took on a new lease on life. William introduced Alison to those of us who hadn't met her and then, with her knowledge of the better places to go in the city, we headed in that direction. It was to be 'Roxie's', a dance hall on Lothian Road. To begin with it wasn't busy, but as the night wore on it was standing room only. Findlay did dance with Catherine, but only once. He had his eye on a girl and danced with her most of the night. John was the same. We didn't see much of either one of them after the first hour. The four of us sat together but when we weren't dancing Catherine and Alison were like long-lost friends, they seemed to hit it off immediately. When I thought about it, I shouldn't have been surprised. Dancing with Catherine I asked her what she thought of Alison. Thinking for a few moments and then, with a serious look on her face, she gave me her opinion.

"You're right, she is very attractive. She's smart and fun to be with. I like her. But I told her if she ever makes eyes at you she's going to be in trouble."

Catherine waited for a comment but I didn't make any. She began to laugh.

"I never said that to her, I'm just teasing you. As far as I can see, she's madly in love with William."

Before the night was over I danced with Alison. She was easy going and fun to be with, but I'd also seen the other side of her, the no nonsense officious side that group captain McKenzie needed to help him get through his days. As we danced around the floor I asked her how long she'd been at Turnhouse, but she didn't want to talk about work. She was more interested in Catherine and I.

"Catherine says she's known you for a long time."

"Quite a long time," I answered, smiling, thinking about the little boy in short trousers who was in her class. It seemed like a very long time ago now. Alison wondered where we had met.

Knowing that Catherine felt a little uneasy about people knowing she had been my teacher, I thought for a moment before I answered.

"We were in the same class in school, actually."

"Isn't that romantic, childhood sweethearts. Well, I can tell you this much," she went on. "She is totally devoted to you, body and soul. And there's something else I know," she said, grinning at me. "You feel the same way about her."

We smiled and danced on.

Then, our evening together was over, it was time to go back to Turnhouse. William and Allison said goodnight on the steps of the dance hall and then we got the last bus back to the aerodrome. Walking Catherine to the commander's house I told her Alison wondered where we met. Catherine asked what I'd told her.

"I told her that we'd met in school, that we had been in the same class."

Catherine looked at me and laughed. "Yes, we did meet in school and we were in the same class."

And then, shivering, she kissed me and whispered in my ear. "I love you James and I've enjoyed every minute of our day, but I'm freezing and I'm going to have to go in."

We met the next morning as planned and over breakfast Catherine said that she'd like to go to the golf course, Mrs McKenzie said we could borrow their clubs. Although the weather was a bit on the cool side, it looked like it would stay dry, so that's what we decided.

All too soon our time together was over. Before boarding the train she asked when we'd see each other again. I told her that if everything went to plan I'd be home in two weeks.

Then she was gone and it was my turn to stand on the platform and watch her disappear into the distance.

For the next three months we settled into a bit of a routine, either I went home or Catherine came to Edinburgh. Flying as well became routine, patrols and instructing. Squadron Leader Timmons had his week off and he's had a few more since. I spoke with Group Captain McKenzie on a more regular basis so I didn't think anything of it when Alison, Miss Jenkins, called to say that he wanted to see me. She didn't sound her cheery self on the phone nor did she look it when I saw her. Waiting only a moment before the commander called me in, I didn't get the chance to ask her what was troubling her.

"Squadron leader, your time with us is almost over," he began. "I'm just waiting on confirmation but sometime in the next day or two you'll be heading back down to Eastchurch. I wanted to let you know so you can prepare and also I'd like to say how much we've enjoyed having you here. You and your squadron have done a good job. We're going to miss all of you."

As always these meetings were brief and to the point. On the way out I spoke to Miss Jenkins. Now I knew why she didn't sound too happy earlier; her William was leaving.

As I spoke to her she shuffled paper from one pile to the other, trying not to make eye contact, but when she answered I could see she was on the verge of crying.

"How do Catherine and you do it?" she began. "How do you manage to say all those goodbyes? William hasn't left yet and I miss him already."

"It is difficult," I answered. "But somehow we get through. We write a lot of letters."

We didn't speak long. Nothing I said was going to make her feel any happier. We knew that sooner or later we would be posted. Catherine and Alison knew that as well, but it didn't make it any easier when the time came.

The first thing to do was to round up my squadron and give them the news. As I brought them up to date there was a stunned silence. All of us commented from time to time about flying patrols, hours in the air and seeing no action but at the same time we all liked flying out of Turnhouse and the relative safety of it. As we left the briefing we were all feeling a bit down but there was nothing we could do about it. Later on in the day, the briefing officer informed us that we were to leave first thing in the morning to go back to Eastchurch.

At least we'd be in familiar surroundings.

The weekend coming up would have been my turn to go and see Catherine; instead she would only get a letter. Writing the note I could picture her eyes fill and spill over as she read. 'It won't be long until the summer,' I wrote. 'Maybe we can rent the cottage so you can come down and stay again.' A person could get really depressed, I thought, sealing the envelope. The moving and wrenching from the people who meant the most to us, the uncertainty of all our futures and how hopeless our overall situation seemed to be. Then the image of the two little girls in that bombed-out house in London flashed into my mind. Gritting my teeth I thought again about how far we'd come. 'We will win,' I told myself. 'With every passing day we get stronger.' Admiring Catherine in the picture before packing it away, I tried to touch her under the glass. "You have to be strong," I told her image. "We *will* win and I *will* come home."

In the morning the squadron had breakfast early, it was a grey damp start to the day but reading the weather reports it looked like it was better further south. Feeling refreshed after a good night's sleep I was ready to go. Our aircraft were sitting on the apron, fuelled and ready to go. John was beside mine, waiting to help me strap in and start, but before that I shook the commander's hand; he'd come to see us away. Beside him stood Alison, needless to say she was upset. Giving her a hug I told her to keep her chin up and suggested she give Catherine a call. With tears running down her cheeks she said goodbye to William. And then it was time to go.

"Take care little brother," John said. "We'll see you sometime," and then cleared me to start.

Pushing the start button, the engine fired and thoughts of emotional farewells subsided as we focused on the task at hand. Checks complete I advanced the throttle and waved to John and the commander and Alison.

Climbing out to the east, Edinburgh looked inviting, even under her familiar blanket of smoke. Suddenly she disappeared as we climbed up into the thick overcast. 'Until the next time,' I thought, as the cloud enveloped us. William's voiced filled the radio.

"Why didn't we stay? We could have."

Knowing what he meant and to whom he was speaking I felt momentarily guilty but dismissed it immediately. I couldn't do anything about it now.

"Too late for that now," I answered. "Hopefully we'll all be back before too long."

We were at fifteen thousand feet before breaking through into brilliant sunshine. We stayed just above the mass of white that stretched into the distance. Slowly, just like the weatherman predicted, the farther south we got the better the conditions became. When we landed at Eastchurch there wasn't a cloud to be seen.

Checking in with the briefing officer first I then called Group Captain Thomson at sector to let him know we'd arrived. Other than to say he'd be out to see us, he didn't give me any indication as to what our long-term role at Eastchurch would be.

The next day or two was a carry-over from what we'd been doing at Turnhouse. Convoy escorts and patrols.

And then there was a visit from the commander...

11.   Posted to Gibraltar

"Hello again squadron leader," he began, as we sat in my office. "I trust you had a nice relaxing time in your native land?"

"It was good to be back in Scotland sir, but between one thing and another we were quite busy."

"So I've been hearing. I spoke with Group Captain McKenzie on the phone the other day. By the sounds of things they're going to miss you and your squadron. He was telling me that he'd given you and Pilot Officer Grey the chance to stay."

It wasn't surprising that he knew what we'd been up to, there really were only a few handfuls of senior officers in the RAF and they stayed in touch with one another and all knew what was going on in each other's area. It was their job and they were good at it.

"Yes sir, he did give us the opportunity to stay. It was a difficult decision to make but we felt our place was with the squadron."

"Well," he smiled. "You should know that the commander spoke highly of all of you."

"Thank you sir, I'll pass your comments on to the squadron."

"There is something else you should let them know about, squadron leader. We're sending you to Gibraltar. There's a bit of a push on in the area and we need to have more of a presence there. All the arrangements have been made. Your aircraft will be crated and put aboard the aircraft carrier *Ark Royal* where you'll join them. They'll be reassembled on the way and once you get close enough you'll leave the carrier and fly into the aerodrome."

"You mean a carrier take-off sir?"

He saw the look of apprehension on my face. We'd never flown off a carrier before. Immediately I had visions of attempting a take-off only to drop off the end of the deck and be run over by the ship.

"I wouldn't worry about it," he continued. "It's been done often enough already with Spitfires. The crew on the flight deck will keep you right. There are a number of squadrons going but you're not all going to Gibraltar."

He stood up to leave and we shook hands. "If I don't see you again before you go, squadron leader, have a safe trip and take care. If there's anything you need and you think I can help, don't hesitate to let me know."

As I walked with him to his car a number of lorries and personnel arrived.

"Looks like the mechanics are here to prepare your aircraft, squadron leader. Take care now, hopefully we'll see you again before long."

As soon as the commander left, I summoned my clutch to the briefing room. I didn't beat around the bush.

"Group Captain Thomson was here to tell us that we wouldn't be doing any more flying in Britain, at least not for the time being. The mechanics are here already to crate our aircraft. We've been posted to Gibraltar."

None of them said anything. We had been expecting it for a while now and were thankful it hadn't happened sooner. For myself, I was glad it was the Mediterranean we were going to and a reasonable climate. For the next day or two, other than write letters and watch the mechanics dismantle our aircraft, we didn't do much. In an effort to stay as fit as possible we kept up with our early morning runs. As always there was the odd complaint from those of us who shall remain nameless, but he enjoyed it once he got going. I'd asked the briefing officer to find out as much as he could about aircraft carriers. After he'd made some phone calls he advised me of what he'd found out.

"Everyone I spoke to, sir, said the same thing. When it comes time for a take-off they'll point the ship into wind, you open the throttle and you'll be airborne before you know it."

'Easy for them to say,' I thought, 'it's not them who's going to get wet, or worse, if we didn't make it...' but I decided I wasn't going to think about it until the time came. In one of our quiet moments before we left I talked with Findlay.

"There's something I've been meaning to ask you," he began. "When we left Edinburgh the other day, what was that wee exchange between William and you all about?"

I couldn't help but smile and wondered why he hadn't quizzed me about it sooner.

"If I tell you, you have to keep it to yourself."

"My lips are sealed, won't say a word."

"I mean it, if word ever got back home neither one of us would be very popular."

He promised me again he wouldn't say anything so I went on to tell him about how we'd been given the opportunity to stay at Turnhouse to be instructors. He sat for a moment, mulling over what I told him and then he shared his thoughts.

"And then, after that, he got hot and heavy with Alison, so when it came time to leave he wished he could have stayed."

"That's exactly right. There are only a few people know about what happened. If Catherine or my family found out, especially now that we're being posted overseas, they wouldn't be very happy."

"That's a bummer," Findlay went on. "If I'd gotten the chance I don't know, I think I would have stayed."

"Well maybe. I don't know if you would have. We both wanted to stay with the squadron and I still feel that way and I think William would say the same thing. There's something else he said when we were discussing our dilemma. He said that he liked flying with you and that he wanted us to stay together. He would likely have been promoted if he'd stayed."

"Well I have to say I'm touched," Findlay went on. "I think the two of you are as daft as a brush for not staying but I'm glad you are here."

That was all that was said about it but I did observe for a long time afterwards that Findlay looked up to William more than at him. I don't think he had realized until then just how tight the bond between we three especially had become.

Three days later we were on our way to the channel port of Folkestone where the *Ark Royal* was tied up. She and other ships of the royal navy had been in port there for a week already, loading supplies for allied bases in the Mediterranean. As we went aboard we watched what appeared to be legions of men, franticly working, being chased by time, preparing a huge floating monster to sail on the evening tide. I was in awe at the logistical nightmare of it all.

As we were escorted to our quarters for the voyage, I discovered that for the first time in a long time I'd be sharing space with the rest of my squadron.

"Thank the lord it's only for a few days," I said to Findlay. "I still haven't forgotten how loud you snore."

"Funny," he answered facetiously. "In the night, when you get lonely don't come slipping into my bunk."

As we laid claim to the bunk we wanted, the rest of the squadron had a good giggle at our bantering. Once our belongings were stored we went for a wander around the ship but I decided it was more interesting to watch the ship's crew getting ready for our departure, so I found a place out of the way where I could watch the comings and goings on the flight deck. Still in possession of Catherine's camera, I took a few pictures. There likely wouldn't be another opportunity.

Right on schedule the ship was untied, pulled this way and that by tugs a fraction of her size, and we were soon heading out into deep water. 'Catherine would like to be here to see this,' I thought, and then I thought again. She would have received my letter telling her about our posting to Eastchurch, then another one saying about going overseas. God alone knew when we'd see each other again or when we'd be back on British soil. Amidst the blaring of claxons and foghorns heralding our departure and as the ship began to make way on her own, one of Dad's little phrases flashed into my mind. It didn't make the task at hand any less difficult but what it always seemed to do was give me comfort. 'Do what you have to do, this too will pass.' The war would end, none of us knew just when yet but, God willing, I'd be back. Back to my family, to the peace and tranquillity of my Perthshire home and to the beauty and companionship of the woman I loved.

Gathering speed now, this steel giant, along with her escorts and other supply ships, steamed towards Brest on the north western tip of France. From there we would go down the west coast through the Bay of Biscay. There had been numerous reports about U-Boats lurking there, hopefully not when we're there, I thought. It was also a body of water that was reputed to be quite turbulent and it wasn't difficult to understand why. Between it and the coast of North America there was nothing to stop the entire wrath and fury the Atlantic Ocean had to offer. Again, hopefully not when we're there, then I decided to go back to our quarters. The squadron were back there already, thinking about finding something to eat. William said he'd been talking to a couple of the ship's crew who'd told him that the weather forecast for the next day or so wasn't good and that it could get a bit choppy. We looked at one another, all wondering, I think, what their definition of 'choppy' might be.

"I've been on a ship before, don't worry about a thing," said Findlay, swaggering. "This is a big boat, we'll be fine."

It had been a long day. After our meal we were all tired and decided to turn in. We had just gone to bed it seemed when we were awakened to the most ear-piercing noise. Getting the fright of our lives we then discovered it was the six am wakeup call. The ship was doing a bit of rolling and pitching so before we went for breakfast we decided to go topside to see what the weather was really like. When I looked outside I was glad I was on the carrier. It was a windy, grey, overcast day and sometimes the ships around us almost looked like they were submerging as they dropped into troughs. All the hours I'd spent flying I never once felt queasy, but at that moment, if I'd really thought about it, I could have been seasick.

"It's not too bad," Findlay snorted. "Just a wee breeze. Come on, let's go and see if they serve breakfast on this tub."

After we'd eaten we decided to see if the mechanics were putting our aircraft back together. I'd gotten used to the ship swaying around and had forgotten about how rough the weather was outside. Unfortunately Findlay hadn't and in an instant was sick everywhere.

Finding a door to take us outside I ushered him to the side of the ship where he retched and heaved for a while. When he didn't have anything left to bring up I took him back to our quarters and bed.

"Will you be wanting anything to eat?" I asked him jokingly.

Unable to speak, he pulled the blankets over his head. Leaving him in peace I went to explore the ship. Later on in the day I got together with some members of other squadrons. Most of them had come from aerodromes in the south of England and, like us, for the last while they hadn't seen much action.

After that the day seemed to drag, but eventually it passed and as we prepared to turn in the ship was still swaying. Findlay, whether or not he'd slept all day I couldn't say, but he was certainly snoring loudly enough when we went to bed. In the morning we were awakened yet again by the same awful din. Right away there was something different, looking around, trying to think what it was, Findlay was sitting on his bunk, looking at me.

"You woke me up with your snoring,' he said. "I never slept a wink all night."

"You were sleeping when we went to bed last night. How are you feeling now anyway?"

"Aye a lot better, but my belly hurts with all that heaving."

"Well you definitely had something you wanted rid of. Having been on a ship before I didn't think you'd have been sick like that."

"Neither did I," he answered innocently. "But they don't have waves that size on the Clyde."

I looked at him in disbelief. "You mean to tell me that the furthest out to sea you've been is a sail on the Clyde?"

He shrugged his shoulders and said nothing. The rest of the squadron tormented him, saying that for a seasoned sailor he had been pretty green looking. As usual the taunts ran off Findlay like water off a duck's back. Then it dawned on me.

"The ship isn't rolling."

"No," Findlay answered. "About midnight it began to ease, it's fine now."

We went for breakfast and for obvious reasons Findlay said he was eating nothing. He did concede however and felt the better for it. Later on we went up to the flight deck for a walk and were relieved to see the sun shining and a calm sea. But there wasn't anything to do but wait until we got close to land. One thing we discovered as the time dragged, none of us ever wanted to be sailors.

Then the day came for us to leave the ship, first thing in the morning there was a briefing about what was expected of us on the flight deck, emergency procedures, and heaven forbid what to do in the event of an engine failure on take-off. After breakfast we went to check on our aircraft, they were ready to go. And then it was time. Gibraltar was fifty miles to the southeast. As the captain turned his floating airfield into wind the Spitfires first in line started their engines. All the pilots were apprehensive about the take-off but it had to be done. The signal was given and with its engine screaming the first Spitfire rolled down the deck towards the precipice, but even before it got to the end it looked like it had been lifted by some invisible hand. It limped into the air and climbed away. 'Thank the lord,' I thought. 'If he can do it so can I.' One by one the aircraft took off, the deck cleared and then it was my turn. With a few degrees of flaps I released the brakes and with the throttle pushed hard against the stop, together we rolled down the deck and were lifted by the same mysterious hand. Circling in a pattern just behind the carrier I waited for the rest of my squadron. It wasn't a difficult job finding the aerodrome, it lay at the base of the almost vertical rock. It was more difficult after we landed to taxi on the congested aerodrome. If the Germans could have bombed Gibraltar at that moment there would have been a lot of scrap aeroplanes.

For the first few days everything was a shambles. 'Organized chaos' Findlay said. Even our accommodation was vastly different to what we were used to. We were sleeping in tents. But as the days passed things became more civilized. The aerodrome became a lot less congested as the squadrons we came with were slowly dispatched to either Malta or North Africa. Malta was a thousand miles away. To be able to get there in one hop the Spitfires were fitted with another fuel tank. For the pilots, in case they needed to pee on their long flight, a receptacle was installed in which to store it. As we sat in the warm sun, watching the mechanics fit these tanks, Findlay once more didn't miss the opportunity.

"What if you missed?" he said. "You would have a wet leg and all that liquid sloshing around in the cockpit would play havoc with the electrics. It wouldn't be good."

We looked at him and then at each other. After he'd thought for a minute, with a straight face he shared more of his thoughts.

"The night before their trip I think they should drink only whisky, then if they got fitted up with a pipe they could whiz right into the fuel tank. That way they wouldn't need to fit these other tanks. With the high octane content they'd likely get another fifty miles an hour out of these planes."

As this brainwave dribbled from his mouth it was difficult to tell whether or not he was serious and thought his idea would actually work, there wasn't the slightest hint of otherwise. Again we stared at him and started to laugh.

"Tell me," I asked him. "Did you think of that all by yourself or did you have help with it?"

He laughed with us and then said he had another theory.

"You know how they've got women ferry pilots? Well sometimes they go on long trips. They could do the same thing. I just can't think how they'd connect the pipe. With their premium grade they'd likely get seventy five miles an hour more."

That was Findlay and his quick-witted Glaswegian humour, he hadn't changed in the time I'd known him. From time to time he got under everybody's skin with his incessant nattering, he knew it but didn't seem to care. Maybe it was his way of relieving the stress. On days like today when he was in good form I know he relieved ours. In spite of this trivial personality flaw he was a good person, what was more important was that he was a good pilot, we all liked flying with him.

In the weeks that followed it looked like the RAF had forgotten about us. Convoys passed through the straits, aircraft came and went but we stayed, our existence on the rock apparently forgotten. We flew yet more patrols and a lot of escorts but saw nothing of the enemy. We knew their submarines were passing through the straits into the Mediterranean but they did the deed at night or were submerged at the time. Again we longed to be somewhere else, somewhere we'd be contributing more to the war effort. We knew the authorities hadn't forgotten about us, it just felt like that. We knew as well they needed a presence on the Rock and for the time being, along with about thirty thousand other military personnel we were it.

During our stay at Gibraltar we were under the direction of group captain William Douglas and our briefing officer was sergeant Alex Simpson. Between them they made our stay as pleasant and comfortable as possible and kept us informed about what was happening with the war in other parts of the world.

There was still turmoil everywhere. All the countries of the world were at war. If they weren't, they sympathized with one that was. There were few people who weren't affected by it in one way or another. One exception was Spain, right next door to the north. The aerodrome was sandwiched between the sheer face of 'The Rock' and the border. Everybody was concerned that she would enter the war on the enemy's side. After all, Hitler had helped their current leader, Franco, sweep to power in a bloody civil war. But so far she remained neutral.

Contact with home was intermittent. Ships did come with our supplies, fuel and food. The harbour was a hive of activity day and night as ships of the Royal Navy and merchant ships alike called into Gibraltar with either supplies or for repairs. But what we yearned for more than anything was letters from home. It was proof there was still a world out there and that our families still existed. My correspondence to home was ready every week but it didn't go every week, sometimes there could be four or five letters at a time. When we got mail it was usually a bundle and I would read each letter over and over. A few days later we would do the same thing again, reading the same bundle until the next one came. Catherine told me about when she first learned of our posting, how she couldn't believe that it had happened or how quickly. She had wondered why she hadn't been getting mail from me when Alison phoned her. Bella as well wrote to me faithfully every week keeping me up to date with their lives. Dad was buying more breeding cows, still convinced that the enemy, if they couldn't beat us into submission would starve us. By producing more it was his way of contributing to the war effort.

In my letters to them, other than to confirm I was all right, I couldn't divulge anything about what we were up to, or the fact that almost the entire civilian population of Gibraltar had been evacuated, or about the miles of tunnels that had been dug into the Rock and the underground fortress she had become. These details would have to wait until I went home.

The Rock of Gibraltar stood like a beacon, rising almost fourteen hundred feet above the Strait. When we got here it had been somewhat green but with the searing heat of summer and the lack of rain it had since turned a drab brown colour. On closer inspection, however, away from congested areas, the landscape resembled a giant rock garden gone wild. Although I'd helped Mum and Catherine dig and plant in their respective gardens, plants and flowers just weren't my forte but walking in the more remote areas of the peninsula there was no escaping the fragrance and blaze of colour offered by the wild flowers that grew there. Lavender and orchids, for example, growing and flourishing in abundance in the rocky arid terrain. Then there were the dolphins that played and raced with the many ships that came and went. The pods of whales in the Strait seemingly heading out into the Atlantic, treading water only they were keeping pace with the easterly flow of the upper currents in the Strait. Then there were the swarms of birds that sometimes made flying hazardous. The 'Rock' was their home. Peregrine Falcons soared on thermals, scouring for their lunch. No, this place wasn't Pitlochry but it was fascinating nevertheless.

We were into mid-July now and although there was plenty to do, the last few days seemed to be dragging. It was hot and when it was like that our aircraft didn't perform well. Oh for a shower of rain! As usual, when we felt like that the topic of conversation between us was that we'd like to be somewhere else and see some action. Then there were reports the war wasn't going well. Malta was on her knees. If she didn't get help soon she'd be overrun. The supply ships sent there in the last few weeks never made it, torpedoed or bombed they were at the bottom of the Mediterranean. Reports that the squadrons we had come to Gibraltar with and had moved on to Malta had been considerably reduced in numbers. Some had been shot down, but the majority had been damaged or destroyed by the relentless pounding of the island by both German and Italian aircraft. We decided that flying patrols around Gibraltar maybe wasn't the worst thing to be doing.

A week later our commander advised us that we were being posted. A convoy was coming into port on its way to Malta and we were to go with it. We had wanted more action and there was no doubt that now we'd see it. I told my clutch they should be careful what they wish for, it might just come true.

It was nearly two weeks, but under the cover of heavy fog the convoy arrived and as soon as the carrier tied up there was no time wasted loading our aircraft. Dozens of aircraft were hoisted onto the flight deck and parked.

Then, saying goodbye to Gibraltar, we were underway.

It was August 11th 1942.

Once out in open water, 'Operation Pedestal' was an impressive sight. Fifty ships in convoy, all with the same goal, a last ditch attempt to save Malta before she fell into enemy hands.

Just hours after leaving Gibraltar, however, the convoy was attacked by submarines. We watched in total disbelief as one of the carriers disappeared under the water. We didn't know how many men or aircraft were on board, the only thing we did know for sure was that only four aircraft managed to get airborne before she sank. They flew back to Gibraltar. We were too far away to know the fate of the sailors or the rest of the men on board. We steamed on, unable to stop.

Unfortunately, that was only the beginning.

That night I don't think any of us slept a wink, terrified that our carrier would be next. As dawn broke we were still intact. Shortly thereafter, enemy bombers and torpedo planes attacked the convoy, sinking two freighters. Hours later they were back and sunk another two. We stood watching, anxious to be airborne. We knew we could blow the slow, cumbersome dive-bombers and torpedo planes out of the sky. But we couldn't. We didn't have arrester hooks on our aircraft to be able to land back on the carrier. Nor did we have enough fuel to fly to Malta after tangling with the enemy, so we watched, unable to do anything. Then the unthinkable happened. Somebody saw the wake of a torpedo and shouted. We waited for the explosion but it never happened. There had been a torpedo all right and it did hit the side of the ship, but it didn't explode. What were the chances of that, we wondered.

Later on in the day as we got ever closer to Malta Spitfires began leaving one of the remaining carriers. As soon as they were all up the carrier turned around and went back the way she'd come. We should have done the same. As far as I was concerned it would be the safest thing to do. We stood more of a chance in the air than we did on the carrier if she was hit. As night came we felt a little better. Maybe the enemy submarines wouldn't find us in the dark, moonless night. And then, all pilots were summoned to a briefing. It had been decided that first thing in the morning we would leave the carrier and make for Malta. I was relieved.

For the second night in a row none of us got any sleep, but thankfully it too passed without incident. In the morning I don't know if it was fear or adrenaline but we were all wide awake and anxious to get off the carrier. In the grey light of day the order was given. One after the other we got airborne and flew east. About an hour later the Maltese islands came into view. From that distance they looked insignificant, lying alone in the blue water of the Mediterranean, but they were crucial. 'Whatever the cost' the wing commander had said before we left Gibraltar, 'the islands must not fall into enemy hands.'

All of us landed safely and with some assistance from the ground crew found a place among the devastation to park. The aircraft were immediately refuelled and at the same time there was a briefing describing the hastily devised plan as to how all of the squadrons now at Malta could provide continuous cover for the approaching convoy. One squadron left, followed by another fifteen minutes later. We would go later in the morning. Until then, a less than personable briefing officer, Sergeant Robert Brown, advised us of the current status of what bore no resemblance to an aerodrome. As he went on to tell us there was enough petrol and food for only a few more days it was clear there was something else on his mind. It wasn't just petrol and food that were close to exhaustion.

And then, until it was our turn to go, we went out into the heat of the day and familiarized ourselves with the aerodrome. As we walked, Findlay commented,

"What was that beggar's problem? By the looks of him you'd think he'd been fighting the Germans by himself. What a grumpy sod."

To me sergeant Brown looked pale, like he was feeling under the weather. In light of what he and the rest of the island inhabitants had endured in recent weeks, and months for that matter, I could understand why, so I didn't say anything to him about his abrupt manner.

"Well he's likely been here a while," I responded. "He's likely fed up with the pounding they've been getting in the last while."

"You would have thought then," Findlay went on. "Now that more help is here he would have been a bit happier looking. Hopefully the rest of the natives will be more friendly."

As we walked about and viewed the devastation for ourselves we realized that all we had heard was true, the aerodrome was a shambles from one end to the other. According to sergeant Brown there were still daily raids.

And then it was time for us to go out and provide cover for the convoy. Just as we were leaving we got the grim news that another two supply ships had been sunk earlier in the day; enemy aircraft had attacked the convoy before our Spitfires got there.

As we flew west to meet the convoy we could see the thick black smoke in the distance. We passed one of our squadrons going back to Malta to refuel and just as we got on station we watched mortified, the flames quickly extinguished as another ship, the source of the smoke, slipped under the water. There was nothing we could do but keep our eyes peeled in case the enemy returned. Because of the damage inflicted on the ships by the aerial attacks, what was left of the convoy was now reduced to a crawl. The tanker bringing petrol to the island had been hit and was now under tow. To keep her upright and afloat she was lashed to two other ships, one on either side. They were a long way from safety yet; at their present speed it would be at least another day before they made port. We could protect them from above but no one knew where the enemy submarines were. More than anything else Malta needed the fuel in the tanker, if it didn't get there the island was finished.

There were no more attacks on the convoy during our stint as escort and with another squadron now on station we set course for Malta. Getting closer to the island we could see smoke rising and as we prepared to land we were informed that there had been another raid. We were low on fuel and needed to land so thankfully we didn't run into any enemy aircraft. As soon as we landed our aircraft were refuelled and we went to debriefing. This time, however, it was a Sergeant Robert Gilmore who quickly took what details we had and advised us that the base commander was having a briefing in a few minutes and gave us directions to an air raid shelter a couple of hundred yards away. Descending the steps into a hole in the ground it opened up into a giant underground chamber. This was the nerve centre of the island defences. Radar, radio communication, planning and decision making was all done here.

The commander, a short, fiery-looking man, began almost immediately. As he introduced himself there was an unmistakable Scottish accent and warmth about him.

"Good afternoon gentlemen," he began. "My name is Group Captain John McLean. First of all, for those of you who have just joined us today, I'd like to welcome you to Malta. It goes without saying that we're glad to see you. Unfortunately I've got some bad news. Just moments ago there was a radio transmission from the convoy. Another ship was hit by torpedoes from a submarine; it sank almost immediately."

For a moment there was a hushed silence in the room. Everybody knew the consequences if the convoy didn't get here. Then, in his quiet Highland accent, the commander continued.

"There's a little bit of good news though. Some of you will have met my briefing officer, Sergeant Brown, when you checked in. I'm happy to say he's going to be alright, but an hour ago he collapsed in his office and had to have an emergency operation for an appendicitis."

Instantly I was transported back in time. Memories of Mum and our family's great loss flooded my mind. There was a need to see my family and home and especially a desperate longing to see Catherine, to hold her and talk to her. Then I felt guilty. We had been so engrossed in this move to Malta, survival uppermost in all our minds, that in the last little while I hadn't given home or Catherine a thought. Before I knew it the briefing was over and I never heard a word. As the commander made his way among us we shook hands and said hello.

"Well now squadron leader, and what part of Scotland is home for you?"

"Perthshire sir, Pitlochry in Perthshire."

"I'm envious, squadron leader, that's a nice place to come from. Why don't you come by my office later and we can have a chat?"

Arranging a time, he left the rest of us together to get better acquainted. There were only a few of us from Scotland, the rest of the pilots were from a number of other countries, Australia, New Zealand, Canada. But there was one thing we all had in common, a longing to see home again. Even if it were only for a few days then we would come back and continue the fight. But we knew that wasn't going to happen. We talked for an hour or so and then I went to keep my appointment with the commander.

"Have a seat squadron leader, make yourself comfortable. Now first things first," he began. "Tell me what was on your mind at the briefing?"

I was a little taken aback that he'd been watching me. Apologizing for my lack of attention, I explained.

"Aye, I can see how that would distract you. I'm sorry about your mother. I can see she meant a great deal to you."

He paused for a moment, looking out of his office window and then he went on.

"It's good to talk to somebody from home. I'm glad that you're here. You know, I was born on the island of Mull. She's just about the same size as Malta, I suppose. My folks had a croft there, just outside Tobermory. When I was ten we left and went to live on the mainland. My father had bought a bigger place, a mile or two from Oban but I can remember those early years on the island, about going to Iona and how peaceful it was there." Again he paused, still looking out of the window. "When this war is over I'm going back to spend time there, away from this devastation and destruction."

He turned and looked at me, then sat at his desk and began to smile.

"When you were in pilot training you had Wing Commander Campbell for an instructor."

"Yes sir," I answered. "You know him?"

"We haven't seen each other for a wee while but aye, I know him well. We trained together. I was at his wedding and I've even held his daughter on my knee."

"You know Catherine?" I asked, staring at him in disbelief.

"Aye, I know her well squadron leader," his smile broadening.

He looked at the clock on the wall and said he would have to go; something else had come up and would have to cut our meeting short.

"Don't worry about the briefing, squadron leader, there's another first thing in the morning. Take care now. I'm glad that you're here."

We parted company and I went to round up my squadron. As I did so, I couldn't help thinking that the commander knew about Catherine and I. It felt strange for a commander to speak so openly about his personal life with a junior officer and a virtual stranger. But then I thought he was just like the rest of us. He missed home and wanted to be back. When we talked he didn't speak to me as a subordinate or a stranger, he spoke to me as a fellow Scotsman who, like him, was far from home.

Locating my clutch we sat and discussed our new posting and collected all the information we could about the island and the small ones around it. Also about the island of Sicily, the enemy stronghold which lay about eighty or so miles to the north. At the same time I reminded them we'd had it pretty easy during our stay in Gibraltar and that this was a different kettle of fish. 'You have to stay alert and focused,' I told them. Findlay raised his hand.

"Respectfully, squadron leader," he said, smiling. "We know."

Looking at my squadron I smiled and nodded. Yes, they did know.

"There's going to be another briefing first thing in the morning to discuss strategy," I told them.

"Respectfully, squadron leader," Findlay grinned. "We know that too. The commander said so at the briefing. You were with us at the briefing but your mind was somewhere else. It wasn't like you. What was wrong?"

"When the commander told us about Sergeant Brown it threw me. It brought back some unpleasant memories. An appendix complication was how my mother died."

They sat looking at me as I again thought of home and a desperate longing to be there. They didn't know what to say.

"But that was a long time ago now and fortunately Sergeant Brown isn't going to suffer the same fate."

"The poor bugger must have been in a lot of pain when we spoke to him earlier," Findlay remarked, looking a little sheepish. "I should learn to keep my big mouth shut."

Just at that moment Sergeant Gilmore interrupted us.

"Just thought you'd like to know sir," he began. "Four ships from the convoy entered Grand Harbour a few minutes ago, that only leaves one. She won't be here until tomorrow."

"But there were six left," I answered.

"Yes sir, but there was an attack by a U-Boat about three hours ago and another freighter was sunk, the remaining freighters that still had some speed and half the escorts made a run for port, the rest of the escorts stayed to protect the tanker."

"The tanker is still afloat sergeant?"

"Yes sir, but only just, she's sitting pretty low in the water. Sir, there's something else, one of the squadrons that is up at the moment is getting low on fuel. If you could be ready to go in fifteen minutes..."

We went immediately to start our aircraft and for the next hour or so until it got dark we patrolled around the island to keep any would be attackers at bay. It had been another eventful day and between one thing and another I was tired, but before I turned in I started a letter to Catherine.

In the morning we went for a short run and also had breakfast before the seven a.m. briefing. Group Captain McLean, true to RAF tradition, started the briefing right on time.

"Good morning gentlemen," he began. "First let me apologize again for the condition you find my aerodrome in but I'm sure you're aware that we are only eighty miles from Sicily. As a result, the enemy have bombed us steadily for quite some time. Quite frankly, we're at a loss to know why they haven't invaded the island but that's behind us now. Now that you're here, Jerry's going to get the message quickly that we will not be giving Malta up."

He went on to say that for the next few days we would play a defensive role around the island, but after that we would be going on the offensive, going to Sicily to beat on the enemy's door. 'I expect to be in Italy within the year' were his words. At that there was a thunderous cheer, just as the commotion died down the commander was handed a memo. He read it and then for a few moments he looked at us, you could have heard a pin drop. Speaking slowly and with the detection of a new assertiveness and determination he told us what was on the memo.

"Gentlemen, you have no idea how much pleasure it gives me to be able to tell you that the tanker bringing our desperately needed fuel has just been towed into Grand Harbour."

The room erupted. 'Operation Pedestal' had succeeded. How hopeless their plight had looked, how dangerously close Malta had come to being invaded, but now she could go on and continue to fight. We all left the briefing jubilant and with renewed optimism, but at the same time we were acutely aware that of the fourteen merchant ships to leave Gibraltar, only five had made it all the way to Malta.

Until now we had always been on the defensive. To be going on the offensive was a new thing for the majority of the pilots on Malta. There was something else none of us had seen before, and that was particularly awe inspiring, the congregating of more than two hundred fighter aircraft, over half were Spitfires. The Luftwaffe was in for a shock. As well there were reports that a few American heavy bombers, B17s and Liberators, had flown into allied bases in North Africa. We didn't know why they were there but the fact that they were lifted everybody's spirits higher still.

Over the next eight weeks or so, a pattern emerged. The daylight raids on Malta virtually ceased but it was a sure bet there would be activity of some kind at night. Sometimes there was damage, other times nothing at all. During that time we flew patrols, helping to protect torpedo planes attacking enemy merchant ships being used to supply the German army in North Africa. Thankfully, even with our increased exposure to the risks of war, my squadron so far was unscathed.

Also during that time, Sergeant Brown was fully recovered and back at work. I'd got to know him better and thankfully he was nothing like his first impression. As well, I'd had the opportunity on a number of occasions to speak with Group Captain McLean. I liked him and looked forward to our chats. He was easy to talk to and I found him to be a lot like Catherine's dad. It turns out they had been two of only a handful of Scottish trainees to become pilots and officers in the RAF between the First and Second World Wars. Although he was my superior officer I never felt intimidated by him. Whether it was because we came from the same place and both had farming backgrounds, I don't know, but I admired him; we all did. A symbol of true courage and determination, he was respected. He was a warrior. Most would have succumbed to the enormous pressure he found himself under as Malta teetered. I'm sure there were times he felt their stand was futile. But if he had flinched there never had been any evidence of it. It was because of him and people like him that the island had held on under the constant bombardment, overwhelming odds and constant threat of invasion. We talked about it often and couldn't understand why the enemy didn't just storm the island and be done with it.

On one of the times we got together I showed him a picture of Catherine and I together in the house at home.

"My, she's a fine looking woman," he began. "It's a while since I've seen her but I would know her anywhere. She's the spitting image of her mother, you know." For a few moments he admired Catherine and then he continued. "When her mother died, a part of Catherine died with her. She was a sad wee lassie for a long time and wouldn't let her Dad out of her sight. But somehow she managed to let her Mum go and the next thing we knew she was finished school and away training to be a teacher. It seemed like no time at all she was finished her training and right away she had a teaching job up in Pitlochry where she met you."

As he said it, he was watching my reaction. "You know about that?"

"It's my job to know about the pilots under my command," he went on. "But I know a lot more about you. I know that you're likely the youngest squadron leader in the RAF. That the woman in this picture thinks about you night and day, and because of that her father asked you to look after her if anything happened to him. Wing Commander Campbell also told me that Catherine and your stepmother have become really close friends. He told me also about being invited into your home and the good times he's had there. I can tell you he appreciated that and everything else you and your family have meant to his."

As he spoke affectionately of Catherine and a family he didn't know, I could feel a lump in my throat and then, as he always did at some point when we talked, he revealed just a little bit more about himself and what his plans were after the war. Ordinarily one's commanding officer would have kept themselves at arm's length but these were no ordinary times. These were times of great hardship when everyone's patience and endurance were tested. Times when, if one shared a dream or aspiration with someone, it somehow carried you on and gave you the strength to keep going. The commander wasn't as revealing with everybody, I know, although he was my superior officer and a generation older, we did get along well, but it was because of Catherine that we'd become friends.

"James," he went on. "I'll let you into a wee secret. I've made myself a to-do list. It's a list of things I want to do after the war. It gets longer by the day," he laughed. "So long, in fact, I don't think I'll get half of them done. But when Catherine's Dad was here and he was telling me again about Pitlochry and how much he likes it there, I decided I wanted to go back and see the place again. Maybe at the same time I'll get the opportunity to meet your family."

"I know they'd like to meet you sir. And as for Pitlochry... after the war there's no other place I want to be."

"Well it could be a while yet before any of us are home, but keep your chin up. We will win this war. Good will triumph over evil."

Even though we were a lot busier than we'd been in Gibraltar, I still found time to take some pictures of the places we'd been and, as often as we could, we went swimming in the Mediterranean. The warm, crystal-clear water was the perfect place to unwind. We discovered, however, that although we always had enough to eat, the civilian population of the islands were being subjected to serious food rationing and hunger. We all felt genuinely sorry for them, but the only thing we could do to help them was to keep on doing what we were doing and try to end their suffering as quickly as possible.

Then the daylight raids started again. For two weeks the enemy were relentless and in that time we lost thirty aircraft, three of those being from my squadron. Thankfully pilot officers Simpson, Grey and Smith all survived. Unfortunately three pilots from other squadrons weren't so lucky. Enemy aircraft shot down in the same period totalled more than a hundred, with the crews either killed or captured.

We were now at the end of October 1942 and the air raids on the island all but stopped. We didn't know it at the time but those two weeks were the last major offensive against the island.

As the weeks passed and Christmas got closer we knew that this was one we wouldn't be home for. But what we did have between Christmas and New Year was a concert. Only a few people knew about it until a day or two before, then at a briefing one morning, the commander laid all of the speculation to rest.

"We're not going to be home for Christmas and New Year," he said. "So we've arranged to have a little bit of home brought here." Everybody had been down in the dumps but after the announcement our spirits lifted and we couldn't wait until the night. On the morning of December 27th three DC3s landed and for the rest of the day, in one of the few buildings left standing on the aerodrome their occupants prepared to entertain us. Anybody who could be in the building that night was there. There was something for everyone, but there were two things that I enjoyed more than the rest. I'd heard Vera Lynn on the wireless and I liked her music but I'd never seen her in person before. As she sang of 'The White Cliffs of Dover' and 'A Nightingale Sang in Berkley Square', it was she who was the nightingale. To finish off the lights were dimmed and two pipers marched in to the sound of their own music. What or how long they played I don't know. I just remember the lump in my throat and a hundred images of Scotland and home flashed through my mind as the music filled the night air.

All too soon it was over. We could have listened and laughed twice as long. In the morning the aircraft left with their occupants, going somewhere else to boost morale. As the drone of their engines grew quiet and the planes disappeared there was an emptiness, a void. There was nothing else to do but get on with the war.

There was one thing that was sure to lift spirits and that was mail from home. As we checked in with our briefing officer, asking him if we were scheduled to fly, he pointed to the bag on his desk.

"It's either Santa Claus or the postman who's come sergeant, which is it?"

"Well I'm quite sure it's the latter sir," he answered, smiling. "But I think getting a letter from home is as good as any present."

As Sergeant Brown distributed the bag's contents my euphoria was short-lived. I didn't get one letter. To say I was disappointed did not describe how I felt at that moment.

"There's nothing for you squadron leader but we're expecting another aircraft in a day or two," he remarked, seeing the disappointment on my face. "I'm sure there will be something on that one."

Since getting to Malta I saw and worked with Sergeant Brown almost every day but I really didn't know him, so I took the opportunity to get to know him a little better.

"Are you fully recovered from you're operation?" I asked.

"Yes sir I am. Thank you for asking. It all happened really quickly, you know, I don't think I'll ever forget that day. In the morning I felt fine, lunchtime I felt terrible and by the middle of the afternoon I'd such a pain in my gut I couldn't begin to describe to you what it felt like. It was so bad I flaked out. The next thing I remember was waking up in the hospital hours later with the doctor telling me I'd had an operation to remove my appendix. Apart from a bit of discomfort from the operation I felt a whole lot better. I told the doctor I didn't care what it was, anything that hurt that bad I didn't need."

"Well I can remember when we checked in you looked pale, then later on when the commander told us about your operation I was a bit stunned, to say the least."

He went on to tell me that he came from North Yorkshire. There were rolling hills and dales there, big trees and dykes. But best of all there was peace and quiet. I knew by the tone in his voice that he was, like the rest of us, passionate about his home and longed to be back.

"If you don't mind me asking sir, why would my condition that day affect you so much?"

Deciding I'd go back to our quarters, I got up and made my way to the door, but before I left I told him.

"A few years ago my mother died of an appendix complication. It's a day I know I'll never forget. Keep looking for a letter for me sergeant," I said smiling, then I opened the door and left him.

Although it was the last day or so in December it was quite warm and the aerodrome was the quietest I'd ever seen it, hardly a soul in sight. As expected, the squadron were reading their coveted letters. Findlay was beaming from ear to ear.

"Look," he said. "A letter from your sister."

"One of these days I'll have to tell Isobel what you're really like."

"Save your breath, she won't believe you anyway. I'm not going to let you read it but I'll tell you a wee bit of what she's saying. She's finished her training and is working in a hospital in Edinburgh, going home for Christmas. She's asking after you, and oh aye, the best bit. She's been thinking a lot about me."

"That's great Findlay," I answered, feeling sorry for myself. "I'm glad you're happy."

"You didn't get any mail, did you?"

"No, and I'll bet you a pound I'm the only person on this aerodrome that didn't."

"Well you know that happens sometimes," he replied, in a somewhat consoling tone. "There will be another plane in a day or two. You'll get a stack of mail then and we'll get none."

Sitting beside him for a few minutes, I couldn't settle, so I went to check on our aircraft. Just because it was the festive season the war didn't stop. We were scheduled to go out in an hour to escort some torpedo planes. There had been reports from a Catalina flying boat about an enemy convoy steaming between Italy and North Africa and we were going to give them some grief.

The time came and we took off, heading east on a course to intercept them. It was a nice day for flying, not many clouds, good visibility and with the cooler air at this time of year our aircraft were performing a lot better. About fifty miles out we spotted the convoy and immediately the torpedo planes set themselves up for their attack. It had been decided that half our squadron would attack with them and the rest would stay aloft to keep a lookout for enemy fighters. Instructing William in red two and three other aircraft to stay aloft, Findlay and I, along with two other Spitfires, would attack the escorting ships in an effort to draw fire away from the torpedo planes.

The attacking aircraft broke formation and descended. As we got closer I could see the flashing of the anti-aircraft guns on the ships. They knew we were coming, all right. We returned fire and I could see my ammunition make contact with its target. I looked at the other aircraft just as their torpedoes went into the water. All five ships were attacked at the same time. Maybe we'd get lucky and hit all five. As we broke off the attack and pulled up to go over the top of the ships, the anti-aircraft was still firing at us. There was a dull thud and a burning searing pain in my side as enemy fire hit my aircraft. Pieces of the fuselage came flying off at the same time and a few seconds later the engine spluttered and lost power. Climbing as much as I could while my aircraft still had momentum I managed to get to three thousand feet. The engine, coughing and spluttering, was producing just enough power to keep me airborne. There was no doubt I'd been hit and I could feel my backside getting wet with what could only be blood. Looking around I couldn't see any of my squadron.

"Red Two, Red Two, where are you?" I shouted into my radio.

"Right beside you Red Leader," he came back immediately. "Are you alright? You're trailing smoke."

"Just point me in the right direction for home Red Two. Let's see how close I can get."

"You're good Red Leader, stay on that heading."

"Where's the rest of Red Wing and the torpedo planes? I can't see any of them."

"They're fine Red Leader, we're all right behind you. I'm going to call ahead to see if there's a seaplane in the area, just in case you have to ditch."

Concerned more with the pain in my side and my engine's every sound, I didn't answer. It didn't seem to be getting any worse so I decide I'd stay with it. Limping slowly home I could hear the other pilots chattering on the radio, but feeling a bit light headed and queasy I wasn't listening. For a few moments I wasn't sure where I was, I could have sworn I heard Mum's voice.

"Come on James, you can do this, listen to William, listen to William."

"Red Leader, Red Leader, come on now, you're drifting off course."

With this voice shouting at me I was jolted back to reality.

"William, is that you?"

"Yes it's me, look out of your starboard side, I'm right here. Stay with me James, we're almost home."

There was more chatter on the radio but all I wanted to do now was sleep.

"Red Leader this is Red Two." I heard my call sign but I couldn't really be bothered answering. Again he shouted at me.

"Red Leader, Red Leader, we have to land. Come on now, this is William, you have to listen to me."

Somewhere I'd heard that before. 'Listen to William.'

"This is Red Leader, go ahead Two."

"Sir you have to lower your undercarriage and put some flap on, we're going to land in a couple of minutes."

For some reason I felt a bit better and was more aware of my predicament. The flaps lowered but the undercarriage was a different story. It wouldn't budge. Again William's voice filled my headset.

"Flaps are good Red Leader, but you have to lower your undercarriage."

"Won't go Two, it's stuck."

For a few moments the radio was silent and then I heard him instructing the squadron to land. Then I heard my call sign again.

"Red Leader this is William, I'm going to get you down now. It's going to be a belly landing but you'll be fine."

"William, I can't see a thing out my windscreen."

"It doesn't matter, I'll get you down," he answered, in a slow, calming but assertive voice. "Make a slow turn to the left till I get you lined up with the runway. You don't have to answer me, just do what I tell you and we'll be down before you know it."

Entering a slow turn to port we seemed to be in it for ages.

"You're looking good Red Leader, bring her back level now, the runway's dead ahead. Ease back on the throttle and reduce your air speed."

Easing back on the throttle I could feel the plane slow and start to sink.

"You're looking good Red Leader, runway dead ahead, ease back on the throttle a little more."

Again the plane sank and as I looked to the side I could see I was almost down.

"You're over the threshold and a hundred feet till touchdown, pull the throttle all the way back now and switch off your ignition. Fifty feet to go now, ease back on the stick just a little..."

The engine stopped and all I could hear was the whooshing of the air around my plane.

"Almost home Red Leader, twenty feet till you touch. Ten feet..."

The tail wheel touched and then we were down on the belly. The noise of the scraping and grinding as the plane slid along the runway was deafening and seemed to go on forever. All I could do was wait till it stopped. As soon as it did someone jumped on the wing and slid my canopy back, helping me out of the cockpit.

The last thing I remember was seeing an ambulance and a fire engine beside my plane and wondering why they were there, then a Spitfire screamed over us, doing a victory roll.

12.   The Road to Recovery

When I eventually woke up in the sick bay I'd lost three days of my life but even then I only stayed awake long enough to have something to eat then promptly fell asleep again. When I woke the next time it was when a nurse was straightening my bed.

"Well, sleeping beauty awakes," she said. "How do you feel?"

"To be honest, I'm starving."

"We're just about to have supper, could you eat that much?"

I told her I could and she left, saying she'd be back in a few minutes. She seemed to be away for ages but finally the tray arrived, carried by Group Captain McLean himself.

"How are you feeling squadron leader?"

"Feeling quite tired sir, and hungry."

"Aye, I'm sure you are and here I am holding on to the tray. Here you go. You eat and I'll talk. Your patrol did a fine job the other day. Four of the five ships you went after sank. The other sat dead in the water till we sent another patrol out and finished her off too. By the way, would you like a visitor?"

With my mouth full of food, I could only nod. He motioned to someone at the door but I was so intent in satisfying my hunger I didn't see who it was until he was standing right by the bed.

I was absolutely dumbstruck. It was Catherine's father.

"What's wrong?" he asked. "Cat got your tongue?"

"What are you doing here? How did you get here?"

"We're here to take some pictures in the area," he answered. "So we'll be around for a week or so. You eat and get some rest, we can talk again tomorrow."

They both turned and left, but Catherine's dad came back in, carrying a parcel.

"Almost forgot. I know it's late but this is your Christmas mail," he said, shaking my hand. "Merry Christmas. I'm so glad you're going to be all right."

By the time I'd finished eating I again felt the overwhelming need to sleep. When I awoke there was a dim light on in my room and although the blinds were drawn I could see it was dark outside. Just then the nurse looked round the door.

"Well, you're awake. What else are you good at besides sleeping?"

"Are there no other nurses work here besides you, I've never seen anyone else," I asked.

"Well if you didn't sleep all the time you would. I've been off shift and back on again. You've been sleeping for more than twelve hours."

Maybe it was her uniform, but she was attractive, not unlike Catherine and about the same size. The biggest difference was her English accent and she certainly talked a lot more. Taking the chart off the end of the bed she looked at it.

"You know, it doesn't say anything on here about you being Royalty."

"Royalty?" I blurted. "What makes you say that?"

"Well, your squadron's been here I don't know how many times to see you. Group Captain McLean just about as often and then there's another officer who flew in the other day in one of those blue coloured planes, he's been out and in all the time as well. He even brought your mail. I'd say you were royalty of some kind."

"I'm nobody important," I laughed. "What's your name anyway?"

"I'm nurse Mills, I'm from London." Just at that moment another nurse appeared. "And this is nurse McIntosh, she's got the same accent as you, so you'll be able to reminisce."

Standing beside my bed, this new nurse took my hand and checked my pulse.

"So, are you going to stay awake today?" she asked, smiling.

Her voice sounded like her skin looked, soft and mellow but with a defined Aberdonian accent. Her eyes were the colour of the Mediterranean and she had long black hair tied back in a ponytail. She was very attractive. She knew I was looking at her but she just smiled and asked me again.

"Well... are you going to stay awake?"

"Hopefully. What day is it anyway?"

"It's New Year's Eve. You came in here four days ago and so far you've been a model patient. It'll be daylight in a little while. I'll change your dressing and get you freshened up. Maybe then we can have breakfast. How does that sound?"

"It sounds great, I'm starving."

Rolling over on the bed she removed the bandage and cleaned my wound.

"Mmm," she said. "You had a nasty cut here but it's healing nicely. You could get up after breakfast and stretch your legs if you like."

"That's sounds nearly as good as breakfast, my back is aching lying here, I need a walk."

She finished the dressing then rolled up the blinds on the windows.

"Right, I'll be back in a bit then," she said, disappearing out of the door.

Lying there in the quiet, I looked out of the window and watched the sun peep over the horizon, gradually becoming a blazing ball of orange and red. My mind was quickly flitting from one thing to the other and then silence was broken as she came back with my breakfast.

"Do you need help?" she asked, laying the tray on the bed.

"No, I can manage. But why don't you stay for a bit and tell me where you're from."

"I'm from Banchory," she answered, sitting at the end of the bed. "Have you been there?"

With my mouth full of food I could only shake my head.

"It's just to the west of Aberdeen, not that far from Balmoral, actually. I love it there and can't wait to get back. There are nice green fields but the hills are right there so there's a ruggedness to it too. The only thing I don't like is that it can get cold in winter. But you know, in all the years growing up there I never knew what we had until I was posted overseas to places like Malta. Each to his own I suppose."

As she spoke affectionately of home she was no different than the rest of us. She missed it and longed to be back. And then her tone and expression changed.

"In a few days it'll be a year since Mary and I came here. It hasn't been as bad lately, but earlier on in the year, with all the bombing and everything, this place was just hell on earth. The devastation and the suffering, not just on the aerodrome, it's terrible. Civilians on the island are starving and nobody except the military has any petrol. Bloody Germans, who do they think they are anyway?"

I stared at her and she wondered what was wrong.

"It's just that you said exactly what Catherine said."

"Who's Catherine? Is she you're sister, girlfriend, what?"

"Girlfriend... no, she's more than that."

As I finished my breakfast she took my tray, saying she'd find something for me to wear so I could get up. Again I lay in the silence. Banchory wasn't all that far from Pitlochry, I thought. She had grown up in the same countryside as I had.

"Here you go," she said, reappearing. "You should be able to find something in this bundle that'll fit you."

No sooner had I got dressed than the commander and Catherine's Dad walked in.

"Well, you certainly look better today. How do you feel?" he asked.

"I'm feeling a lot better sir. I thought I'd go out for a breath of fresh air though."

"That sounds like a good idea. You two have a wander and I'll see you later."

"You haven't opened your mail yet," Catherine's Dad remarked, looking at the unopened parcel.

"I would like to open it, I just haven't been able to keep my eyes open long enough yet. Have you got time for a walk?"

"Today, as it happens, I've got all day."

Just as we were about to step outside, nurse McIntosh advised me that I shouldn't be long. Assuring her that I wouldn't be, we stepped out into the morning sunshine. It was quiet. With a clear blue sky and no wind it was a nice morning for flying. Standing by the door for a minute, I took a couple of deep breaths and then we sauntered on. I asked him what he'd been doing since we last spoke.

"This last year has been busier than ever. There's a new squadron been formed with new, faster aircraft to keep up with the workload. I've still got my Spitfire but the other aircraft that came with me is a Mosquito. It's very fast, there's nothing can catch it. I'll introduce you to the pilot, he'll take you up, I'm sure."

"I've heard about the Mosquito, I wouldn't mind going up in her."

Making our way back to the sickbay, he told me he'd been to Pitlochry just before Christmas.

"That's why you didn't get any mail in the post. I knew I was coming here so I said I'd deliver it."

"Did Group Captain McLean know you were coming?"

He just smiled. 'The sly old fox,' I thought. He's someone else who likes to spring surprises. Then I asked how Catherine was.

"She's the picture of health but as usual she's missing you. When she knew I would be seeing you she jokingly asked if she could come. She's a bit fed up with the post though, sometimes three weeks will go past and she doesn't get any letters, then she'll get four all at once."

"Did you go to the farm while you were there?"

"Of course, no visit to Pitlochry would be complete without going there. They're all fine and send you their love. Bella sent you mail, it's all in the parcel."

By the time we got back to the hospital I'd been out for about half an hour. As I opened the door and went in nurse McIntosh was waiting.

"You've been out far too long," she said, waving her finger. "Come on back to your room and I'll get you some tea."

Sitting on the bed as we waited on her bringing the tea, Catherine's dad said that my squadron had been to see me a few times.

"Maybe if they come in after lunchtime, you'll have had a snooze by then."

"Thanks, I could do with another forty winks to be honest."

Nurse McIntosh brought our tea and we chatted a bit more.

"By the way," he went on. "You'll have to thank William for getting you home. He did a first class job." Looking at me, he paused for a moment.

"He most likely saved your life. We lost aircraft and we had aircraft damaged, but because of his efforts everybody came home."

"We lost aircraft? I had no idea."

"You don't have anything to feel bad about. The attack on the ships was a success and everyone came home. Convoys aren't just going to let you attack them without firing back, you know. Sometimes there are casualties and damage. From the planning, execution and success of the attack, and yes, even your crash landing back here was handled with professionalism, so I don't want to hear any more about it."

In all the years I'd known Catherine's father I'd never heard him so vocal about anything. He reminded me of Dad. He finished his tea and then got up to leave.

"You have some rest and I'll see you later."

Before he left he said that Findlay had lost his aircraft. On the way back his engine stopped so he had no alternative but to bale out. William didn't think you were going to make it back and had called ahead for a PBY. You made it but Findlay didn't. Just as he baled out the seaplane arrived, so he was in the water for only a few minutes. He doesn't know how or when it happened but he's got a broken arm and a shiner of a black eye. But like I said, as far as your commanding officer and I are concerned the mission was a success."

With that he gave me a smile and left. Immediately thereafter nurse McIntosh came in.

"Right," she said. "Get those clothes off and back into bed."

"Well, if you give me some privacy I'll do that."

"Huh! You want privacy? Who do you think undressed you when they brought you in here in a pile? Me," she said, giggling. "You've got two minutes to be in there."

Leaving me to get undressed it was no more than two minutes before she was back. As I lay down she tucked the bed covers in.

"Could I open some of my Christmas mail please," I asked, as she was about to leave again. "You could help me if you've got a minute."

She looked at me and then smiled. "Alright, just for a minute."

Laying the box on the side of the bed she unwrapped it and began to remove the contents. There were letters on top then underneath there was a thin rectangular cardboard box. Handing it to me I opened the flap on the end and slid out the contents. Instantly my eyes filled as they gazed on a recent picture of Catherine. Nurse McIntosh wondered what was wrong. Unable to speak I turned the picture around so she could see it.

"So this is the lucky girl."

As we looked at each other I could only manage a feeble nod.

"Listen," she went on. "Why don't I put these letters back in the box and we can open them later."

Again I nodded and she left me. Looking at the woman in the picture smiling at me I missed her more than words could say. Slipping back under the bed covers I lay thinking about the things we'd done together, dreaming about the things we would do together and every minute or so looked at the picture to see if by some miracle she had come to life. The next thing I knew it was lunchtime, I'd fallen asleep yet again. Just as I was trying to wriggle out of what resembled a straightjacket nurse McIntosh came in, carrying a tray.

"Did you have a nice snooze?" she asked.

"Why am I so tired? I'm always falling asleep."

"You lost a lot of blood, that's what's doing it. But you're fine and healthy. If you eat and drink plenty you'll be as right as rain in no time. By the way, I put the love of your life up here beside your bed, where you can see each other. She is very attractive."

"She is, but that's not the only reason I think the world of her."

"Do you know what I'd like. I'd like to find someone I could have a relationship with like you two obviously have."

"Nurse McIntosh, I think you're pulling my leg. I'm quite sure you have a long list of eligible young men on a string."

"Not a one," she sighed. "Would you like to know what I think? I think the loss of blood has affected your eyesight. Now eat your lunch and I'll come back in a bit for the tray."

No sooner had I finished eating when my 'clutch' came for a visit and as usual, even although he was looking the worse for wear, Findlay was the first to speak.

"Well now, Rip Van Winkle is actually awake. Do you know how many times we've been to see you?"

We talked about the attack on the ships and they brought me up to date with what they'd been doing since. Then they told me they were having a bit of a get together to see the New Year in and wondered if I felt up to it.

"It'll depend if my nurse will let me out," I answered.

"Bring her," said Findlay. "If that's what it takes to get you there, then bring her."

"Let me have a bit more sleep then and I'll be there."

With that, everyone except William left. I asked him to stay for a minute. We looked at each other and smiled. I could feel a lump wanting to plug my throat but somehow I managed to say what I needed to.

"Thanks for getting me home, you saved my life."

"You would have done the same thing for me. We're going to see this war through together. I wasn't about to let you go that easily."

"Thanks," I said again extending my hand, "I owe you."

As he turned to leave he had only taken two steps when I asked him if he had heard from Alison at Christmas. He stopped dead in his tracks. Why I asked him I don't know. I hadn't heard him speak of her for a while. He turned around and looked at me with a particularly sad expression.

"Alison and I haven't been corresponding since August."

"You haven't? I didn't know. What happened?"

"Apparently, about a month after we left Edinburgh she went dancing again to Roxies. She met some navy man, in port for a few days and looking for a good time. Alison gave it to him and now she's pregnant."

"Oh man, William, I'm sorry. I know you liked her. Why didn't you say something?"

"Nothing to say really. When she wrote and told me I couldn't believe it. I really didn't want to talk about it anyway. It's over."

"You'll meet somebody else. When one door closes another one opens, eh."

"Maybe, but I don't think I'm likely to be finding a girlfriend here now, am I?" he said, as he turned to leave. "I'll see you tonight at the party."

After he left me I thought about how much he cared for Alison and about how much she seemed to care for him. I could see her still, standing on the apron at Turnhouse hanging onto Group Captain McKenzie's arm, distraught at William's imminent departure. I couldn't believe she intentionally meant to hurt him.

No sooner had William left than nurse McIntosh came back for my lunch tray. Now was as good a time as any to tell her about the party later on and ask if she'd like to go.

"Squadron leader, first of all you're in no fit state to go to a party, and second, your girlfriend is right there watching you," she said, pointing to the picture, "and you're asking me to go out with you. I don't think so."

"Well, I am asking you to go to look after me, but that's not the only reason. There's someone I'd like you to meet, you could say it was a blind date."

"The answer's still no, it will be too much for you. And besides, I've never been on a blind date before."

"Ah come on, please. I'd really like to go and have a bit of fun and I know you'd like William. He saved my life, you know. Didn't you see him? He just left."

"Just a side view," she replied, hovering and clutching the tray. "Did he really save your life?"

"He did indeed. If it hadn't been for him I wouldn't be here."

"You get some rest and I'll think about going to your Hogmanay party."

Reminding her that I'd slept most of the morning and I didn't feel tired I suggested that if she had a few minutes she could help me dig a bit deeper in my Christmas parcel. She quickly agreed. Secretly I think she was just as eager as I to see what was in the parcel still. Handing me the box, she sat on the bed and watched as I dug deeper into it, finding a small bottle of Catherine's favourite perfume with a note attached. 'This is one of the smells of home,' it read. Opening the bottle I sniffed the contents and closed my eyes. For a second Catherine was right there, and then, just like before I exposed my soft sentimental underbelly to nurse McIntosh.

"What is it this time," she asked.

Handing her the bottle I told her it was the perfume that Catherine wore.

"Mm, that's nice," she said, breathing deeply. "It's like fresh flowers. She is one romantic lady," she continued, looking at Catherine's picture. "I'll have to talk to her. Maybe she can tell me where I'm going wrong with men."

Opening an envelope from inside the box there were a handful of pictures and another note. 'And these are some of the sights of home.'

Showing them to nurse McIntosh, I explained their significance. Catherine leaning on the wall outside our tearoom in Pitlochry, another of her sitting on the big stone by the river. There was yet another of her sitting beside Bella on the garden seat at the farm, giggling about something. Keeping me company as I thumbed through the memories, she looked at me like Catherine often did, flitting from one eye to the other.

"Do you know how lucky the two of you are?" she smiled. "There are people who spend their entire life looking for what you two have and never find it. Hang on to it, it's precious. "Hopefully one day I'll be as fortunate."

"You'll find your white knight, I know," I told her.

"Never happen," she answered, getting up off the bed. "And look at the time. I've sat here for an hour. You get some rest, I'll see you later."

Still not feeling tired I decided to read one of my letters and picked one at random out of the bundle. It was from Isobel. I was surprised as she'd never written to me before but then I'd never written to her either. She had finished her training and was now a fully-fledged nurse. I could tell she was happy about that. Now she could work in a field hospital and she was thinking about joining the army or the air force. Findlay had written to her a few times during the year. She liked him but didn't really know him. 'Catherine and you are like peas in a pod,' she said. 'A perfect fit.' She just didn't know if Findlay and she would ever be like that. She wasn't seeing anyone else though. By the time I finished reading I was tired so I slid down the bed and closed my eyes.

When I awoke the blinds were drawn and a dim light was on, obviously it was night and over the chair beside my bed my tunic hung, freshly pressed. Whoever did it had done it before. Even my shoes were shining. Just as I thought I was the only one in the building, nurse Mills walked into my room, wondering if I'd had a good day. Telling her I had, I asked her if I'd missed the party.

"No, you haven't missed it," she smiled. "It's supper time though, if you're ready for it."

She went on to tell me that nurse McIntosh was changing and getting ready to go to the party, and, because I was the only one in the hospital at the moment, nurse Mills had got permission to go as well. After eating, I got dressed and had just finished when nurse McIntosh came in. She looked great and completely different in her RAF uniform.

We chatted and kept each other company until nurse Mills changed. I asked her how my tunic came to be there.

"I called your briefing officer, he brought it over and then I gave it a quick press."

"You didn't need to do that."

Thanking her, I asked if she'd given any more thought to the blind date. Giving me a mischievous smile I could see that she had. The trouble with this date was that William didn't know anything about it yet. Reaching for the perfume that Catherine had sent I suggested she try it.

"No, I'm not wearing it. You're girlfriend sent it to you to remind you of her."

"She did, but I know she wouldn't mind if you used it. Besides, you'll be doing me a favour, it'll smell a lot better on you than it does just sniffing the bottle."

"Do you think it will have him spellbound?" she asked.

"Guaranteed... I know I was."

Confessing she'd run out of her own perfume months ago she agreed to try Catherine's. Just then nurse Mills came back. She too looked completely different.

"Mm, what is that smell? It's like flowers."

Nurse McIntosh and I looked at each other and smiled but didn't make her any the wiser.

"Are we ready to go to a party?" I asked them.

And so, with a girl on each arm we made our way to the building where the get-together was to be. Getting inside, Findlay was the first person we met.

"Well I don't believe it. The two best looking girls on the aerodrome and you come with both of them!"

With a welcome like that, my two escorts were giggling and enjoying things already. With the recent concert still quite vivid in everybody's mind, one of Vera Lynn's records was playing on the gramophone. At a table off to the side, Group Captain McLean and Catherine's dad were sitting with another pilot I hadn't seen before. Before I talked to them I introduced my nurses to the rest of the squadron and managed to get William and nurse McIntosh sitting together. When it looked like they'd relaxed a bit I went to speak with Catherine's dad and the commander.

They introduced me to the other pilot. Quite a stocky individual, with piercing blue eyes and wavy black hair, he had a handlebar moustache and must have been all of six feet tall.

"Squadron Leader Somerville, this is Squadron Leader Baxter; he flies the Mosquito."

"You had a lucky escape the other day squadron leader," he said, still shaking my hand with a vice-like grip. "We watched you land."

"It would seem that way, but frankly I don't remember much about it."

I sat beside them and we talked for a while. First of all they pulled my leg about coming to the party with two girls but then I got to ask Squadron Leader Baxter about his aircraft.

"She's fantastic," he answered, his eyes lighting up with enthusiasm. "There isn't a plane built that can catch me. Except maybe another Mosquito," he bellowed. "I'll take you up if you like. I need to do a check on one of the engines anyway, one of the magnetos, you know," he laughed again and winked. "It's not quite right."

We knew what he meant. Any excuse to go flying and show off his plane.

With that, I excused myself and went to get hold of Findlay, telling him what I was trying to do.

"You're trying to set William up with your nurse," he laughed. "Can't see it happening. Besides, he's got a girl back in Edinburgh and really he's more scared of women than he is of Germans."

"I know you're like that when Isobel's around, but I don't think William's that way."

"All right,' he conceded. "Maybe I am a bit. What do you want me to do?"

"Just go and find a nice record and put it on the gramophone and I'll go and ask nurse McIntosh to dance. Once we've been up for a minute you come and cut in."

Dancing slowly around the floor I watched William watch us and at the same time I asked her what she thought of him.

"Well so far so good. He is a bit quiet but I like him."

Just at that moment Findlay cut in so I didn't get the chance to ask her anything else. Sitting beside William I tried to start a conversation with him but it was quite useless, his attention was on Findlay and Nurse McIntosh.

"Why don't you go and cut in on Findlay?" I suggested.

No sooner had I said it than he was gone.

Making my way back over, I sat beside Catherine's Dad.

"You may have come with these two girls," the commander laughed. "But they're not going home with you."

"That was the plan sir."

We talked a little about the war and I asked them how they felt it was going. They agreed that hanging on to Malta was a significant step in the right direction. They felt that allied forces would be in Italy by the end of the incoming year. And then the New Year was upon us. Standing together looking at the clock on the wall we watched 1942 slip into history and as we wished each other a happy New Year and sang 'Auld Lang Syne' I wondered what the new year would hold. Watching William and nurse McIntosh I smiled. For the first few seconds of the year, at least, they held each other. I asked her if I would have to find my own way back to sickbay.

She smiled and let go of William's arm, saying that she would take me. This had been the longest spell I'd been awake in days but now I was tired and had trouble keeping my eyes open.

"Come on," she said, taking my arm. "You need to get back into bed."

It was just as well I hadn't walked on my own. By the time I got there I felt drained.

It was mid-morning the next day when I woke and nurse McIntosh was back on duty. When she discovered I was awake she brought me a late breakfast. Sitting on the end of the bed she talked as I tried to satisfy my seemingly insatiable appetite and thirst.

"Thanks," she said, smiling. "Thanks for introducing me to William. I had a good time last night."

"So the perfume worked for you too then," I answered between mouthfuls.

"It seems to have... for the time being at least."

Talking for a while longer, she wanted to know more about William. Then she took my tray, giving me my Christmas parcel, saying I still had letters to read.

The next one I read was one from John. He hadn't written to me before either. It was short and to the point but I was glad to get it just the same. He was still at Turnhouse but was thinking about applying for a transfer. He told me to keep up the good work and that it had been all over the news about how effective the RAF had been against the enemy recently. Catherine's father would have told Catherine and my family where I was but it was against regulations for me to write and tell them. It was a positive note on which to start the day. Feeling a lot better, I needed to get out for some air and wanted to find out if the mechanics had fixed my aircraft.

Promising nurse McIntosh I wouldn't be long, she let me go. First speaking with the briefing officer, I asked him if my plane had been fixed but he didn't know anything about it. He suggested I speak with the mechanics directly. On my way over there I met Group Captain McLean and told him I was going to check on my aircraft.

"Squadron leader, your aircraft won't fly again. It's in the scrap pile."

"Scrap pile sir? I know it was damaged but it got me home."

"Squadron leader,' he went on. "I don't think you fully appreciate just how fortunate you were the other day. You must have a guardian angel watching over you. Everyone is amazed you made it back. Your aircraft has bullet holes in it from end to end and how your engine kept running is a mystery. There were only a few cupfuls of oil left in it. If that wasn't enough, it's just as well you didn't bail out because whatever it was that cut your back also damaged your parachute. If you'd tried using it, it would never have opened."

As I tried to comprehend what he'd just told me he suggested I go and see the aircraft for myself.

Making my way to the 'scrap pile,' I met William and Findlay on the way.

"You're going to see your plane," said Findlay. "We'll come with you for a walk, but there's not much to see, I can tell you that."

He was right. There were chunks of fuselage missing and holes in it from end to end. The propeller was bent and it was lying on its belly. It was a sorry looking sight. Looking into the cockpit, it was blood-stained and it was quite impossible to see out of the oil-smeared windscreen. Sitting beside Findlay and William on the wing it was beginning to sink in just how lucky I'd been. If it hadn't been for William I wouldn't have survived.

"Thanks for getting me home William. If it hadn't been for you I know now I wouldn't be here."

"Getting that P.B.Y. out there you likely saved my bacon as well," Findlay added.

"She trailed smoke all the way home," William commented. "I expected her to blow up at any minute, then two or three times you were drifting off course and wouldn't answer when I called you. You scared me. Thankfully, you began to talk to me again and when I got you turned onto finals I knew you would be all right. What you did though, not being able to see anything, listening to somebody else talk you down, that took guts. I admire you an awful lot."

William, in some respects, was like Catherine's dad, or my own for that matter. He did what had to be done without looking for recognition. He didn't say a lot but what he did say he meant. If he said he admired you it came straight from the heart. We stood looking at each other for a moment and then I shook his hand. Findlay slapped his hand on the top of ours.

"All for one and one for all!" he shouted.

William and I looked at him and laughed. "We will survive the war," I told them, "to see peace and go home."

Then it dawned on me. I was going to be in trouble with nurse McIntosh for being away so long. Before we parted company I asked William if he'd had a good time last night.

"It was good, I really enjoyed it."

"Maybe you'd like to come back to the sick bay with me for moral support. I was only supposed to be away for fifteen minutes. I'm going to catch it."

"What I don't understand is," Findlay commented. "Why are you chasing another girl if you've got a girlfriend back in Edinburgh? You could have left nurse McIntosh for me."

William looked at me. He knew his secret was safe. Neither one of us made Findlay any the wiser.

"What about Nurse Mills, Findlay?" I said. "You could keep company with her."

"Not my type, she's nice and all that but she talks a lot."

We both laughed at Findlay's comment. He just said how he saw it.

There was no getting past nurse McIntosh. When she saw William with me she just smiled and said I should get back into bed. Getting into bed I went out like a light. I'd been told that with the amount of blood I'd lost it would be a month before I'd fly again. I was beginning to believe it. Nurse McIntosh brought me lunch and again she sat on the bed and talked as I ate. I nearly choked when she said she wasn't letting me out of sickbay again.

"You were out far too long this morning," she scolded. "There's nothing wrong with a walk in the fresh air, but the more you exert yourself the longer it's going to be before you will fly again."

"You're right, I'll try to be good."

We looked at each other and laughed, and then she left me to finish my lunch. Five minutes later she was back, smiling again when we made eye contact.

"Can I go for another walk in a little while?" I asked her.

"Sorry, you didn't keep your word this morning."

"Please, there's something I need to do."

"What could be more important than your health?"

"Well, there's a new aeroplane on the aerodrome. It's only here for a few days, the pilot was going to show it to me."

"You mean he's going to take you up in it."

Were all women blessed with intuition, I wondered, or was it only the ones I met. She knew what I was thinking and hoping for; it was futile to try and pull the wool over her eyes.

"Well, I have to confess he said he would take me up. But if you're saying I can't go, that will be the end of that."

"You can go, but there are conditions. You cannot be in control and you have to instruct whoever is that it has to be straight and level. It's not long since you lost all that blood. If he was pulling a lot of 'g's, you could quite easily black out."

She is smart, I thought. She knows about the effect 'g's have on pilots. Even with a full complement of blood it's common to black out when manoeuvring aggressively.

After lunch I went looking for Squadron Leader Baxter. He had been away somewhere in the morning taking pictures and I found him eating a late lunch.

"I was hoping you would show up," he bellowed, twisting at his moustache. "We still need to check that magneto."

Choking the rest of his food down we then practically ran to where his plane was parked.

"Two Rolls Royce Merlins in her," he began. "She'll climb to over forty thousand feet and do over four hundred miles an hour. There isn't a thing yet that will catch me. I've never felt as safe. Come on, I'll take you for a spin."

"Try the left seat for size," he said, as we climbed up inside.

It was a lot different from the Spitfire. There were two of everything and there was no big long nose to try and see around.

"They nicknamed this bird 'The Wooden Wonder,'" he went on. "Come on, change seats and we'll get going."

Starting the engines we taxied to the runway and then, with his checks complete, he looked at me with a wry, boyish grin, asking if I was ready.

I gave him a nod and he pushed the throttles forward. Slowly at first, babying his engines, he then released the brakes. As soon as we left the ground he brought the undercarriage up and let the speed build. With engines screaming he pulled back on the stick and with the plane hanging on the big propellers we were at five thousand feet in a flash. Levelling off, he turned and looked at me, grinning like a Cheshire cat.

"If I could get a bed in here I'd sleep in her," he laughed. "I love this kite. We'll head back now, I don't want to keep you up here too long. Besides, I got permission from the commander to do a low-level pass."

Cranking her hard to port he headed back to the aerodrome, descending and lining up with the runway. With the airspeed indicator showing over four hundred miles an hour we went steaming through the airfield two hundred feet above the runway.

He was enjoying himself, but I was beginning to feel a bit queasy and by the time we landed I'd had enough. After parking the aircraft we got out and I thanked him for the ride.

"No bother at all. Next time you can drive. You'll be feeling better then."

We parted company and I made my way back to sickbay. Nurse McIntosh would be waiting.

"Well, did you enjoy that?" she asked.

"I did enjoy it, he really loves that plane. But you're right. By the time we got down I was feeling a little iffy. From now on I'll do everything you tell me."

So that's what I did and slowly but surely my strength returned. Eventually I could stay awake all day without feeling the overwhelming need to sleep. Catherine's Dad and Squadron Leader Baxter went back to England and for the next month or so Findlay and I sat around and played cards and wrote letters. During that time William had assumed responsibility for the squadron.

As well as writing letters, I finished reading the mail I had got at Christmas. Bella's letter was crammed with bits and pieces about my brothers and sisters. Dad was buying a few more cows. That didn't surprise me. So far he'd been right, the enemy were trying to starve Britain and as a result farmers were getting a good price for what they produced. Dad as well had bought a few more acres of land, although Bella didn't say where it was. Another thing that surprised me was that my brother William had a girlfriend. I couldn't imagine it somehow. Her name was Jean Galbraith, a farmer's daughter from Dunkeld. Bella finished by saying they missed me and wished I could go home for some time off. If she only knew how much we all wanted that.

There was still one more letter to read, the one I was anxious to open but left till last. Looking at the handwriting on the envelope, how the letters flowed together, consistent and precise, I decided the penmanship was a true reflection of Catherine's personality. The flowing together part showed me she was flamboyant and easy going, the consistency part showed me she was dependable, and precise that she was neat and tidy. Catherine was all of those things and more and I missed her. Wanting to savour every letter of every word, I read slowly.

'My dearest James, how I miss you,' it began. 'It's Christmas and you're not here.' She went on to tell me what she'd been doing since she last wrote. Working on a scrapbook with pictures and facts about the war, it would make interesting reading someday there was no doubt. The pictures and the perfume she had sent so I'd know that the places and people I knew were still there waiting, and to remind me of happier times. She had been going up to the farm regularly. If she got really lonely and worrying about me she went more often. As well she thought about what mum had said to me in the cemetery that day. Just in case you've forgotten, 'be careful, there's someone here waiting for you.' I read her letter half a dozen times and then reluctantly I put the pages back into the envelope. As always after reading everybody's news I felt a bit down. Not by anything they'd written, I just missed everybody and couldn't go and see them, not now and not for a while yet. Maybe it was because of the war and how it ate into all our lives I felt that way. In normal times we wouldn't have been away from home for so long, we would have been rotated with another squadron. But these were not normal times. The war was being fought on many fronts and the RAF needed pilots on those fronts. We knew that and knew also that with us being so far away they wouldn't send us home for a few days just because we missed it. We were all in the same boat and found solace in each other.

During that first month or so of 1943 there were disturbing reports that the Germans were conducting an 'ethnic cleansing' in Europe, that they were rounding up hundreds of thousands of Jews and sending them back to Germany where they were being gassed. Everybody was mortified; the reports had to be false. Surely the enemy wouldn't stoop that low? Group Captain McLean spoke about it at a briefing one morning.

"It is difficult to believe that one human being would engage in such an unspeakable atrocity against another," he began. "There are no words to adequately describe an individual or country that would partake in such a horrible act, inflicting so much pain, grief and terror on another. If the reports are true it is absolutely shameful."

The unfortunate thing was that, at that moment, we could do nothing about it. If it was really happening only the allied forces fighting doggedly on could put an end to it. We didn't forget about the reports but neither could we dwell on them. We had to focus on the moment and the task at hand.

It was the only thing we could do.

13. Operational Again

In January a number of new Spitfires arrived – Mark Nines. They were no bigger to look at but had bigger engines, so better performance, but it was the middle of February before Findlay and I would be cleared by the doctor to fly again. We were relieved. Our convalescing over, the first thing we did was to take our new machines up to see if we could still fly. With the bigger engine and other little refinements complete with the new aircraft smell, there was no doubt they handled better and more importantly were faster. She fitted like a glove and was a dream to fly.

During the winter months it was reported that the war on many fronts had slowed and North Africa and the Mediterranean were no exception. Rain had made things difficult for both sides but the weather had now taken a drier trend and as a result some squadrons had been moved out of Malta to other airfields in the Mediterranean and North Africa. Rumour was that there was going to be a concerted effort to finally roust the enemy from the area. Because of our effectiveness at disposing of them, the enemy convoys supplying their ground troops in North Africa had ceased, but in an effort to keep their troops supplied with aviation fuel and ammunition the latest move on their part was to try and keep their supply line open with aircraft. The plane they used was a ME 323 heavy lift, a monster with six engines and about as manoeuvrable as a beached whale. There was always fighter cover with them but with the massive build-up of allied aircraft in the area they weren't the threat they once had been. Consequently a large number of the transports never made it to their destinations; in March alone the allied air forces had destroyed more than four hundred of them. Large and slow-moving, they were sitting ducks and because of the very nature of their cargo they often blew up in a spectacular fireball when we shot at them. Getting too close to them was hazardous. It was almost certain death for their crews who often had no time to bail out.

At the same time the US Air Force was bombing Sicily and parts of Southern Italy in preparation for an allied landing there. And then, on 12th of May 1943, we got news that the enemy in North Africa had capitulated. For days after there was jubilation. At last we were making headway.

In the midst of all the activity and excitement I had another milestone, my 21st birthday. My squadron arranged a bit of a get together and my two nurses from sickbay were also present for the gaieties. What I wanted to know was Heather's (nurse McIntosh) version of how things were going between William and her. I did know they were seeing each other regularly, but William being the way he was didn't give much away. When I got the chance I asked her.

"Things are going great," she confided. "They couldn't be better, thanks to you."

Although we still missed home lately there hadn't been as much talk about it. We had been too busy flying patrols and escorts and we were preoccupied with the fact there could be an allied landing on Sicily. The American heavy bombers had been pounding the island for weeks, so it didn't come as much of a surprise when we learned that they had, in fact, landed there. It was July 10th 1943. A few days later a number of spitfire squadrons were sent to the island, and we were one of them. Not knowing if or when we'd be back on Malta, for Heather and William it was a tearful goodbye.

For a while the aerodromes we operated from in Sicily were, to put it mildly, very basic. Runway surfaces that only hours before had been bomb cratered as a result of the allied bombing were poor and, there were virtually no buildings left standing. We slept in tents. Because we were into the height of summer and because we were making headway nobody seemed to mind. For the next six weeks or so we chased the remaining enemy forces out of Sicily and attacked some of their positions on the Italian mainland. Then, on the same day as Catherine's birthday, September 3rd, the allies landed there. This date was memorable for another reason; Britain had now been at war for four long agonising years. Six days later, on September 9th, more allied troops landed at Salerno in Southern Italy. Later that day Italy surrendered. It was a major boost to everybody's morale. Group captain McLean's prediction had been correct. Just days after that, with the need for a more effective air cover in the Salerno area, we were on the move again. The airfields there were no better than the one's we'd just left.

Although Italy had surrendered, Germany had not, so there was still fierce resistance on their part. As a result of that and the different kind of terrain in Italy, and also with the onslaught of winter, the pace of the allied advance slowed. It had been a busy summer with significant progress made, but with all the flying we'd been doing we were tired. Consequently, for the fear of losing pilots through fatigue we came to an arrangement with the other squadrons. We would have definite days off when we could relax and recharge.

After settling into a bit of a routine, although there had been damage to our aircraft, we had gone for some considerable time with no injuries. On the 16th December that changed. Pilot officer David Simpson, one of the original squadron graduates at Turnhouse was shot down while strafing enemy positions. I watched his aircraft lose height and belly-land in a small field but I was relieved to see him slide his canopy back and get out. Unfortunately the euphoria was short-lived as I watched a number of enemy soldiers run across the field towards him. There was nothing any of us could do but fly on. Being behind enemy lines and so close to the ground there was a distinct possibility we could be hit by enemy ground fire.

Tragically, a few days later, on the 20th, it happened again. Doing the same thing in the same area, Ian Rankin's aircraft crashed and exploded on impact. There was no doubt he was gone. Climbing up to a safe height I circled the billowing smoke but there was no sign of life. I tried to keep those in my command as safe as I could but the harsh reality was that we couldn't be effective and safe at the same time.

When we lost someone my loathing for the enemy deepened a little more but it also deepened our resolve to rid humanity of this scourge and avenge those of us who fell. That was of little comfort, though, to the recipient of a telegram and a letter of condolence conveying the sad news. If there were words that would adequately console parents at such a time I knew not of them. I could only tell them that I considered him to be my friend and that my friend had died gallantly fighting for freedom and honour. A symbol of true courage he knew that each time he flew there existed the possibility it could be his last, but he went anyway.

Closing the envelope I thought of their grief and sorrow, and of the waste. He was a good person and pilot. The squadron would miss him and the contribution he made. Until he enlisted, Ian had lived with his parents in Wishaw in Lanarkshire. His father had a painting and decorating business there.

There was still a letter to David Simpson's parents. I'd been putting if off because there had been no word as to his fate. Before I started to write I thought I'd have some tea and was in the midst of getting it when an American army lorry drove onto the aerodrome. The two occupants talked for a minute and then the passenger jumped out and the lorry left. From a distance I had no idea who the bedraggled-looking character was but as he got closer it looked like David. But it couldn't be. I had seen him taken prisoner. Only a few feet away and now there was no mistake.

"You look like you've seen a ghost," he smiled.

He went on to tell me that I had indeed seen Germans running across the field towards him. He had run the other way towards a clump of trees and was stood behind one of them, wondering what to do next, when an American voice told him to get down and take cover. The Germans were about fifty feet away when the thicket erupted in gunfire. The enemy soldiers had fallen before they knew what hit them. It turned out that an American platoon had been lying in wait. He hadn't seen them when he ran in there and unfortunately for the Germans, neither had they.

Shaking his hand I welcomed him back – and then gave him the sad news about Ian.

Christmas 1943 came and went with none of us getting any mail; we had been moving around so much I don't think it could find us. The craving for home was greatest at this time of year. I missed the family gathering and Bella's cooking and baking. But until such times as we did get mail I consoled myself with reading a few letters I'd got earlier, looking at Catherine's picture and sniffing at what was left of her 'Summer Blossoms'. But with the top having been off the bottle so many times, the aroma was fading. It had been such a simple but thoughtful gesture on Catherine's part; smelling the fragrance had lifted my spirits often, bringing back memories of her and happier times in a peaceful place.

Over the festive season none of us had done much flying; the weather hadn't been the greatest either. We didn't complain, it gave us a chance to relax. And then, just when we thought everybody had forgotten we existed, the correspondence from home arrived. Bella told me that everyone was well and that nothing had changed at the farm. William still had his girl-friend. That was more than a year he'd been seeing her now. It must be love, I thought. There was my annual note from John. He was disappointed he didn't get a posting to another aerodrome. He did however get promotion and was now one of the kingpins in maintenance at Turnhouse. He wrote also that he'd been seeing a girl for a while now. They'd met at a dance somewhere. Like William's girlfriend she too was an only child and a farmer's daughter. She lived with her parents not that far from the aerodrome at Turnhouse. Her name was Mary Johnston. Well there was one thing, I thought, there may still be a war on, but life to some degree goes on. Isobel's letter was short and sweet. She had now joined the R.A.F. and had been working in a hospital in the south of England to which injured aircrew were taken. I was proud of her. She had accomplished what she set out to do. She said also that she had written to Findlay. 'He writes to me,' she said. 'So I answer.' With her being so far away from home she wouldn't be back for Christmas this year either.

Then there was my letter from Catherine, purposely left till last. It started as it always did. As I read on I got the feeling she was a bit down. She didn't know how much longer she could go on without seeing me, hoping for the best but fearing the worst. How unfair everything seemed to be and wishing the war would end. The only bright spot in her life was every other day when she went to the farm to see Bella and the rest of my family. She wasn't sure if he would make it, but was hoping her dad would be home for a few days at Christmas. Just at the end of her letter, she wondered if it would be possible for me to get a posting to the same squadron her dad was in. 'He at least gets home sometimes,' she said. Putting the letter back in the envelope I was concerned. I knew she missed me, but this didn't sound like the Catherine I knew. Except to write back and be positive and optimistic there wasn't anything I could do about it. Just at that Findlay made an appearance; he too was looking down in the mouth. I asked him what was wrong.

"It's Isobel, she's joined the R.A.F. and is working in a hospital down in England. She's going to meet somebody else, I know it."

As I listened a dozen thoughts were going through my mind. The war had gone on long enough, even if we could go home for just a few days it would make such a difference, we had made significant progress in the last year, now we could see that there could be an end to the nightmare, but it wasn't over yet.

"Are you listening to me?" Findlay grunted.

"Yes I am. Isobel is still writing to you so that's a good sign and she didn't say anything about seeing anybody else, did she?"

He shook his head. In an effort to take his mind off his dilemma I told him about mine, about how Catherine sounded in her letter.

"You are the luckiest man I know," he began. "You have someone at home who desperately wants to spend the rest of her life with you. She is an attractive, funny, intelligent person who loves you." And then, as was typical of Findlay, he'd hit you broadside with a question that would leave you somewhat stunned. "Have you asked her to marry you yet?"

Looking at him I could hear myself drivel as I tried to comprehend what he'd just said.

"You haven't, have you?"

Shaking my head I told him I was too young to be thinking about getting married.

"You know James, you're one of the best pilots I know, but when it comes to women you're not that swift. Where did you think you're relationship with her was going?"

Then, for the first time we talked seriously about what we would do after the war was over. He asked me where I'd like to live. Instantly a dozen images of Pitlochry flooded my mind.

"That's easy, I want to live where I grew up. There's peace and quiet and then there's a cottage not far from the farm with a view of the valley. I'd like to buy it and stay there."

"And who's going to keep you company in that little cottage. Going home isn't just about being in a place you want to be, a place where you feel secure and has happy memories, it's the people, your family and friends. That's what makes home what it is, that's what binds everything together. You come from a happy home, but I know, if by some miracle you could go to the farm this minute there would be tears of joy and cuddles. But as soon as you had that done with you'd be down the road to Pitlochry to see Catherine. You would have to see her."

Mulling over everything he'd just said I concluded he was right. But for some reason the thought of getting married just never entered my head, I don't know what I expected to happen.

"Do you love the girl?" he asked.

Without hesitation I told him that I did.

"Well there's absolutely no doubt she feels the same way, the logical thing to do is to ask her. One thing though, don't write and ask her. Wait till you go home."

"Did I ever show you what she gave me the day we got our wings, or what she gave me for Christmas when I was last home?"

Showing him the compass and the pen and the inscriptions on them he looked at me and slowly shook his head.

"She is one special lady, you could search the world over and never find again what you have right now. God grant that I will be as fortunate."

Findlay left me to finish my note. *Don't get discouraged,* I told her, *We've made huge gains against the enemy in the last few months, we'll be home before you know it.* But as I sealed and addressed the envelope I wondered when, exactly, would we be allowed home again?

In the weeks that followed I thought a lot about what Findlay had said. Asking Catherine to marry me felt right. Why hadn't I thought about it?

To my surprise, a couple of weeks later I received another two letters: one from Bella and one from Catherine. Catherine's was in sharp contrast to her last. Her dad had been home at Christmas for a few days and had told her that the enemy was being thrashed and that she shouldn't worry. Putting her note back in its envelope I was relieved. Bella's letter confirmed what I'd thought. Catherine had told her what she had written at Christmas. *With it being Christmas and you not being here again she was feeling down. She is fine now, I'll make sure she's all right.* As there was no chance of us getting home for the foreseeable future, I could only hope that she would be.

At the end of January and beginning of February 1944 the weather was terrible. There was snow and it was bitterly cold at times, so bad that there was no movement by either side. It was a big enough job just trying to stay warm. By the time the weather had got better I'd had another birthday and we were now facing another summer in Italy. Ordinarily it was a nice place to be at that time of year but under the circumstances it was sometimes difficult keeping everybody's spirits up. As we watched the American heavy bombers fly north to bomb enemy strongholds in preparation for the offensive that lay ahead we were encouraged and tried to stay focused. Maybe if we made as much progress this summer we'd be home by Christmas.

On the 11th of May it all started again and there was a big effort to push the enemy north. On May 18th there were reports that a Polish regiment had won a hard fight at Monte Casino, which had been an enemy stronghold for months. On June 4th the allies took Rome and pushed the Germans up into Northern Italy to what is known as the Gothic Line but here everything stalled. It didn't seem to matter how hard we hit them, we couldn't get them back any further. As the stalemate continued we were getting reports that on June 6th the allies had landed on the beaches of Northern France and were heading inland. News of the invasion boosted our morale no end. Literarily thousands of aircraft and ships had been involved. As the summer progressed the reports kept coming. The allies were advancing. It was good to hear that somebody was. It didn't matter what we did, we made little or no progress. The enemy had become firmly entrenched in the area, determined to protect factories that were still making a valuable contribution to their war effort.

The scenery in this part of Italy is breath-taking, with rivers running through forested valleys and winding roads. It would have been nice to be a tourist. But we were fighting a war and the type of terrain we found ourselves in made that difficult. September turned very wet and quiet, meandering streams turned into raging torrents. What used to be dust turned into deep mud. Although we were disappointed about not making progress, we consoled ourselves with the fact we'd pushed them this far. Knowing our armies had made giant strides since landing on the beaches at Normandy was a comfort, there was no doubt the picture was a lot brighter now. We were going to win the war in Europe. It was only a matter of time. But because of the weather it didn't look like it was going to be this year. We were facing yet another Christmas away from home. We felt bad enough but we'd met Hurricane and Spitfire pilots from New Zealand, Australia and Canada who'd been away from home since the beginning of the war. What kept us all going now was the fact it looked like we would win.

As autumn turned to winter the temperature fell like the snow. Once again our main objective wasn't the Germans, it was to stay warm. At least there was no excuse for not getting our Christmas mail away on time, and surprising as it was we actually got our mail from home a few days before Christmas instead of weeks after.

Bella told me everybody was in good health and spirits because of how the war was going. 'You'll be home before long,' she wrote. 'We can't wait to see you'. Catherine's letter was the same, upbeat and positive. She wondered if I'd been checking my compass. 'Hopefully it still works, so you'll find your way home. Everybody's sure this hell will be over soon. I hope and pray they're right.'

Isobel and John wrote again but there was nothing new from them either; John was still at Turnhouse and still has his girlfriend and Isobel was still working in the R.A.F. hospital down in England and still writing to Findlay occasionally.

It was obvious that Findlay had got a letter from Isobel. I asked him if it was a good one.

"The best yet. She's saying the war will be over before long and says she's looking forward to seeing me again."

It was clear he liked Isobel. Although from time to time he'd met other women in our travels, his feelings towards her were unwavering. William and Heather were still corresponding; apparently there was a fire burning there. I was happy about that.

As the weeks turned into months we were still making little progress in Italy, at the end of February we were basically at the same place we were six months before. How we'd made it through the winter was a miracle in itself. It was certainly the coldest we'd endured, with endless amounts of snow. The enemy had heavily fortified the country. That, coupled with the terrain and the winter weather, made the situation extremely difficult. As we flew over parts of the country that used to be enemy strongholds like Cassino and its monastery, it was sad to see they had been reduced to rubble. Devastation was everywhere. The only things that kept us going were the almost daily reports of the allied progress through France. We couldn't get enough of them. Although they were making significant headway we wished they'd go even faster. It seemed like years since they had landed in Normandy, eventually freeing Paris in August 1944.

In the next four weeks the weather got better and again we hammered the enemy and at last we managed to make some headway. At the same time, March 10th 1945, we heard our armies were standing on the west banks of the Rhine. A few days later, on the 23rd, they had crossed the river. We were excited, it wouldn't be long now, but at the same time we wondered why the enemy, in light of their now hopeless situation, to preserve human life, why wouldn't they just surrender.

Into the third week in April we definitely had the enemy on the run in Italy. Weather conditions were very much better so we used it to our advantage. Frontline aircraft were flying two and three missions a day and were regularly fired on but the squadron did not lose any aircraft. For that I was thankful.

Still more reports of the allied advances. On April 16th they had liberated Holland, only to discover that thousands of men, women and children had perished there during the winter. They had run out of food and fuel. The country had been occupied by the enemy from almost the beginning of the war and now, with the end in sight, it was tragic that so many had died.

We were now at the end of April and everything was moving quickly. There were still pockets of resistance in Northern Italy. Why the enemy didn't surrender was a mystery; it was clear they had absolutely no hope left. Reports now were telling us that on April 25th, American and Russian troops had met on the banks of the river Elbe in Germany. And then, into the first week in May came a report that had us all jumping for joy. With Russian troops encircling his bunker in Berlin, Adolf Hitler had committed suicide. *Please let it be true,* we thought.

In the days that followed the reports were confirmed and then on May 7th 1945, at Rheims in France, Germany signed surrender documents. Suddenly the world was a much brighter place. The war in Europe was over. We were ecstatic, now we could go home. In the next few days we got the word, prepare to make the flight to England.

There was still a dark cloud in the Far East, however. The Japanese were fighting on. *Will we be sent there next?* I wondered. *Don't think about that now,* I told myself. *Savour this moment.* There were more reports coming out of Germany from the allied armies there, of atrocities and crimes against humanity. *This is only the beginning of that,* I thought.

14.   The Flight Home

Finally the long-awaited day came; we were leaving for home. I gathered what belongings I could safely take with me, making sure I had all the things that had given me the strength to keep going, the things that had reminded me what I was fighting for. Looking at Catherine's picture and the compass she'd given me, the needle seemed to be pointing in the right direction. Findlay caught me.

"Well, are you going to ask her?"

"Ask her? What do you mean?"

"You know what I mean," he grinned. "She's in a long white dress and there's rings and bells and things."

"Ah, I don't know Findlay, we've been away from home for a long time now. Will everything be as it was? Maybe she's been seeing somebody else."

"We have been away for a while but I'll guarantee you she hasn't been seeing anybody else. Come on, let's go, the sooner we get out of here the sooner you'll be able to ask her."

Crossing the Alps in Northern Italy and heading northwest towards Switzerland I looked back and thought maybe someday I would go back and see the country again in a happier time. It was a nice day for flying; good visibility and not many clouds. Without the fear of being blown out of the sky we could actually relax a bit and watch the countryside go by. We would fly over Paris on the way, with the Eiffel tower sticking up into the skyline the city wasn't difficult to find. As we flew over we could clearly see the Louvre, the Champs Elysees and the river Seine meandering through the city. With the warm spring weather the trees and grass were nice and green. Paris had been home to thousands of German soldiers for much of the war. How much pain and suffering did they inflict there? I wondered.

We landed at an allied airfield not far from Paris for fuel, but spent no longer than we had to. Pressing on, flying almost due north now, I think all of us had our hand on the throttle, pushing it hard against the stop, hoping for a few more miles per hour. In a short while the Channel came into view and a few minutes after that, the familiar white cliffs of Dover and the green fields of Kent. We were almost there. We would be landing at our old aerodrome at Eastchurch. They were expecting us and as soon as we landed they were all over us, welcoming us back. We shook hands with and hugged strangers, all of us bursting with excitement, dancing around on the grass. But there was someone else waiting for our return. Someone we hadn't seen for more than two years. As the excitement calmed down,

Catherine's Dad made us aware of his presence. We stood looking at each other for a few moments and then we shook hands and embraced. I was a bit choked and could barely speak as he welcomed the squadron home. As we spoke the groundcrew fuelled our aircraft and then he suggested we have something to eat. In the midst of filling our bellies he stood and, with a glass of water, proposed a toast.

"Gentlemen," he began. "A salute to all who fought but didn't see this day. Their memory will live on."

With our toast we paid a simple homage to those who wouldn't be coming home. Then Catherine's Dad asked if we were ready. Ready for what? we wondered. He didn't keep us in suspense long.

"Effective immediately, we all have three weeks off."

The room erupted. Findlay was swinging everybody around and stepping like he was doing the Highland fling. When the commotion had subsided, Catherine's father continued.

"But we have to be back. Some squadrons may have to go to the Far East to help deal with the Japanese."

"No problem," said Findlay. "We creamed the Jerries, we can send the Nips packing as well."

The squadron dispersed. The Scots among us were flying on up to Turnhouse and as we made our way back to our aircraft Catherine's dad's light blue Spitfire was sitting beside ours.

"That wasn't there when we came in," I said to him.

"No, she was in the hangar," he said, smiling.

"You still like surprises."

"Only when they're nice surprises," he chuckled, patting me on the back.

Getting to my aircraft my mechanic shook my hand, saying how glad he was to see us home. He had been my mechanic when I had been at Eastchurch before and was still there. As he helped me strap in I could see there was something on his mind.

"What is it?" I asked him.

With his eyes welled up, he was going to have difficulty saying anything, but he cleared his throat and began.

"You are one of the few. We all owe you so much. I just wanted to say it's been a privilege knowing you and to say thanks."

As he shook my hand a tear rolled down his cheek. He and the rest of the mechanics had been through so much as well. We flew the planes but they had worked, day and night sometimes, to keep them serviceable so that we could fly, at times bearing the brunt of someone's wrath because for whatever reason maybe they weren't ready.

"Hey, come on now, don't do that. You'll have me doing it to."

Forcing a smile, he let go of my hand and jumped down off the wing. I pushed the start button, the propeller turned and the engine sprang into life. Giving him the thumbs up, he pulled the chocks from in front of the wheels and saluted me as I advanced the throttle.

Heading up the coast of England and crossing the border into Scotland, it wasn't my imagination. The grass definitely was getting greener with each passing mile. And then, in the distance, I could see the greyish haze, with Edinburgh underneath. Beyond that the Firth of Forth and the railway bridge were clear to see. Flying over Arthur's Seat and the castle, everything looked just the same. Only a few miles from Turnhouse it was time to call the tower for a clearance to land.

"Welcome home sixteen squadron," came the reply. "The circuit is wide open. Land at your discretion."

An open invitation for a low-level pass if ever I had heard one. Instructing the squadron to follow my lead, I descended and made the pass and, with the original mother hen at the rear, we peeled off to land.

There were a lot of people milling around as we taxied to the apron and as we parked and shut down our engines a crowd came running towards us whistling and cheering. Getting out of my aircraft there was a familiar face standing there waiting.

"You're looking pretty good, little brother," John smiled.

Jumping down we stood hugging each other and then Group Captain McKenzie approached.

"Welcome home squadron leader Somerville, it's good to see you."

"Thank-you sir, it's good to be back."

He welcomed Catherine's father and the rest of the squadron and told us we were the first squadron from overseas to be back in Scotland.

"We'll have a drink later in the mess to celebrate," he said.

It took a while for everybody on the apron to disperse, all of them wanted to shake our hand and congratulate us. With John still at my side we made our way to the briefing room. After attending to the small amount of paperwork we were shown where we'd spend the night. It seemed to me that they had been prepared for our arrival. When I mentioned it to Catherine's Dad he smiled and said he'd contacted them earlier in the day.

"What other little surprises have you got up your sleeve?" I asked.

"None for you. But neither your family or Catherine know you're back. I thought I'd let you surprise them yourself."

Later on we sat in familiar surroundings with familiar faces and talked for a while about the war and Hitler's demise. Then group captain McKenzie insisted on buying us a drink. Aware of the effect the stuff had on me I suggested to him that I'd have some tea instead.

"Tea!" he snorted.

Everybody laughed. At that minute, if there had been a hole somewhere I could have crawled into I'd have done that.

"Squadron leader, James," he said, still grinning. "Your accomplishments call for something a wee bit stronger than that. I'm not going to be drinking to your health with tea!"

Passing the glasses he made the toast.

"To all of you and your continued good health. You maybe don't know it yet but in the years to come you'll look back and realize just what a significant contribution you made to mankind and just how monumental your achievement has been. We are deeply indebted to you all. Your health gentlemen!" He raised his glass.

"Come on now squadron leader," he said, laughing. "Tilt that glass. This is a time to celebrate!" I swallowed and almost at once I could feel the warm glow and felt relaxed. But the commander wasn't finished and in a much more sombre tone he proposed another toast.

"Gentlemen, I'd like also to drink to the health of those of us who lie in a hospital somewhere recovering from their injuries, who will come home bearing the scars of war, I wish them a speedy recovery," he paused for a moment and then continued, "And to those who paid the ultimate price and will not be coming home at all, who died for freedom and honour. Gentlemen, let us make a pledge that we will not forget them. To the fallen," he said, raising his glass high.

The room reverberated with his sentiments as we toasted our comrades. Then, as usual, Findlay felt he had to say something and stood on a chair.

"Your attention gentlemen. I too would like to propose a toast. I'd like to drink to the health of the instructors here at Turnhouse who taught us to fly. They taught us well. But especially I'd like to drink to the continued good health of two people who led by example, who showed no fear. By their attention to detail they kept themselves and many others alive. Gentlemen I give you our fearless leaders, Wing Commander John Campbell and Squadron Leader James Somerville."

There were times I felt I could have choked Findlay. Clearly this wasn't one of them. Although we didn't always think it he did have a high regard for those he flew with.

As we sat talking about some of our experiences when we were overseas, John couldn't wait to tell me about his girlfriend.

"She is absolutely gorgeous," he said. "I know you'll like her, we're planning on going home this weekend. She's dying to meet you."

He went on to tell me again that she was a farmer's daughter and didn't live far from the aerodrome. Things he'd already told when he'd written.

"Did you phone home today telling them I was coming back?"

"No I didn't. I was sorely tempted though, but I thought you'd like to do that yourself."

Leaving John chatting with William and Findlay I went to find a phone. The operator connected me and I listened as the phone on the other end rang.

"Hello, who's calling?" someone asked.

"This is James, who am I speaking to?"

"It's Margaret," came the reply.

And then there was another voice.

"Hello, this is Bella. Who's calling?"

"Hello Bella, it's me, James. I'm just phoning to say I'm at Turnhouse and I'll be home tomorrow."

"Oh my!" I heard her say and then there was yet another voice.

"James, it's Dad, is it really you?"

"It's me Dad, I'm phoning to say we're getting the train in the morning and should be home after lunchtime."

He sounded a bit upset and I just managed to hear him say he'd be at the station before he hung up the phone. Then I phoned Catherine. As I waited for her to answer I suddenly felt nervous and apprehensive.

"Hello, who's calling?"

"Catherine, it's James."

There was a long silence and for a moment I thought we'd been cut off.

"Catherine, it's me. I'm just phoning to tell you we're at Turnhouse. We're getting the train in the morning and will be back after dinner time."

Apart from the faint sound of her crying there was silence. When I asked her if she'd be alright she managed a feeble 'yes', so I said I'd see her tomorrow and hung up the phone.

On getting back to our celebration, Catherine's father asked if I'd spoken to her.

"Yes, but she was a bit upset."

"I thought that would happen," he answered. "She likely won't sleep much tonight now."

It was getting late and I was feeling quite tired, so I went to bed. Once I got there it took ages to get to sleep. Staring into the darkness I thought about what Findlay had said. Should I ask her? Instantly the little voice that had always kept me right answered with a resounding YES. Do I love her? Does she love you? What stupid questions. And then it was morning.

15.   Home at Last

Maybe it was the Scottish air but I was starving although Findlay complained about having a headache and didn't feel like breakfast. Obviously a wee bit too much Glenfiddich.

Other than those also suffering the after effects of the 'Highland Nectar', we all had breakfast. Catherine's Dad, John, even the commander was with us. As soon as we'd eaten we collected our belongings and made our way to the bus that would take us to the station. Beside it there was a young piper playing the same tune I'd heard the pipers play at the concert in Malta a lifetime ago. Why it stuck in my mind I don't know but I listened and waited until he was finished and then asked him what the piece was called.

"*Going Home* sir. It's called *Going Home.*"

Shaking his hand I boarded the bus and as we went the short distance into the city I thought about him and his music. He didn't look old enough to be aware of just how significant the piece was he had chosen to play.

Getting to the station Catherine's Dad and I parted company with the other members of the squadron then boarded the northbound train. It had been a while since I'd made this journey. Determined to see as much of the countryside as possible I got a window seat. Neither one of us said much as the train rumbled on. Who knows where his thoughts were. Mine were on the conversation I had had the previous night with whoever it was that lived inside of me. *Maybe she's found somebody else* it began but immediately I heard it again: *Don't be ridiculous!* Glancing at her dad I saw he was miles away. *If I'm going to ask her I have to ask him first,* I thought. The more I thought, I couldn't think of a reason why I shouldn't ask her. My heart was telling me yes but in the next instant there were doubts. *Hang on a minute Somerville, what makes you think she wants to marry you?* To and fro in my mind it went and then I remembered what mum had said. *There's someone here waiting for you.*

Looking at her Dad I discovered he was looking at me. Just as well he didn't know what I was thinking.

"You look like you've got something on your mind," he said.

"That's what I was thinking about you."

He looked at me for a few moments and then peered out of the window again, but he couldn't settle.

"There's something I should tell you," he began. "I'd like to tell you before we get to Pitlochry because I don't know when I'll get the chance again. Yesterday I told you I didn't have any other surprises. That wasn't quite true. For the last eighteen months or so I've been up at Turnhouse just about every other weekend. At dinner one night in Group Captain McKenzie's house I was introduced to someone and I've been keeping company with her since."

"Sir, if you've met someone you like, I'm glad."

"Well I just wanted to let you know before we got home. Catherine doesn't know anything about her either. I didn't know how to tell her or how she would take it. She's going to find out before long and I know she'll talk to you."

"When are you going to tell her?"

"Before the weekend. I've arranged with my friend to come up to Pitlochry then."

For a moment we looked at each other and then began to smile.

"Congratulations," I went on. "Everybody needs somebody and if you've found her, I'm glad."

"Thanks, but for the moment we're just good friends. That could change though."

"So is that it – or do you still have more surprises?"

He looked at his watch and smiled, saying we didn't have much longer to go now until we were home. Opening one of the carriage windows I stuck my head out into the wind. Yes, we were almost there. Weather-wise it wasn't the brightest of days and with the smoke from the engine hanging just above the carriages it didn't help. Nevertheless, everything looked green and fresh, the fields and the trees bursting with new life. Nature can teach us a lot about life, we should take heed. It's so resilient. It doesn't matter how long dark or how cold it gets in the winter, it always perseveres and triumphs again.

We were just about to start the climb up to Pitlochry, the fireman obviously shovelling coal furiously into the engine as she was now belching a trail of thick black smoke and greyish steam. We were climbing and the river Tay was going the other way. I could see the junction, where the Tummel flows into the Tay. *Another few minutes,* I thought. Closing the window I sat down and immediately Catherine's Dad went into a fit of laughter. Between his spasms he suggested I pay a visit to the men's room.

When I got there and looked in the mirror it wasn't difficult to see what had triggered his gaiety, I looked like a chimney sweep. My eyes had been watering in the wind and with the train pumping out so much smoke my face was absolutely black. If I hadn't known who it was in the mirror I'd never have guessed. Quickly running some water in the sink I franticly scrubbed in an effort to remove the grime. Another quick look in the mirror revealed I'd have to scrub harder and then I heard the train's whistle. *Oh my Lord we're almost there.* A bit more soap might do it. Rubbing harder still I then washed off the lather. The train's whistle blew again, now we were there. Standing looking at myself for a moment I thought, Somerville, what an idiot you are. With scrubbing so hard now your face is redder than a baboon's backside.

Getting back to my seat Catherine's dad started laughing again.

"We'll just tell them you got too much sun in Italy," he sniggered.

"Hopefully dad will be on time and I'll make a hasty retreat into the car."

"Ah, don't worry about it. In a week or two you'll be back to normal."

As the train came to a stop he went into another kink of laughter. Collecting my belongings I followed him to the door. As soon as he opened it I could hear bagpipes. I'd sometimes seen a piper playing at the station on a Sunday, but never on a weekday. There was more than one piper I could see, and there was a small crowd as well. Catherine's Dad stepped onto the platform and with my head down I quickly followed, staying as close to him as I could. But the crowd started whistling and cheering and made a beeline for us. Catherine's Dad stopped in his tracks and looked at me over his shoulder.

"What the devil's going on here?" I asked him.

Before he could answer, a short, untidy-looking man intervened.

"Squadron Leader Somerville," he began, "I'm with the *Pitlochry Gazette*. What's it like to be home sir?"

"It feels good," I answered, keeping my head down, trying to hide my face.

Then there was a blinding flash; a photographer had just taken my picture.

"They tell me you've just come back from Italy sir."

"Yes, that's right, we got back yesterday."

"Looks like it's warm there at this time of year sir."

I glanced at Catherine's Dad, who was grinning from ear to ear.

"Yes it is," I replied. "Very warm."

"Welcome home sir," he said, shaking my hand. "You did a fine job."

Just as quickly as he'd appeared he vanished but then the members of the small crowd gathered there all shook my hand and welcomed me home. The pipers played the same melody the young piper had played earlier at Turnhouse. When they were done, on the pipe major's command they saluted me. Taking the salute everybody could see my red face now but I didn't care, I was proud to be there. These people had come to see me, the pipers had played for me. The pipe major shook my hand.

"Good job squadron leader," he said. "You kicked Jerry's arse."

"Thanks. And thanks for being here and playing. Your choice of music was appropriate."

"You know what that piece was called?" he asked.

I nodded. He got his pipers tuned up again and they marched out of the station to another pipe tune I knew, with the crowd that had gathered to see me home following them. The train left to continue its journey on up to Inverness, leaving one small group on the platform. I'd expected only Dad to be there but, with the exception of John and Isobel, the whole family had come. They had stayed back until everybody else had gone. Walking towards each other, Bella and Dad looked just the same but my brothers and sisters had changed so much I hardly recognized them. Only a step away now and somehow I managed to keep my composure, then we all started hugging each other. Bella was so overcome she couldn't say anything and when I gave Dad a hug, my eyes filled too.

One by one I hugged my brothers and sisters and by now Bella wasn't quite so choked-up and managed to ask how I was.

"Couldn't be better," I answered. "Just a bit tired maybe."

"It's just that your face is a wee bit red."

"Mmm, I'll tell you about it later," I replied, having forgotten about it. "Did Catherine come?"

Bella and Dad looked behind them and then I could see her, standing beside her Dad, hanging onto his arm. She looked absolutely stunning. He let her go and we walked the few short steps towards each other. We paused briefly to look at each other, neither one of us saying anything, then her image blurred.

After almost three years we held each other again. Crying uncontrollably, she didn't care who saw or heard and quite frankly neither did I. We were together again, that's all we cared about. Eventually she settled down a bit and asked if she was dreaming.

"No it's really me," I said. "I'm home."

We looked at each other. Her eyes were red and puffy.

"Findlay was right," I told her. "The first flowers of spring can't compete with you. You're much better looking than they could ever be."

She put her head on my shoulder and I heard her sniffle.

"I love you with all my heart James Somerville," she managed to say.

How long we stood there I don't know, but when we gathered our thoughts together we were alone.

"They've left us,' I said. "We'll have to walk."

"Then we'll walk slowly,' she smiled for the first time. "The longer it takes the more time I'll have you to myself."

Holding on to my arm we sauntered out to the front of the station where we found her Dad and Bella sitting on a bench. Bella looked at Catherine.

"Well, are you feeling better now?" she asked her.

Catherine looked at me and smiled.

"After you phoned last night this young lady phoned the farm absolutely bawling. I thought somebody was choking her. Couldn't make out a word she was saying, so I got your Dad to bring me into the town and I stayed with her last night."

Catherine turned and buried her head in my shoulder. Just at that Dad appeared, he'd taken the rest of the family home and had come back to pick us up.

"We're all going to the farm," Bella went on. "We're going to have tea and relax and do absolutely nothing, how about that?"

Dad got out of the car and sat on the bench. He stared at me for the longest minute, and then I could see his eyes beginning to cloud.

"It's good to see you home and safe," he managed to say.

Bella held his hand and, still hanging onto Catherine, I took his other. "I'm glad to be back."

Catherine was holding her Dad's hand now and when I looked at him I could see he too was emotional.

"There are two little secrets I'd like to share with you all," I said. "First, you're the four most important people in my life. I don't know what I'd do without either one of you. And second, I don't have sunburn. Coming up the valley I had my head stuck out of the carriage window and got covered in soot off the engine. My face is red because I scrubbed it. As the train pulled into the station I was still scrubbing."

They looked at me and then at each other and giggled.

As we got into the car and made our way back to the farm I wondered how all these people would know I was coming back. Then I noticed Bella and Catherine glance at each other.

"You two," I said.

"We only mentioned it to one person," Bella responded. "We thought it would be nice if we could have a piper there to play when you got off the train. We asked the wee man in the post office if he knew anybody that would do it, he said he could arrange it. We wondered what all the folk were doing at the station when that wee man from the Gazette appeared and was asking about you. A few minutes after that the man from the post office showed up with all of these pipers saying he hoped we didn't mind that he brought more than one piper. We just had a laugh about it all."

Getting back to the farm Dad pulled up in front of the house and everybody except me got out. I sat for a minute, looking around the yard. I was finally home. Feeling a lump in my throat things got a bit hazy. Catherine looked back into the car then sat down beside me and held my hand.

"You know, there were times when I wondered if I'd ever see this place again."

"I know, but you're home now," she answered, wiping my eyes with her dainty little hanky. "Your face isn't red anymore," she smiled.

"What an embarrassment. I tried to hide behind your Dad, they even took my picture."

"It doesn't matter, come on, let's go and have some tea," she said, pulling me out of the car.

"Did I tell you how nice you smell today," I said, hanging on to her.

"Come on, you daft thing, let's go and have that tea."

Sitting around the kitchen table we talked, drank tea and consumed some of Bella's baking. My little sister Margaret was staring at me, hopefully because she hadn't seen me for a while and not because of the amount of cake I'd devoured.

Later, Catherine and I walked up to 'the gate', her hand in mine. Every now and then she would look at me and smile. 'Just checking I'm not dreaming,' she said. The view from our vantage point was as I remembered. Malta and Gibraltar had what they had, but none could compare with this.

"Someday I'll take you to the places I've been and you'll see how lucky we are to live here."

"Is it how you remember it?"

"No, it's like you – even prettier than I remembered."

Rolling her eyes she suggested we go back to the house. It wasn't a bad idea; I was about ready to eat again.

"You must have smelled the food," Bella quirked as we went in the door.

As we all sat around the table to eat I'd forgotten one thing, the monumental workload facing Bella every day. But she took everything in her stride and never got flustered.

There was another little surprise in store. Bella put a cake on the table, complete with icing, candles and happy birthday written on it. We sang happy birthday and at the same time I tried to sort out in my head who's birthday it was. Then I discovered it was in honour of me.

"But it's not my birthday," I protested.

"Not today, but it was a few weeks ago," Bella answered.

"You poor thing, you forgot your own birthday, didn't you? That means you didn't get the mail we sent you either."

Somewhat stunned at forgetting I wondered aloud how old I was. Twenty-three came the reply.

Twenty three, what happened to twenty two, I'd lost a year somewhere.

After we'd eaten we all went to sit in the front room. Although Bella had kept me up to date with what everybody had been doing while I'd been away, I still wanted to hear it from them. Starting with the youngest I asked Margaret how she was getting on at school.

"It's all right I suppose, I like seeing my friends but I don't like the work much. We got a day off today because you were coming home."

Grace and Lisa were still at school but didn't have much longer to go. Heather had now left school. Wanting to be a teacher she was planning to start college after the summer. Since leaving school Mary had worked at home and for the time being was content to do that. She liked working with the cattle and sheep. When she told me she was getting another dog I asked how our two old dogs were. Dad said that they just had Sally now and went on to tell me that about a year ago Meg had been kicked by a cow and had only lived for a few days after. About a month after that Mhairi died. Mary had gone to get her one morning but she didn't come out of the shed and when she opened the door she found her curled up in her bed. 'It looked like she was pining,' Dad said.

"It was a shame," Bella added. "She just missed her sister too much."

Out of the corner of my eye I saw Catherine glance at me and her grip on my arm tightened.

Still anxious to know what the rest of the family had been doing, Jean continued by telling me she had been training to be a manager in a hotel in Pitlochry and hoped one day to have her own. She loved it, she said. When I asked her if she had a boyfriend she just said she didn't have time for men.

"Maybe you just haven't found the right one yet," I joked.

Again I felt Catherine cling a little tighter. Richard was still working in the bank as a trainee manager, he too liked the work, hoping in a few years to have a branch of his own. When I got my wings, I'd made arrangements with the R.A.F. to have most of my pay sent to his bank in Pitlochry, other than some pocket money I didn't need it. Since starting work there he had been looking after it. I'd have to have a word with him about it. Jokingly I said I might need a loan.

"You can forget that," he said, laughing. "Fighter pilots are a bad risk."

For a moment the room hushed and Catherine pulled me tighter. Richard, I could see, was wishing he could retract. It was a harmless statement, spoken in jest, but that was the perception. If you were a fighter pilot nobody rated your chances of survival very highly. It was a stark reminder the war wasn't completely over.

"John told me he'd be home at the weekend and that he was bringing his girlfriend. He seems to be keen on her."

"She's been here quite a few times now," Bella answered. "She's a nice girl."

Turning to William I asked him when I was going to meet his girlfriend.

"She's anxious to meet you so she's coming up this weekend as well. But she isn't my girlfriend anymore," he paused. "We got engaged a month ago."

Grinning, I could see he was more than happy. Shaking his hand and giving him a hug I congratulated him, telling him I couldn't wait to meet the person who'd be my first sister in-law.

"Do you have any date for a wedding?" I asked.

"We did think about later on this year, but we'll see."

Sitting beside Catherine she held on to my arm. I wondered what she'd say if she knew what I had in my mind. Briefly I heard the voice inside. 'Somerville, you have to ask her.'

We sat talking for a while longer and then Catherine said that she should go home, she had work in the morning. Dad gave me the keys to the car so I could drive them into the town. On the way Catherine's Dad asked me if I'd like to play golf one day.

"I wouldn't mind trying again, I haven't played in years."

"It doesn't matter, we're going to go and unwind. In fact," he chuckled. "We may have to go quite often."

When we got to the house he shook my hand and said he was glad that I was home at last and then left Catherine and I together on the step. As soon as her Dad went into the house she threw her arms around me and we kissed, a long lingering kiss. Once again I heard the voice. 'So you think she's been seeing somebody else Somerville.'

"Will you come in and see me tomorrow."

"I'll stay at the farm in the morning and then I'll come in after dinner, how's that?"

"Maybe you could go golfing with Dad tomorrow?"

"Maybe, we'll see. You didn't tell me about William getting engaged when we went for our walk this afternoon."

"It was William's news to tell you, it meant a lot to him that he told you himself."

Half an hour had passed and we were still standing there, hanging onto each other.

"This is silly, why don't we go in? You could sleep on the couch."

"Maybe tomorrow, I'll stay tomorrow."

Reluctantly we parted. When I got back to the farm everybody except Bella was in bed.

"You got them home all right then."

"Yes, but Catherine wanted me to stay, I said I would tomorrow."

"I'm surprised she let you out of her sight. When you phoned last night she immediately phoned here, she was almost hysterical. I went in there and got her calmed down, all she could say was she couldn't wait until tomorrow. This morning she was up at the crack of dawn and must have tried on ten different outfits before she decided on what she'd wear."

Giving Bella a hug I said that she was a good friend to Catherine.

"She's been a good friend to me, in spite of the war and all its hardships we've had some laughs."

As we stood there I heard her sniffle and swallow.

"Hey, what are you doing?" I asked her softly.

"We're all so happy to see you home in one piece. Sometimes we'd listen to the wireless and hear about how badly the war was going and how many pilots we were losing, we thought we'd never see you again."

When I leaned back and looked at her she was more upset that I'd ever seen her.

"Did you forget what mum said?"

"No, but there were times we doubted it. I can't believe it's over and you're back."

"It's going to take a while for all of us to get used to it," I answered.

We talked for a few more minutes then went to bed.

16.   Asking the Question

Like many of the nice things of home I'd forgotten just how comfortable my own bed could be. For the last years we'd survived somehow on R.A.F. rations and lots of nights sleeping in a tent on the hard ground. But as tired as I was and as cosy as the bed was it took a while to get to sleep. I lay thinking about Catherine and if I would ask her. We would have to go back to Turnhouse in three weeks and, maybe back to war. If I asked her, would she be able to cope? Round and round in my head it went. Then the birds were singing and it was daylight. When I got up everybody was either away to school or out working. Following the familiar smell of baking to the kitchen, as usual I found Bella there.

"You're up at long last, you were tired."

She made us some tea and toast and then, just like old times we sat at the table and talked. Talked about the picnics we used to have and the fun we had playing hide and seek. We talked about the war and what would happen next, and then I said there was something I wanted to ask her.

"Oh my, this sounds serious," she said, smiling.

Sipping on my tea I thought for a moment.

"Come on, out with it, what's on your mind."

"This is difficult, but I need your advice."

Again I hesitated. Bella reached across the table and held my hand.

"Come on, just say it," she said softly.

"All right, I want to ask Catherine to marry me."

As Bella looked at me her eyes filled and then, like the day before, I watched them boil over. She leaned over the table and with her cheek pressed hard against mine she whispered in my ear.

"I don't know of any other two people who are better suited. I know you'd be happy," and after a moment she sat and looked at me. "But if you're asking me if I think you should ask her, I can't say. Only you can decide that. Catherine and I have shared many little secrets since we became friends, in all of the times she's spoken of you there hasn't been one occasion when she said anything about marrying you. But, she didn't need to. I know there's nothing she wants more. Your Dad and I have talked about this day. We could see it coming. If it happens I can tell you we'll both be thrilled about it."

"But there's a problem," I interrupted her. "We have to report back to Turnhouse in three weeks and could be sent to the Far East. If I ask her and then have to go there, how will she handle it?"

Bella thought for a moment and then said what she thought.

"Whether or not you're engaged, she couldn't possibly love you any more. If they send you there she's going to hurt, but she certainly won't love you any less. Your Dad and I had a long chat with Catherine's Dad yesterday when you were away for a walk. He doesn't see the war going on much longer, and even if it did, he's quite sure they won't send a squadron to the Far East that's seen so much action already. If you want my penny's worth I think he's right."

Bella leaned over the table, squeezing my hand and smiling

"I'd like to see her face when you ask her. I won't be able to make the dinner now for thinking about it. Speaking of which," she said, looking at the clock on the wall, "I'd better get a move on."

She gave me a hug and said she was glad I was home at last then I went outside for a walk, ending up in the garden. Sitting in the seat I marvelled at the spectacle spread out in front of me. It was a warm May day and the valley was responding to it. Although I'd been told in good authority that I'd come back from the war there had been times I very nearly didn't. Jolted from my thoughts I turned around to see Mary knocking on the window waving at me to go in.

"You scared the living daylights out of me," I told her as we sat at the table.

"Aye, I could see you jumped a bit," she said, laughing.

It was a very much smaller gathering than it had been the night before. There was just the five of us. As we ate Dad asked if it had sunk in that I was home.

"No it hasn't, it could take a while. We've been away for so long and then last winter in Italy, if I live till I'm a hundred I still won't know how we got through it."

"Well, for the next three weeks," Mary chirped, "you can help me with the sheep. That'll keep your mind off the war."

"And if you run out of a job," William added, "you can come and help me with the cows."

Dad sat in his chair and grinned as Bella glowered at Mary and William.

"Will you two stop. He's only been back a day and you want him to work already!"

"Actually, I'm quite looking forward to doing something, just not today. I might go to the golf course with Catherine's Dad this afternoon."

After dinner I did go into the town, I found Catherine's Dad working in the garden.

"James, you made it, I was hoping you would. I've been digging here all morning, you're my excuse to stop. Let's go and have some tea."

Sitting at the table he showed me an article in the paper with the headline 'War veteran comes home. Squadron leader James Somerville yesterday arrived home from Italy, although sun tanned and tired he was in one piece and healthy'. There was more but I'd read enough. Catherine's dad was grinning.

"You're famous," he grinned. I just don't know what they'd have written if they'd seen your face a few minutes earlier."

We laughed and then headed for the golf course, where probably we'd have another.

"The last time I was on a course was with Catherine at Turnhouse just before we were posted overseas."

"I have to confess, it could be a couple of years since I last played. I don't know if I'll be able to hit the ball either. But it doesn't matter, we're going to have a bit of fun and relax."

As we made our way around the course we accomplished what we set out to do, and didn't do too badly at hitting the ball either. Foremost in my mind though was the thought that today I was going to ask him if I could marry his daughter. After getting around the course we sat in the clubhouse and had tea, where I could talk to him one on one and in peace and quiet.

"Do you think they'll send us to the Far East?" I asked him.

It was clear to me he'd been giving it some thought; his response was rapid and decisive.

"My opinion is that they will not. You and your squadron have seen enough action and you've been away far too long. There are plenty of other squadrons they can send without you going. It's my belief that the war there will be over before long. The Japanese are beaten. They just don't have the good sense to throw in the towel. There's no doubt you and your squadron will have to report back in three weeks but I think for you the war is over."

Mulling over in my mind what he'd just said I prayed he was right. And then I had another thought. In the past, as long as the war was going on, something was driving me. There was always unfinished business to attend to and somehow I found the stamina to keep going. Suddenly I realized the feeling was gone. It was time to move on with my life and I wanted company.

"There's something else I'd like to ask you."

Sitting forward in his chair he gave me his full attention. Hesitating, I heard the voice inside of me again. 'Somerville, get on with it, he isn't going to eat you.'

As he asked me what was on my mind I looked around to see where the nearest exit was, just in case I had to bolt for it.

"Sir, I'd like to ask Catherine to marry me but I wanted to ask your permission first."

He sat looking at me for the longest minute. I was just about to run when he answered.

"You're a fine young man James, I've long admired you. There's nothing would give me greater pleasure than to see the two of you get married. Permission granted."

Sighing a sigh of relief, I felt drained.

"We should have a dram to celebrate."

"If it's alright with you sir, I'd rather ask Catherine before we celebrate. She might say no."

"We can wait. Anything's possible, I suppose."

When we got back to the cottage Catherine was in her kitchen.

"Well you two, did you have a good game?"

"We had a good time," I answered, "but I don't think the golf course will be the same again."

She gave her Dad a hug then put her arm around my waist and said that supper was ready.

"After we eat we can sit by the fire. It was cool in here when I came back, so I lit it."

After supper Catherine's Dad insisted that he would tidy up and that we should go and relax.

"Go for a walk or go and sit by the fire," he said. Catherine shrugged her shoulders and agreed.

There were perfectly good chairs in the sitting room but we sat on the floor. With my back against an armrest Catherine sat between my legs and together we watched the fire flicker.

"Did you have a good day at school today?" I asked her.

"It was a good day but it passed much too slowly. I wanted to get back home to see if you were here. I looked at the clock every five minutes. Oh, and Mrs Dunlop saw your picture in the paper and said to say welcome home. She wants you to go and see her one day." She looked over her shoulder and smiled. "You're famous now you know."

Catherine was speaking but watching the fire I was in another place, having a conversation with this other person who lived inside me. 'Somerville, come on man, have I steered you wrong before, it's not complicated, just ask her.' Slipping my arms around her waist I rested my chin on her shoulder and whispered there was something I wanted to ask her. Hesitating yet again I heard the voice once more. 'Come on, you know this is the right thing to do. She is your future.' Just at that Catherine looked over her shoulder.

"What is it?" she asked.

"Will you marry me?"

Instantly her eyes clouded. She cuddled into me and I heard her sniffle. After a few moments she gave me her answer.

"I was beginning to think you'd never ask me. I love you James Somerville. Yes, I'll marry you. There's nothing I want more in the world. I can't wait."

Drying her eyes she got up.

"Come on, we have to tell Dad," she said, pulling me into the kitchen.

Sitting at the table the day's paper was spread out before him.

"Dad, we've got something to tell you," she said, hanging onto me. "James and I are going to be married."

For a moment he looked at the two of us and then with a little nod and an approving smile he hugged his daughter.

"Congratulations, I'm so happy for you, you were meant for each other. I know you'll be happy."

"I just love him so much Dad."

"Yes, I know you do," he answered.

Suddenly she released the stranglehold she had on him, wiped her eyes and blurted.

"We have to go and tell Bella and your dad. I'll get my coat."

Leaving her dad and I alone for a minute we shook hands.

Congratulations. I know I don't have to worry about her, she's in good hands."

Seconds later she reappeared, took my hand and pulled me towards the front door.

"We'll be back later dad," she said as we went out the door.

And then, with Catherine sitting on the bar of the bike, we made for the farm. The night wasn't any warmer than the day had been, but peddling the bike for two I didn't feel the chill. Catherine did however.

"Come on, you sit on the bar and I'll peddle for a while, I'm freezing, plus my backside is sore."

We traded places, but to be honest we'd have been quicker walking.

"It's difficult keeping your balance when there's two on the bike," she said, laughing as we weaved all over the road.

At least she got warmed up. Getting to the farm there was just Dad, Bella and Margaret there. Surprised to see Catherine and I, Bella asked what we were up to. Again we stood with an arm around each other and Catherine told them why we were there.

"James and I are going to be married."

"Well if that's not the best news I've heard for a while," Bella said, giving us a hug.

"If ever there was a match made in heaven this is it. You were made for each other."

Dad shook my hand and hugged Catherine.

"This calls for a wee dram," he said.

Getting the seldom seen whisky bottle out of the cupboard he poured a little into the glasses. Standing with his arm around Bella he proposed a toast.

"Here's to your future, to your health and happiness always."

Remembering my experience with whisky in the past I felt the best plan was just to down it in one. Unfortunately Bella noticed and I was immediately subjected to a reprimand of sorts.

"Where did you learn to drink whisky like that?" she demanded. "If that's a habit you've picked up somewhere you can just get rid of it again!"

"You can relax Bella," I answered, laughing. " I haven't picked up any drinking habits."

Telling them about my previous experiences they were amused. We didn't stay long, it was getting late so I said I'd go back into the town with Catherine and stay the night.

It was May 16th 1945 and as I lay contorted on Catherine's couch thinking about the day, I realized I'd reached another milestone in my life. I had just proposed to the woman in my life who was my life. I felt good, happy and content.

In the morning we had breakfast together before Catherine went to work.

"Will you be here when I come back?" she asked.

"Actually, I was going to go home for the day."

"We might come out to the farm later then. Come on, walk me to the door."

Holding onto my arm as I walked with her to the garden gate she said she didn't know why she was going to work, that she'd never be able to teach anything, 'I'm going to be much too engrossed about becoming Mrs Somerville' she said, giggling. Reluctantly she let go of my arm and walked along the pavement towards the school, looking back every few steps. After Catherine left I talked with her Dad for a while and asked him when he was going to tell Catherine about his friend.

"This afternoon, I'm going to tell her this afternoon when she comes back from work."

"She'll be happy about it, I'd like to see her face when you tell her though."

"You can be here if you like, why don't you come back in later and we can have supper together, I'll tell her then."

I spent the rest of the day helping Mary. The first thing she did was to congratulate me on our engagement and then asked if I remembered how to work with sheep. What I could remember was that as lambs they looked cute and were amusing to watch. As they grew up though they seemed to become increasingly more stupid. As the day progressed it quickly became apparent that none of that had changed.

Working with Mary was a new experience. We had played a lot together when we were little and had happy memories of those times, but she had grown up a lot since then, she wasn't a little girl with pigtails anymore. Now she was an attractive young woman, much the same build as Catherine, but she had dark brown hair and blue eyes. How she managed to man handle the ewes with her slender frame was quite amazing. Taking a break for a while we found a place to sit out of the cool May breeze and had a chat.

"You seem to like working with the sheep," I said.

" It's a challenge but so far I'm enjoying it. This is the second year I've done it."

"Wouldn't you like to do something else, like Isobel and Jean?"

"I did think about it when I left school but I didn't know what I wanted to do. Dad was really busy at the time and jokingly said I could be the shepherd if I wanted. That's how it started, and for the time being I'm content."

"And has this shepherdess got a boyfriend?"

"Not yet. One of these days maybe. If I'm lucky I'll find somebody and be as content as you and Catherine are. When do you think you'll get married?"

"We haven't got that far yet. It'll take me a while to get used to the fact that we're engaged. Unfortunately there's still a war going on and the squadron may have to go overseas again."

Making our way back to the house I spoke with Bella briefly, telling her I was going into Catherine's for supper and that I might even spend the night again.

"That's fine, but you should change before you go in, you've been working with smelly sheep all day."

Catherine and her Dad were waiting for me. She greeted me at the door with a smile and a hug. Sitting down at the table Catherine's Dad looked uneasy and all the way through supper he was noticeably quiet. He was concerned about what he had to tell Catherine. After eating Catherine went to fix the fire and as we tidied up I asked him when he was going to tell her.

"In just a few minutes. Hopefully after that I'll feel a bit better."

"Aye, I wondered if that's what was troubling you."

There was no reason for him to feel the way he did, but there was no doubt he was worried about how Catherine might react. Since her mother died there had just been the two of them, maybe he thought that Catherine would feel he'd forgotten about her mother. Going through to the sitting room he sat in the big chair beside the fire and put his feet up on the stool. Catherine sat beside me on the couch and told me about her day. Apparently my little sister Margaret had gone to school and told everybody that Miss Campbell was going to marry her big brother.

"It's all over the school," she said, smiling, "but I'm glad. I want everybody to know."

All the while we sat talking her Dad stared into the fire. I whispered to Catherine to go and ask him what was on his mind. She went over and knelt beside his chair and held onto his arm.

"What's wrong Dad, you've hardly said a word all night."

Looking at her he said he had something to tell her. He hesitated as Catherine stared at him.

"Tell me what it is Dad, you're scaring me."

"You don't have to be scared," he answered, taking her hand. "It's just that I've been carrying around a secret for a while. I never told you because I didn't know how to tell you."

"Tell me now then," she smiled.

"Well as you know, for the past year or so I've been up at Turnhouse every other weekend and on one of these visits I had dinner with Group Captain McKenzie and his wife, they introduced me to someone. Since that night I've seen quite a bit of her and have grown quite fond of her."

Catherine looked at me and then back at her Dad then began to smile.

"You've been seeing a woman for a year and you didn't tell me. I always hoped you'd find someone but I don't know why you'd keep it a secret all this time. You had me worried for a minute there," she smiled, throwing her arms around his neck. "I'm glad you've found someone, this calls for a toast."

"There's nothing to celebrate,' he said. "I like her, that's all there is in it."

Catherine came back and sat beside me on the couch, held my hand and looked me straight in the eye.

"You knew about this, didn't you?"

Before I could answer her Dad came to my defence, telling her that he'd just told me coming up on the train. She asked him what his plans were, would we ever meet her. Her Dad looked at me and smiled.

"All right, there's something else you haven't told me," Catherine went on.

"Yes, you will meet her. She's coming up on the train on Saturday."

The expression on Catherine's face was hilarious, her mouth fell open and her eyes were the size of saucers, but after a few minutes she seemed preoccupied, now she was staring into the fire.

"Why don't you tell us about her," I suggested.

As he'd said before, they had met in the Commander's house. She was a widow and her name was Frances Dunsmore. Her husband had been a flying instructor and was killed while on a training flight. They'd had a son together. He had flown bombers but he too had been killed in the war while on a mission. After her husband had died she had bought and still owned a confectioners in Edinburgh. Catherine never heard a word. She was miles away. Her Dad noticed. He got up, saying he was going out for some fresh air. As he closed the door behind him I thought, suddenly, this isn't going so well. Putting a bit more coal on the fire I then pulled a stool over and sat in front of Catherine. Holding both of her hands in mine I asked her if she was all right.

"I'm fine," she answered. "Where did Dad go?"

"He's gone for a walk, he'll be back in ten minutes. You don't seem happy about him seeing somebody."

"I am, I really am. I always hoped he'd find someone else. It's just that for years after Mum died there was just the two of us. We needed and clung to each other for support, now we both have someone of our own and I was just thinking it's like the book has just ended."

"No the book hasn't ended. It's more like a chapter in the book. We're going to turn the page and discover there's a new chapter about to begin."

For a moment she looked at me, 'soul searching', then gave me a hug and whispered 'I love you' in my ear.

"You have to talk to your Dad when he comes back. He was really worried about telling you. He may have found somebody but he isn't going to love you any less."

After giving her a cuddle I said I'd put the kettle on. She pulled her legs up onto the couch beside her and watched the smoke from the new coal disappear up the chimney. When I returned a few minutes later she was looking at a picture of her mum and dad on their wedding day. Holding her hand I could see she was upset.

"She was a good person, I'll never forget her."

Slipping my arm around her waist we looked at the picture together and I told her that her Dad wouldn't either.

"You are your mother's double. Every time he looks at you he can see her. You and your Dad share something special, nobody wants to change that."

The kettle began to sing in the kitchen and as I went to make the tea the front door opened and Catherine's Dad came back in.

"It's a bit cool out there tonight again."

"It's a lot warmer in here now," I said, giving him a smile.

He smiled back, hung his coat up and went back into the sitting room. Catherine never told me what they said to each other, it didn't matter, the only thing that mattered was that when I went back in with their tea they were sitting on the couch together, Catherine wanting to know all about this person who he'd been spending time with and who had obviously become a big part of his life.

"I'm looking forward to meeting her," said Catherine. "I know if you like her I will as well."

Shortly after her Dad said he was going to turn in. I was tired myself. But tired or not, we sat talking gibberish and watching the fire slowly fade. Squeezing her hand I asked her if she wanted to know something.

"No, I don't think I do," she answered.

"Well, I'm going to tell you anyway. Do you know we've been engaged for a whole day already."

She nodded and her smile broadened. And then I asked her if she would like to see about getting an engagement ring on Saturday.

"I'd love to, it's a date."

"You know, other than the few times going into Edinburgh to the pictures or to the dancing we haven't been on a lot of dates."

"Well, this could be the start of many. Talking about dancing, I heard about Alison getting pregnant, I couldn't believe it. How did William take the news?"

"He said nothing about it to anybody. You could say I found out by accident about six months later. He hasn't been in touch with her since."

Catherine got up saying she should go to bed. She still had another day of work before the weekend. Giving me a blanket she asked if I'd be warm enough. I said if I wasn't I'd put more coal on the fire. She gave me a hug and whispered in my ear and giggled.

"Once we're married, I'll keep you warm."

Morning came quickly. We had breakfast together and then Catherine went to work. Before going up to the farm I talked with her Dad, he thanked me for the support the night before.

"Telling Catherine about Frances was the hardest thing I've done in a while."

"If you think that was difficult you should try asking a girl's Dad if you can marry his daughter."

"*Touché*," he said, laughing. "Hopefully everything will go all right on Saturday when Frances gets here."

The first person I met at the farm was William. I hadn't seen him the day before so the first thing he did was to congratulate me on our engagement and joked about having a double wedding. Maybe I thought, but knowing how John feels about his Mary it could be a triple. At lunchtime, when we got a chance to sit and chat, Bella wondered how Catherine and her Dad were.

"This morning they're fine, but last night wasn't so rosy for a little while. For the past year her Dad has been spending time with a woman he met. She is coming this weekend to meet Catherine."

"My, my," Bella remarked. "The news just gets better and better. Now that you and Catherine are getting married he needs somebody of his own. I can understand her being apprehensive, but nothing will change what the two of them have shared or how they feel about each other. I think that's great news."

Up until now Dad had just been sitting listening, not contributing anything to our conversation.

"When are you buying Catherine's ring?" he asked smiling.

"Tomorrow, we're going to look in the town first. If we can't find anything there we will go to Perth."

"Jean and I went to a wee shop she knew about in Dunkeld," William added. "She found a ring there she liked. The bit I liked was that I'd to pay less than I thought."

Bella looked at William and shook her head.

"Well, maybe you'll find something in Pitlochry," Dad went on. "Get her something nice, that's the main thing."

We looked at him. Statements like that were a little out of character for Dad.

"This is going to be a busy weekend," I commented. "We're going to buy a ring, Catherine's Dad's friend is coming, John and Mary are coming up from Turnhouse, and William's fiancée is coming up from Dunkeld."

"It's going to be busy all right," Bella smiled at me. "We'll have to get another bottle of whisky, there will likely be another toast of some kind."

Dad stood up, saying it was time to get back to work and that if I wanted something to do I could either go with him or go with Mary to the sheep. As Mary was trying her new dog I decided to go with her.

Jip was a friendly thing and looked like a lot of collies do. White legs and a white stripe down her face. But that first day for Mary and Jip wasn't a happy one. Mary couldn't get her to do what she wanted and was disappointed and annoyed with her on more than one occasion. Between running after sheep ourselves and trying to calm Mary's frustration I was fully employed for the whole afternoon.

Catherine and her Dad arrived and when they were there dad got his whisky bottle out to have a dram with Catherine's Dad to celebrate. This bottle that sits in the cupboard for weeks on end never seeing the light of day is suddenly exposed twice in one week! It would be out again over the weekend. Before they went home I asked Catherine what time she wanted to go shopping in the morning.

"Just as soon as you can get in I'll be ready," she beamed.

After they left I sat at the kitchen table with Bella. The setting for most of the little chats we had was about to witness another.

"You know," Bella began. "I don't think I've ever seen Catherine as happy as she is right now. And that's the way it should be. She can't wait until the two of you are married so you can share a home and your life with each other."

"Who knows when that will be, the war isn't over and we still have to report back."

"Maybe so, but the worst is over. It's time to look to the future."

"Catherine and you have become really good friends."

"Since you've been away we've spent many a long night together, talking about you and anything and everything, helping each other along so we could get through all of those dark days. Sometimes when you talk about everything you reveal little secrets about yourself that ordinarily you wouldn't do. Because of the mid-night sessions she's the best friend I ever had."

We sat for a few minutes longer then Bella suggested we get to bed.

"Tomorrow's going to be a big day for you, a milestone in your life. Get some rest so you can savour every minute."

"Did I ever thank you for everything you've done, for all the letters you've written to me when I was away."

"Aye you have that, in more ways than you know. Now go to bed, it's late."

Morning came quickly. I would just have gone into the town and had breakfast with Catherine and her Dad but Bella said she had it ready.

"You have to eat somewhere so it might as well be here. The way things are going we won't have you for breakfast many more days, you'll have your own table."

"Who knows how many more there will be, but I won't forget the ones I've had or the fun we've all had with you over the years."

"Last night you asked if you'd ever thanked me. You just did again," she commented. "You don't realize it, but you say little things like that to me all the time. It makes my day. But you're right. We did have fun and I wouldn't have missed it."

On my way out the door she asked me to remind Catherine they'd to come for dinner the next day.

"It's a special day and I want everybody to be here."

"You can't do all of that," I said, doing a quick calculation. "There would be seventeen of us."

"Don't you worry about a thing, it's all been arranged. You go and get that ring."

When I got to the cottage, Catherine and her Dad were in the garden, neither one heard me. For a minute I admired her and wondered how I got to be so lucky. When she saw me she smiled and came to meet me.

"Hello handsome," she said, giving me a hug. "I thought you'd never get here, you look great."

"You're the one who looks great."

"Thanks. I'm wearing your favourite perfume."

Her Dad and I exchanged good mornings but we didn't spend a lot of time in the house. We wanted to have as much time to ourselves as possible, he was going to meet his friend off the train at one.

There was only one shop in Pitlochry where we could look at rings. We'd only been in the shop fifteen minutes when Catherine decided on the one she wanted. When the lady let her try it on Catherine was disappointed. It was loose.

"Don't worry about a thing," the lady said. "If that's the one you like we can adjust it, it'll only take an hour."

"You don't want to look at anything else?" I asked her.

Catherine shook her head and said that was the one she liked, so the lady said to be back in an hour that it would be ready then.

Catherine could hardly contain her excitement. Wondering what to do for an hour she suggested we go to the café. That sounded like a good idea. I hadn't been in it for ages. Walking down the street Catherine laughed and giggled at the slightest thing. In the café she looked at my watch every two minutes wondering what time it was.

"I didn't think this day would ever come, I'm so happy."

"You certainly didn't waste any time in deciding on the ring you wanted."

"Well, I've got a confession to make. Every time I went into the shop to get perfume I admired that ring and I told myself that if you asked me to marry you that was the one I'd choose."

An hour later we were back in the shop.

"It's done," the lady said. "Try it on."

"It fits perfectly, I love it."

"Do you want to put it back in its box or do you want to keep it on," the lady asked.

"Most definitely keeping it on," Catherine answered, oozing happiness.

When I went to pay the lady she asked if I was the same person who'd come into the shop years ago and bought all the bottles of perfume. Telling her I was she went on to say she'd seen my picture in the paper. Remembering what I looked like that day I didn't know whether I should own up or not, but I didn't get the chance to deny it.

"That's him all right," Catherine answered.

"It's a pleasure to meet you again," she said, shaking my hand. "We all owe you a great debt."

As she wrote the bill I thought 'this isn't right, it was more than that when we first looked at it.' Pointing to the bill I was about to say she must have made a mistake, but she interrupted.

"Hopefully everything is in order, squadron leader. I just know the two of you will be very happy." I thanked her and she shook my hand and for a moment she held on. "No. Thank *you* squadron leader."

Catherine held her hand out to show me what the ring looked like on her finger asking if I liked it.

"It looks great," I answered. "But it pales in comparison to you."

"I love you James Somerville. Always have and always will," she said, throwing her arms around my neck.

"May you always be as happy as you are at this moment," the lady congratulated us.

Standing outside the shop door I wondered what she wanted to do next.

"My plan is just to be with you, look at my ring and feel it on my finger."

Radiating happiness she slipping her arm through mine and we walked up the street. With it being a kinder day weather wise there were quite a few people out walking, most I'd never seen before, but they'd seen me, in the Gazette. Shaking my hand they welcomed me back.

"We need to find a quiet place," Catherine said, thinking for a moment. "I know. Let's go to the church where we'll get married."

It was quiet inside the church; you could have heard a pin drop, that is until Catherine started humming the wedding march.

"Come and stand by me," she smiled, walking up to the altar.

Holding my hand she quoted parts of the marriage ceremony.

"Dearly beloved, we are gathered here today. Do you James take thee Catherine to be thy lawfully wedded wife? Do you Catherine take thee James to be thy lawfully wedded husband? Will you love him?" She paused for a moment. "I swear I will love him always."

She turned and kissed me. We stood hanging onto each other, listening to the silence and then she whispered. "Have you been to see your mum since you got back?"

"Not yet," I said shaking my head.

"Come on then, we have to go."

Leaving the church we walked up through the churchyard. It was peaceful and the sun was warm on our backs. When we reached mums grave I looked at the grass knowing that she lay somewhere underneath and then I looked at her headstone. Any other time I'd tried to read the inscription I couldn't get past the line 'beloved wife and mother', but it didn't trouble me today. What I had trouble with was the date she died, October 26th 1933. I knew that's when it was but I just couldn't believe it was eleven and a half years ago. I could remember it like it was yesterday.

All the time we stood there, Catherine never said a word. She held my hand and kept me company, but knew my mind was somewhere else.

Leaning forward I touched Mum's headstone and said that I missed her.

We turned to leave and had only taken a few steps when I felt the same sensation and shiver I'd had once before when I was here. I heard my name and stopped in my tracks. It was a familiar voice but it wasn't Catherine's. Turning around I looked at the stone, the shiver grew a little more intense then I heard my name again. 'James, I'm glad you're back, for you the nightmare is over, Catherine and you will always be happy, she loves you as much as I do'. In an instant it was over.

"James, are you all right?" Catherine asked. "Your hand is sweating." Shaking my arm I heard her ask again. "James, are you alright? Say something." And then she pulled at my arm. "Come on. Let's go to the café and have some tea."

Making our way to the cemetery gate I looked over my shoulder a couple of times towards Mum's headstone, half expecting to see her there.

Although Catherine shot me the odd fleeting glance she didn't say anything until we got to the café. We ordered our tea and as we waited Catherine held my hand and asked me again.

"Did your mother speak to you?"

I responded with an insignificant little nod.

"What did she say?"

"Catherine this is silly. If folk knew I thought my mother who's been gone for more than eleven years spoke to me they'd say, poor soul, the war got to him and have me locked up in an asylum somewhere."

"Well first of all they're not going to find out, and second, it's nobody's business. All of us have gotten comfort in what she told you before you went to war, and she was right, wasn't she. You did come back." Squeezing my hand she asked me again. "Please James, if your mother talked to you tell me what she said. *Please.*"

"She said she was glad I was back and that for me the nightmare was over. What does that mean?"

"I don't know. Did she say anything else?"

"Just that you loved me as much as she does and that we'd be happy."

"Well that much I know," Catherine said, smiling and squeezing my hand tighter. "But the nightmare part I don't know."

Our tea came and as we drank Catherine admired her ring and then she looked at me and smiled.

"I know what it is. You're not going to the Far East. For you the war is over."

"Well there's no guarantee we're not going. Only time will tell."

"No, you're not going back to war, I know it."

Drinking her tea she was convinced that was the explanation. I told her about another time I thought Mum had intervened.

"When we were in Malta there was another time I think Mum spoke to me. I can't be sure, I don't remember a lot about it. We had attacked ships and my plane got quite badly shot up. A piece of it cut my back and I must have drifted in and out of consciousness."

Catherine laid her cup down and grasped my hand between hers, the happy face gone. "You were injured that badly?"

'Apparently. As I say, I don't remember much about it. I had to land wheels up. If it hadn't been for William, well who knows. I vaguely remember a voice saying, 'Come on now, you can do this, listen to William.'

"What happened next?"

"William got me down and I spent a few days in the hospital, sleeping a lot as I recall, until I was fit to fly again."

"Don't tell me any more right now, save it for some other time."

Although what had just happened in the cemetery was uppermost in our minds, it was overshadowed by the events at hand. I glanced at my watch. It was one. I asked Catherine if she wanted to go back home or whether there was something else she'd rather do.

"Let's go for a walk down by the river, then we'll go home. It'll give Dad time to be back."

There was nothing to rush for so we casually strolled down the hill. The sights and sounds of spring were everywhere and there was still the odd daffodil that had almost forgotten to wake up. The huge beech trees were almost in full leaf. In places the sun had difficulty penetrating the foliage. Sitting in our usual place Catherine made a daisy chain and stuck it on my head, saying it should be a new custom, that when a couple get engaged they should have to wear one so everyone would know. I made one and put it on her head as well. It was quiet, but downstream a bit someone was fishing, and closer at hand two blue herons waded into the river trying their luck. Sitting observing nature Catherine began to smile and asked what my nurse in Malta was like.

"Actually there were two of them, Mary and Heather. Heather and I got along especially well. Believe it or not she comes from Banchory. She is quite attractive."

Getting up off the stone Catherine gave me a hug.

"Come on, we should go back."

As we made our ascent back to the heart of the town I told her about introducing Heather to William, that they'd seen a lot of each other.

"Personally, I think the perfume had a lot to do with it."

"Perfume?" Catherine asked with a curious look.

"Yes, your perfume. You remember that little bottle of perfume you sent at Christmas one year. Well a few times when they were going out I let her use it, apparently it had the same effect on him as it had on me. Listen," I said, stopping briefly, "you have no idea how much that meant. The aroma inside that little bottle did more to keep me going than anything else."

We stood for a moment hugging each other. I closed my eyes and for a second I was back in sickbay in Malta, remembering how I felt when I opened the bottle. The burning desire to do then what I was doing right now. I could feel a lump in my throat.

"I love you James Somerville, there isn't a thing I wouldn't do for you. When I did it I thought what a silly thing to do. But I needed to somehow let you know I was still here waiting for you. My heart ached for you so much there were times I thought I would die."

Both a little misty eyed we continued on up the hill.

"I'll have to meet this nurse of yours sometime," Catherine continued.

"Maybe you can. I was thinking that some of the people I've served with we could invite to our wedding."

"That's a good idea, we should make a list and get addresses so that we can."

"You haven't changed have you? You like to be prepared."

She just pulled my arm a little tighter and smiled. But this rendezvous we were about to keep she hadn't a lot of time to prepare for and as we got closer to the house she became increasingly agitated. I asked her how she was feeling.

"Just a bit apprehensive. I've never seen Dad with another woman before. I don't know what to expect or how to handle it."

"You'll be fine," I said, squeezing her hand. "Just be yourself. If you do that everything will be just fine."

Standing outside the garden gate, she took a deep breath.

For some reason we thought they'd be in the house, but as we made our way up the path we heard voices from the far end of the garden. Looking in that direction for a few moments we watched, unobserved, as her Dad showed his friend some of the plants.

"What do you think?" Catherine asked.

"She looks like a nice person from here. Come on, let's go and meet her."

We were almost beside them before they realized we were there.

"Catherine, James, we didn't hear you," her Dad said.

His friend turned around and he introduced us. She was young looking for her fifty years and had a warm smile.

"Frances, I'd like you to meet my daughter Catherine and her fiancé James."

"I've been looking forward to meeting you," she said, as we shook hands. "I've heard so much about you both."

"Frances was just telling me she's never been to Pitlochry," her Dad continued. "She was comparing some of the plants you have in your garden to what's in Edinburgh."

"It's my first time here. I didn't realize how beautiful it is. It's quiet and peaceful. I like it."

Catherine, in the meantime, was unconsciously playing with her ring. Her Dad noticed.

"So you didn't have to go to Perth then?" he commented.

Catherine smiled then held her hand out so he could see the ring.

"It's beautiful. I hope you'll always be as happy as you are right now," he said, giving his daughter a hug.

Catherine made eye contact with Frances and for a second they looked at each other, then she too admired the ring.

"Your Dad is right, it's stunning. Congratulations to you both. I wish you all the happiness in the world."

We thanked her and Catherine asked if she'd like some tea.

"Yes please," she replied. "The tea on the train was awful."

As we sat around the kitchen table, making small-talk, my first impressions were that she was a nice person. How could she be anything else if she'd made such an impression on Catherine's dad. She wasn't intimidating nor tried to create the impression of being something she wasn't. Already I could see similarities between them. She too was soft spoken and had the same easy-going nature. I liked her. After a while Catherine said we were going to the farm but would be back to have supper with them.

"Your daisy chain might get blown off peddling up the road," her Dad laughed at me.

Feeling my head it was still there. I'd forgotten about it.

"I may as well leave it now," I said. "Half the town will have seen me with it on."

"You might get your picture in the paper again!" he snorted.

On our way up to the farm I asked Catherine what she thought.

"She seems like a nice person. I just don't know what to say to her."

"She most likely feels the same way," I reassured her. "Give it time. Just be yourself. They're happy and I think she is what he needs."

Looking at the view of the valley for a moment, suddenly my thoughts were of William and his fiancé, Jean, and John and his girlfriend Mary. As we continued on up the road I asked Catherine what they were like.

"They're two very nice young women," Catherine began. "They're attractive. Mary is quieter than Jean but I like them both."

When we got to the farm John met us at the house door. He immediately congratulated us on our engagement.

"Come on in," he said. "I've got a surprise for you too. I want to introduce you to Mary."

"James, I'd like you to meet my fiancée Mary," he said, holding her hand, "Mary this is James."

At first it didn't register with me what he'd said. As I shook her hand it dawned on me.

"Did you say fiancée?"

As I looked at him he was just beaming.

"Well congratulations to you both as well," I said, giving him a hug.

Mary looked a bit overwhelmed by it all and stood beside John whenever she could. And then Bella introduced me to Jean, William's fiancée.

"Hello," she said. "I've heard so much about you, it's nice to meet you at long last."

Shaking her hand I congratulated her on her engagement to William. Catherine was right, they were attractive and Jean was more outgoing than Mary.

"Come on," Bella said to Catherine. "Let me see this ring then."

"You've waited a long time for this day," Bella said, admiring the ring and giving her a hug. "I'm so happy for you."

It was an emotional moment. Drying their eyes the four of them sat around the kitchen table admiring rings and talking about weddings and things. John and I decided to go for a walk. As we went up through the yard we met William coming down, heading for the house.

"There's no point going in there just now," John said. "The women are having a discussion about weddings."

"So you met Jean then?" William asked.

"Yes. Bella introduced us. She's nice, I like her."

Going into the shed we sat and talked for a while. John asked William if he and Jean had decided on a date for their wedding.

"We haven't done anything about it yet, but we thought about later on this year. What about you?"

"We talked about it on the way up on the train. Neither of us want a long engagement so it could be later on this year as well."

"What about you and Catherine?" William asked.

"We've never talked about when. I have to report back to Turnhouse in about a couple of weeks, they might send us to the Far East yet. If the war was over we could make plans but until that happens I don't think we can."

My comments put a damper on our conversation. Although the thought was never far from my mind I decided then and there I wouldn't mention the war again. Our chat resumed when John asked William if he'd thought about where they were going to live.

"I'm not sure yet. The land dad bought last has two cottages on it so we could live in one of those. We should get cracking and make some decisions I suppose. What about you? Where would you and Mary live?

"Mary's parents are older and apparently have been thinking about retiring. When we got engaged they asked us if we wanted to move into the farmhouse and take over the farm. If we don't they are going to keep it going for another year or two and then sell. It would mean me leaving the R.A.F., but both Mary and I would like to carry on with the farm so I think that's what we'll do."

"You lucky beggar!" William chimed in, smiling at him. "You found a woman who has no other brothers or sisters and whose parents just happen to own a farm they want to give it to you!"

"It's my personality," John laughed. "From the very first time I met them they just took a real shine to me."

"Mary seems quite shy," I commented.

"She is but once she knows you she's fine. It took me a while to get to know her. She's been dying to meet you. She's got a great sense of humour, she's kind, plus she's gorgeous."

There was a brief lull and then John asked me where I was going to live.

"You've got as much idea about that as I have. One thing I can tell you for sure is that it'll be somewhere around Pitlochry. Neither Catherine or I want to live anywhere else, we love it here. Catherine has a house, I suppose we could live there, but there's that old cottage down the road, if I could buy that, I think that's what I would do."

William and John were shooting glances at each other so I asked them if there was anything wrong.

"No, nothing," William answered. "Come on, let's head for the house."

Getting into the kitchen Catherine was pouring tea.

"Well, well," Bella said poking fun at us. "You three have decided to come back. We were going to send a search party to look for you but then we decided the best plan was to make tea and you'd come back by yourselves."

We smiled at each other then sat beside our fiancées. As we sat and devoured some of Bella's creations she was watching us.

"I was just thinking," she went on. "All we need is for Richard to come home with a girl and that would be all the Somerville males spoken for."

None of us really knew if he had a girlfriend. Of the four of us I suppose he was the odd one out. He didn't like any aspect of farming and never did help at home. Working in the bank was all he was interested in. From when I'd gone into the R.A.F. they had sent my pay back to the bank in Pitlochry, after Richard started working there he had been looking after it. I had no idea how much money I had. I would have to talk to him. Finishing our tea, Catherine put her arm around my waist and said we should get back into the town, that she would have to make supper. Thanking Bella for tea she reminded us to be at the farm the next day for dinner.

Getting back to the cottage we were surprised to find that everything had been done. Frances and her dad were just putting the final touches to the dinner they'd prepared.

"You two didn't have to do this," Catherine said.

"It was our pleasure," Frances answered. "All you have to do is sit down and eat, I just hope you didn't mind me working in your kitchen."

But before we started to eat Catherine's Dad wanted to propose a toast.

"Congratulations on your engagement," he began. "You are totally devoted to each other. I couldn't wish for a better son-in-law. Have a long and happy life together. To Catherine and James."

"Let's eat," Frances said. "No more speeches or toasts, I get too emotional."

It wasn't difficult to see why Catherine's Dad liked her. She was sensitive and caring and as we ate I thought, if the old adage was true about the way to a man's heart being through his stomach, she was definitely on the right road.

After supper we sat in the sitting room and although the fire wasn't lit it was as cosy as ever. We were almost at the end of a perfect day, a day when so much had happened. When bedtime came I wished for my bed at the farm, but either Mary or Jean would be sleeping in it. It had been decided I'd stay at Catherine's. With Frances staying the night both Catherine's Dad and I were sleeping in the sitting room.

Thank the lord it was only for one night, I had been tired but I didn't sleep much.

Going into the kitchen in the morning Catherine was there already and starting to make breakfast. We hugged each other.

"You look tired, did you get any sleep?" she asked.

"Not much. Tonight I'm sleeping in my own bed."

Minutes later her Dad appeared, followed by Frances. He didn't look like he'd slept either. I jokingly asked him if he was well rested.

"Not really," he answered. "It's not the best place in the world to sleep."

"You poor dear," Frances smiled putting her arm around him. "You can have your bed back tonight."

Since getting to Pitlochry Frances hadn't seen anything of the town, so after breakfast we went for a walk. All the time she commented about how beautiful, quiet and peaceful it was. Later in the morning we made our way to the farm. Catherine had promised Bella she'd be there to help prepare dinner.

When we got there Bella, as expected, was in her kitchen. Catherine's dad introduced her to Frances, they shook hands and spoke for a minute, Frances offering to help.

"Thank you for asking, but I've got an army of girls here and three future daughters-in-law. Maybe John could take you into the sitting room and introduce you to William."

For the first time ever Bella looked a little harassed, so I asked her if I could do anything to help.

"Yes there is something you can do," she said, putting her arm around my waist. "You and your brothers can go for a walk and come back in an hour."

Like she said, she had lots of help and just needed space to organize everybody and everything. For years she had cooked for thirteen, a few more wasn't going to make a difference to her. An hour later the kitchen table was a sea of faces and under Bella's expert supervision everything went like clockwork. The only family member missing was Isobel. When we had finished eating Dad stood up, saying he wanted to propose a toast, everybody getting a glass with a little whisky in it. Bella smiled and said she'd be watching me ... and then Dad began.

"There will be few days in our life that will be as memorable as this one and so it's appropriate we have a toast in its honour. First of all I'd like to congratulate our three sons and their fiancées on their engagements. William and Jean, John and Mary, and James and Catherine, I hope you live happy and long, healthy and wealthy together."

We all stood and chinked glasses and congratulated each other. But Dad wasn't finished.

"We should drink also to the war ending, and thank the lord that our family and friends came through it unscathed." Catherine held my hand as Dad continued. "And now that it is almost over we should drink to all our futures and hope we never know anything like it again."

Again we chinked glasses and were just about to sit down when Frances spoke.

"I hope everyone still has some whisky in their glass and I hope you don't mind Mr Somerville," she said, looking at Dad. "But I too would like to propose a toast. Let me start off by saying that proposing toasts isn't my forte. To be honest I don't think I've ever done it before. But I couldn't let this moment go by without drinking to the health of a very special lady. Bella," she said, smiling at her. "We've never met before today but since meeting John he's told me so much about you and about how much he admires you. He told me about how you helped Catherine when he just couldn't be here and about how you've raised your family. You are a legend. It's an honour to meet you finally."

All our eyes were on Bella as she stood at the end of the table and listened as Frances continued.

"How you cope with all you have to do every day, well I don't know how you do it. Then today you prepare a feast for seventeen. You are to be complemented and commended. I wouldn't know where to start! Your continued good health Bella," she said, raising her glass.

Bella was stuck for words. She didn't know where to look or what to say. Catherine squeezed my hand and whispered in my ear, 'I think I like Dad's friend'.

In what was left of our time together Frances got to know Bella a little better and I got to know my future sisters-in-law better. Catherine's Dad took pictures of the newly engaged couples – and the rest of the family for that matter.

All too soon it was time for the ones that had to, to get to the station to catch the train south. Dad and Catherine's Dad took them into the station and Catherine and I sat with Bella and talked.

"What do you think of your dad's friend?" Bella asked Catherine.

"There's no doubt she's a nice person, I like her. It's just strange seeing him with another woman."

"It's the first time you've met her, it's natural for you to feel the way you do. The next time you meet you'll get to know each other better. There was just too much going on this weekend. For what it's worth, my first impression is that she is a genuine person. She's just what your Dad needs."

"There's one thing she was right about," I said, taking Bella's hand. "You are a legend. I don't know where any of us would be without you."

"And I'll never be able to repay you for all you've done for me either," Catherine continued. "How you managed to find time for me when I came crying on your shoulder I don't know. Looking back it was selfish of me."

"Your world was falling apart," Bella answered giving her a hug. "But he's back now. It makes all of us happy to see the two of you together at last. I'm glad you picked my shoulder to cry on."

"You're my best friend," Catherine answered, looking at her. "I won't ever forget all you've done."

There was a long pause as the three of us sat there. I could only assume that Catherine and Bella's thoughts were with mine, reflecting on the day. At that moment I wasn't thinking much about what lay ahead, I knew that having survived the dark days of war and all its hardships the future was bright, it beckoned and I was excited by the prospect.

We were still there when Dad and Catherine's dad came back from the station.

"This is as good a time as any," Dad smiled. "There's another bit of news we haven't told you. I know the two of you haven't had a chance to discuss anything yet, wedding plans or where you might live. But Bella and I wanted to let you know so you would have some options to think about. That wee house down the road you've always had your eye on was sold a couple of years ago."

As Dad paused my heart sank. I didn't know what it was about the place, I'd never been there but there was something about it. Bella saw the look of disappointment and said to Dad to tell me the rest.

"Well, the lady who owned it died. But before she passed away she sent word that she wanted to see me. When I met her, although she was elderly she was the picture of health and as sharp as a pin. She introduced herself as Mrs Fraser. She had heard I may be interested in buying more land and wondered if I'd be interested in hers. Her family lived in Perth and wasn't interested in the farm. It had been rented to another farmer who'd had it for years. When she approached him about buying it he told her he wasn't interested. There are a hundred acres and two cottages. When she told me how much she wanted for it I couldn't refuse. A week later all the paperwork was done and the ownership was transferred. Part of the agreement was that she could stay in her cottage for as long as she wanted. Sadly, a month later she died in her sleep. Since she passed away I've had people renting it, but if the two of you decide you'd like to live there, it's yours."

My eyes welled up and boiled over. I couldn't speak. Looking at Catherine she was the same way. Bella put an arm around both of us.

"You don't have to decide right now," he went on. "But if you want to go and look at it, just let us know."

Dad and Catherine's dad went into the front room. When they'd gone Bella asked if I was all right.

"It's just that I haven't been home a week, but so much has happened."

"None of us can believe you are home, and home in one piece. Every day you were away we lived in fear of the postman bringing us a telegram. The night you phoned to say you were coming home your Dad was quite upset after. His son was coming home. And then this young lady phoned. I'd some time with the two of them. But it's over, I can feel it. For you the nightmare is over, at last we can go on."

Catherine and I stared at each other. That was the second time we'd heard those words this weekend.

"What is it?" Bella asked. 'The two of you look like you've seen a ghost."

Neither Catherine nor I said anything and so she continued.

"If it's a secret you have, forget I asked. I didn't mean to pry."

"Actually, it is a bit of a secret," Catherine answered looking at me. "But you're not prying. In fact, I don't think James would mind if I told you. Would you?"

"It doesn't matter about Bella and Dad knowing, I just wouldn't like word getting around or people will be thinking I'm certifiable."

Both of them had a giggle at the thought of it, and then Catherine continued.

"Well yesterday, after we got my ring, we went to the church where we'll get married. When we were there we walked up to see James's mum's grave. We had been there a while and had actually turned to leave when James just froze to the spot. I kept asking him what was wrong but he wouldn't answer. He had this weird look on his face and his hands were sweating. When I did eventually get him to speak he told me he was sure his mum had spoken to him again. What you just said is what she said to him."

Bella looked at me for a moment and then gave me a hug.

"You're a special person James Somerville. You wonder what you would have done without me. I don't know what I would have done without you. You and your brothers and sisters and your Dad. My life would have been one big void. All of us are here on earth for a short time and only get a little while to make a difference. Some of us do it, some of us never do it, but you have accomplished so much so young. Your country and all within owe you a great debt, I feel privileged to know you. And there's something else I can tell you. There never was a prouder man than your Dad when you stepped off that train the other day and he witnessed all these people around you wanting to shake your hand. You don't realize what you've done yet but someday you will."

Bella looked at Catherine and smiled.

"You're both special people and you mean so much to each other. If there's one thing I'm sure of it's that you'll always be happy together. Now I don't know about you two but I need some tea," she said, putting the kettle on.

Waiting for it to boil she went into the front room to see our dads. Catherine slid over beside me, staring at me for the longest time.

"What is it?" I asked her. You're miles away."

"Frances told Bella today that she was a legend. She isn't the only one. You're a legend, a legend in your own lifetime. I'm marrying a legend."

"You're marrying little simple old me," I smiled.

The kettle started to sing and Bella reappeared. We helped her make the tea and then we all sat in the sitting room. An hour later Catherine said she'd have to go home, she had work again in the morning. She asked me if I was going with them to stay at the cottage.

Telling her I was going to stay at home so I could sleep in my own bed, we arranged to meet the next day.

The next week was spent helping around the farm and at some point every day I saw Catherine. Catherine talked to her dad about Frances, he told her for the time being at least he just wanted to keep company with her. Catherine told him she liked Frances. That of course made him happy, it was important to him that they got along. When the weekend did come around again Frances came up to stay on the Saturday night. Catherine and I took a picnic and climbed one of the hills behind the town. It had been years since I'd been on a hike so I was looking forward to it. It was a tough climb in places but the view from the summit was worth it. Finding a sheltered place out of the cool wind we had our picnic. This was Scotland at its best. In the valley below I could see the silver thread of the Tay flowing gently on. On either side there were gently rolling lush green fields, lined with the big beech and sycamore trees, a bit higher up there were the heavy stands of Douglas Fir and Scots Pine. Higher still the landscape was more rugged, with bracken covered rocky outcrops. And above us we maybe didn't have Peregrine falcons like Gibraltar, but we had Kestrels. They were just as fascinating to watch as they soared on their own thermals. This was one of the rewards of freedom, to go where one wanted, and to spend as much time there as one wanted. Catherine was looking at her hand. Not wanting to lose it, she had taken her ring off and left it at home.

"Somehow I feel naked without it. I've only had it a week but I've missed not having it on today.

She paused for a moment and I wondered what was on her mind.

"Would you like to go and see your cottage tomorrow?"

Although I'd given it some thought it hadn't been uppermost in my mind. I think maybe I was preoccupied with the thought that the war in Europe was actually over and for the first time in years I was home.

"To be honest I haven't given the cottage much thought this week. More on my mind was what mum said, I hope and pray your interpretation of it is correct. I love flying and can't imagine not doing it, but I've had enough of flying combat, being on edge all the time."

"She was right before, I'm not going to doubt her. I have to believe it."

Looking across the valley she didn't say anything for a minute. But there was something else on her mind.

"Did you ever wonder about what you might do now that the war is over?"

"Well, I love flying. I don't think I would like to give it up, so I've never given any thought to what else I'd do if I left the RAF."

"Maybe they'd let you be an instructor. You've done that before."

Again she paused. It was a good idea, maybe they would. But before I could answer Catherine changed the subject again.

"Why don't you ask your Dad about us seeing the cottage tomorrow. I'd like to see it."

"All right, I'll ask him. But if we moved into it you wouldn't mind leaving your little house?"

"It's as much Dad's house as it is mine, maybe he would move into it. Why don't we take one step at a time? We can look at the cottage; if we don't like it there's nothing more to discuss. If we like it it'll be a new start for both of us."

Looking at her I began to smile. I maybe hadn't given a lot of thought to what we would do next but it was obvious Catherine had. It was one of the things I loved about her. She always had to have a plan.

"You've got it all thought out already, haven't you?"

She smiled and then looked upwards at the darkening sky.

"You know, I'm disappointed in you, James Somerville. I thought all pilots were supposed to check the weather before they left base."

It was getting threatening looking and so I agreed with her that we should head for home. We didn't get very far before we felt a drizzle, and then the drizzle became rain. By the time we got to the house it was absolutely pouring. Needless to say we were soaked to the skin. Catherine's father had lit the fire and both he and Frances were sitting beside it when we went in.

They eyed us up and down as we stood at the door making a puddle on the floor.

"You two look a touch wet, we thought you might have taken shelter somewhere."

"We were soaked before we got close to shelter," Catherine answered. "Once you're wet you might as well keep going, how much wetter can you get?"

"Why don't you go and have a hot bath and I'll find some dry clothes for James," he replied.

Catherine disappeared and in fifteen minutes she was back, warm and refreshed.

"Maybe you should go and have a quick bath as well James, before you catch pneumonia."

A hot bath sounded great, so Catherine gave me a towel and ran the water, instructing me not to spend all night in it, that supper would be ready.

After we'd eaten I looked out the window for a minute. I don't think it could have rained any harder if it tried. Catherine put her arm around my waist and smiled.

"You'll have to stay here tonight, you'll get soaked again if you go home in that."

"We could trade," I answered, looking at her. "You sleep on the chair and I'll sleep in your bed."

But I could see by the expression on her face that wasn't going to be happening. The four of us sat talking about all sorts of things as the rain continued. I asked Frances about her shop in Edinburgh.

"It's just off Princes Street. I've got two ladies who help when its busy, the biggest problem I've had is because of the war. It's almost impossible to get chocolate and sugar."

And then Catherine asked her dad a question that I was sure Frances was interested in knowing the answer to. Now that the war was over, what were his plans? Would he stay in the R.A.F?

"Those are pretty big questions, but yes, I have given it some thought. Nobody knows what will happen yet. Clearly a lot of personnel will not be needed. If I got the chance I might leave."

Catherine and Frances were as surprised as I. The R.A.F. was his life. What would he do?

"There's a possibility a few officers will be kept on in an advisory capacity, if I was asked I may look at that. But I've gotten quite interested in aerial photography, maybe I'll buy an old plane, James can fly it and I'll take the pictures."

Catherine wondered how much need there would be for something like that, who would want the pictures. It was just an idea as yet he said, and that he would have to do some research. There was silence for a few minutes as we sat digesting what he'd just said. Catherine had her ring on again and was spinning it around on her finger when she changed everybody's train of thought, saying she wanted to go and see the cottage. Catherine's dad must have been thinking about it too. His response was immediate.

"Well if you like it and decide to move in, I'll move in here."

Frances was listening intently, probably wondering if she fit into his plan somewhere. All at once my mind was occupied with one thought. If the war was over what would I do. There were options I suppose. Maybe I could stay on and be an instructor, or maybe there would be something for me to do at the farm. Clearly I would have to make some decisions.

After Catherine and Frances went to bed, I asked her dad if he meant what he said about leaving the air force.

"It's early days yet but I think I might leave. I've given the air force a big chunk of my life, it could be time for a change. I can feel it in my bones. But I'm not going to make any decisions until I find out what the R.A.F. are thinking."

The last thing I heard as I drifted off to sleep was the rain hammering on the window.

Catherine woke us in the morning, bright and cheerful.

"Breakfast is ready," she said, pulling back the curtains letting the sun in. "It's a lovely morning, it's stopped raining and the birds are singing. Did the two of you sleep all right?"

Apart from the crick in my neck I felt fine, Catherine's dad said he could have slept for another hour. But Catherine had a bee in her bonnet, she wanted breakfast out of the way so we could go and see the cottage. As we were eating she asked her Dad and Frances if they'd like to go with us.

"Maybe go by yourselves the first time. If you fall in love with it then we'll go. We'll go for a walk down by the river until you come back. It'll be a ragging torrent today after all the rain."

Parting company we went to the farm where we found Dad and Bella sitting at the kitchen table drinking tea.

"We're having a lazy morning," Dad said. "What are you two up to?"

Catherine looked at me and took my hand, then at Dad, almost bursting with enthusiasm.

"You want to go and see the cottage," he said, reading her mind.

"Can we go today?"

"Sure. In fact Bella was just saying she hasn't been there either. We can all go together."

Ten minutes later we were there and Dad knocked on the door. Nobody answered. He knocked again and a few moments later a sleepy eyed, and most likely the scruffiest looking character I'd ever seen opened the door. Dad and him exchanged a few words and then the door closed.

"We can look around the outside first," Dad said. "Then we can go in, he wants a few minutes to tidy up."

It didn't look bad from the front but as we went around behind we were all a bit stunned.

"My Lord!" Bella remarked. "Everything is so overgrown."

"It's a while since I've been here," Dad added. "I'd forgotten just how big this garden was. I should put some sheep in it for a day or two to eat it down."

There was a small burn running through it and on down past the side of the cottage there were a few fruit trees and evidence of a winding path.

"You can see it's been nice at one time," Bella went on. "But it's years since anybody's done anything in here. I'm almost frightened to go inside the cottage."

"It's a while since I've been in it," Dad answered. "But it was certainly very homely when Mrs Fraser was here."

Making our way back around to the front Dad knocked on the door, this time it opened almost at once. The man, who was just as scruffy looking, ushered us in. What a shock we got. His appearance should have been fair warning as to what to expect. It was a dark, dingy hole and stunk of goodness knows what. There were dirty clothes lying around and the windows were so dirty there was barely any light coming through. This character had wanted a minute to tidy up but you could have spent a week in the cottage and still not know where you'd been. Pigs kept themselves cleaner than he did. I was embarrassed to have taken Catherine there. I could see Dad was annoyed and as we made our way back out of the door he didn't mince any words. He told this poor excuse for a human being he had a week to tidy the place up and get out.

Getting into the car and as we went back to the farm, Dad apologized for taking us.

"If I'd known it was in a state like that I wouldn't have taken you."

We sat at the kitchen table and talked about the condition it was in. Then it dawned on me that Catherine hadn't said a word.

"You've gotten such a shock," I said, grinning at her. "You've lost your voice."

"No, I'm fine. I was just thinking," she began to smile. "I like it. I know there's some kind of animal living in it just now, but it can be cleaned up."

"You must have a fever after getting wet yesterday," I said, feeling her forehead.

"There's nothing wrong with me," she answered, holding my hand. "It's got water running through the garden, I've always wanted that. You like the view of the valley and it's got that big tree in the front garden. We could put a seat under it so we can sit and admire the view. The house is bigger than mine and with the south-facing kitchen it would be nice and bright."

She had that look she always got when her mind was made up. When she had it she was usually right. Dad and Bella were looking at me and I looked at Catherine, asking her if that's what she really wanted. She answered with the faintest of smiles.

"All right. But it's going to take years to tidy it up."

"It doesn't matter how long it takes," she said, throwing her arms around my neck. "We'll put the little house back on the map; it just needs somebody to love it."

"Right then," Dad said. "It's settled. Whenever that character leaves you can have the key."

We had supper with my family and then we went back into the town, telling Bella before I went that I'd be back later to sleep in my own bed. Catherine's Dad and Frances were just getting home when we got there.

"You've had a long walk," Catherine said to her Dad.

"Not really, we went down and watched the river. There's a lot of water going down it today, you should go and see it."

"Actually, it's a bit scary," Frances added.

Catherine put the kettle on and then her Dad asked us what the cottage was like.

"It was disgusting. When I saw it I was glad that you didn't go with us. It will take a long time to tidy it up – and to think I've admired the place for years..."

"So you're not going to go into it then?" her Dad asked.

Looking at Catherine I wondered if maybe she had changed her mind after getting back to her own little mansion. Holding my hand she began to smile, telling her Dad that she'd never seen a place so overgrown and dirty.

"It's too bad it's not what you expected," he answered.

"It will be a big job," Catherine went on. "But I like the place and I know James does as well. He's always been drawn to it. We can work at it together. I'm looking forward to it already."

There was a brief pause and then Catherine asked her Dad if they'd spent all that time at the river.

He looked at Frances and they exchanged smiles and then they put an arm around each other.

"Well actually, we spent some time in the café down the street, we had some lunch and talked."

He paused for a moment looking at Frances.

"There's something we want to tell you,' he went on. "I've asked Frances to marry me and she said yes."

Although I had a feeling he would ask her some time, at that moment there was nothing farther from my mind. I couldn't believe it. They looked at us, waiting for a response.

"Well, I can see we've given you something to think about," he added.

"I'm sorry," I said, shaking his hand and giving Frances a hug. "Congratulations."

Although I had no objections to them getting engaged, clearly it was too soon for Catherine. She was stunned. At that moment there was nothing further for her mind either, especially after her Dad telling us before he just wanted to keep company with Frances. She gave both her dad and Frances a hug and congratulated them, trying to look happy. But there was no doubt she was in a state of shock. Looking at Catherine I said we should have a toast. Catherine slid off her seat and went to get a bottle.

"It doesn't look like Catherine is ready for this," he remarked.

"She'll come around when she gets used to the idea."

Catherine came back with a toast and we drank to their future.

As Catherine put her empty glass back on the tray her dad caught her hand. She looked at him and gave him a feeble little smile.

"I'm sorry, we shouldn't have told you for a while. You only met Frances a week ago, you haven't had a chance to get to know her. It was a bit insensitive of me."

"It does seem a bit sudden. It's just that it's strange seeing you and Frances together."

Frances and I sat with our tea as Catherine and her Dad had a brief exchange. There was no argument or heated debate, no animosity, but it was clear there was something niggling at Catherine; he knew it and wanted to address it. Her Dad was getting married again. Maybe she felt something would change between them. Whatever it was, how Catherine had taken the news was totally out of character for her. In the midst of their exchange Frances intervened.

"Your Dad is right, he and I have known each other for a while now and we enjoy each other's company immensely. You've only known me for a week, we probably shouldn't have said anything until you and I had gotten better acquainted. But we were both excited and wanted to share our news with you both."

Catherine's eyes welled up as Frances continued.

"There's a deep bond between you and your Dad. I have no intention of trying to change that. I just want to share what's left of my life with him."

They looked at each other for a few moments and then Catherine apologized.

"I'm sorry, I didn't mean to spoil your special day. I've been hoping for a while that Dad would find someone else but now that he has it feels like I'm losing him."

"You're not losing him," Frances smiled. "What the two of you have is special. No one can take that away. Whenever we met he spoke of you all the time and after things became a little more serious between us, I realized if we ever did get married I'd have to share him. But I don't mind," she said, reaching for his hand. "I'd rather share him than not be part of his life."

Catherine smiled and then I asked them if they'd given any thought to when they might get married. Catherine's Dad answered, saying that they had no immediate plans.

"But if I leave the air force we'd like to live in Pitlochry; we both like it here."

"Maybe you could open a small confectionary here," Catherine added. "There isn't one in the town."

"That's a good idea. I might just do that."

"You'll have to go if you want to catch the train," Catherine's Dad said, looking at the clock.

Frances gathered her belongings then Catherine walked with them to the door. The door closed and Catherine came back into the kitchen, put the kettle on and sat beside me.

"That wasn't very nice of me," she commented. "I feel terrible. If she was nasty there would be some excuse for the way I acted, but Dad couldn't have found a nicer person."

The kettle boiled and she made the tea, muttering as she went. "What an idiot you are Catherine Campbell. You're a selfish stuck up prude."

When she brought the cups to the table I caught her hand and sat her on my knee, slipping my arm around her slender waist.

"Don't you think you're being a bit hard on yourself? Your dad was right. We only met Frances a week ago and now they're engaged. We think they're moving too fast but they're happy because they've known each other for a while. Don't worry," I said, squeezing her. "Everything will be fine. We'll be the closest family she'll have now. Both her husband and her son are gone, remember."

Catherine asked me what I thought she should do.

"Do what you always do. Be yourself. Follow your heart."

By the time her Dad came back from the station we had finished our tea. Whenever he came in the door she went and hugged him.

"That wasn't very nice of me Dad, I'm sorry. Will you forgive me?"

"It was our fault. You only met Frances last weekend and now we're engaged. We should have waited a while."

"It's no excuse for the way I acted. If you give me Frances's address in Edinburgh I'll send her a note and apologize."

As we sat talking for a while he was visibly more relaxed and happier. He too was entering a new phase in his life. He'd found someone he wanted to share his life with, but it was important to him that his daughter and Frances liked each other.

Although I hadn't really done anything over the weekend I felt tired, so I decided to go back to the farm and have an early night. I felt as well that Catherine and her Dad needed some time on their own. When I got back to the farm Bella and Dad were sitting at the kitchen table.

"Are you feeling alright?" Bella asked. "You look like you could be coming down with something".

"I'm just a bit tired. I thought I'd have an early night."

Dad asked me how Catherine and her Dad were.

"They're fine now, but earlier on things could have been better."

Dad wondered what the problem was. When I told him that Catherine's dad and Frances were engaged he just about fell of his chair. Bella was equally as surprised. I told them that Catherine didn't take the news very well and that I felt everything was moving too fast for her.

"Well I can understand her Dad wanting to get on with his life," Bella went on. "His daughter is getting married and he wants somebody of his own to keep him company. But I can sympathize with Catherine as well, she'll be feeling rushed all right."

The next week I spent at the farm helping where I could, some days with Mary and other days I helped Dad and William. In the course of conversation with William he told me that he and Mary had talked about when they may get married, that it could be late September or October. He wondered if I'd be there. I told him that as long as the R.A.F. didn't send me overseas again to fight the still warring Japanese nothing would keep me away. One afternoon I helped Bella in the garden, as we sat on the garden seat taking a breather she told me that she'd spoken to Catherine about her Dad and Frances.

"As you know I've only met Frances once. She seems like a nice person and I know her Dad wouldn't rush into anything. You have to remember she lost her husband and her only son in the war. That would be pretty hard to take. Now she too has found somebody she likes very much, and if they're engaged, obviously loves and enjoys spending time with him."

Another development during the week was that Catherine's Dad went down to Edinburgh to meet Frances so they could buy her ring. Then the weekend came around, our last before we had to go back, and again Frances arrived on the midday train. Catherine, wanting to make a fresh start met her and the two of them went to the café for lunch. When I went into the town at night they were getting on famously and we all spent a relaxing evening together. Catherine produced two big red books. Written on the front in bold print were the words 'The War Years'.

"These are my scrap books," she said. "Anything I could find about the war is in here. From time to time we can look back on it and say we were part of it all."

Inside the front cover of the first one were a host of quotes and defiant words by Winston Churchill, 'Never in the field of human conflict' and 'We shall fight them on the beaches' were just two. Sitting together we leafed through the pages. There were pictures of me I'd forgotten about, like the day we got our wings at Turnhouse. Pictures Catherine had taken when she spent that summer at Eastchurch, of people we met in the air raid shelters in London, of Jock and Fergus on their boat in the channel. As well she had newspaper clippings, the years of stories and pictures of how the war progressed in different part of the world – Italy, North Africa, Pearl Harbour, stories as well about the reports of the mass extermination of Jews. At the back of the second book there were still pages waiting to be filled. The war with the Japanese was still raging. On the very back page she had included a fitting conclusion. It was a poem entitled 'In Flanders Fields' and was written by an officer, John McCrae, he had fought and died in the First World War. When we closed the book Catherine's Dad and I looked at each other.

"How did we make it through?" he remarked. "Against all odds we survived, Britain and her allies have won the war and we survived."

Frances had viewed the books with as much enthusiasm as we, but after Catherine's Dad's comment she was visibly upset.

"I'm sorry," he said. "I wasn't thinking."

"I'm sorry as well," Catherine added. "It was too soon to bring the books out when memories of your loss are still so vivid."

"It's all right," she said, "I'll be fine, I have lots of happy memories to remember them by. I'll get over it."

Catherine and I said we'd make some tea and as we made our way to the kitchen I thought, when you lose someone who's close to you, you never really do get over it. Waiting for the kettle to boil I slipped my arm around Catherine's waist and complemented her on the good job she'd made of putting the books together. They were indeed a poignant reminder of just how desperate and hopeless Britain's situation was during the first years of the war. As we sat with our tea Catherine's dad and I discussed briefly about the squadron going back to Eastchurch, and as well the three of us were anxious to know if he thought either one of us would be posted to the Far East.

"I can't say for sure. One never knows what the R.A.F. and the government are thinking, but personally for me and for squadrons like yours, pilots who have been in the war from the beginning I think the war is over."

"If I had anything to do with it," Catherine added. "You wouldn't be going anywhere. You two have done more than your fair share. Let them send somebody else."

Now that the time was getting close for us to go back, that's how I was feeling myself. I loved my aircraft and flying, but I'd had enough of combat flying. Before she went to bed Catherine suggested that if the weather was nice the next day she'd like us all to go for a picnic down by the river, and maybe later on go to the golf course. Then I spent yet another night contorted on the chair.

When morning came, high cloud obscured the sun and there was mist. By the time we had breakfast and the picnic prepared, the sun was starting to shine through. It was a nice morning for a walk.

The river had returned to normal after all the rain the weekend before, apart from the sound of the river, it was quiet. Not another soul in sight. This was the third time Frances had been to Pitlochry, but as we sat there having our picnic she quite simply couldn't stop commenting on how beautiful it was. Later, as planned, we went to the golf course. As we made our way around it was plain to see my game hadn't improved any. All too soon though it was time for Frances to catch the train for Edinburgh again. Before heading home myself I had supper with Catherine and her Dad. It would likely be a while before we'd sit together at the table again. As I left, Catherine gave me a hug and said that they'd come out to the farm the next day after work.

Back at the farm Dad and Bella were sitting at the table having tea.

"Just in time," Bella said, pouring me a cup. "How did things go this weekend?"

"Couldn't have been better, we've had a nice couple of days together."

"That sorry-looking character has left the cottage," Dad told me, "but unfortunately he didn't clean it up any. We'll have to get into it ourselves. We just won't rent it out again. By the way, someone phoned from the town hall yesterday, wondering if you could go there in the morning. They want to see you about something."

"Somebody from the town hall wants to see me? What would that be about?"

"You know," Bella smiled, changing the subject again. "It's been quite dull around here this week, no sons coming home, no engagements. Hopefully we don't have to wait long for a wedding."

"It won't be us," I chuckled. " I hear William and Jean will be first, Catherine and I haven't talked about it. I don't want to make any plans until I know what's happening."

"Well I'm quite confident," Bella went on, "It'll all be over soon, the Japanese won't fight long by themselves."

The next day I went into the town hall to find out why they wanted to see me. It turned out that it was none other than the Lord Provost himself, Robert Henderson. One of my nurse's in Malta, Mary Mills, once asked me if I was royalty. During and after my meeting with his lordship I almost felt like royalty. Slightly taller than me, he was a slim man with a clear Highland accent. When we shook hands he held on and kept shaking. Eventually he let go and as we sat in his office his secretary brought us tea. Then he talked for ages, telling me about some of his experiences when he was in the Athol Highlanders, the Scottish regiment whose home is Blair Castle. The place I first met Catherine's Dad, and where I touched an aeroplane for the first time. Then he got to the point of why he wanted to see me.

"Sometime in the not too distant future, squadron leader, the town is going to be remembering those who didn't come home. There will be a memorial service and a wreath laying ceremony. We'd like you to represent all the services by being there to lay the wreath."

Telling him that I'd consider it an honour, I went on to say there was still a possibility I'd be going overseas again.

"Well, we'll stay in touch, squadron leader. We'll adjust our schedule to suit you. Maybe we could liaise with your family or your fiancée as to your whereabouts and go from there. That takes me to my next point, squadron leader," he went on. "Congratulations on your engagement, and please convey the town's congratulations to your two brothers and their fiancées as well. The highland nectar must have been flowing freely in your home the day all that came to light," he smiled. He went on to tell me the town office was planning a dinner in my honour. I told him that I was humbled at the suggestion but that it wouldn't be necessary.

"It's something the councillors and I were all quite definite about, squadron leader," he said, smiling again. "The people of this town and your country owe you a great debt. If it hadn't been for you and the rest of the pilots in Fighter Command, this country would have been overrun. Compared to what you have done for us, having a dinner in your honour is the least we can do to show our appreciation. We want to thank you and rejoice."

It looked like he was quite definite about it, so I agreed. As I got up to leave he asked when Catherine and I were thinking about getting married. I told him we hadn't yet set a date. He said to remember and tell him when we had.

As I made my way home I felt about ten feet tall. The town was planning a dinner in my honour. I couldn't believe it. When I told Bella and Dad at dinnertime they were both a bit misty eyed.

"You don't realize what you've done yet, or how grateful people are for it," Dad said. "But as the years go by you will."

"It's been a short three weeks," Bella sighed. "What a pleasure having you home, when you go this time we'll be able to sleep easier at night knowing you're a lot safer than you have been. This time I know it won't be long before you're back."

"Now when we go flying we'll be able to go with peace of mind, knowing the enemy isn't lurking around somewhere waiting to take pot shots at us. I'm looking forward to that."

As planned Catherine and her Dad came out to the farm later in the afternoon and stayed until after suppertime. The two of us went for a walk up to 'the gate', so I could have a last look at the valley. As we stood there looking at the view I never tired of, I told her about the meeting I'd had with the Lord Provost.

"That's great," she said, hugging me.

She was more excited about it than I was, saying I'd likely get my picture in the paper again. And then she asked me if I was looking forward to getting back.

"In some respects I am. I miss William and Findlay and the rest of the gang. Most of all I'm looking forward to getting into my aircraft. I love flying almost as much as I love you. But I can't explain it. I don't have the burning desire to be there anymore. If there was some way I could be part of the R.A.F. so I could still fly and then be home here with you every night, that's what I would like. Anyway, we'll wait and see what happens."

"Maybe Dad and you could do something together. Start a flying school or take aerial pictures, something so that you can still fly and make a living at the same time."

Taking a last look at the countryside we turned and headed back to the house.

"Making a living is something I haven't given any thought to, but if I'm going to have a wee wife and a house I'm going to have to."

"It's going to be great," Catherine laughed. "We'll manage. I can't wait and don't care if we have money, you're my dream come true. The only thing I've wanted for years now is to be married to you and for someone to call me Mrs Somerville. After all you've been through keeping your little wife and a house is going to be easy."

"You know, I've just had a thought. I don't know how much money I have. Other than a bit of spending money from time to time I've never had my pay from the R.A.F., there was nowhere to spend it. I remember arranging with the briefing officer at Turnhouse at the start of the war to have it sent up to the bank in Pitlochry. After Richard started working there he's been looking after it. I'll have to talk to him."

"That's almost six years of pay," Catherine said in amazement. "You could be in for a surprise."

When we got back to the house we had tea with our parents, then Catherine's Dad said they should get going. I arranged with him to catch the early train in the morning.

It took a long time to get to sleep, I lay thinking about all the things that had happened in the last month. The war in Europe had ended, I got home for the first time in years, Catherine and I had gotten engaged and my brothers and their girlfriends had done the same. There could even be weddings this year yet.

When Bella woke me it seemed too early. There wasn't enough daylight.

"No, it's time,' Bella said. "It pouring rain outside, that's why it's a bit dark."

Dragging myself out of bed I peered out of the window. Pouring was putting it mildly. When I got to the kitchen Dad and Bella, William and my sister Mary were waiting on me so we could have breakfast together. Dad asked me if I was looking forward to getting back.

"It'll be good to fly again and to see the rest of the crew, but hopefully there won't be any more combat flying, I don't think I could do it any more. Looking back I don't know how I lasted to the end."

"Catherine's Dad doesn't think you'll be sent overseas again. Maybe you'll get the chance to enjoy the flying you do now."

Finishing breakfast William and Mary thanked me for helping them since I'd been back and then, sadly, it was time to go. Bella gave me a hug and said that when she got the chance she would go to the cottage and start to get it cleaned up. Bolting to the car I managed to get in before getting too wet. Making our way into the town it was evident it had been raining for a while.

"There won't be much done on the farm today," Dad remarked, both of us engrossed with the windscreen wipers trying to cope with the water. "Maybe we should go by Catherine's house and see if they've left yet. They're going to get soaked if they walk to the station in this."

Pulling up to the gate I ran to the door. Just as I got there Catherine and her Dad came out.

"We were hoping you'd come by," Catherine said, as we ran back to the car and got in.

It was only a couple of minutes to the station in the car, but in that time Catherine's Dad must have thanked Dad half a dozen times.

The train was at the platform when we got there so there wasn't a lot of time for goodbyes.

"Take care now," Dad said, giving me a hug. "It's not over yet."

"I'll be careful, you can count on it. Thanks for getting me the cottage."

"We'll get it tidied up a bit by the time you get back," he smiled.

Looking at Catherine her face was wet. It could have been the rain.

"Another goodbye," she managed to say. "If it was just a day or two I wouldn't mind so much."

Taking her hand I looked at her ring and then into her misty eyes.

"Do you remember what Mum told me about the nightmare being over. Believe it. When I come back we'll find a wedding ring to go with this one."

"I love you James Somerville," she said, hugging me again.

The train whistle blew and the conductor shouted. Picking up our belongings we ran across the platform to the carriage, a few seconds later the train began to move. Catherine waved only once and just as I lost sight of them through the rain Dad put his arm around her.

Finding a place to sit Catherine's Dad said the first thing we had to do was get a cup of tea and disappeared in the direction of the buffet car. Ten minutes later he came back with a pot and some toast, enough for two.

Watching the rain we didn't say a lot on the way south, it was raining just as heavily when we got off the train in Edinburgh. It was a dreich Scottish day.

"We won't be flying south in this," Catherine's dad said.

Just at that Frances appeared out of nowhere. Whenever they caught sight of each other they just beamed. If ever I had had doubts about their union it was certainly gone now.

"Hello James," she said, smiling and giving me a hug. "The two of you look so handsome in those uniforms."

We found a café and sat chatting for half an hour over tea, and then we had to get to the aerodrome. Sitting on the bus that would take us out we couldn't see much out of the steamed up windows.

"Frances is a really nice person," I commented, as the bus splashed through the puddles. "I can see you're both happy."

"To be honest James, I didn't think I could be this happy again. In fact, I've made up my mind. The war will be over soon, and when it is, I'm going to retire and spend time with her. The R.A.F. has had enough of me."

Getting to the aerodrome and into the briefing room we discovered the rest of the squadron were already there. They stood to attention and saluted as we went in.

"At ease gentlemen," Catherine's Dad said.

"It looks like everybody had a good leave," I remarked.

"It was great," Findlay answered. "Wherever I went I was treated like royalty. With all the food and beer I've consumed I must have gained a stone in weight, all my old friends wanting to take me to the pub every other day to celebrate. To be honest, I was glad it was time to come back, if I'd stayed any longer I wouldn't have needed to walk anywhere, I'd just have laid down and rolled there."

"Some things never change," I said, smiling at him. "You still talk as much."

"He's been like that since we got here," William said. "He's wound up tighter than a fiddle string. I think the real reason he's glad to be back is because he missed us."

We all stared at him, wondering how he'd respond, but he just looked at each of us in turn and then shrugged his shoulders.

"I did miss you all. I thought the third week was never going to end."

Everybody said the same thing, about how they'd been welcomed back by their family and friends, but as time went on they had looked forward to getting back to flying, and to each other. Having been to hell and back we had become more than acquaintances, more than friends, a deep bond had formed. The regard in which we held each other we knew would go with us where ever we went in our lives.

"Has anybody checked the weather?" I asked.

"I did," William answered. "They're saying it's going to be like this the rest of the day, with a slow clearing tonight. It's the same in the south of England so it looks like we'll have to stay here tonight."

Agreeing with him, I looked at the briefing officer but before I could say anything he said he'd already sent a signal to sector control in London telling them we were storm-stayed.

"It's been taken care of sir. I've also arranged for accommodation for you here tonight."

Catherine's Dad and I looked at each other.

"They've got everything covered, there's only one thing left for us to do," he laughed. "And that's to have lunch. When we got to the mess hall it looked like everybody else had the same idea, the building was almost filled to capacity. Standing there dripping, wondering where we would sit, I heard a familiar voice saying we could sit beside him.

In the sea of faces I saw John grinning at me. We got our food and then went back to his table, where he'd made space for us. Sitting beside him I poked him and told him he was supposed to salute a superior officer.

"I've made a space for you at my table," he answered, grinning. "Does that count?"

As we ate lunch and talked he asked if I enjoyed my leave.

"It's been great, so much has happened since I've been back. Meeting my future sisters-in-law, getting engaged myself."

Findlay overheard our exchange and staring at me asked if he was hearing right. Grinning at him, I didn't say anything, so he asked again.

"Tell us, did Catherine and you get engaged?"

"You might as well tell them," John said. "The cat's out of the bag now."

They were all waiting for an answer, so I gave them the news.

"Congratulations!" Findlay said, leaning across the table, shaking my hand. "You're a lucky man, she's a lucky girl. A match made in heaven if ever there was."

William asked when the big day was going to be.

"We have no plans yet, it won't be for a while."

"Whenever it is," Findlay went on, "I'm going to be there to witness it. I can't believe it, at long last you've asked her."

We continued with our lunch, the only distraction was Findlay muttering away to himself.

Catherine's Dad left us, saying he'd see us later and John and his mechanics got up and left as well, saying he'd have to get back to work. As soon as John left Findlay started again.

"Did you tell Catherine how loud you snore? I think I'll get her earplugs for a wedding present. Did you get down on one knee when you asked her?"

"I'm not telling you a thing. In fact, I'm not telling you when we're getting married either."

"You won't keep *that* a secret," he grunted. "We'll find out when it is and we'll be there."

"Never mind me. Are you still writing to Isobel, or were you keeping company with some of your old flames when you were home?"

"There are two questions there. The short answers are yes and no."

"What would be the long answers then?"

"Well, I wrote to her and told her we were home for three weeks and then she wrote to me, twice, so things are looking up. And no, although I could have been out with a dozen girls I didn't go out with any of them. I'm quite sure my mother thinks there's something wrong with me."

We all had a laugh and then I asked William if he was still corresponding with Heather.

"We're writing often. She and Mary applied for a posting back to Britain. They got it and if they're not already home they will be in the next day or two."

"You'll be getting engaged next."

"If the war was totally over, I'd ask her. We'll just have to wait and see what happens."

"For goodness sake!" Findlay interrupted. "Everybody's getting engaged except me."

"That's because *everybody* knows how loud *you* snore," I said, getting up from the table.

Leaving them sitting there I went to the hanger. Still it rained, and for the time of year it was cold. I found John in his office, keeping track of everything that was being done to the aircraft.

"It was more fun in here when I had an engine apart," he sighed. "All this paperwork, I don't care for it."

"Paper comes with the promotion," I answered, smiling at him.

We walked to where our aircraft were parked. They were shining like brand new and said it looked like they'd been busy.

"We touched them up a bit and they're all serviced and ready to go."

"I love this aeroplane," I said, running my hand up the leading edge of the propeller. "We've been through a lot together."

"Maybe if the war is really over the R.A.F. will sell her to you. They've got thousands of aircraft all over the place that might never be used again."

He was right. What would happen to them all? John said he would have to get back to work and left me to admire my aeroplane a little longer. Sitting in the cockpit I felt a desperate urge to start her up and take her for a spin. I'd missed her.

Feeling at a loose end I went over to the briefing room. When I walked in the briefing officer had a message for me.

"Group captain McKenzie would like to see you sir, right away."

17.   The Nightmare is Over

Making my way over I wondered, *is this good or bad?*

On reaching his outer office I was surprised to be greeted by the same happy face that sat behind the desk the last time I was here. She looked just the same.

"Squadron Leader Somerville, how are you?" she smiled.

"Alison, I'm fine, how are you? I didn't expect to see you here."

"Oh, I'm still here. I'll tell the commander you've arrived."

As she rang through to his office I wondered what she'd been doing since we'd last seen her. Had she been pregnant? Had she thought of William?

"The commander will see you right away," she said, getting up to open the door for me. "Do you still take both in your tea?"

Somewhat surprised that she'd remember that small detail, I smiled and nodded. Entering the commander's office I was surprised also to find Catherine's dad sitting there.

"Ah, Squadron Leader Somerville,' he began, as I saluted him. "How nice to see you again. I trust you had a good leave?"

"Excellent sir, it couldn't have been better."

"I hear congratulations are in order."

Looking at Catherine's Dad we exchanged smiles.

"Congratulations squadron leader," the commander continued, shaking my hand. "You're two fine people."

There was a knock on the door and Alison came in with three cups of tea.

"Have a seat squadron leader and I'll get to the point of why I wanted to see you. Now that the war is all but over, Wing Commander Campbell and I are discussing the possibility of a Spitfire and Hurricane squadron touring Scotland, going to different aerodromes, and on the day of the visit these aerodromes would be open to the public, so they can see first-hand the aircraft that saved this country in the Battle of Britain and can speak to some of the young men who flew them. We can't do it yet. We'll have to wait until the Japanese are beaten, but that won't be long, I'm sure of that. What do you think?"

"It's an excellent idea sir. I think a lot of people would like to see them first hand."

"Good, so we're going to sort out some kind of itinerary. If you and your squadron can put a few manoeuvres together so that the public can see some of what was involved. It'll be low-level, but we don't want anybody pulling any stunts."

"You want *us* to do this tour sir?" I asked, somewhat surprised.

"There's no one more fitting than you, squadron leader," he went on. "You've been in the war from the duration, you survived, and you're quite possibly the youngest squadron leader in the R.A.F. A shining example of courage and determination. You're the perfect representative for your peers who flew along with you in defence of your country. You and your squadron are outstanding ambassadors for the R.A.F."

Thinking for a minute, trying to digest all he'd said, I reminded him that we may yet have to go to the Far East.

Catherine's Dad and the commander looked at each other and smiled and then he continued.

"You won't be going to the Far East, squadron leader, I'll see to that. You've done your bit."

Speechless, I looked at Catherine's Dad.

"For you the nightmare is over,' he said, smiling warmly.

Feeling a little shiver the hair on the back of my neck stood on end. That was the third time I'd heard that. Sitting motionless and dumbstruck, a dozen things went through my mind. Mum was right again. I have to phone home. In the midst of my thoughts Catherine's Dad was shaking my arm, asking me if I was alright. Looking at them both I apologized.

"I'm sorry sir, my mind was somewhere else. It's difficult to believe it's over."

"Believe it squadron leader. Take your squadron back to Eastchurch, but the only thing you need have on your mind is this tour and putting a bit of a programme together. For the time being don't tell any more people than you have to about it. It's not that it's a big secret but it would look better if the war in the Pacific was over before we do the tour, then we can really celebrate. We'll stay in touch, have a good flight south tomorrow."

Thanking him and with Catherine's Dad saying he'd see me later I left the office. Outside his office I stood with my back against the door. Still somewhat dazed by what had just happened, staring at the floor I couldn't think straight.

"Are you all right squadron leader?" Alison asked.

"You know the scary thing about life, Miss Jenkins, you just never know what's around the corner."

She had a mystified look on her face but there was a faint indication of a smile when I asked her how she was. We spoke for a few minutes but there was no doubt she looked a little uneasy, so I said for her to look after herself and headed for the door.

"How's William?" she asked.

Turning around, her happy face was gone and somehow I felt a little sorry for her. She looked vulnerable and helpless somehow.

"He's fine," I answered, struggling for words. What could I say? She knew William would have told me about what had happened.

"When I heard you and your squadron were coming back I wanted to see him. But when I told myself he wouldn't want to see me my heart ached. I know I hurt him. After he left I just missed him so much, I couldn't stand it". She paused for a moment and again a faint smile returned. "But now I have a little boy. I wouldn't trade him for anything. He's two and a half now, you know."

She knew William was on the aerodrome, a stone's throw away. She would like to have seen him, maybe even hoping they could start over. But William didn't know she was here, there was nothing further from his mind and I wasn't going to tell him.

"Alison, when we were in Malta William met somebody else. I know it's in his mind that when the war is over he will ask her to marry him."

She was staring at the floor now and I really did feel sorry for her.

"I'm sorry Alison. Take care"

After leaving her office I needed some tea so I made my way to the mess hall. Then it dawned on me it had stopped raining. I stopped for a moment taking a few deep breaths. Everything smelled and looked so fresh. *A chapter has ended* I thought, *and a new one is about to begin.*

It's difficult to explain how I felt at that moment. On one hand there was total disbelief that we didn't have to go back to war and on the other I felt like I could have burst with excitement at any second for the same reason. The thought of our squadron going to different places representing the R.A.F. was also an exciting prospect and I was already looking forward to it. I felt like shouting it out, telling everybody. It was going to be difficult containing my excitement. Continuing my walk to the mess hall, I consciously felt a spring in my step and an overwhelming sense of relief. As well, that little voice inside was telling me that my life within the R.A.F. was going to be changing, I was quite sure of that.

Poking my head inside the mess room door I discovered that my 'clutch' had left. Not wanting to sit on my own I decided to go to the briefing room. I'd only gone a few steps when I heard Catherine's Dad call me. We went back to the mess hall and got some tea.

"Well, how do you feel now?" he asked. "You had me worried there for a moment, you looked like you got quite a shock."

"I can't believe we're not going back to war, I honestly can't believe it. It's going to take a while to sink in. I wish I could let them know at home. And the thought of touring Scotland with the squadron is really exciting."

He looked at me for a moment.

"Maybe you should let Catherine and your family know; they've been through enough and they'll sleep better at night knowing that you're not going away again."

"It's too bad the war wasn't totally over, there's still a dark cloud there yet."

"There is,' he answered. "But it's only a matter of time before the Japanese are beaten into submission. It won't be long."

"It's difficult to believe we've survived almost six years of war. Did you ever wonder how we made it and so many others didn't?"

"Yes I have,' he answered, sipping his tea. "But that's a question I think we'll ask ourselves for many years to come."

"There's something I was wondering about. Did the commander think of this tour or was it your idea?"

"It didn't take a lot," he answered, smiling. "I mentioned that it might be good for public morale if they could see the legendry Spitfire and Hurricane at first-hand. That was enough. He liked the idea right away. When it came to which Spitfire squadron would do the honours I didn't have to make any suggestions, he thought of you right away."

Taking a sip of my tea, I thanked him for everything he'd done for me.

"No James, thank you. You've been and still are an inspiration to us all. You and your family for a long time have been a big part of Catherine's life and of mine and it's been a pleasure knowing all of you. Trying to keep you safe now after all you've been through is the least I can do. Besides, I want to go on this tour with you, it'll be good fun."

Sitting with our own thoughts for a minute he then asked what had happened to me in the commander's office.

"For a minute there, you looked like you'd seen a ghost."

Looking at him I thought that was the second peculiar thing he'd said to me today and was truer than he knew.

"Maybe I had," I answered.

He was waiting for an explanation so I asked if I could tell him something in confidence, wondering if I should tell him at all. Hesitating for a moment I began.

"Did Catherine ever tell you about an experience I had in the cemetery in Pitlochry when the war started?"

"Actually she did,' he answered, smiling. "But she asked me to keep it to myself."

"You'll be thinking I'm some kind of nutcase."

"Now why would I think that? I go to church when I can and I believe in life everlasting. There's more to life than just life you know. If I believe in that why wouldn't I believe your mother reached out to you. Besides, everybody drew a lot of strength from that encounter and, at the end of the day she was right."

"Did Catherine tell you we went to the cemetery the day we went to get her ring?"

"No, she never mentioned that."

I told him about my experience and about Bella saying the same thing. When I was done he sat looking at me for a minute and then he answered.

"You're a special person James Somerville, I don't think you realize that yet. You not only have a guardian angel, you know who she is."

I said there was something else I had always wondered about.

"What do Dad and you get to talk about all the time? You don't have anything in common but somehow you can sit and talk for hours."

As he sipped his tea he looked at me over the top of his cup.

"Your Dad and I do walk a different path but I have the deepest respect and admiration for him. He is a very interesting and knowledgeable individual and we never run out of things to talk about. Believe it or not, outside of the R.A.F. he's the only friend I have. One of the few things we have in common is the love we have for our families. He's got a very much bigger family than me but there's no doubt he loves each and every one of you."

Sitting listening to Catherine's Dad speaking of Dad I thought back. Dad, as far as I knew, had never been ill a day in his life. He was never up later than six in the morning, out feeding his cattle and doing whatever needed to be done. He didn't say much and rarely played with us when we were growing up, but he was always there. Until that moment I'd never given any thought to how he must have felt when he got married and went with Mum up to Pitlochry to start on his own. It must have been daunting. But I'd never heard him complain about anything. He lived as he'd taught us, 'do what you have to do, this too will pass'. Thinking of his easy-going nature and his big calloused hands my eyes blurred. I loved and admired him and I made a pledge to myself right there and then that now the war was over I would spend more time with him.

"And Bella," Catherine's Dad went on. "You know how I feel about her. She's the salt of the earth. For her to step into your mother's shoes and raise all of her family was to say the very least a daunting prospect. She deserves a medal for the contribution she has made. Your Dad knows that, we've spoken about it often. They think the world of each other and because of that and their approach to life your home is a happy one and I enjoy each and every minute I'm in it."

We sat with our own thoughts for a minute and I smiled as I thought back to the long gone summer days when my siblings and I went for picnics and played hide and seek with Bella out on the hill. The giggling when we jumped out from behind a Douglas fir to give her a fright. And then there were the sad times, when Mum died and shortly after when Bella herself left us to get married. How empty it felt and how unfair life seemed. But she came back to us and I knew I'd never forget that day either, the jubilation. Again my eyes grew hazy as I thought of all the letters she'd written to me when I was away. In spite of all she had to do I don't think she'd missed a week. Then I discovered where Catherine's dad's thoughts were.

"You know, I should phone Frances. As we're not going south now maybe we could meet somewhere. Would you like to come?"

"I'll stay here with my 'clutch' and catch up with what they've been doing. Besides, two's company, three's a crowd."

He went to phone Frances. Ten minutes later he came back to say that he was indeed going to meet her.

Eventually I caught up with my squadron but my mind wasn't with them. With all that had happened since we got back I was in a bit of a daze, I just couldn't believe it. The nightmare was over. Not able to contain my excitement any longer I had to phone home and tell them. Catherine answered and right away she wondered why I was phoning. Was there something wrong?

'There's nothing wrong. I had to phone and tell you. Both Mum and you were right, the nightmare is over. I'm not going back to war."

She didn't answer. I knew what she'd be doing so I said I'd call her back in a little while. Phoning home, Bella answered, and she too was surprised to hear me. When I told her why I was calling she sounded upset so I said I'd write in a day or two and let them know what was happening. Calling Catherine again I asked if she was alright.

"I just got a bit of a scare when I heard your voice. Is it right, you're not going away?"

"It's right, but I'll send you a note and give you more details. There's something else, I love you and miss you."

There was a feeble 'me too' reply.

"We can make some plans now," I said, with a lump in my throat. "We could get married later on this year if you want."

There was no reply so I said I'd write in a day or so and laid the phone down. Sitting there for a few minutes I thought, it was just this morning when I'd seen her last, already I missed her desperately. Although I didn't know exactly when we'd see each other again, I knew it wouldn't be too long. It had been another monumental day in my life, so instead of going back to spend time with my squadron I decided to turn in. Needless to say it was difficult falling asleep.

In the morning yesterday's preoccupation came back to mind. I felt a renewed hope and an inner peace and happiness that I almost felt guilty for having. *The* briefing officer was the only person in the briefing room when I got there.

"Good morning squadron leader."

"Yes it is sergeant, it couldn't be better. Good morning."

Asking him if he could round up the rest of my squadron so we could go for an early morning run, I went to get the weather report. It was a sleepy looking bunch who greeted me when I got back fifteen minutes later.

"Are we really going out for a run?" Findlay asked.

"We need the exercise," I answered, grinning at him. "We've all had a lazy three weeks, it's time to get back at it. Besides, it's a lovely morning, you'll be ready for your breakfast when you get back."

"The way I'm feeling right now I don't think I will get back."

If they knew what I knew they'd be a bit livelier, I thought.

Visiting the briefing room one last time before we left, I noticed that our aircraft had been taken out of the hanger and were sitting on the apron. Catherine's Dad was in the briefing room and after we exchanged good mornings he asked if we were ready to go.

"We're ready, I just wanted to check there were no signals or changes."

"There's nothing," he answered. "We can go anytime."

Before I got into my aircraft I ran into the hanger to tell John we were leaving. He walked back with me to help me start. Almost ready to climb in group captain McKenzie appeared.

"Have a good flight squadron leader," he said, shaking my hand. "I'll be in touch sometime in the next few weeks."

As John helped me strap in he said he hoped I wouldn't be going overseas again. I hadn't told him what was happening, it would have to wait. This wasn't the time.

"There's something I wanted to ask you before you go. Mary and I are thinking about getting married later on this year and I wondered if you would be my best man."

As he stood on the wing of my aircraft we looked at each other and smiled. All the engines except mine were started now and when I answered him I had to shout.

"There's nothing I'd like better," I said, shaking his hand.

"Have a good flight," he shouted back, grinning.

Pushing the button and with a few puffs of smoke from the exhausts the dependable Merlin started. Pushing the throttle ahead the engine immediately responded and we began to move. I remembered vividly doing the same thing when I first flew in a Hurricane about six years before. I was inexperienced and intimidated. So much has happened and changed since then.

Waving to John and commander McKenzie, with the rest of my squadron and Catherine's Dad behind me, we taxied to our take off point. Climbing up to five thousand feet, in the clear morning we had a good view of Edinburgh off our port wing. There were still a few barrage balloons aloft and the city was shrouded in its seemingly permanent smoky haze. *We'll be back before long* I thought, as it slipped away behind us. Smooth and clear, it was a good day to fly, but evidence of the weather the day before lay everywhere below us. We kept each other company on the radio on the way south and in no time at all we were on the ground at Eastchurch. Later on in the day we had a surprise visit from Group Captain Thomson from Sector.

"It's good to see you again squadron leader, I trust you had a relaxing three weeks at home?"

"We did sir, it was good to get home. We'd been away for a long time."

He went on to tell me that Group Captain McKenzie from Turnhouse had called him and had discussed our proposed tour.

"It's an excellent idea," he said. "We'll likely do the same thing in England. If there's anything you feel I can help you with to put your show together just let me know."

After he left I had the briefing officer round up the squadron for a meeting. It was time to tell them.

"Tell us the worst then," said Findlay. "When do we leave?"

Looking at each one of them in turn I could see they feared the worst.

"Are you ready for this?" I began to smile. "For us the war is over. We will not be going to the Far East."

Dumbstruck, they stared at me and then at each other. We had been expecting to be sent overseas again and were mentally prepared for it. Whether it was relief or disbelief that we weren't going I couldn't say, but they all looked like I must have when I was first told.

"Could you repeat that?" William asked.

"Believe it, it's true, it's official. We're not going overseas. For us, the war is over."

The briefing room erupted with cheers and hoorays. When they settled down they wanted to know what we were going to be doing.

"The powers that be think the war in the East will be over before very long as well. With the full might of the allies directed at them the Japanese have to see their situation is hopeless. When that day comes the R.A.F. want to have open days at a number of aerodromes around the country to show the public some of the aircraft that flew in the war. Our squadron has been chosen to do the tour in Scotland."

They were feeling what I had felt, disbelief and immediately excited at the prospect. I had always enjoyed flying but for the first time since getting our wings we would be able to fly and have a bit of fun.

"This could be exciting," Findlay remarked.

"You're just thinking about all the women who'll be there and you hope will be drooling over you," William retorted.

"There could be a lot of them couldn't there?" Findlay grinned, looking at me. "But I'm spoken for, so I won't be interested at all."

"We don't have to do anything more about it today," I continued. "Today you can relax and let what I've told you sink in. Any ideas you have that could make the tour more exciting and memorable I'd be interested in hearing them."

After our discussion we went and had supper. Later on I talked to Findlay. Was there something going on between he and Isobel he hadn't told me.

"Wishful thinking on my part, we did write to each other when we were on leave and I told her we were stationed at Eastchurch. She wrote back and said that if we were going to be here for a while she might come and see me."

"Well, things are looking up, you'll be able to write back and tell her you will be here."

"Will it be me she comes to see or will it be her brother?"

"Likely a bit of both. Maybe the two of you will get to know each other better."

Since Findlay met Isobel he had never talked about any other women. Over the years they have written to each other from time to time, but they've never had the chance to build any kind of relationship. Only time would tell if there would ever be anything between them.

The next morning we were up at six and went for a run, and then after breakfast it was into the briefing room to toss some ideas around. An hour or so later we had enough to start with and by the end of the week we had a fairly good programme put together, it was just a case of practicing the manoeuvres.

Catherine's Dad paid us a visit again. There wasn't as much need for aerial pictures so he had time on his hands. He approved of our programme but suggested I try and get a few different types of aircraft, like Squadron Leader Baxter and his Mosquito, a Lancaster or an American B17. He said he'd talk to Squadron Leader Baxter and left me to try and get the bombers. Group Captain Thomson I remembered had told me that anything I needed to let him know. Calling him he said to leave it to him, as it turned out it was nearly two weeks before I heard from him again.

"I've got you two Lancasters, two B17s, a couple of Liberators from Coastal Command and a couple of Dakotas from Transport. Do you think that's enough squadron leader?"

"Those are the aircraft that people have heard most about sir. That should be adequate."

He gave me the names of the commanding officers at the aerodromes the aircraft would be coming from and said he'd stay in touch.

We'd been back at Eastchurch for a month already and until now we'd never had any correspondence from home. Needless to say we were eager to open our mail and all of us retreated to some quiet corner where we could read the latest news in peace.

Catherine's letters were full of information and excitement, she wrote that she had been getting my mail all right and how relieved she was about us not going overseas. She had also been to see the minister about when we could get married and what we needed to do. She'd been looking at wedding dresses and that Bella and Frances had said they'd make it for her. As well she'd asked somebody to be her matron of honour but didn't say who it was. She had spoken to the Lord Provost and that the town were now planning to have their dinner for me in September. They had been at the cottage a few times trying to clean it up. 'It's disgusting,' she wrote, 'how that person could live in it is beyond me. But I love it, it's such a homely little place.'

Where Catherine got her energy from to do all the things she'd been up to I didn't know, I felt exhausted just reading about them. Bella's letters were similar, everybody was so relieved that I wasn't going away again. 'It's so exciting,' she wrote. 'All these weddings and things going on, I've got goosebumps'. It was an exciting time, for everybody. I was no more than finished reading my mail when Findlay disturbed my peace.

"What date is this?" he asked.

"It's July the 10th. Why?"

"Isobel wrote saying that she and a friend have a few days leave and is planning on coming to see me July the 10th."

"Well you better go and get yourself tidied up then, make a good impression."

For the next while he ran about like a hen on a hot brick, wondering if he looked all right. It had been a long time since either one of us had seen my sister.

Later in the afternoon when I was in my office there was a knock on the door. It opened and in walked two young women in uniform; we stood looking at each other for a few moments. I barely recognized either one of them.

"Are you going to give your little sister a hug then?" Isobel smiled.

We held onto each other and then I leaned back and looked at her. Her eyes were full and about to spill over.

"Come on now," I said softly. "Don't do that. Stand back and let me look at you."

I told her how smart she looked in her uniform and she cried and grabbed onto me.

"I've missed you," she sobbed. "There were times I thought I'd never see you again."

The friend Isobel had come with was none other than Heather McIntosh, my nurse in Malta. She too was teary eyed and as I held onto Isobel I held out my hand for Heather. Giving her a hug, immediately I smelt it. 'Summer Blossoms.'

"The two of you not only look great you smell great. How do you know each other anyway?"

Heather went on to tell me that when she came back from Malta she'd been posted to the hospital where Isobel worked, they met one day and had become instant friends. 'The type of person you meet, somehow you just fit', she said, smiling at Isobel.

"We discovered we had a lot in common," Isobel added. "She told me her boyfriend's name was William and that she'd been introduced to him by his squadron leader, someone she'd been caring for. A few days later I realized the squadron leader was you."

"Aye, it was me," I answered still holding Heather's hand.

Heather smiled and went into her tunic pocket and then handed me a small bottle.

Recognising what it was I said for her to keep it, that it smelt better on her than it did on me. We laughed and then Isobel said she'd got a letter from home a couple of weeks before with all the latest news. Her eyes glistened again as she gave me another hug.

"You finally asked her. I'm so happy for you both. Congratulations on your engagement. All my big brothers getting married. The next thing I know I'll be an aunt."

As we laughed at the thought of it Heather congratulated me too, saying she'd have to meet Catherine.

"How are you and Findlay getting on?" I asked Isobel.

"He always writes and I look forward to his letters but I don't really know him.

"But you've never met anybody else either?"

"No, I haven't," she smiled. "I've met a lot of doctors and, since coming down here, a lot of aircrew as well, and you know how everybody loves their nurse."

"Yes, I can remember that," I answered, looking at Heather.

"When Findlay wrote, telling me your squadron was back and going to be at your old aerodrome, I thought, they're not all that far away, I'll go and see them. When Heather and I got talking she wanted to come and see William too, so here we are."

"How are William and you getting on?" I asked Heather.

"Everything is great. I think the world of him."

"You'll be anxious to see him. I'll get the duty officer to find the two of them."

A few minutes later there was a knock on the door and as it opened my regret was that I didn't have my camera at the ready. William stared at Heather, not believing his eyes. They hadn't seen each other since Malta.

"Heather, is it really you?" he asked. "How did you get here?"

After the hellos the two of them disappeared. That left Isobel, Findlay and I in my office, the two of them stood staring at each other. Leaving them there, I stayed out of their way for a while. An hour later they were still in there.

Standing outside the door for a moment I could hear them talking and laughing. *Sounds like it could be safe to go in now,* I thought, so I knocked on the door and went in. Findlay was sitting in my chair with Isobel sitting on his knee. Isobel wondered where I'd gone earlier.

I told her I'd some things to attend to I then asked if she and Heather had somewhere to stay for the night.

"Actually, no we don't. We thought we might have to go into London to find a place."

"If I found you a place to sleep here tonight we could all go into London for the day tomorrow. How about that?" I said.

"You could do that?" Isobel asked.

"If the two of you give me my office back I'll make some calls and arrange it."

Isobel got up off Findlay's knee then pulled him up.

Phoning sector I spoke with Group Captain Thomson and arranged to have the next day off.

"You've never been to sector control have you?" he said. "Why don't you come by for an hour tomorrow and I'll show you around?"

Arranging a time to meet I then had the briefing officer arrange transport for the morning. Curious as to where the four lovebirds were I had a look outside. Heather was sitting in William's aircraft. Isobel and Findlay were nowhere to be seen. We usually all ate together, but it wasn't going to be today. Locating the rest of the squadron we went to have supper, at the same time I told them we were having the next day off and going into London. It was later on in the evening before I saw the love-struck couples again. Sitting chatting I told them that everything was set up for the next day. They didn't care where they were going, just as long as they could spend time together. It was getting late and Isobel and Heather wanted to retire, so the briefing officer showed them their quarters. William, Findlay and I sat talking for a while longer.

"So, I take it you had a good afternoon," I said to them.

"It's been great," Findlay answered. "Your sister smells good enough to eat. Spending the whole day with her tomorrow, I can't wait."

"Thanks for arranging the day off," William added.

"It's overdue. It just makes it all the better when Isobel and Heather are here to share it with us. There's something else about tomorrow," I went on. "We're going by sector control for a visit, Group Captain Thomson asked us to go for an hour so everybody has to be ship shape and looking their best.

We have to show him that for this tour we're worthy representatives of the R.A.F. And one last thing, I don't want anybody getting the idea I'm running some kind of dating service at the aerodrome, all the commander needs to know is that Isobel's my sister and Heather's her friend and they came to visit me."

Both of them assured me I had nothing to worry about and then they too retired for the night. Staying up a bit later myself I scribbled a note to Catherine, telling her of the day's events.

When morning came we strayed from the norm. There was no run round the aerodrome, no briefing and no flying. The only thing on our minds was our day in London. Isobel and Heather graced us with their presence at the breakfast table. We had just sat down but when they appeared everybody stood, giving them admiring looks. They were a perfect example of how the military wanted and expected us to be; both looked stunning in uniform. As they sat beside me I told them that. They smiled and thanked me for the compliment.

As soon as we'd finished we made our way into London and our rendezvous. It had been years since we were last there, for Isobel and Heather this was their first visit. We could remember the destruction and although we were surprised at how much more widespread the damage was, we knew what to expect. Heather had seen bomb damage in Malta, but nothing on this scale. Isobel had only read about it, she'd never seen it first-hand. Both were mortified.

"These poor people," Isobel said over and over. "Where do you go when you emerge from an air raid shelter and discover your home and your memories are destroyed?"

We didn't linger in that part of London. The first port of call was sector control to meet with Group Captain Thomson. After introducing him to Isobel and Heather and the rest of the squadron he then took us on a tour of the underground control rooms used to plot aircraft movements both enemy and friendly.

"It's quiet down here now," he said. "But during the summer of 1940 especially, it was pretty intense. I can tell you what it was like but you had to witness it to know. The pilots of the fighters came face to face with the enemy in the skies and overcame the overwhelming odds, a true David and Goliath story. But the people whose job it was to plot the enemy and then get our fighters into a position to intercept them, all of them flew with the pilots of the Spitfires and the Hurricanes."

It was evident by the way the commander spoke he was immensely proud of these nameless people and of the R.A.F. fighter pilots. Together they undoubtedly saved Britain from certain invasion, we were all acutely aware what that would have meant.

After our tour of the underground control room we had tea with the commander and then we moved on to spend the day sightseeing in London. We had a good time together but as is so often the case, sometimes it was more tiring relaxing than working. William and Heather and Isobel and Findlay stuck to each other like glue all day. Watching Isobel and Findlay they seemed to be enjoying each other's company, it was up to them now if they wanted to see more of one another. It was late when we got back to the aerodrome and I for one wasted no time in getting to bed.

In the morning Isobel and Heather had breakfast with us again and stayed for a while but sadly they had to get back to their hospital.

"It's been great seeing you," Isobel said, giving me a hug. "Hopefully we'll get posted back up to Scotland and we can be a family again."

Heather and I hugged each other and I said I had never thanked her for looking after me in Malta.

"You don't have to thank me, it was my job. Besides, I think I owe you more than you owe me," she said, looking at William.

"Keep my little sister out of mischief now, hopefully I'll see you again soon."

Saying cheerio I left the four of them to do the same. In the afternoon it was back to the grindstone, planning and flying the routine we intended using for our tour.

18.   The Tour Begins

Another month passed. We had visits from the commander and Catherine's Dad and I visited the aerodromes where the aircraft were coming from that would accompany us on the tour, but still there was no word as to when it would be.

Then came August 6th 1945, and with it the news we'd just entered a new more terrifying than ever age. The American air force had dropped the mother of all bombs on Hiroshima in Japan. It had obliterated a third of the city and the rest lay in ruins. One hundred thousand people lived there. At first none of us could believe it. What kind of bomb razes a whole city? It couldn't be true, we thought. Three days later the city of Nagasaki ceased to exist, totally destroyed by another single bomb blast. The very next day Japan called for peace and later that same day the commander phoned to say that our tour of Scotland had been arranged to start within the week and for us to fly back up to Turnhouse, the venue for our first open day.

We were at Turnhouse when, on 14th August 1945, we got the news that the Japanese empire had surrendered unconditionally. Now it was time to celebrate. After almost six years, the Second World War was finally over and our tour of Scotland was to be part of the celebrations. It was advertised in the newspapers and the wireless, 'Come to your local R.A.F. aerodrome and see the legendry Spitfire and Hurricane. Shake hands with some of the young men who flew for your country' the advertisement read. Now I could phone home and tell them that my squadron was doing a tour of Scotland.

When Catherine answered she was so excited she could hardly speak.

"It's finally over ... and you're safe. I'm so immensely proud of you. I wish there was some way you could fit me into your aircraft so I could come with you."

Then I phoned home. Margaret answered and would have talked all day but eventually Bella spoke and wondered where I was. When I told her we were back at Turnhouse and what we were up to she sounded a little emotional.

"So it's *your* squadron who's going to be flying?" she asked. "It's been on the wireless umpteen times today about it."

"Why don't you all come down to Perth for the day when we're there?" I asked.

After telling me that they would, she hung up the phone.

The next day the aircraft that would accompany us on our tour arrived. It was an exciting time for all of us. After the last plane landed there was a briefing for all of the pilots and navigators to discuss the format for the tour and the aerodromes we would visit. At each venue the aircraft would be parked where the public could get close to them and the aircrew would be on hand to answer any questions that might come up. In the afternoon all the aircraft would fly, with the Spitfires flying last. For our part we wanted to show just how deadly the aircraft was, why it deserved the accolades it got and why it was every fighter pilot's dream to fly one. We were going to include a simulated dogfight and strafing attack, and an inverted low-level pass among other things, concluding with the missing man formation. It would be interesting to see just how many people would come. All we needed was the weather...

And when the day came it was quite unbelievable; none of us were expecting what happened. Long before the gates of the aerodrome were to open there were long lines of people waiting to get in. When they did finally open they just kept coming. Who knows how many thousands of people turned up. As we stood in front of our aircraft they milled around, looking at them and asking questions. Different people but the same questions, over and over.

What's it like to fly in a Spitfire?

'Exciting.'

What's it like up there when you know the enemy could be there, somewhere, waiting to shoot you down?

'Frightening.'

How do you feel now that it's over and you're home?

'Lucky'.

But it seemed people were determined to have a happy, carefree day. Older people, some who said they'd fought in the last war, would have talked all day; there were also middle-aged couples and young couples with families, their kids running around with arms outstretched. Some sat or lay on the grass, listening to the pipe band, enjoying the weather and the picnic they'd brought. Frances had come, and at one point was sitting in Catherine's dad's plane. John had the day off, so he showed his fiancée Mary around the aerodrome; after that they stayed with me.

When the flying actually started, the expressions on faces as the bombers started their engines and took off had to be witnessed. Some were excited, some looked emotional, some terrified. But there was one thing we all had in common; this was an experience none of us would ever forget.

And then it was our turn. Starting our engines we taxied to our take off point past a sea of happy, cheering faces. We couldn't hear it but they were cheering for us. More than anything else, they'd come to see the Spitfires. For years they'd heard about them and their pilots, now they'd come to see for themselves. Everything went as planned and after we landed again dozens of people wanted us to sign autographs. Every minute of the day was more remarkable than the one before it. Hours after the day was officially over there were people still hanging around, taking a last look at what had become a legend. The day was deemed a roaring success.

Every venue was the same. Although there was the odd shower of rain at night the weather during the day was ideal for flying.

Then it was Perth's turn. Phoning home to make sure they hadn't forgotten, somehow it made me nervous. Catherine had seen me fly but other than John the rest of my family hadn't. Getting the early train down from Pitlochry the Somerville clan were among the first in the gate.

After introducing the squadron to my family one by one they wanted to see my aircraft.

Margaret had gone with Catherine's Dad. She asked him why his plane was a different colour.

Catherine had been in my plane before but she wanted to take another peek anyway. She looked at everything inside and then grew quiet as she looked out either side at the wings, towards the front at the great long nose and then with misty eyes, at me.

"Do you know how proud I am of you? You're my hero."

Leaning inside the plane I put my arm around her and held her.

"I know, but I couldn't have done any of it without you. You're *my* hero." Still holding her, I continued. "It's all over. The war is finally over. Now we can get on with our lives. Come on, let's go and see the other aircraft."

"We brought a picnic," she smiled.

"I was hoping you would. I'm looking forward to it."

Wandering along the line-up we talked and laughed and when lunchtime came we had the picnic they'd brought. When the flying started I stayed with them for a while and then it was our turn. John helped me strap in and with the engine start, pulling the chocks from in front of the wheels, he gave me the all clear. Making my way to the take-off point with my squadron behind me, I waved to my family as I passed, bursting with pride. If I live to be a hundred it was a moment I'll never forget. Taxiing out, everybody was waving, once again, more than anything it was the Spitfire they'd come to see.

Our routine went as planned and when we landed it was like every other venue, hundreds of people wanted our autograph and after the day was officially over they just didn't want to leave. Eventually I made it back to my family, who were waiting patiently. My sisters hugged me and my brothers patted me on the back. Dad and Bella were a bit emotional and didn't say much. Margaret wondered why I didn't fall out when the aircraft was upside down.

What my family didn't know was that I'd arranged with one of the Dakota pilots to take them flying for half an hour, to go up over Pitlochry and the farm. John and Catherine's Dad knew and helped me get them into the aircraft.

"Come on," I said. "I've arranged with the pilot for you to see inside one of the Dakotas."

Getting inside the plane the pilot showed them the cockpit and then he asked them if they'd like to go up. I laughed as Bella made a hasty retreat for the door.

"You'll be fine Bella," Catherine's Dad said. "I'll go with you."

She understandably was a bit apprehensive but sat down anyway and he helped her with her seat belt.

"Here," she said. "I don't want to be flying upside down."

"Don't worry," he laughed. "Guaranteed, you won't be upside down".

Dad sat and never said a word. I helped him with his seat belt and then took his hand.

"Don't worry about a thing," I said, smiling at him. "He's a good pilot, you'll be fine. He's going to take you up over the farm."

The rest of the family, along with Jean and Mary, giggled with excitement. Checking again on Bella I held her hand and told her she'd be fine.

"Why don't you or Catherine's Dad drive this thing, I'd feel better."

As the starboard engine started Bella's hand squeezed on mine like a vice. Telling her again she'd be fine she reluctantly let me go and I got out of the aircraft just as the port engine started. Catherine and I waved as the aircraft began to move.

"Are your dad and Bella all right?" Catherine shouted.

"They're a bit apprehensive, but your Dad's there for reassurance."

As the plane took off and headed northwest towards Pitlochry Catherine and I sat on the grass and talked.

"Well, did you have a good day?" I asked, taking her hand.

"This has been one of the best days in my life," she answered quietly. "For lots of reasons I won't forget it. Like witnessing a profoundly proud man with tears rolling down his cheeks as he watched his son wheeling around the sky, Bella hanging onto his arm doing the same. For the way the public cheered as you took off. For the way we're all here together celebrating. None of us will forget it. The Spitfire and her pilots beat overwhelming odds and gave Britain a chance to fight on. Because of that chance we're here today. It's down in history, it never will be forgotten."

Smiling at her I looked in the direction of the Dakota, straining to see it in the distance, it was beginning to sink in just exactly what we'd accomplished.

"It certainly looks like people have fallen in love with the Spitfire doesn't it?"

"They have, but not nearly as much as I love you," she smiled. "There's so much I have to tell you, but we don't have time right now. Are you going to be getting any leave?"

"We haven't been thinking about leave to be honest but now that you mention it, I wouldn't mind."

"Guess what?" she grinned. "I talked to the minister about us getting married and he says any Saturday in October is fine with him. What do you think?"

In the distance I could hear the drone of the Dakota coming back.

"Does that give you enough time to do all the things you need to do?"

'There isn't all that much left to do. My dress is made, and my brides-maid's dress, we just need a date so we can invite who we want to be there."

The Dakota's engines were much louder now and as I turned to look the aircraft was on short finals. We watched the main wheels touch and the tail settle.

"Who did you ask to be your bridesmaid?" I asked, squeezing her hand.

"Who do you think it could be?" she teased.

At that moment I couldn't think, the plane was almost on us and had to shout to be heard over the engines. Catherine wriggled closer and put her arm around my waist.

"Who is the best friend I have? Whose shoulder did I cry on when you were away?"

"Bella's your best friend, it was her shoulder you cried on." I looked at her and began to smile. "You asked Bella?"

The engines stopped and the plane's occupants got out. Catherine pulled me closer still as we watched them walk towards us, both Dad and Bella were laughing.

"She was the only person I wanted to do it," Catherine went on. "I'd made up my mind a long time ago that if you asked me to marry you she'd be the one I'd ask."

My family were upon us now, all of them giggling with excitement.

"Are you happy because you liked it or because you're glad to be back on the ground?" I asked.

"It was great!" Bella said, hugging me first.

"It was better than great," Dad echoed, putting his arm around my shoulder. "I can see why you like flying. It's been a great day altogether."

For a while we sat together and talked and laughed, hoping the day wouldn't end. Sadly the time came for them to go. Catherine's parting words were 'get some leave and come home.'

The next morning after breakfast there was a briefing for all the aircrew who had been involved with the tour. The powers that be merely concurred with what we already knew, that the tour had been a resounding success. It had been an experience none of us would forget. We'd never had as much fun since getting our wings and we were in fact a bit sad that it was over. Later in the morning my squadron, along with Catherine's Dad and Squadron Leader Baxter went back to Turnhouse. Checking in with the briefing officer he told me that Group Captain McKenzie wanted to see the squadron as soon as we got back. *This doesn't sound good*, I thought, as we trooped over there. As we entered his outer office I'd completely forgotten that Alison would be there. When William saw her he froze on the spot. He hadn't an inkling she'd still be in the R.A.F. or that she'd still be working for the commander. She glanced at him a few times but as always she carried out her duties with professionalism.

"Squadron Leader Somerville, the commander is expecting you, I'll tell him you're here."

Almost immediately the commander invited us in.

"Squadron leader, I wanted to have a word with you and your pilots to congratulate you on a job well done, I've been following your tour with great interest. There's nothing but high praise from everyone at the aerodromes you visited and the reports on the wireless and the newspapers, well, they're just phenomenal. All of you are a great asset to the R.A.F. and your country. On behalf of all I thank you".

Shaking all of our hands he dismissed the rest of the squadron saying he'd see them in the mess later. 'We'll have a drink to celebrate,' he said, but there was something else he wanted to discuss with me.

"Squadron leader, if you don't mind me asking, what do you see yourself doing now that the war is over? What are your plans?"

"Plans sir? I'm not sure what you mean."

"Now that the war is over, would you like to stay in the R.A.F. or have you had enough?"

His question hit me like a torpedo hits the broadside of a ship. I wasn't expecting it but I gave him the thought that had gone through my mind a number of times.

"To be honest sir, if there was some way I could stay in the R.A.F. so I could still fly and then go home every night, that's what I would like. I love flying and can't imagine the day when I won't be able to."

"That's the answer we were hoping for, squadron leader. Now that the war is over there's a vast number of aircrew who sadly we just don't need any longer. But men like you and your pilots, men who are leaders, the R.A.F. will always need." He paused for a moment and looked at me. "What about on a personal level? What are your plans?"

"On a personal level sir, Catherine and I would like to get married sometime in October."

"That's what I heard," he answered, smiling. "So if you had three months paid leave, that would give you enough time then?"

"Yes sir," I smiled.

"Right then, advise your pilots. The same thing applies to them. In three months if they want to stay in the R.A.F. there will be a place for them, but if they want to leave and pursue other things, that's fine too."

Our meeting over, he shook my hand again and smiled. "Go home and marry that girl James, you're two fine young people."

Leaving his office I was surprised to find William still in the outer office, speaking to Alison. On getting outside I stood on the path for a minute looking around the airfield. There were aircraft sitting everywhere. John was right, there were a lot of them that might not fly much again. Moments later the door opened behind me and William emerged. He too looked out across the airfield.

"You didn't tell me Alison was still here."

"No," I answered, pausing for a moment. "I'm sorry, I should have."

"No, it doesn't matter, it wouldn't have changed anything. I loved her at the time but now I just feel a bit sorry for her. No, Heather's the girl for me. I'm going to ask her to marry me."

"Heather's a lucky girl, does she know that?"

We laughed, then walked together to the briefing room, where we found the rest of the squadron.

"Good, I'm glad you're all here. There's something I need to tell you."

After conveying to them what the commander had just told me they weren't sure what to think. In spite of their best efforts and the praise just bestowed upon them by him, initially they felt dumped. But then they could see they were in the enviable position of being able to stay in the R.A.F. if they wanted to.

Later on in the officer's mess, the commander did join us for a bit of light-hearted fun. Catherine's Dad was there as well, and when I told him about my chat with the commander and our extended leave, he said he'd been speaking to him as well and he'd told him he would be retiring from the R.A.F.

"It's a good time for me to go. It's time for a change."

"There's something else you should know," I went on. "Catherine and I are thinking about getting married."

"Yes I know,' he answered smiling. "In October, she told me yesterday up in Perth."

Thinking for a minute it dawned on me, retirement wasn't the only thing the commander and he had talked about.

"We've got you to thank for our leave, haven't we?" I said, looking at him wryly.

Again he smiled. "Well, I might have had something to do with it. Are you going to go home tomorrow?"

"Likely, I should go and phone though, and let them know."

"I'm going in to the city tomorrow to meet Frances, so I'll take you in if you like."

Saying that I would I went to find a phone. When Catherine answered she was so excited she could hardly speak. She had so much to tell me when I got back, she said. Phoning the farm, as usual Margaret answered. I spoke with her for a minute, telling her I'd be home the next day and to tell her Mum. When I got back to the mess, Catherine's Dad was gone so I sat with William and Findlay.

"There's been nothing mentioned about weddings and the like lately," I said. "But I wanted to let you know Catherine and I are planning to get married in October."

"You said you weren't going to tell us," Findlay quirked.

"Well, if you're going to be my best men I should really tell you when the day is."

They looked at each other, and what was known to happen only once in a blue moon, Findlay was stuck for words.

"You want *both* of us to be your best man?" William queried.

"Actually, there could be three of you. I'm going to ask my brother Richard as well."

"You must be planning on having a wild day if it's going to take three of us to keep you in line," Findlay laughed, finding his tongue again.

"I for one will do it," William answered.

Findlay thought for a few moments and then he too gave me his answer.

"Thanks for asking, I'm flattered, but you don't need three best men. William and your brother will do it for you, but I still want to be there, just to make sure you go through with it."

Findlay went to bed and left William and I sitting there. We talked and talked. He spoke briefly of Alison.

"It was a bit of a shocker seeing her there. If she had waited I'd maybe have asked her."

"Did she tell you she had a little boy?"

He shook his head and for a minute we had our own thoughts.

"Do you think you'll stay in the air force?" I asked, changing the subject.

"Probably, but I'll have to ask Heather what her plans are and see if we can be stationed together. Maybe I should ask her if she wants to get married first. Maybe she wouldn't have me."

"There's no fear of that", I snorted, and thought of the first time they met and the circumstances surrounding it.

"Thanks again," I said, "for saving my life when we were in Malta. I know if it hadn't been for you I wouldn't be here."

"Ah man James, if the shoe had been on the other foot you'd have done the exact same thing for me. You know, I'm glad the war and the killing is over. We've had some bad days and seen some terrible things, but there have been a lot of good days when we had some good laughs, I'm going to miss that."

When we eventually went to bed although I was tired I felt great and inside a great sense of accomplishment and, I was going to be getting married. Life couldn't be better.

19. Three Months Leave

At breakfast the next morning we all sat together for as long again, it was like nobody wanted to leave. Maybe it was because we knew that another chapter had ended and that none of our lives would be the same again. Telling them I would be inviting them to my wedding we exchanged addresses and then reluctantly we went our separate ways. Before I left I went to the hanger to see John, where as usual he was up to his armpits in paper and not looking all that happy.

"Thankfully I don't have much more of this," he said.

He went on to tell me he too had been approached about either staying in the R.A.F. or leaving, but he'd decided to leave.

"Two more weeks and I'll be done. I'm glad you came by. Mary and I are getting married on the second Saturday in October. You're still going to be my best man aren't you?"

"I am," I answered smiling. "The second Saturday you say? Catherine wants us to get married on the third one."

"I know, and William and Jean are tying the knot on the first one."

"You're kidding aren't you? Three weddings in three weeks?"

"Yep, it's going to be great, the whole family together; even Isobel's coming home," he answered, rocking back and forth on his chair.

"Well, I just came by to say we've been given three months leave. I'm on my way home, so anything I can help you with, I'll be there."

This really was a year none of us would forget. Not only had the war ended but there was going to be a major change to the Somerville clan structure as well.

Leaving John to his unenviable chores I went looking for Catherine's Dad. I didn't have to look far; he was walking into the hanger as I was going out.

"Well Squadron Leader Somerville, are you ready to go to the station?"

On the way there he told me he had to take his aircraft back to London and that he'd some things to attend to while he was there.

"But I'll be back in a few days. My daughter's getting married you know," he said, grinning. "I have to be there to help her where I can."

"Thanks for everything you've done for me, I replied. "I know there are untold things you've done. Thanks for helping me fulfil a dream. But most of all for Catherine, she means the world to me."

"James, my boy, I know that. I've known as well for a long time how Catherine feels about you, I couldn't wish for a better son in-law. I'm happy because she's happy. When you were flying I hoped and prayed nothing would happen to you. If it had I didn't know how she'd ever get over it. You know what she's like, she's focused and strong, she knows what she wants and goes after it, but at the same time she has a soft heart. My only regret is that her Mum won't see her on her big day and to see the fine person she's become."

As we drove on through the traffic I had another thought.

"You know, I've heard about some instructors who put the fear of death in their students when they were training, but you've always been so easy going."

"Students don't learn anything in that kind of hostile environment. A person can be easy going and still have the respect of those around him. I found out a long time ago that if things aren't going the way you'd like there's no point going off the deep end about it. That always makes a bad day worse. When things are like that I just tell myself that this too will pass."

"That's what Dad always says," I answered, shaking my head.

"That's why your Dad and I get along so well," he smiled. "We think along the same lines."

Getting to the station he shook my hand and said he'd be back in a few days and then I boarded the train.

It wasn't a long trip. Just a few miles out of Edinburgh I entered into the land of nod and the next thing I knew the train was slowing down as we went into Perth and, a short while after that we were in Pitlochry where Dad, Bella and Catherine were waiting. Although there was no pipe band or newspaper reporter, somehow this time I got even more of a sense of being home. As the four of us stood on the platform holding each other, I could tell the three most important people in my life felt the same way.

"Now, finally you're home," Catherine said. "Now we can go on."

Slowly we walked to where the car was parked and equally slowly Dad drove us home. It had been a long time I'd been away to war, none of us knowing if I'd return. I wasn't a repentant waster like the prodigal son returning home, I'd been away for a cause, but now I was back to where I was loved and welcome. They wouldn't need to kill the fatted calf to celebrate my return, we just needed peace and harmony. That was one thing I knew for sure I'd find in this place.

Stopping at the house door Dad and Bella looked at Catherine and I in the back seat. As I got a little misty eyed, they got out and left the two of us sitting there.

"No tears my love," Catherine said, holding my hand. "It's all over. That was a sad chapter in all our lives, but remember what you once told me, we're going to turn the page. There's a new chapter just about to begin. I don't know what twists and turns this one will take, but I know it's going to start off well. We're going to get married in a few weeks, we're going to live in that little house down the road and I'm going to love you always. You fill me with pride James Somerville. I know we'll always be happy because your Mum told us. Remember?"

We sat there for a while, holding each other, then Bella came out and got into the front seat of the car, looked back at us and reached for my hand.

"I've made tea," she smiled. "Why don't you come in? Come on, it's over and you're home."

Dad was sitting at the table when we went in but he got up and came over and gave me a hug. He didn't say anything. The embrace said it all. We were all a bit emotional as we sat drinking our tea.

"Would you look at us," Bella said, beginning to smile. "You'd think we were at a wake or something. Come on, we're supposed to be happy."

Looking at one another we began to smile.

"So, what do you think then?" Bella went on. "Three Somervilles getting married in as many weeks, is that not some work? There's going to be nothing done but celebrating. William and Jean's invitations have been sent out already, John and Mary's are going this week, now you'll have to help Catherine with yours."

Catherine wondered if I had thought about who to ask to be my best man.

"I have actually, just yesterday I asked William and Findlay. Findlay declined but I'm going to ask Richard too. And a little bird told me you were going to be a bridesmaid," I said, squinting at Bella.

"Your little bird was right," she answered, grinning at Catherine. "And I'm really looking forward to it."

"I've got a list of names," Catherine went on. "Of people I thought you might want to invite. You'll have to look at it and see if I've missed anyone. If you came to the cottage tomorrow afternoon we could go over it." She paused for a moment, looking at Dad and Bella. They smiled at each other and then said there were a couple of other things she should tell me.

"First of all, I've kept in touch with the Lord Provost. They plan to have a dinner for you in three weeks. It's all been arranged. There could be about a hundred people there. You might have to say a few words, so you should be prepared."

"You mean a speech? In front of a hundred strangers? I don't think that's a good idea."

"It's only a few words," Dad added. "The dinner is in your honour; it's the least you can do."

"There's another little thing," Catherine went on. "This really took the wind out of my sails. Apparently the whole town knows we're getting married, I don't know whose idea it was or how it got started but there was an article in the paper. The reporter who wrote the story about you before wrote another one. He talked about the dinner the town is having for 'one of its sons', and about us getting married. As a token of their appreciation, any individual or business who felt inclined could make a donation towards a wedding present. There's a list being kept of where the donations have come from, I can tell you it's getting quite long. What do you think about that then?"

Sitting in stunned disbelief I asked why they would do that.

Dad reached across the table and put his hand on mine.

"It's quite simple really," he began. "They see a young man who's been away to war, he along with a few handfuls of his comrades saved this country from certain invasion. They feel indebted to you. You went and could have given your life, they feel that giving you a few pounds for a wedding present is a small price to pay for what you did."

"But there are other people went to war and came home."

"Yes there were, but there are no other pilots from Pitlochry who made it through the war. None who have been in the war from the beginning and certainly none your age. In their eyes you're a hero. Their hero. You have to let them do this."

Looking at Catherine her lip trembled; Bella reached across the table and held onto my arm.

"You're a special person James," Dad went on. "I don't think you fully realize what it is you've done yet but in time you will. It's not only we who are proud of you."

Thinking for a moment I then asked what I should do.

"Just take a day at a time,' Bella answered. "We've all been through so much, just take a day at a time."

Catherine wondered how long I was home for. When I said it was for three months they couldn't believe it. She wondered as well what was happening after I went back.

"To be honest I don't know. I don't think the R.A.F. know themselves yet what's happening. There are a lot of people leaving, but the squadron and I, if we want, can stay on. If there was some way I could be there two or three days a week and be home every night, that's what I would like. But if they want me to be somewhere miles away I wouldn't be interested. We'll just have to wait and see what happens."

The day wore on and Bella got up, saying she'd have to be making supper. William and Mary came in from work and welcomed me home. I ribbed William a little bit, saying he didn't have a lot of days off freedom left.

"No, but neither do you," he laughed.

"My, would you listen to them?" Bella quipped. "You'd think that instead of exchanging vows they were going to be fitted with a ball and chain."

"I've got one for James," Catherine answered, with a wry little smile.

William had a good giggle at the thought of it.

Catherine spent the night at the farm and in the morning I kept her company as she went to work.

"Will you come back into the town later, I'd like to make sure the chain fits properly," she said, laughing. "In a few weeks I won't be Catherine Campbell any more, I'll be Mrs Somerville. I've waited so long I can't believe it's actually happening. Mrs Somerville, I like the sound of that."

We hugged one another again and then she said she'd have to go.

When I got back to the farm Bella was alone. She poured two cups of the freshly made tea and we sat together at the table.

"In a few short weeks you'll have your own little house and your own table. I'm going to miss these little chats."

"We will have our own place but I don't see the chitchats stopping. I thought now that I was home we'd have more."

"It's been quite a year so far between one thing and another," she went on. "And it's not over yet. Your honorary dinner is coming up, you and your brothers getting married. It's going to be positively dull around here after it's all over."

"So are William and Jean moving into the other farm cottage then?"

"They are, but as you know, Jean is an only child. The two of them could go to Dunkeld and take over her Dad's farm sometime."

"Would William do that? Leave Dad with all that work I mean?"

"Your Dad and I have talked about it. If it was to happen we'd just change things around a bit but we'd manage. If you're going to be part time in the R.A.F. you could spend some time at home."

"I'll have to do something if I'm going to have a house of my own and a little wife. I'll have to support her somehow."

"Oh, you and your little wife will manage just fine," Bella went on smiling.

"What about the cottage? I know Catherine and you have been cleaning it but are we going to be able to live in it?"

"You go and see it with Catherine," she smiled again. "See what you think. But first things first, see to your invitations and you have to go and see the Lord Provost. There's a fair bit to do, you know what Catherine is like. She likes to be organized. She's got everything written down and the two of you will likely manage, but if you need any help you know we're here."

"She asked you to be her bridesmaid."

"She's some girl. We were sitting right here when she asked. I just about fell off my seat. I told her I was too old and that there must be somebody else she could ask, but she wouldn't take no for an answer. Frances helped us make the dresses, we've all been quite busy, but we've had a few laughs at the same time."

The kitchen door opened and Dad walked in, followed by William and Mary. Bella looked at the clock on the wall.

"Oh my Lord," Bella exclaimed. "Look what you made me do, James Somerville. I don't have the dinner ready."

As she jumped up off the chair the rest of us looked at one another and laughed.

"Don't go to a lot of bother now Bella," Dad said, grinning at her. "Just a cup of tea and one of your cakes will be fine today."

As the five of us sat around the table William wondered where Catherine and I were going on our honeymoon. A honeymoon was something else I hadn't thought of and obviously William could tell.

"You haven't thought about a honeymoon yet have you?"

"No I haven't," I answered, shaking my head. "Where are Jean and you going?"

"It's supposed to be a secret but we're just going to get on the train and go down to Edinburgh for a few days. Jean has booked us into a guest house and we're going to do some sightseeing. We would have liked to go out to the west coast, to Mull or Skye, but we would have needed a car for that. With the petrol rationing we couldn't."

"It won't matter where you take Catherine James," Bella added. "As long as she's got you all to herself she'll be happy anywhere."

"Maybe we should just spend a few days in Edinburgh as well, there's plenty to do there and we can walk everywhere."

Dad, William and Jean went back to work and Bella and I talked for a bit longer.

"If we go on like this," I laughed, "in a day or two we'll have nothing left to talk about."

"You think so?" she answered, grinning. "I don't know, I think we've got a lot of catching up to do."

The day rolled on and soon it was time to go into the town to meet Catherine. Telling Bella I'd be back later, I jumped on the bike and got to Catherine's house just as she was opening the door.

"Well James Somerville, you made it," she said, smiling.

Getting into the house she took her coat off and let it fall on the floor behind her and then threw her arms around me, hugging and kissing me.

"All day you've been on my mind. I don't think I've taught the kids anything."

We stood for ages swaying to and fro, and then she went on.

"Why don't we have something to eat then I'll show you what I've done with our wedding plans."

Setting the table for two I joked with her that it was like a rehearsal for when we get married, I'd be home every night and we'd have tea together.

"For a while it'll be just the two of us," she answered grinning. "But hopefully one day we'll have ten little Somervilles running around."

"Ten? You have to be kidding!" I blurted. "Couldn't we just have a dog?"

"We'll have a dog as well," she teased, slipping her arm around my waist.

As we sat eating she grinned from time to time, obviously still amused at my reaction. After supper she got her paperwork onto the table and started off by showing me a list of all the things she had thought of to do, like making a wedding dress, making bridesmaid's dress. She had been busy but there were still things to do. The dress was made and so I asked her where it was.

"It's here," she smiled, squeezing my hand. "But I'm not showing it to you, it's bad luck for you to see it until I walk up the aisle. The other big thing is we need to decide where we want to have our reception. I've spoken to four hotels, any one could do it. Personally I like the one that Jean works in best, but we have to choose. Wedding rings. We could do that tomorrow. The other big thing is furniture, we'll have to get some furniture for our little house."

"Is it even liveable?" I wondered. "The last time I saw it I just couldn't imagine living in it."

Holding my hand and her face smiling she said I wouldn't know the place. Nothing had been done to the garden. That would have to wait till we were living there. I said if she was happy with it I would be as well.

We ran through the rest of the list and then as it was getting late I said I should go back to the farm and come back in the morning.

"Maybe I should stay?" I said, smiling at her. "That way I won't be late in the morning."

Holding my hand she walked with me to the door where we stood holding each other for a while.

"On you go before I change my mind," she said, opening the door.

When I got back to the farm Dad and Bella were having their usual cup of tea together before going to bed. Bella wondered if we'd gotten everything done.

In the morning at breakfast I asked Richard if he'd like to be my best man. With a faint smile he sat looking at me for a moment.

"Isn't there somebody else you could ask? I'll help you in any other way I can, it's just that I don't like being in the limelight like that."

That was true, it's how he's always been, so I didn't pressure him.

"That's all right," I answered, smiling at him. "I would have liked you to do it but I know how you feel."

"We should have a chat about your bank account though," he went on. "You might want to look after it yourself now."

"I've been meaning to ask you about it. I need some money to buy furniture and the like."

"Well," he hesitated, "I hope you don't mind but I invested most of it. But it's done all right."

Richard went to his room and a few minutes later he was back and handed me a little blue book with Royal Bank of Scotland embossed on the front. Looking at it I ran my fingers over the letters.

"Go ahead then,' he said, grinning. "Open it."

Opening the book I looked at the modest entries for the first few months I was in the R.A.F., and then when I got my wings and a pay increase the total grew a little faster. When I was made squadron leader it grew faster still. There were withdrawals, and details of where the money had gone. He had invested it in war bonds and a handful of other companies. With the demand during the war for what they produced their value had grown significantly, and consequently, so had my bankbook. I asked him if the total was correct. Smiling he said that it was. It was quite unbelievable and another surprise. He'd worked away quietly in his own way, a Somerville trait, taking my modest pay and making it into a significant amount of money. He obviously had a flair for it and judging by the expression on his face he was proud of his achievement.

"If this is what you can do, you can continue to look after my money. I'm impressed. Did you invest in the same places?"

"I did, but with the war ending everybody's focus is changing, so I've changed things around a bit."

"Keep on doing what you're doing, you're obviously good at it."

Giving him the book back I went to keep my rendezvous with Catherine. When I got to the cottage she was sitting at the table writing invitations.

"That was one thing you didn't show me last night," I said, looking at the list of names.

"No, I forgot, but have a look now and see if there's anyone you feel I've forgotten."

Going down the list, all the obvious ones were there, Catherine's friends and colleagues from school, including Mrs Dunlop, her Dad and Frances, and then there was the Somerville clan. From the R.A.F. there was my squadron of course, Group Captain McKenzie and his wife Jean from Turnhouse, Group Captain Thomson from sector control in London, and then there was Group Captain McLean, our commanding officer in Malta, it would be good to see him again, he was a canny Scot, I liked him. And then, at the end of the list there were two names that made me chuckle, Jock and Fergus. Just seeing their names there made me smile, they worked well together and obviously liked each other, but I don't remember ever meeting two people whose personalities were so different. I was looking forward to seeing them again.

"You found Jock and Fergus's address? How did you do that?"

"It helps when your Dad knows people," she answered, smiling.

"Hopefully they can come, it'll be nice to see them again."

"Do you think I've missed anyone, or is there anyone on the list you don't want to ask?"

"It looks fine, but I feel a bit guilty. You've done all this work in preparation for our wedding and I've done nothing."

She came around to my side of the table and sitting beside me she slipped her arm around my waist.

"Now why would you feel guilty you daft thing. How could you help if you weren't here? Besides, there's still lots to do. Did you ask Richard to be your best man?" she asked in the next breath.

"I did, but he doesn't want to do it."

"To be honest I wondered if he would, but you've got William. Do you think he'll bring his girlfriend?"

"He'll bring her alright, but she won't be his girlfriend much longer, he's going to ask her to marry him."

"He is, how nice, I'm so looking forward to meeting her."

"You'll like her, Isobel and her have become great pals."

"Do you know whatever became of Alison?"

"Believe it or not she's still working at Turnhouse for Group Captain McKenzie, I couldn't believe my eyes when I walked in there one day and there she was."

"It's too bad what happened, she's a nice person, I hope she finds someone else."

We sat with our own thoughts for a moment and then Catherine said she'd make tea before we went out shopping. I wondered where she wanted to go for her ring.

"You mean where do I want to go for our rings," she answered grinning. "You're mine now James Somerville and you have to wear my ring so that the world knows you're off the market."

"So where are we going to go for them then?" I smiled back.

"We'll go to the same little shop where we got my engagement ring. She'll have something I'm sure."

Wandering down the street and into the shop, the owner welcomed us in.

"So, your wedding is in a few weeks," she remarked. "You must be excited."

"We are," Catherine answered. "We came in to see if you had wedding rings we liked."

"When I read about your upcoming wedding I wondered if you'd come in. Someone approached me about making a donation to your wedding fund but I thought I'd wait and see if you came."

Catherine and I sat together as the lady let us see one and then another until we found ones we liked. When it came to paying it was the same as before, she charged us half price. We thanked her and as we left the store she hugged Catherine and I.

"You'll always be happy," she smiled. "I can feel it."

Outside the shop we stood for a moment. Catherine asked if I wanted to go to the café for tea.

"Maybe another day, I'd rather go and see the cottage."

We got on our bikes and raced each other along the road. Five minutes later we were there.

"Are you ready for this?" Catherine asked, turning the key in the lock. "Come on, give me your hand and close your eyes."

Leading the way she took a few steps in the front door.

"Alright, you can open them now."

Looking around it didn't appear to be the same place. All the old furniture was gone, there was new paint and wallpaper and the sun could actually shine in the windows again. It still needed carpets and furniture but now it was clean and fresh. Now I really was feeling awkward.

"You've done all this work and I wasn't here to help you with it."

"You don't have to feel bad because you weren't here," she said, giving me a hug. "Bella and I have had a lot of laughs in here, neither one of us had ever done any wall papering before. The first few pieces we tried to put up were more on us than on the wall. Don't worry, there's still plenty left to tackle, now that you're home for a while you're going to be busy. There's still the outside to paint and tidy up. The main thing is, do you like it?"

"It looks great. The change is miraculous. Once we get some furniture in here it will be as cosy as your cottage in the town."

Before we left we peeked around the corner of the house into the garden; it still looked like a jungle. We'd get to it some time.

Deciding to go to the farm it seemed the rest of my family were in the kitchen drinking tea.

"You're just in time," Bella said, grinning and pouring us a cup. "So did you get another little job done this morning then?"

Catherine took the boxes out of her pocket and gave them to Bella.

"My, my, they're lovely," she beamed. "You'll have to get them engraved after the big day."

And then she wondered if we'd been to the cottage yet. I told her we had and that I couldn't believe the difference.

My sister Jean wondered if we'd decided on which hotel we'd want to have our reception in. Catherine and I looked at each other and said we didn't know yet.

"Well," she went on. "I've got a surprise for you. After the story about you in the paper the other day, about your honorary dinner, getting married and donations, the manager of my hotel and I got talking and he came up with an idea. He spoke to the other hotels and they're all prepared to work together on it, all you have to do is choose which hotel you want to have your reception in and instead of a donation they'll all contribute, so the reception won't cost you anything. There's a condition," Jean continued. "The guest count cannot be more than a hundred. If it's less than a hundred instead of making a donation towards a wedding present the hotels will pay for the reception."

"Why is everybody being so generous?" I wondered.

"It's like your Dad said," Bella added. "Everybody wants to show their appreciation for what you did, that's the sum and substance of it. There are people in the town you know and there are some you don't know, but because of the story in the paper they all feel they know you, you've touched all of their lives. You can't stop what they want to do, that wouldn't be right either, so why don't you accept it and savour the moment."

"You think that's what I should do?"

Holding my hand in hers she smiled and slowly nodded.

I couldn't believe it. Catherine thanked Jean and said we'd let her know in a day or two. Finishing our tea we went back into the town to work on our wedding plans. As we sat at the table I said to Catherine I just couldn't believe what the people of the town were doing, that I didn't know what to think about it. She just smiled.

As we sat together writing invitations I said there was another name I wanted to add to the list. I wanted to ask the lady from the shop where we got our rings. Then I said there was something I might need my teacher's help with and that was to prepare a speech for my honorary dinner. She laughed and said she'd almost forgotten she had been my teacher.

Over the next weeks Catherine and I worked together more closely than we'd ever done and eventually all of the items on her "to do" list had been addressed. We bought furniture for the cottage, sent our wedding invitations, decided we would have our reception in the Atholl Palace, the hotel where my sister Jean worked. And then the day came for William and Jean's wedding. The ceremony and reception were being held in Dunkeld and so the Somerville clan went down on the train. The service was to be held in the old Dunkeld Abbey church. It sits right on the banks of the river Tay. With all the big trees surrounding it and the river, it's almost as nice there as it was in Pitlochry.

The minister's voice echoed and reverberated into every corner of the old building and as William and Jean exchanged vows Catherine held my hand. My brother and his fiancée had just become husband and wife, it was a touching moment. Their reception was held in a hotel not far from the church, close enough to be able to walk to. As we ate and drank to their health and future they looked incredibly happy. It was the first day of the start of their life together.

A week later we did the same thing again. John and Mary's wedding day was no less spectacular. The big difference for me was that this time I was the best man. John and Mary, if it was at all possible looked even happier than William and Jean had done the week before. In the course of the evening I joked with Catherine that she only had one more week of freedom left and asked her if she was going to change her mind and leave me standing at the altar.

"Well," she answered, smiling. "I did think about keeping you waiting and wondering, but no, I'll be there. You're looking at the next Mrs Somerville. What about you, will you be there?"

Looking at this person who had shared so much of my life I felt the beginnings of a lump in my throat. Slipping my arm around her waist she knew I'd be there.

Sitting hanging onto each other we watched Dad and Bella dance around the floor, it was certainly something they hadn't done much of over the years, they'd been too busy farming and providing for their family. I thought of all they'd done for us. I loved them very much and was proud to be called Somerville.

"It seems like only yesterday when we all played together and went for picnics out on the hill with Bella. I miss those days, but here we were getting married. Where did the time go? In another way it feels like a life time ago, so much had happened since then."

"A lot has happened since then," Catherine answered, squeezing my hand. "None of us should ever wish our lives away but I'm glad the last few years are over. If there's one positive thing we should glean from the war it's that all of us should now realize we have to make the most of every day, every precious moment of our lives has to count."

She was right, we owed it to all of the people who died for our freedom to do at least that.

After we'd seen John and Mary off on their honeymoon everybody began to leave the reception and go home. We, on the other hand, had decided to stay the night in Edinburgh and go back to Pitlochry the next day.

20. Wedding Vows

Over the next couple of days Catherine helped me put the finishing touches to the speech I'd prepared for my honorary dinner. And then, accompanied by clouds and rain, the day came. It was to be held in the Atholl Palace, the same hotel we would be in on the coming Saturday for our wedding. Dad and Bella, Catherine and her Dad and Frances were also invited. We arrived right on time and were met at the hotel door by the Lord Provost himself. Leading us into a small room he introduced us to the dignitaries waiting there. There were a few familiar faces among the council members, and our minister, the man we'd meet again on Saturday was also there. Right on seven, to the applause of the invited guests, his Lordship led us into the banquet room. It was a little intimidating when I saw how many people there were there. Glancing at Catherine she instinctively knew what I was thinking and discreetly winked at me. As we sat his Lordship addressed the gathering and then introduced us. When he got to me, everybody, including Catherine, stood and applauded. The room blurred and there was a lump in my throat bigger than an apple. In an effort to keep my composure I thought of how bad the weather had been all day. It helped and eventually the applause stopped. Finding Catherine's hand under the table I held it and looked at her, whispering that I didn't think I could do this.

"Yes you can, I know you can," she whispered back.

The moment his Lordship sat down the feast began. Sitting immediately to his right and with Catherine on mine I didn't get the chance to think or worry much about the speech I'd be making shortly. Looking along the table towards Dad and Bella they seemed to be enjoying themselves and I thought. *Everybody is here for me.* "The weather, think of the rain and the wind outside" the voice inside of me said.

And then, with the meal over, the Lord Provost stood up. It was time for the formal part of the evening.

"Good evening again ladies and gentlemen," he began. "It's time to get to why all of us are here this evening."

He went on to say that some months previously, just after the article in the paper when I'd come home after the war ended, there had been a resolution made and passed unanimously that my contribution to the war effort and subsequent homecoming shouldn't go unrecognized. According to the Lord Provost I was the only one from the Pitlochry area who'd joined the R.A.F., gone to war and come home. He spoke about the sacrifices people around the world had made, the loss of life and atrocities, the wanton destruction. As he spoke you could have heard a pin drop, everybody's memory of the hell still vivid.

"But it's time now to rejoice and move on, to welcome home one of Pitlochry's sons. Churchill spoke of The Few, well Squadron Leader Somerville is one of them, so let us welcome him and thank him."

He turned to me and I stood. As he shook my hand there was a flash of light and I recognized the reporter from the paper, and as the Lord Provost presented me with a plaque and shook my hand again there was another flash.

"Squadron leader, on behalf of the citizens of Pitlochry it's my pleasure to welcome you on your safe return and to thank you for the significant contribution you made, not only for us but for your country. We're all immensely proud of you and will be forever in your debt."

The camera flashed again and his Lordship sat down and as I looked at the wood and bronze plaque with my name and an inscription on it, I felt quite emotional. Glancing at Catherine she knew it and held onto my trouser leg under the table. Thinking of the rain outside, I laid the plaque on the table and took the speech from my pocket. The applause stopped and the faces waited for me to begin. Looking along the table at Dad he smiled and gave me the faintest little nod. I knew what he was thinking and cleared my throat.

"Dear Lord Provost, council members, family and guests," I began, with an unfaltering upbeat tone. "It is indeed an honour for me to be here this evening to be the recipient of this dinner and presentation."

Catherine let go of my leg and I could see her out of the corner of my eye, looking at me and smiling.

"You know," I went on. "We are all so lucky to be able to call Pitlochry home. It's quiet and peaceful, somewhat removed from the terrors of war. Thinking about my loved ones and this place kept me going all the years we were away. I longed to be back to walk down by the river or up in the hills behind the town, to be able to bask in the summer sun. Believe it or not I even missed weather like we have today. I might have been away but my heart was always here."

Suddenly the room blurred and I faltered, as Catherine again held onto my leg I tried to continue.

"To be honest, as I flew every day and encountered the enemy I never really thought about how fortunate I was to be surviving, although each time we went up we were all scared and sometimes wondered if this would be the flight we wouldn't come back from. But now the war is over and with each passing day I do think about how privileged I am. In fact, Wing Commander Campbell and I talked about it recently. We wondered why we were spared when so many other pilots perished. When you really analyse it, it's an amazing feat to have survived almost six years of war. Certainly, one had to have skill to outmanoeuvre the enemy, but it wasn't all about skill. To begin with there was training and discipline. Wing Commander Campbell played a big part in my training and was, for a while, our squadron leader during the Battle of Britain. He too has flown Spitfires for the duration of the war. I owe a big part of my survival to him. But more than that, you have to have faith in the other pilots who fly with you. I had that. A few of the pilots in my squadron have also flown throughout the war and countless times each of us has held each other's life in the palm of our hand. Recently we had the honour of representing the R.A.F. at different venues around Scotland, some of you may have been there. The tour was Wing Commander Campbell's idea, everybody thought it was a good one, but none of us knew how it would go or what to expect. I can tell you we were all quite staggered by the public response. Everywhere we went people wanted to see the aircraft they'd heard so much about. But more than any other it was the Spitfire they'd come to see. Different places brought different faces but the questions were the same. What's it like to fly in a Spitfire? Well, I can tell you it's exciting, it's every fighter pilot's dream. When I sat in the cockpit she became an extension of me, with her frightening power and response. I felt safe in her and I feel I owe another part of my survival to my aircraft. Not being able to fly in her every day is certainly one thing I'll miss about the war.

"The next question was, 'what is it like to go up every day knowing the enemy could be waiting?' As I said before, we were scared, we knew it didn't matter if you were the most skilful. Every day we'd see skilful, experienced pilots go up and not come back. No, there was a degree of luck involved. If you were in the wrong place at the wrong time it was over. It was bad enough for us at the front line to lose somebody who'd become a colleague and friend, but to then have to write and tell his parents their son wouldn't be coming home was the most difficult thing I've ever had to do. There aren't enough words in the English dictionary for me to begin to express how profoundly sorry I was for their loss."

Pausing for a moment I felt drained.

"And the last most frequently asked question was, 'how do you feel now that it's all over?' I feel lucky, privileged, fortunate, blessed. With each passing day the gravity of what we did sinks in a little more. I honestly can't believe I made it through. The last winter we spent in northern Italy, just staying warm was the biggest challenge. But thoughts of home kept me going and these thoughts were kept alive by the letters from my family. They wrote faithfully every week, keeping me up to date with what was happening here. From the bottom of my heart I thank them for that. We all looked forward to the mail from home and read our letters over and over. All of us missed home desperately. But there has to be another reason I survived the long dark days of war. Along with the training, luck and the best aircraft, the only thing I can think of is I must have had a guardian angel."

"So you see, having survived wasn't just about me, many people and factors contributed to my survival and I'm thankful for each and every one of them. If any of them hadn't played the part they had, maybe the outcome would have been different. But the war is over and it's time to move on with our lives. For my part I'm looking forward to being here and being part of this community.

In closing I'd like to thank each and every one of you for coming out tonight, making for me a night as monumental as it's been. As we make our way home and carry on with our lives tomorrow, next week and the week after that, let us not forget all the men and women who will not be coming home, who paid the ultimate price for our freedom. It's important that we do not forget. Maybe if we don't the same thing won't happen again. Nor should we forget the countless thousands of injured and wounded; I wish them a speedy recovery. To all those not yet home, I wish them a speedy return. To the hundreds of thousands who find themselves homeless or orphaned, I wish them well and hope that they soon find peace and a renewed purpose in life. May we all find peace, thank you all for this memory, I won't forget it."

As I sat, relieved that my address was over, everybody stood and applauded, and then as it slowly died, his Lordship said a few words to end the formal part of the evening. But the guests lingered and before we left I think I'd been introduced to and shook hands with everybody in the hall. They wondered what I'd be doing now, would I stay in the R.A.F.? I just said I hadn't decided yet and left it at that.

As we were leaving I thanked the Lord Provost for everything he'd done. His response was that I should go to the town chambers one day soon to have tea and discuss the laying of a wreath on behalf of the town and of its citizens in memory of the war dead.

It was still raining as we piled into the car to go home. Getting to Catherine's cottage we went inside to have tea.

"That was a pretty good speech squadron leader," Catherine's Dad remarked. "You keep doing that you could end up being a politician."

We laughed and then we talked briefly about our big day coming up.

"Is there anything left to do," he continued.

"We think we've got everything seen to," Catherine answered. "At the end of the day as long as James and I are there, the minister and our guests, that's all that really matters. We're staying the night in the hotel and then getting the train in the morning to go to Edinburgh where we're booked into a hotel. I can't wait to see my new name on the register," she said.

She was excited, we both were. I was glad I was getting married and was looking forward to us being together, waking up together.

The next morning was Thursday, and just two more days. Meeting William at the station the first thing we did was go to Catherine's. She said that everybody who had been invited to our wedding had now replied and were coming. The hotel needed the information so in an attempt to make ourselves useful William and I went there, after which we went to the farm. On the way I asked him if he'd popped the question yet. For a moment I watched him smile and then he squinted at me.

"Well congratulations," I said, shaking his hand. "She's a great person, I know you'll be happy."

What he didn't know was that Isobel had invited Heather to the farm to stay for a few days before the wedding. She had told me they were engaged but until we got back to the farm I couldn't let on that I knew. She was going to the wedding with him but he was expecting her to arrive on the train on Saturday morning. Getting into the house we sat at the kitchen table and were about to have tea when Isobel and Heather appeared. To say he was surprised was an understatement. For a few moments he was speechless.

"When you live here," I told him, "these kinds of things happen to you all the time."

"You quite enjoy all the wee surprises," Bella laughed.

Smiling at her, I didn't say anything but she was right. It wasn't just the enjoyment of the surprise, it was that they were proof we were loved and thought of all the time.

Later on in the day Catherine came out to the farm. She had heard a lot about Heather but they'd never met until then. As expected they took to each other like ducks to water. In the course of conversation Heather thanked Catherine for sending some of her perfume to me when the squadron was in Malta. William, until then, knew nothing of the conspiracy to net him. As we laughed about it he just sat and smiled, shaking his head.

The next day, Friday, about all I did was pack some clothes for going away. In the afternoon Isobel, Heather and William and I went into the town to visit Catherine. When we arrived she too was packing.

And then, our big day came. As planned, Bella went into Catherine's early while the rest of us lazed around, drinking tea. William laughed, saying it wasn't too late for me to change my mind and run. Heather, sitting on his knee, elbowed him in the ribs and asked him if that's what he was thinking about doing. He was pulling my leg, she knew that and it was plain to see by the way he looked back at her he wouldn't be running either. As the hour approached Dad had to make several trips getting everybody to the church. Life was going on but rationing was still with us and with all the weddings and whatnot he'd done more running around than normal in the last three weeks. To conserve what precious fuel he was allotted he let the car coast down the hill into the town. Meeting the minister outside the church he showed William and I into the vestry. As we sat waiting for his return William wished me luck and checked again to make sure he still had the ring in his pocket.

"Do you think she'll keep you waiting," he asked smiling.

"She said she was thinking about it, but to be honest I think she'll be right on time."

Just at that the minister reappeared and escorted us into the body of the church where we stood in front of all our relations and friends. There was still a minute or so and as we stood there I had a last minute conversation with whoever it was that resided inside of me. I wasn't very old to be getting married, was this right I wondered? 'Somerville, you're an idiot, you're here because you're going to marry the person who's your destiny, the person you love more than any other, who's been your guiding light. This is just last minute jitters, you know it's the right thing to do.'

Suddenly I was jolted back to reality as the organist began to play the wedding march and as I looked at the minister he smiled and motioned for me to look towards the door of the church. Turning around I watched in awe as Catherine on her Dad's arm slowly walked up the aisle. In her long white wedding gown she looked absolutely stunning. Holding my hand she squeezed it. *How did I ever get to be this lucky?* I wondered, as I looked at the smiling face under the veil. Bella, standing beside her in a long pink dress, smiled at me. I hardly recognized her. I'd never seen her dressed like that before. The music stopped and then, with our minister's voice resonating in the church, our wedding began.

"Dearly beloved, we are gathered here today in God's house, to join together this man and this woman in holy matrimony."

Catherine squeezed my hand as the minister continued. It was the third Saturday in October 1945 and with our guests bearing witness, Catherine's Dad gave his daughter away and we exchanged vows and rings.

"I now hereby pronounce you husband and wife," he said at last. "You may kiss the bride."

As Bella helped Catherine with her veil I could see she was a bit misty eyed. Kissing her lightly we hugged and she whispered in my ear.

"I'll love you forever James Somerville."

With Bella and William bearing witness we signed the register and then, with her hand in mine, we walked through the smiling faces and outside to the front of the church. It had been cloudy and cool in the morning, but now the sun was shining and it was quite warm for late October. Our taxi whisked us the short distance to the hotel and for the first time as Mr and Mrs Somerville we shook hands with our friends and relations, some of whom I hadn't seen for years. Jock and Fergus with their wives were no exception, and as he shook my hand in a vice-like grip, visions of the day he hoisted me out of the Channel came flooding back. He was just the same.

"Aye man, how are you, it's nice to see you again, congratulations. I said to Fergus after you visited that day, man she's a bonnie lass, they'll be a wedding there for sure."

He would have stood there and talked all day but after a few minutes his wife smiled, slowly shook her head and gave him a little push. For the first time in a while I spoke to and shook hands with the other members of my squadron. Hugging Catherine they told me what a lucky beggar I was. All of them with the exception of Findlay had come with a partner. He would be sitting beside Isobel at the reception but according to what both she and William had been telling me they had lost touch in the last while. Isobel hadn't been seeing anybody else but apparently Findlay had. He and Alison had somehow gotten together the day we had gone on leave and had been dating since. He'd asked William why his relationship with Alison hadn't gone anywhere. William had told him but it didn't discourage him. Telling him that she had a little boy was one of the first things Alison did when they started dating. Although he'd been invited to come with a partner he didn't bring her. Maybe he'd asked her and she'd decided not to. I'd have to ask him sometime.

As the line progressed we shook hands with Group Captain McKenzie and his wife Jean, Group Captain Thomson from Sector Control in London along with his wife and then there was Group Captain McLean from Malta. All three had decided they'd retire from the R.A.F. There were the newly-weds and the rest of my family, Isobel Heather and Mary, the three nurses in our midst. Mary I hadn't seen since we'd left Malta. It might have been an autumn day but the scent of 'Summer Blossoms' was wafting everywhere.

As we sat at the head table, with the minister saying grace and officiating, the next part of our day began. After we'd eaten came the speeches, first the minister and then me.

"Ladies and gentlemen," I began. "On behalf of my wife and myself..."

For a few moments that was as far as I got, the room erupted with applause whistles and shouts, the main instigators being the members of my squadron, spurred on by Findlay, of course.

He'd been strategically placed at a table beside Isobel and I smiled as I watched her poke him in the ribs for his outbursts. As the room quietened I went on to thank all of the people who had touched my life in one-way or another, and all of the people in the town who had contributed in some way to our wedding.

"But I want to say a special thanks to my squadron. We'll be forever connected by memories of the time we spent together."

As I spoke I looked at each one of them. We had shared a time in history and camaraderie that few would ever experience. We were more than brothers. None of us had done anything without wondering how it would affect the other. There were a number of our squadron who wouldn't be coming home. Pausing briefly I looked along the table at Catherine's Dad and he smiled as I thanked him for allowing me to marry his daughter. I thanked Dad and Bella for their love while I was growing up, for their support when I announced I wanted to join the R.A.F. Letting me do something I wanted to do, knowing in all probability there would be a war, took courage.

"And then there's Catherine, my guiding light. I want to thank you for everything you've done for me and I want to say how beautiful you are, especially today. I'll love you always."

Catherine stood and with her eyes glistening she threw her arms around me.

"Now look what you made me do," she managed to say.

After a few moments Catherine and I sat and then my best man, William, began.

"James, Findlay and I became the best of friends," he started. "All of us became fighter pilots together and as the war progressed James became squadron leader. He might have been the youngest in our group, but he was the natural successor to Wing Commander Campbell."

He spoke of Catherine and how he watched our relationship stand the test of time and the strains of war, watching our love blossom and grow.

As William finished Catherine's Dad got up. He too had something he wanted to say.

"Catherine and James and guests," he began, "I'd just like to say a few words to welcome James as my son in-law. I know my daughter is in safe hands." He went on to say a few words about the war and me as a pilot, but his tribute was to Dad and Bella, thanking them for taking the time to look after Catherine when we were away and for all of the happy times he himself has had in our home.

"Please everybody, be upstanding and toast with me to all the Somervilles, and to the latest Mr and Mrs Somerville. I know your years together will be happy. I pray they'll be many."

With the official part of the proceedings over, we mingled with our guests and then, as the music began, to cheers and jeers, again mainly from the members of my squadron, Catherine and I danced our first dance as husband and wife.

"Did I tell you how absolutely stunning and beautiful you look today?"

"No, but I haven't told you either how happy you've made me. I've wanted to be Mrs Somerville for so long. Tonight you don't have to go home.

Tonight we can sleep together and in the morning we'll wake up together to start our new life."

Since the war had ended and I'd been home more, Catherine had been happy and content, but today in her wedding dress she was glowing.

Our big day seemingly passed in a flash, our guests began leaving and we went to the luxury of our hotel room. In the peace and quiet of the room we held each other for a while and then we went to bed. You can tell someone you love them often, but it means nothing without showing it. It's the little things that one does for the other that shows the measure of love, neither one of us did anything without wondering how it would affect the other. That day and night our love and lives entered a whole new chapter, over the years we'd gotten to know each other intimately, but now we were one.

In the morning we had breakfast, arranged personally by my sister Jean and then later on we made our way to the station to catch the train for Edinburgh. It had been years since we'd made the trip together, Catherine usually stood on the platform waving goodbye as I went to war. The days we spent in Edinburgh were the most relaxing an enjoyable I could ever remember spending. There was nothing to rush for and no set day to be back home.

After getting back we stayed a few days in Catherine's cottage in Pitlochry, in that time we moved the things she wanted to take with her to our new home. As well I made contact with the reporter from the paper and thanked him for all his kind words. I asked him if there was one more thing he could do for me. I wanted to put a notice in the paper thanking everybody in the town for their generosity. He said he could arrange for that and to leave it to him.

The first night we spent in the cottage I'd always been drawn to was a weird experience. I woke up a number of times in the middle of night wondering where I was. But it was only one night. Catherine was on cloud nine. It was going to be a while before she came back to earth. There were still things she wanted to do with the cottage and so we worked on them together. We looked at the garden for days on end and eventually came up with an idea of what we would like to do with it.

"We'll fix up the front garden first," Catherine said. "We'll put a seat under the big beech tree so that when the weather's nice we can sit in it and look at the view."

And then, unbelievably, my three months leave was over. When I got back to Turnhouse Group Captain McKenzie was still there. We talked for a while, he thanked me for inviting him to our wedding, and at the same time confirmed that he was retiring at the end of the year.

"Something else has come up, squadron leader," he went on. "I'm not going to twist your arm but the R.A.F are flying food and supplies into

Germany. The bottom line is they could do with more pilots to keep everything ticking along. Is that something you'd be interested in doing."

Thinking only momentarily, I gave him my answer.

"Personally sir, it's not something I'd be interested in, but I can ask the rest of the squadron to see if any of them would like to go. Have you got something for us to do if we stay here?"

"Well, I can remember you saying you'd like to be home every night, so for the time being you could go to Perth; they need someone to coordinate their flying training up there. I can't tell you how long it would be for but the post is available at the moment."

"What about the rest of my pilots sir? What will happen to them?"

"We still need part of a squadron to fly costal patrols, the powers that be want to continue with that for the moment. But as well we could do with a couple of instructors here. Talk to them and let me know as soon as you can."

Leaving his office I spoke briefly with Alison. She had heard Catherine and I had married and wished us luck. She also said she was leaving her job when the commander retired at the end of the year. Reading between the lines I think in some ways she wished she could turn the clock back, but I didn't ask her anything about her relationship with Findlay. Hopefully it would blossom. Findlay and she were quite alike in a lot of ways.

Rounding up my 'clutch', we had a meeting in the briefing room and told them about the possibilities of flying transports to Germany. They looked at each other and made a decision almost as hastily as I made mine. Findlay, as always, was quite vocal.

"We just spent nearly six years fighting them. I'm not doing it, not me."

That's all that was said on the matter and I went on to tell them what else the commander had talked about.

"So if you go to Perth you won't be flying with us then," William commented.

"That's what it would mean, but you've most likely had enough of me now anyway," I answered, smiling.

Calling back to the commander's office I told him we'd made our decision, none of us wanted to fly to Germany.

"Well I can't say I blame you, but I thought I'd give you the option anyway."

He went on to say that effective immediately I was to fly up to Perth and assume my new responsibilities, but added he didn't know how long I'd be able to keep my Spitfire. There was no doubt things were changing, when the day comes I can't fly in her, flying just won't be the same. William and Findlay were to report to the commander personally for further instructions and what was left of the squadron were to report to the briefing officer for details as to what their duties would be. Back in the briefing room I conveyed the information to my squadron and then they walked with me to my aircraft where we said our goodbyes. We were all feeling a bit choked. We had been together and looked out for each other for a long time. I was going to miss them. Starting my aircraft I advanced the throttle and began to taxi, waving to them as I passed. They were like family. All of us had so many memories of our years together. Memories we wouldn't forget.

Climbing up and away from Turnhouse I had an emptiness in the pit of my stomach. The war was over, I was glad of that, but things wouldn't be the same. Flying wouldn't be the same without the company of my comrades.

Checking in at Perth I discovered I was to head the flying training there for a while. The basic training would be done by other instructors and I would teach some advanced manoeuvres. 'Share some of your expertise,' I was told. But the best part of my new posting was that I would be able to go home every night – and as the weeks progressed I discovered I didn't need to be there every day. One of the advantages of the responsibility I suppose. For the time being I had what I wanted.

Before the end of 1945 there was yet another development on the home front. Just a few days before Christmas Catherine's Dad and Frances were married and after a short honeymoon they were back in Pitlochry for Christmas day. They went to the farm with Catherine and I and spent the day there. William and Jean went to Dunkeld to spend a few days with Jean's parents and John and Mary stayed down at Edinburgh. At New Year the whole family were at the farm to see the New Year in. The year that had gone none of us would see anything like it again, the biggest single change affecting everybody was the war ending but there were big changes to the Somerville family structure as well. It wasn't just that we were starting a new chapter, we were starting a new generation.

Catherine's Dad and Frances were going to be living in Catherine's cottage in Pitlochry. Frances had sold her confectionary shop in Edinburgh but had decided to keep her house there for the time being. The café in Pitlochry that Catherine and I considered ours was up for sale so Frances bought it. Catherine's Dad had retired from the R.A.F. and helped her get started, but he was still looking into the possibilities of doing something in aviation. Catherine was still teaching but between us we got our cottage finished off inside. The garden in front of the house looked like someone, in fact, did live there now, as yet we hadn't ventured into the wilderness at the back. The days I didn't go to Perth I went to the farm to do what I could there. It was on one of these days I had a heart-to-heart chat with Dad. As we looked down the valley from 'the gate' I remembered having a conversation with him there at the start of the war.

"You know," he began, "I don't think I ever thanked you."

"Thanked me for what?" I asked him.

"For all you've done and who you are."

"You made me who I am," I answered. "I'll never be able to repay you for all you've done."

These days at the farm also gave me the opportunity to talk to Bella, like old times, just the two of us at the kitchen table.

As the weeks rolled on into spring Catherine's Dad, after doing a fair bit of research, felt there was going to be a need for a passenger service between Edinburgh and London, as he had joked about before he wanted me to help him with it. His plan was to buy two surplus DC3s to provide the service, as had been rumoured the R.A.F. were disposing of or indeed almost giving away some of the aircraft they no longer needed. Both Catherine and Frances had reservations about the need for the service, but they knew as well he wouldn't be doing anything if he didn't feel confident about it.

21. A Year Later

A few weeks later we were into the first part of May. Unbelievably it was a year since the war in Europe had ended and slowly but surely our lives were beginning to take shape and meaning. Frances was enjoying her café. Pitlochry was vastly different from the hustle and bustle of Edinburgh but she said she felt quite at home and didn't miss living there. Catherine's Dad bought the two DC3s he had talked about and formed a company of which he made me part owner. He called it 'Highland Air'. Flying was flying but piloting a DC3 was a bit different from a Spitfire, so we both had to go for a few hours of type conversion. Both of us realized that we wouldn't always be able to both fly the service and manage it as well, we would need pilots to make the flights when we couldn't, so I asked William and Findlay if they would like to work for this new airline. Neither one had any hesitation. They needed a change, they said. We explained that we didn't know how busy it would be, that we were all taking a leap of faith, but if the worst came to the worst all that was spent was the modest amount for the two aircraft. For the first few weeks of the flights things didn't look too promising but Catherine's Dad remained positive, saying it just needed time.

Catherine was still teaching but now, in the last few weeks she's been hinting about wanting to be a mother. She has always had the uncanny knack of knowing when it was the right time to do things so I don't expect this time will be any different.

We have worked a bit in the jungle behind the house but with midsummer's day upon us and our parents coming to have dinner with us we decided to have a day off from the digging and hacking. Sitting together in the garden seat at the front of the house looking down the valley then, off in the distance a familiar voice was calling my name.

"James, come on wake up, everybody's here and dinner is ready."

On waking, Catherine was still sitting beside me and still holding my hand.

"Come on sleepy head, we're waiting on you."

"Where is everybody?" I asked.

"They're inside," Catherine answered, getting up and pulling me out of the seat. "They've been here for a while already. We tried to wake you earlier but you were a hundred miles away so we decided to leave you in peace."

"More than a hundred miles. I was dreaming about the war and the places I've been. How long have I been asleep?"

"Not long, maybe an hour or so."

As she pulled me up, her hair, like her smile, sparkled in the afternoon sunshine.

"Have I told you today how lovely you look?"

Her smile broadened. "No, but you can tell me later."

Inside, Dad and Catherine's Dad were sitting reading the paper, Frances and Bella were chatting.

"Well if it isn't sleeping beauty," Bella chirped. "We come to visit and you sleep."

"There's nothing to beat a wee nap in the afternoon," Catherine's Dad added.

"It was nice, in the heat of the day I just drifted away."

As we sat at the table I looked around at my family. With my dream and recollection of the war years still so vivid I thought again about how fortunate I was to have survived the war, how fortunate we were to live where we live. There are still inconveniencies, things that are rationed and will be for a while, petrol, sugar and chocolate to name a few, but we as a family didn't starve or were ever in any danger of it. Because of the shortages, anybody with food to sell sold at a premium, and Dad built up his farm as a result.

We, as a squadron, had been fortunate. What I mean is, we could have been sent to the Far East to confront the Japanese, we could have been sent to the Mediterranean sooner, or maybe even to North Africa. Flying in the searing heat on one hand or monsoon rains and malaria on the other. As it turned out the losses we endured were about average, of the seven original red wing pilots four of us came home, all of us had been shot down more than once and often we had come so very close to not being back. The other two members of our squadron to come home, John McDonald and John Ferguson had been replacement pilots. Altogether, counting Catherine's Dad there were thirteen of us who flew with the squadron at some point, six died, the rest of us having scars of one type or another. Some of us had survived the biggest airborne battle in history, we maybe didn't always know it at the time, how physically and emotionally drained we were, but it took us a while to recuperate from it. I've always admired our superior officers in the R.A.F., seemingly always finding the right people for the job at hand. Sometimes we felt we could have been doing more, but they knew how tired we were after the Battle of Britain, and although we were still doing something that needed to be done, flying patrols, boring and tedious as we felt it was at the time, it was their way I think of giving us a bit of a rest. Sometimes I think Catherine's father had a hand in some of the decision making about what we were doing, trying to protect us a little bit until we got over the summer of 1940, I asked him if he did but said he was like the rest of us, just a small cog in a big wheel.

As far as my contribution to the war effort goes, I'm glad I was in the R.A.F. I wouldn't have survived had I been in the navy or the army. It was no less dangerous flying, but at least I was a little more in control of my own destiny. When I shot at an enemy aircraft I never once had second thoughts about doing it, I saw a machine and knew there were young men like me in it, but it was different somehow, I wasn't shooting at them directly.

Then there was my aircraft. For the time being she is still at Perth and I fly her once or twice a week, with her sleek slim line and speed she's still exciting to be with. She isn't just an aeroplane. She's a lady. I think of her and miss her when I'm not in her company.

But before her there were three other ladies in my life. First there was Mum, first and foremost she gave me life. She was everything and I miss her still. If ever there were doubts in my mind about there being an afterlife she certainly has vanquished them. Even in death she was watching over me. My first experience in the cemetery, although at the time I felt it was a personal one, one I really didn't want everybody knowing about, the people who mean most to me found out about it and were comforted by it. Catherine and I have gone to the cemetery a number of times in the last year but I've never felt she talked to me again. Maybe she feels her job is done and is finally at peace.

Then there is Bella. I can't say that Mum groomed her for the part she has played in our lives. As I recall they worked well together right from the very beginning, differing only in physical appearance they were of the same temperament. One could cook and bake as well as the other, both seemed to have endless amounts of energy, but most of all, their undying love for us. Unfortunately Mum isn't around to share our daily lives, but I know there is no person other than Bella she would rather have had to look after us. After Mum died Bella stepped into her shoes and looked after us like we were her own, for that we will all be indebted to her always. For myself, the chats I had with her over the years, the secrets we shared in the quiet of the morning as we sat at the kitchen table I won't forget them. Nor will I forget the fun we had as a family when we were growing up when we went picnics and played with her out on the hill. These are precious moments.

Finally there is Catherine. I cannot imagine what my life would be like if she were not in it. She has had such a profound influence on it, reaching inside and extracting what I didn't know existed. She made me a better person. Her teaching abilities are unquestionable because of that quality. To be honest, over the years I was unaware of the deep bond growing between us. Findlay was right, I was naïve. Everybody could see it except me. What I do remember is that anytime I was home I needed to see her, to talk to her and confide. I remember also the hurt I felt when I discovered she had been at Turnhouse that summer, when she had gone back to Pitlochry and I hadn't seen her. She had come to tell me how she felt about me and I felt because of my prying I'd lost my dearest friend. Looking back and remembering how I felt I should have known then, but they do say that love is blind. My guiding light, my mentor, my friend, my fiancée and now my wife, she has told me often that if anything happened to me she would die. If anything happened to her I think maybe I would do the same.

In everything she does she is focused, often during the war she felt vulnerable and helpless, but she is strong, she knew there were things she had control over and could do something about. She knew also there were things she had no control over and could do nothing about. Although there was uncertainty and sad times during the war, at heart she has always been a happy person, since the war ended and especially since we've been married she has been even more so. We are happy together and feel fortunate and safe in our little cottage, nothing can touch us now. After being in the war for its entirety and having survived, and all of us enduring all of the hardships and sacrifices that go along with such a monumental conflict, it makes the day to day inconveniences since seem trivial. All of my family have been emotional and shed tears from time to time, some happy, a lot sad. War did that to people, but we made it through. For me it has been a privilege to have been at this point in time, to be able to do what I did for my country and my family, and though I walked in the shadow of death I didn't dwell on or was fazed by it. We had all fought for freedom and honour. What kept me going was that one day the nightmare would end and I'd be going home.

~ END ~